D0651945

DATE DUE

KF Hem	
	PRINTED IN U.S.A.

Shark Fin Soup

Also by Susan Klaus

Secretariat Reborn:
A Christian Roberts Novel

Flight of the Golden Harpy

Shark Fin Soup

A Novel

Susan Klaus

Oceanview Publishing

Longboat Key, Florida

ISBN: 978-1-60809-123-2

Published in the United States of America by Oceanview Publishing,
Longboat Key, Florida
www.oceanviewpub.com

10 9 8 7 6 5 4 3 2 1

PRINTED IN THE UNITED STATES OF AMERICA

To Steve Irwin, the Crocodile Hunter,
a true warrior and champion for wildlife.

To the ocean and its creatures, may they survive mankind.

ACKNOWLEDGMENTS

To my children, Christopher and Kari, their spouses, Crissy and Scott, and my grandsons, Will and little blond Christian. To my family, friends, and the authors who advised, encouraged, and supported me. To Cliff Klaus for legal research; Bobbie Christmas, my Atlanta editor; and Susan Gleason, my agent. To Wade Darby, my friend and guide in Costa Rica and Panama. He was a party right up to the end. And to my muse, Brad Pitt, who has inspired my protagonists, ever since my time with him on the movie set of *Ocean's Eleven*.

Shark Fin Soup

Shark Fin Soup

Ingredients

>One whole chicken or one lb. of Jinhua ham
>Two cups of water
>One cup of Shaoxing wine
>Three dried shark fins

Cook chicken or ham down in the water, creating a broth. Strain and add wine and fins to broth. Simmer for one hour. Stir until fins are broken up into thin translucent noodles. Noodles are tasteless and have no food value.

Serves eight

Note: This Chinese soup is fabled to bring long life; the longer the fin noodle from a big shark, the longer the life of the diner. It might also bring good fortune and is considered an aphrodisiac. Because of the Asian fin demand for this soup, 100 million sharks are killed each year. Sharks grow slowly, some taking more than a decade to mature, and produce a small number of pups, therefore one-third of all shark species are expected to be extinct within the next decade. At this time, three species of hammerhead, the tiger, the bull, the oceanic white tip, and others have been reduced in population by 97 percent. Without these predators balancing the ocean environment, reefs around the world are in decline.

CHAPTER ONE

BAHAMAS, NOVEMBER 2012

Christian gripped the wheel and gazed at the watery dark horizon and fall sunset, the color of blood. Bare feet planted on the pitching deck, he stood as motionless as marble, his tall, lean frame braced in the Caribbean breeze that tugged at his open shirt like an impatient lover. Only his blond hair stirred, the tousled locks flicking at his deep-blue eyes.

Beneath him, the forty-seven-foot Catalina surged under full sail through the swells, but Christian's mind was not on his sloop, the sea, or sky. His thoughts dwelled on Allie and her lifeless body in the forward berth. He dropped his head and closed his moist eyes. *It should've been me. I should be in there instead of her.*

After a while he glanced up, bleary-eyed, and saw the outcrop of islands far ahead. He readjusted his course and brushed the tears off his cheeks. *"Goddamn it, Christian, get your head out of this nightmare."*

The blue waters had turned to black, and the first stars of the evening appeared sharp and clear when Christian's sloop, *Hank's Dream,* entered the bay. Up ahead, Nassau was on the right and Paradise Island on the left. The Bahamian waters mirrored the glittering lights from the docked cruise ships the size of cities and the high-rise hotels of the Atlantis theme park. He pushed the refurl button, and the main sail withdrew into the mast and the genoa sail coiled around the forestay. The sailboat, now driven by diesel power rather than wind, cut through the calm water like scissors through dark satin.

He maneuvered his sloop toward the dock slips filled with a variety of crafts, from small skiffs to large cabin cruisers. Beyond the seawall was a street lined with waterfront shops, restaurants, and the large warehouse of the Nassau straw market.

Unsure where to pull in and mentally drained, Christian cut the engine and allowed his sloop to drift alongside a weathered trawler. Aboard were three Bahamian men, two young black men swabbing its deck, and a bearded old man who sat on a crate and mended a net.

"Could you help me?" Christian pleaded, his voice cracking with stress.

"Grab da boat," said the old man, rising from the crate. The young men dropped their mops and seized the sailboat's side railings to keep the boats from bumping. "What's the matter, mister?"

"My wife . . . my wife . . . she's been shot, killed. Could you call the police?" Saying the words aloud hit Christian hard. His eyes watered and his body quaked, the agonizing reality clawing like a beast at his gut. He sank weak kneed on a bench in the cockpit. Hunched over with his face in his hands, he muttered, "It's my fault, my fault. I'm so sorry, Allie."

For a moment, the three fishermen glanced at one another, apparently too stunned to speak or move. The old man said, "I'll make da call. Drop da fenders and tie his sloop off."

The two men grabbed the Catalina's stern and aft lines, securing *Hank's Dream* to their fishing boat as the old man stepped onto the dock and shuffled to a pay phone on the street.

Within five minutes, the first squad car arrived, lights flashing and siren blaring. Christian saw the old man point at him while talking to two black police officers. They hustled down the dock with the old man trailing and stepped aboard the trawler.

The police officers climbed aboard his sloop. They stared at him, but their gaze quickly shifted to the blood-stained deck. "Mister, your wife was killed?" one officer asked.

Christian swallowed and glanced at the cabin. "She's on the bed in the front berth."

One officer went below. The other remained beside Christian and asked him preliminary questions: his name, his wife's name, address, if he was the sloop's owner, and why he was in the Bahamas.

In a daze, Christian mumbled the answers as the cop wrote on a notepad. The other officer returned to the open deck and whispered into his partner's ear. "Please come with us, Mr. Roberts," the first officer said. "A sergeant will follow up with more questions."

As the two officers escorted Christian down the creaky wooden dock, he felt wobbly, his equilibrium off balance on solid land after days at sea on a rocking boat. He stared at the street that now resembled a carnival. Three more police cars and an ambulance had arrived on the scene. Amid blinking red lights, roughly a dozen policemen awaited him, along with a small crowd of spectators, the commotion drawing the curious out of the local businesses. All eyes focused on Christian. Being a lofty Caucasian, he stood out like a sail on a dusk sea among the Bahamians.

One officer instructed Christian to wait beside a police car. He chewed a thumbnail as he leaned against the fender and watched more officers crawl aboard his boat. He heard the trawler's diesel engine engage and saw the fishing boat motor away from the dock, yielding its space to Christian's sloop. Using the bowline, the police pulled *Hank's Dream* into the empty slot that gave them easier access to his boat, *and Allie.*

"Mr. Roberts," said a man's voice, "I'm Sergeant Drake. Could you please come with me?" Drake was a middle-aged black man of medium height with a thin mustache above a full mouth of large bright teeth. His accent was proper British and lacked the heavy Bahamian twang.

Christian followed him to another squad car.

Drake opened its back door and glanced at the growing throngs of tourists and locals that lined the street. "Please get in. I think it would be better to take your statement at headquarters."

Christian put one foot into the car but stopped, watching a white van arrive with CORONER written on its side. He shuddered and slipped into the backseat, grateful he would not be here when Allie's body was offloaded. Drake and a younger officer took the front seats. The trip through town was short, the riders sullen; no one spoke.

At the station, Christian followed Drake to a small, windowless room with a table between two chairs. Drake told him to take a seat, and he eased into a chair. Although the room was air-conditioned, small beads of sweat formed on Christian's forehead. He swept the moisture back through his collar-length hair.

Drake sat down in the other chair, facing Christian, and thumbed through the preliminary report that rested on the table. "I must inform you," Drake began, "that this interview is being taped."

"Do I need to lawyer up?"

Drake raised a skeptical eyebrow. "That is your choice, Mr. Roberts, but for now, you are not a suspect. It appears your wife died of a gunshot wound. I just need your statement on how it happened."

Christian leaned back in the chair. "I don't know how it happened. Allie was on board while I was diving. We were anchored off the shelf of the Tongue between the Berries and Nassau. When I climbed aboard, I found her on the deck, dead, and the boat was shot up and ransacked. I carried her below, and since everything was gone—cell phones, radio, computers—I couldn't call for help. The GPS was also ripped out and missing, so I dug out some charts and used the compass to get here."

"What time did this happen?"

"This afternoon, around two, I think."

"When you surfaced near your boat, did you see any other boats in the area?"

"No, nothing."

"You didn't hear a boat motor while you were underwater or see another one overhead during your dive? Our waters have a high visibility."

"I told you, I didn't see or hear anything. I did a forty-minute dive and was a good distance from my boat. Hell, maybe the bastards sailed or paddled up to my sloop. Maybe that's why I didn't hear a motor."

"That's rather unlikely," Drake said. A faint smile played on his lips. He questioned and re-questioned Christian, the interview approaching the third hour. "All right, Mr. Roberts, let's move on," he said and flipped to another page. "The old fisherman heard you say that it was your fault. Did you and your wife get into a fight or have marital problems?"

Christian looked up, his eyes burning like hot blue flames. He was exhausted and famished, not to mention grief stricken, and had little patience left. "Fuck you, man," he said. "I loved her. Buying the boat, going on this fucking trip was my idea, so it's my fault she's dead. Now, are you going to find the sons of bitches that killed my wife, or are you looking to pin this shit on me?"

"We will do everything in our power to find your wife's murderer."

"Are we finished?" Christian rose abruptly from the chair.

"For now," Drake said and also stood. "We'll need to take your DNA and fingerprints so we can separate them from others found on your boat. One of my officers will drive you to a hotel and set you up for the night. I'll have more questions for you when our investigation is further along, so don't leave the Bahamas. In fact, I need your passport."

"I don't know where the hell it is. It was on the boat, top dresser drawer in the front berth, but God knows if it's still there—shit's dumped and scattered everywhere."

"We'll look for it. If it's lost, I'll begin the procedure to have your government issue another one." Drake patted Christian's shoulder. "Get some rest, Mr. Roberts."

Christian nodded. *I need to shut up, stop cursing and ranting. It's making me look bad.* "I'm sorry I'm a little short. I'm tired and still can't believe she's gone."

After Christian was fingerprinted and a DNA swab taken, he and another officer left the station, drove along Bay Road, and turned onto a side street to a mid-range hotel several blocks from the coast. Inside the lobby, the officer told the clerk that the Bahamian police department would be picking up his tab for the night.

The officer left, and Christian, barefoot and whipped, walked from the lobby into a small adjacent restaurant that still served food at eleven o'clock. He hadn't eaten since early that morning. His stomach groaned with hunger pains, but his thoughts weren't on food. He was thinking about the police interview. Of course, Sergeant Drake suspected him. Plenty of boyfriends and husbands killed their women, and when the cops found only his and Allie's fingerprints on the boat, they would be even more suspicious.

He sat down at a table away from other diners. As the waitress approached, he realized he had no wallet, no cash, or credit cards.

"Can I put this on my room bill?" he asked.

The waitress said it would be fine, and he ordered a burger, fries, and a Coke. When his meal arrived, he stared at the juicy sandwich and thought of Allie. Only the day before, she had said she was ready for a burger. He took a bite but couldn't taste the food, because of his runny nose and watery eyes. Embarrassed, he quickly wiped his moist face with the napkin and looked around, but nobody had noticed. He managed to eat half the meal.

In his room, he slipped out of his cream linen shirt and Dockers shorts and took a quick shower. Wrapping a towel around his waist, he collapsed on the bed and stared at the ceiling fan. Throughout the day, he had tried to be strong and focused. "Just get through it," he had kept telling himself. At midnight, the day was finished. His resolve toppled like a sandcastle with the incoming tide. He turned on his side and curled up into a fetal position. Burying his face into a pillow, he sobbed. "Jesus, Allie, how did we end up like this?"

CHAPTER TWO

Sergeant Drake returned to the sloop *Hank's Dream* and the crime scene after his interview with the temperamental Christian Roberts. Drake supervised as his small forensic team lifted fingerprints from Roberts's sloop, collected evidence, and took photos of the dead woman, a petite strawberry blond in her late twenties. Standing on the dock, Drake reflected on the handsome husband, his pretty wife, and the luxurious sailboat. *Youth, looks, and money; they had had it all.*

One of his officers approached. "Sergeant Drake, they are done with the forensics and the coroner is ready to remove the body."

"Go ahead, but tell him to hold off on the full autopsy."

Drake's supervisor came alongside him. "What do you think?" he asked, watching the men load the woman's body into the van.

Drake released a loud sigh. "On this one, I called the pathologist in the States. He's flying in tomorrow morning for the autopsy. And since the husband and victim are US citizens, I plan to have the Miami FBI assist us. When I questioned the husband, he was scared, used anger to hide it, and was defensive. Asked if he needed a lawyer. Plus there are flaws in his story. He says he didn't see or hear anything while he was diving. Sound travels a good distance underwater. He also said he carried his wife from the deck into the berth, yet he didn't have a drop of blood on him. Only a person wishing to conceal something washes up and changes clothing after a spouse is murdered. And we haven't found any bloody clothing except hers." He turned to his supervisor. "So what do I think? I think he did it."

• • •

In Miami, Agent Dave Wheeler sat at his desk in the FBI field office and played with his ballpoint pen, clicking the end in and out while he studied the papers. The case was a dead end unless more evidence was found, but more evidence could mean another body. He pulled out the three photos of women, all young, lovely brunettes, and dead. Each had been raped and stabbed in a different part of Florida. Disgusted, he started to close the folder, when he glimpsed his eighteen-year-old daughter in a nearby picture frame. She resembled the murdered girls. Some cases hit closer to home and gave him more incentive.

"Hey, Dave," Ralph, his partner of four years, called from his neighboring desk. "Line two; it's your buddy in Nassau."

"Drake?" Wheeler tossed the pen on the folder and ran a hand over his short, salt-and-pepper hair. On his last trip to Nassau, he had told Drake he needed to hire a good homicide detective for the Royal Bahamian Police Force. The sergeant laughed, said they didn't have the money or enough murders to make it worthwhile.

Wheeler leaned back in the chair and pushed the flashing red light on the phone. "Wheeler."

"Agent Wheeeelerrrr," said Drake, his accent drawing his name out like a song. "This is Sergeant Drake. I have a murder that involves two of your Americans. Last night a young husband sailed into our port with his dead wife. The coroner from the States just finished the autopsy. She was killed with a shotgun blast to the chest and had gunpowder residue on her right hand. The boat was also riddled with shotgun pellets and looted, made to look like a pirate raid. There was no shotgun on board, but we did find a forty-four handgun that had been recently fired, but curiously, no prints. In fact we have yet to find any prints on the boat other than the husband and wife's. According to the woman's body temperature, the time of death was around ten a.m. yesterday, yet the husband claims she died at two in the afternoon." He recited the rest of the details as Wheeler jotted them down.

"I'm certain that Mr. Roberts has been less than truthful," said Drake.

"All right, fax me what you have and the autopsy report. I'll check Roberts out on this end. Hold off questioning him further. I'll fly over tomorrow."

"I will have a Cuban cigar and a nice bottle of Appleton waiting for you."

Wheeler hung up and turned to his computer, performing a background check on Christian Roberts, age twenty-seven of Myakka City, a native Floridian. Roberts's sheet showed that a few years earlier, he was arrested for assault in Miami when he shoved a man named Ed Price at Calder Race Course, but no conviction; the prosecutor dropped the charges. He studied Roberts's features from the arrest photo. *Six two, blond, and good looking*, he thought, *a package that usually reeks of arrogance.*

Ralph walked over to his desk. "What's going on in the Bahamas?"

"Pack your bags. We're taking a puddle jumper over tomorrow. Drake's got a murder, an American woman, and has requested an assist. The husband is a person of interest—lots of circumstantial, but no smoking gun. I'd rather get there before the good sergeant screws up the case. Check on a horse trainer named Ed Price living here in Miami. The husband had a scuffle with him a few years back. Sometimes the friends—or enemies—a person keeps tells a lot about someone."

Ralph looked at Roberts's mug shot on the computer. "That's the husband, Christian Roberts? He looks more like a surfer than a murderer."

"He's a sailor," said Wheeler. "The woman was killed on a forty-seven-foot Catalina sloop registered to the husband. I want to know how this Florida boy could afford that boat. Give the IRS a call. Rich wives with penniless husbands tend to be a motive for murder."

After Ralph returned to his desk, Wheeler did a wider Internet search on Roberts. The previous year, the Bradenton police had filed a boating accident report that took place on Tampa Bay during a hurricane. One man had died, but Roberts and another man survived the crash. Wheeler didn't need Ralph to look up the surviving man. Vince Florio's name jumped off the screen. He knew Florio. He was Italian, mid-fifties with an average build, but more importantly, he was connected to the New York mob and spent his winters in Miami. He was a suspect in several murders, along with loan sharking, gambling, and drug smuggling. For more than a decade, the FBI had been trying to nail the guy, but Vince always managed to slip through the law's fingers. Since Florio had moved from Miami to Sarasota, Wheeler hadn't seen him in more than a year. The Tampa FBI was keeping tabs on him.

Wheeler massaged his chin in thought. *What the heck was Roberts doing on a speedboat with the likes of Florio?* Drugs came to mind. *Maybe that's how the kid got his money or got his wife killed.*

He returned to his search on Roberts and discovered another interesting report. Nine months earlier, the Port Charlotte police had filed a justifiable homicide that had taken place off Pine Key. Roberts had been shot and wounded by Kate Winslow, a twenty-four-year old woman. Allie, Roberts's girlfriend at the time and his now-deceased wife, managed to kill Winslow with a spear gun, and the homicide occurred on his sloop, *Hank's Dream*, the same boat that was now docked in Nassau. Two women killed on the same boat in less than a year. *What were the odds?*

Wheeler did a quick check on Winslow. She was a jealous ex-girlfriend of Roberts with a prior conviction of arson for burning down a horse barn in Myakka City, Florida. The barn belonged to Allie, Roberts's dead wife.

He heard Ralph end his call with the IRS and glanced at him. "So?"

Ralph spun around in his chair to face him. "It's hard to believe, but Roberts got his money from selling one horse, twenty million for a two-year-old Thoroughbred named Clever Chris. The buyer was a Sheik Abdul. But get this. I did a check on Ed Price. Turns out he was the sheik's horse trainer, and he's currently wanted for questioning in Kentucky for fraud. Apparently Price and the sheik raced an illegal horse in a big stake race." He grinned like a cat. "And guess who the horse was."

"Clever Chris."

"Yeah." Ralph frowned. He looked down at his notes. "There's more. Price disappeared a few weeks after that race, but he left behind a Miami home, cars, a barn full of horses at Calder, and untouched bank accounts. He hasn't used his credit cards either. His barn employees suspect foul play and filed a missing person's report on him."

"Twenty million for a colt that couldn't be raced. Maybe Price confronted Roberts, but this time there was more than a scuffle. Our sailor boy has quite a checkered past with some unsavory acquaintances. I'm looking forward to questioning him."

CHAPTER THREE

In the dark, his nude body rested lightly atop her, and his face hung over her shoulder, buried in her shimmering, moonlit hair. He nipped tenderly at her neck and detected her faint moans of pleasure above the heavy breathing. She wrapped her arms around him and pulled him closer, urging him on. He thrust gently back and forth and felt his climax building.

Finger-combing his hair, she gasped. "My beautiful Christian."

Suddenly he was showered with sunlight and found himself kneeling on his swaying boat deck, surrounded by blue sea and sky. His squinting eyes glanced up at a lone gull that circled overhead. Its caws became words. "Your fault, your fault, your fault," the bird squawked. "You killed her."

Salt from his sweat, tears, and the sea stung his eyes, and he stared at Allie, cradled and lying limp in his arms. He set the gun down and gazed in horror at blood, covering him and flowing back and forth on the floorboards with the roll of waves.

He jolted forward on the bed and saw the morning light filtering through the curtains in the hotel room. *It was a dream.* For a moment he sat dazed. He staggered into the bathroom and splashed water on his haggard face, noticing the five o'clock shadow and puffy eyes from crying himself to sleep. Even when his father, Hank, his boat's namesake, had died, Christian hadn't wept this much. He stared into the mirror and saw a stranger, a stranger to himself. *What have I done?*

He trudged to the bedside phone and placed a call to Sarasota. His mother answered.

"Mom, Mom, I've got really bad news." He felt the welling up and the choking, trying to prevent a sobbing fit.

"My God, Christian, what is it? What's wrong?"

"Allie's dead," he blurted out.

"No, God, no," his mother cried. He heard the phone drop and background screaming, hysterically calling for Frank, Christian's stepfather.

"Christian, what happened?" Frank asked, taking over the call.

Frank's steady voice caused Christian to get control. He sniffled and cleared his throat. "Allie was shot to death on my boat while I was diving. I don't know who did it." He explained that he had sailed into Nassau and made a statement to the Bahamian police.

"As soon as you stepped off your boat," Frank said, "you should've called me and never given the police an interview without a lawyer present." Frank, an attorney, spoke in unemotional lawyer tones, treating Christian like a client rather than a son.

"I know, I know, but if I refused to talk, I'd look guilty."

"All right, don't worry about it. Your mother and I will be on the first flight to Nassau and should be there this afternoon. I'll contact a criminal lawyer in the Bahamas, the best they offer. You need someone better than a real estate lawyer like me, and a local who's acquainted with Bahamian law."

"You really think I need a lawyer?"

"If the police had the evidence and you were a suspect, you'd be calling from jail instead of a hotel. But you need to protect your rights, so, yes, you need an attorney." His voice softened, and he became a father again. "Christian, I'm so sorry about Allie. She was a wonderful girl. I'll get you through this and take care of everything."

"Okay, Frank. Ask Mom to bring me some clothes and shoes. I have no money, and everything was on the boat. I'm not sure when the cops will release my stuff."

After the call, Christian put the Do Not Disturb sign on the outside door handle and went back to bed. He curled up in the pillows and stared at the blaring TV, but failed to hear or see the programs. His mind swam with the previous day's details; Allie's last words as she lay dying, his anger and rashness that had caused her death, the gunfire, the blood.

His initial panic and rage slowly turned into numbing devastation. "I don't care if I end up in prison. I deserve it," he said, resigned to his fate, although Frank would do everything in his power to protect him. The man was more than a stepfather. He was a champion. When his mother had married Frank, Christian was an out-of-control eleven-year-old, bitter and confused by his parents' divorce. Frank gave him love and stability and turned his life around.

Christian closed his eyes and drifted to happier times on the farm, Allie laughing and loosening the reins, giving the big red colt his head as they dashed across the green pastures or when she sat on the couch and Christian would lay with his head on her lap. She played with his hair while they stared at the fireplace and listened to the snap and crackle of flames and the howl of a northerly wind outside. His contentment was indescribable. He belonged to her, and now he felt lost.

There was a knock on his room door. Christian stirred from sleep and shook his head. Did he really hear it, or was it a dream? The knock came again. "Okay, okay," he said and rose, hoping it was a hotel maid and not the police. He opened the door.

"Oh, Christian," his teary-eyed mother said and reached up and hugged him. Frank stood behind her, grim, and holding two carry-on bags. The pair made an odd couple. His mother was slender, blond, and beautiful, whereas Frank was short, balding, and toadish.

The first few minutes in the room were awkward. Christian was all cried out and felt shell-shocked, sitting on the bed beside his mother. She rubbed his back and tried to console him, talking about Allie, the tragedy, and the upcoming funeral. Christian could barely focus on her words or answer her questions. He bit his lip, stared at the floor, and nodded periodically. Frank sat in the only chair across the room and watched.

Frank stood. "All right, Angie, your son is not up to talking. Let him deal with his grief in his own way and in good time." He picked up one of the suitcases and handed it to Christian. "Your mother found some clothes in your old bedroom, and we picked up razors, a toothbrush, and other things on the way to the airport. Why don't you clean up? We meet with the Bahamian lawyer in an hour."

"Are you hungry, dear?" Angie asked. "We can catch a quick bite in the restaurant before we go to the lawyer's."

"Okay," Christian said, realizing it was four o'clock. Sporadic meals seemed to be his only measure of time. He picked up the bag and turned in the bathroom doorway. "Thanks, Mom, for bringing my clothes," he said and his gaze went to Frank. No words of thanks were needed. The man understood him and his hopeless mental state.

Christian showered and it felt good to brush his teeth, finally. The sorrow then hit. The last time he brushed was on the sloop with the sound and smells of frying bacon, and Allie standing over the galley stove, a mug of coffee in one hand, spatula in the other. Every little thing he did was a reflection of her and the past. He felt beat despite dozing most of the day. His waking thoughts were befuddled, and his sleep was filled with haunting, terrible dreams. He wondered if he would ever be whole again.

Christian and his parents strolled into the hotel restaurant, more like a tacky diner with a linoleum floor and red, fake leather booths. His mother glanced at the menu. "Frank, we're not sleeping here tonight, and neither is my son."

Christian raised an eyebrow at his pretentious mother. Since marrying Frank, moving into a fancy Siesta Key home, and taking up with wealthy friends, she had become a snob. After eating in the hotel, they took a taxi to the Bahamian lawyer's office.

•   •   •

If the circumference of one's girth were a measure of success, the criminal attorney had done very well. Milford White was black and three-hundred-pounds huge. Once introductions had taken place, White asked the threesome to take a seat in his office. Cheap oil paintings of beach landscapes hung on the turquoise walls, and a neglected potted palm withered near a bookshelf. Christian and Frank sat in the two chairs facing White and his large, cluttered desk. His mother took a small chair against the wall.

Robotically and with dry eyes, Christian repeated the story he had told to the police. Frank and White were quiet, but his mother covered her mouth with a tissue and tried to suppress her sobs. When he finished, Christian asked White, "If I'm charged and convicted of my wife's murder, what kind of jail time would I face here?"

"No jail time, Mr. Roberts," White said and grinned, his lips curling like sausages in a frying pan. "Murderers are hanged in the Bahamas." He riffled through some papers and said more seriously, "But that will not happen to you. I informed the police that I am representing you, and they requested an interview tomorrow afternoon. I agreed to bring you in."

"Is that wise?" Frank asked.

"Bahamians are a very superstitious people, and that includes the police," said White. "To deny them and not cooperate with the investigation raises questions of culpability. Besides, these officers are not experts, and I will be there to make sure your stepson doesn't say anything incriminating. I have also scheduled a hearing in a few days to release Allie's body and the sailboat."

"I don't care about the damn boat," Christian grumbled.

White rocked his large frame from his overstuffed chair and stood. "I would like to speak to my client alone," he told Frank and Angie. "You can take a seat in the waiting room."

His parents left, and White closed his office door. He propped half a butt cheek on the corner of the desk and looked down at Christian, sitting in the chair. "Did you kill her?"

"No!" Christian shouted and leaped to his feet, his defiant stare conveying insult and rage. "I told you the fucking truth."

"You have a hair-trigger temper, Christian; doesn't take much to set you off," White said coolly. "That's good for the police and prosecutor, and a problem for your defense. Now sit."

Christian slumped back into the chair, and White continued, "Understand I'm here to protect you and not accuse you. If you're innocent, we can move forward with this interview. You might be able to tell the police something that helps them find the real killer. But if you're guilty, I need to know now. I can't have any surprises. If you're charged and this case goes to trial, this interview could hurt you. I need to postpone or cancel it."

Christian gazed at the floor, breaking eye contact with White, and said quietly, "I didn't shoot her. I swear to God."

"Okay, then. If you change your mind about talking to the police or recall anything else about the case, call me. If not, I'll meet you here at two o'clock tomorrow. We'll drive to the police station together. I know you're upset and angry, but try to control it tomorrow."

Christian, his mother, and Frank left White's office at six in the evening. They drove to Paradise Island and checked into a lavish two-bedroom suite at the Harbor House. They ordered room service and sat down to a quiet dinner in the room. Angie and Frank talked quietly about the weather, their flight over, and their last visit to the Bahamas. Frank had apparently suggested to his mother that they refrain from discussing Allie or the murder case.

Christian stared solemnly at his plate and picked at the food, but was aware of his parents' concerned glances. He felt like a germ in a test tube, being studied on its mood and manner. They were obviously wondering how he was handling Allie's death.

Christian forced down a fraction of his food and tried to hide the despair. Suicide lurked in his thoughts, an appealing way to end the pain, but he couldn't do it, not yet, not with Allie's dying request clanging like a steeple bell in his head.

He excused himself from the dinner table and explained he needed to walk and have some alone time. He took a short ride in the shuttle bus to the Atlantis theme park. With a destination in mind, he hustled through the extravagant lobbies and passed the crowded casinos, gift shops, and restaurants.

His pace slowed when he strolled around a restaurant dining room and entered a cave with large windows that looked out into the depths of a massive aquarium. A manta ray circled the surface, and tarpon, yellow-tailed snapper, and jacks raced by in schools while a monstrous goliath grouper rested in the rocks among count-less other species of fish. It was almost as good as diving. Christian ignored the other fish and focused on the sharks that patrolled near the bottom. An eight-foot gray reef shark approached the glass. Christian put his hand on the window and whispered to the fish, "Hello, brother. I'm here for you, only for you."

Agent Wheeler, along with his younger partner, Ralph, left Miami in the morning and arrived in Nassau a half hour later. Sergeant Drake met them at the airport.

"Anything new on the case?" Wheeler asked Drake as they walked to a waiting squad car.

"Only that the husband has retained a local lawyer."

"I'm not surprised," said Wheeler, "but is he still willing to talk to us?"

"To me." Drake chuckled. "I failed to mention that I had called in the FBI."

Wheeler and Ralph placed their tote bags in the car trunk, but Ralph kept an evidence kit with him and took the front seat alongside the officer driver. Wheeler and Drake settled into the backseat. "Before we go to the station, I want to see the sailboat," Wheeler said as the car passed a pink wall of a cemetery. He recalled that Anna Nicole Smith was buried there. The buxom actress's funeral had drawn hundreds of spectators, newspaper reporters, and photographers to Nassau. The TV crews and their trucks lined the street. Only a visit from the royal family might have matched the event, bringing so much press to the small island.

The car sped through town on Bay Road, the main drag in Nassau, and came to the dock holding *Hank's Dream*. Wheeler removed his jacket and left it in the car. Even in November, the Bahamas were warm. He loosened his tie and strolled onto the dock with Drake and Ralph. Before climbing aboard the vessel, he took in the sloop and noticed the damaged white bow. He squatted on the dock and examined a large hole, the size of a basketball, in the crushed fiberglass a few feet above the waterline. "You didn't mention this damage in your report," he said to Drake. "Did you question the husband on how it happened?"

"It was dark, and my officers didn't see the damage until after Roberts left for the police station, and during the interview he never mentioned it. The boat probably hit a seawall, docking, days before the murder."

Wheeler leaned closer. "There's some blue paint in the fiberglass. How many blue seawalls do you have in the Bahamas? More likely, the sloop rammed or was rammed by another boat. Ralph, take some paint scrapings. We'll send them off to the Washington lab when we get back." Ralph popped open his kit, slipped on surgical gloves, and went to work collecting samples.

Wheeler inspected a gunshot blast to the outside hull near the railing. "This blast was shot from at least fifty feet away. The woman's autopsy confirms the same thing. The shooter couldn't have been standing on the boat, and with the angles of the blasts, they couldn't have been at water level."

"Maybe the murder occurred off a beach or dock and not in the middle of the ocean, as the husband claims," Drake responded.

"Or maybe the killer was on another boat, and the husband is telling the truth."

"He's lying. I can feel it in my bones."

Wheeler shrugged and stepped aboard the sloop with Drake. He noticed the inside deck was also peppered with gun blasts. "No holes from the forty-four revolver?"

"None, but it was fired recently. Three chambers were empty, but no prints on the weapon. We found the gun here." Drake pointed to the corner of the deck.

Wheeler scratched the back of his neck. "We learned the revolver is registered to the wife, and the pathologist found gun residue on her hand. Looks like she got off a few rounds, defending herself. Did you check the husband's hands and take his clothing?"

"I didn't bother. He had washed all evidence away and changed clothing after carrying her bloody body into the berth."

Sloppy, Wheeler thought. The sergeant should have taken fingernail scrapings. He gazed at the large dark-red stain on the deck. "She was killed here?"

"According to the husband," said Drake.

Wheeler went through the hatch and descended three steps into the cabin. The galley, companionway, and two berths were trashed. Clothes, broken dishes, and papers were strewn on the floor. The console that would normally hold a radio, navigation equipment, stereo, and TV was torn apart and the items had been ripped out and were missing. "Your forensic team still didn't find any prints other than the husband and wife's?"

"That's right," said Drake, standing on the hatch steps.

Wheeler bent down and pushed the clutter aside to reveal a spotted blood trail on the floor that led from the deck to the berth. He thumbed his chin, considering the scenario and evidence. "That feeling in your bones might be right, Sergeant. If Roberts came aboard after a dive and found his wife dead and the boat trashed, this blood trail would be on top of the clutter instead of beneath it. This suggests that he carried her into the berth and then the boat was turned upside-down, made to look like a snatch and grab, although the damaged bow and gunshot blast to the outside hull concern me. I don't think Mr. Roberts told the whole story." He picked several computer printouts off the floor and read them. "This couple seemed to be preoccupied with sharks."

"Many divers come here to see our sharks." Drake grinned. "Long-lining was banned in the Bahamas over twenty years ago, and recently laws were passed to stop commercial shark fishing, so the Bahamas have the healthiest shark population in the Atlantic. We are only one of two countries in the world with the insight to protect those fish, since sharks balance and protect our reefs. Without reefs and fish, our economy would suffer."

CHAPTER FOUR

With a knock on the bedroom door, Christian stirred from a sound sleep. Bright sunlight radiated through the half-closed blinds. He stared at the light with a vampire's dread. *Another crappy day,* he thought and closed his eyes. Despite plenty of rest, he felt wiped out, as if a disease had zapped his strength.

Another knock, and Frank called through the closed door, "Christian, it's noon. You need to get up and get ready. We have to be at White's office in a few hours."

Christian lumbered out of bed. "I'm up, Frank. I'm up."

He took a long, hot shower, hoping it would energize him. Over the bathroom sink, he rubbed the blond stubble on his jaw and reached for the shaving cream. "Fuck it." In the bedroom, he dressed in jeans and a navy-blue t-shirt and stepped into a pair of leather sandals. He found his Ray-Ban sunglasses in the pocket of the linen shirt he had worn the day before. He slipped them on, letting the lenses rest on top of his shaggy wet hair.

He finally emerged from the room to his mother's disapproving gaze. "You're wearing that to the police station? There's a suit and tie in your bag. And Christian, you didn't shave. You look like a beach bum. You need to make a good impression with those officers."

Like I give a shit what they think, he felt like saying, but refrained.

"Angie, he can wear what he wants," Frank said. "He's a grown man."

Angie glared at Frank, obviously irked, but held her tongue and changed the subject. "We ordered room service, your favorite, bacon and scrambled eggs. I can reheat it in the microwave. You hardly ate anything yesterday, and you must eat, Christian. You have plenty of time before we have to leave." She lifted a metal cover off a plate.

The sight and smell of the breakfast nauseated Christian. He sensed his mother was stressed, desperate to help her newly widowed son, but unsure how, so she was treating him like a little boy again. She was also dealing with her own grief since she loved Allie like a daughter. "Thanks, Mom, but I'm not hungry." He kissed her cheek to soften the refusal. "I just want coffee."

Her eyes watered. "Christian, you're not eating, and you're too quiet. And you've never in your life slept until noon."

Christian massaged her shoulder. "It's hard, going through this. Just give me some time. I'll be okay. I promise," he lied.

At two o'clock, Christian, Frank, and Angie arrived at the lawyer's office. Frank had asked Angie to remain at the hotel, since the police would allow only White into the interview room with Christian. She'd snapped at Frank, saying she would be going. Sitting in the hotel room would drive her nuts, she said, and she preferred to wait at the police station and show her support.

Christian rode to the station with White in his silver Lincoln. Frank and Angie followed in a cab. White parked his car and nodded toward the front door at a group of fifteen or more people: blacks, whites, women, and men. "The press," he said. "Money and murder on the high seas always draws them out. If you hadn't moved to a different hotel, a police tip would have put them on your doorstep yesterday." One of the reporters pointed at White's Lincoln, and the group rushed toward them. "Here they come. Stay calm and don't talk to them."

Christian pushed his sunglasses against the bridge of his nose and slipped out of the passenger seat. Before he could close the car door, he was surrounded. The photographers held cameras and snapped pictures. The reporters pressed closer and yelled questions.

"Mr. Roberts, did you kill your wife?" asked a reporter.

"Are you a suspect?" another asked.

"What happened on your boat?" asked a third. "You really want us to believe it was a theft?"

"Mr. Roberts, did you get along with your wife?" said another. "Were you fighting over money? Is that why you murdered her?"

Christian gritted his teeth and clenched his fists. Reporters shouted and pushed against him like buzzards muscling for space on a carcass. White tried to appease them, saying he would give them a statement after the police interview. He placed his hand on Christian's back and ushered him toward the station.

The press followed, still firing questions and accusations. Halfway to the station, and despite White's counsel, Christian had enough and shot back, "I didn't kill her!"

"Sure you did," said a curly haired white guy with an obnoxious grin. He was so close that Christian could smell his bad breath. "Did you shoot your pretty wife because she was cheating on you?"

Christian reeled and punched him square in the face. The man fell backward to the pavement and looked up with a flabbergasted expression and bloody nose. The other reporters shrank back, out of striking range, and stared silently at Christian. His own lawyer had moved away from his side.

Christian removed his sunglasses, swept back his hair, and took a deep breath, more angry with himself than with the jerk he had popped. "I'm sorry, man," he said, "but you crossed the line. My wife would never cheat on me." He gazed at the press snapping more photos of him and his downed victim.

Officers joined the mix, and Frank appeared out of nowhere. "Take him inside," he told White.

White grabbed Christian's arm and escorted him toward the building along with two officers. Over his shoulder, Christian saw Frank helping the injured man up from the pavement. Beyond, his mother stood near the curb, shock on her face.

Christian walked through the door with White and the two officers. "Guess that'll cost me."

"The guy is a local drunk, works for a Bahamian rag," said White. "I'll handle it."

Sergeant Drake walked to them with a smile. "Milford, I heard there was a little trouble outside."

"Yes, Sergeant," said White. "My client was mobbed by reporters. I'm wondering why that happened in front of a police station with no officers around to control the crowd. Unless that was your intention, to goad my client into losing his temper. The press is under the impression that Mr. Roberts is a suspect. Any idea who spoon-fed them that information?"

Drake became grim-faced. "It is regrettable Mr. Roberts was harassed, but you're mistaken if you think my department leaked information on this case."

"Since you agree that my client was harassed," said White, "I assume you won't be charging him with assault for defending himself. Your statement nearly guarantees a dismissal in court."

Christian grinned ever so slightly. *This fat lawyer is good.*

"No, he won't be charged," Drake said, and turned on his heel. "Follow me. They're waiting."

"They?" questioned White as he waddled through the station to the interrogation room, following Christian and Drake.

Drake stepped into the room and said to White, "Agents Wheeler and McKenna are assisting our police department with this case. They'll be questioning Mr. Roberts."

White gave Drake a sideward glance. "You never informed me the Miami FBI had been brought in." He nodded to the agents. "Gentlemen, I'd like a minute with my client before we start." He took Christian down the hallway several feet out of earshot. "I wasn't expecting this. I thought Drake would be questioning you. The interview would have been a breeze, but the FBI changes things. You can still refuse to talk to them."

"No, I want to get this over with," said Christian.

"All right, try not to curse or lose your temper like you did outside, and be as stoic as you can. Answer their questions briefly, carefully, and to the point. Don't give them anything extra. Are you ready?"

Christian nodded. *Stoic,* he thought. *That won't be a stretch.* Except for anger, most of his emotions had been drained out of him, leaving him numb and indifferent. The only thing that kept him moving forward and keeping him alive was the goal Allie gave him. To accomplish it, he had to get past the interview with his freedom intact.

He and White entered the interrogation room, and Christian realized that the four men knew each other. He was the odd man out. He sat down and gazed at the two suits sitting across the table. They, in turn, seemed to be studying him. Drake joined them. White took a seat beside Christian.

The two agents looked like typical FBI, clean-shaven, crew cuts, and detached stares. Wheeler had an average build, graying temples, and had crow's feet near his hazel eyes. He appeared to be in his late forties or early fifties, and his pocked cheeks and double chin gave him a tough, well-seasoned appearance. His partner, McKenna, was younger, maybe mid-thirties. He had a beanpole frame and a weak chin, light brown hair, and pale blue eyes.

Christian leaned back in the chair and got comfortable. Compared to his past terrors, he was hardly intimidated by a couple of FBI guys.

"Would anyone care for coffee or a soda pop before we get started?" Wheeler asked with a southern drawl, not Deep South, but more Texan. Living in Florida all his life, Christian had met people from every state who wanted a chunk of paradise, so he was acquainted with various accents.

No one wanted a drink, so Wheeler looked down at the papers on the table, and said, "Okay, let's get started." He clicked his ball-point pen open and closed. Initially, the agent's questions were as easy and as friendly as his smile. He asked about Christian's life in Florida on his horse farm, the voyage from Sarasota through the Keys up to Lauderdale and across to Freeport, and where he and Allie had anchored and what they had done in the Bahamas.

Yeah, yeah, you're my new buddy, Christian thought. *Sucker must think I'm a fool.*

An hour later, Wheeler's questions turned serious and his demeanor changed. "Mr. Roberts, you told Sergeant Drake that your wife was killed around two in the afternoon?"

Christian knew where Wheeler was heading. With the autopsy, the time of death didn't add up against his earlier statement. He had hoped that detail would slide, with an incompetent Bahamian police department, and he wouldn't have to explain the missing hours. "I never said she died at two. I came aboard after a morning dive and found her, probably around ten or eleven. I tried to revive her and held her a long time. By the time I got it together, dug out charts to navigate here, and pulled anchor, I glanced at my watch, and it was two. Sergeant Drake asked me when everything happened. I thought he was looking for distance and time to pinpoint the location. Guess I misunderstood."

Wheeler flipped back through his earlier statements. "Yes, the sergeant should have been more direct with his questions," he said, giving Drake a headache glance. "You say you held your wife for a long time and then moved her body from the deck to the berth. You must've gotten some blood on you."

"Yeah, I was covered. I couldn't handle it, so I jumped off the boat and stripped. I managed to find some clean clothing in the mess before I got underway."

"What happened to your bloody clothing?"

"I imagine my cutoffs are floating in the ocean somewhere."

"We found a blood trail from the deck through the cabin," said Wheeler. "It must've been made when you carried her into the berth."

Christian massaged his jaw, thinking there was more to Wheeler's question. *He's trying to trip me up.* "Maybe, but I'm not sure. I found Allie's revolver under her, figured that's why the killers didn't see it and take it. The gun was kept in the forward berth. Allie might've been wounded and made the blood trail herself when she got her gun." He stared straight into the agent's eyes. "You have to understand, Agent Wheeler. Allie was fearless, braver than most men. Even wounded, she'd fight back until the very end."

"That makes sense," said Sergeant Drake, "the blood on the floor instead of on top of the strewn clothing."

Wheeler clicked the pen several times with irritation. "Sergeant, I don't think we need your comments."

Christian smiled inwardly, thankful for having given a plausible explanation for the blood trail that should have been on top of the mess.

Wheeler asked the next question. "Can you explain why no fingerprints were found on the sloop except yours and your wife's?"

"No," said Christian. "Maybe the killers wore gloves. I would, if I were robbing a boat."

"And the forty-four revolver?" asked Wheeler. "It was wiped clean."

"Really? Allie's and my prints should've been on the gun. We both handled it. When I sailed here, the gun was sliding back and forth on a wet deck. Maybe the blood and prints washed off."

"That's not likely," commented McKenna.

"Well, you're the detective," said Christian. "You tell me how the gun got clean."

Wheeler chewed the end of the pen and paused, soulfully staring at Christian. "How did the bow of your boat get damaged?"

Christian furrowed his brow. "It's damaged?"

"There's an eighteen-inch-wide hole in the fiberglass two feet above the waterline."

"I used the stern ladder to climb aboard after the dive. I never saw it."

"You don't remember hitting a seawall, dock, or something in the water like debris, a tree trunk?"

Christian grinned cynically. "I think I'd remember hitting something that hard."

"In your earlier statement, you claim you didn't hear or see another boat during your dive or when you surfaced."

"That's right. I know sound travels underwater, but it was a deep dive off the Tongue." He gazed at the floor. "If I had heard the other boat, maybe I'd still have my wife."

"Mr. Roberts," said McKenna, "did you and your wife get along, have any marital problems?"

White put his hand on Christian's arm. "My client doesn't need to answer that."

Christian pulled free. "We got along fine! Anyone who says different is a fucking liar."

Wheeler leaned back. "Son, you seem to have anger issues. You slugged a reporter outside when he pretty much asked the same questions."

Don't wig out. He's baiting me. He shrugged and smiled. "Sure, I get pissed when someone is insinuating shit about my marriage."

"These anger issues—"

Christian leaned forward. "I'd never get angry enough to hurt her, never."

"Can we move on?" asked White.

"We did a background check on you," said Wheeler. "Your wife was the second woman who was killed on your boat in less than a year."

White turned to Christian with a bombshell expression; open mouthed and wide eyed, but quickly collected his wits. "I don't see how that is relevant to this investigation."

"Shows a pattern," said Wheeler.

Christian swept back his hair. "Figured Kate might come up. She was a nut, a firebug I dated before Allie. I broke up with her, and to get even, she burned a Morgan sloop I had and Allie's barn, and then she snuck aboard *Hank's Dream* and shot me. Allie killed her with a spear gun before Kate could finish me off." Christian's eyes narrowed, staring at Wheeler. "But I'm sure you read the police report and know all this. It's listed as a justifiable homicide."

"I know there were no witnesses except you and your wife," said Wheeler as he turned to another page in the file. "What's your connection to Vince Florio?"

"We both owned and raced Thoroughbreds. I met him at the Miami track. He moved to Sarasota and knew I had a boat rental business down the key from his new home, so he hired me as a fishing guide."

"You and Florio were in a boating accident."

"Yeah, we were fishing on Tampa Bay in Vince's Scarab and had motor trouble. By the time I fixed the problem, it was dark and a hurricane was bearing down on us. We were racing in when the Scarab crashed into the hull of a sailboat that had capsized in the storm. It was a hell of a wreck. Vince was injured and one of his friends died. What of it?"

"You have a lot of bad luck on boats, someone always dying, or maybe it's the company you keep that's the problem."

"Agent Wheeler," asked White, "what does this man, Florio, have to do with this case?"

"I was wondering if your client was aware that Vince Florio has ties with the Italian mob in New York. He's a loan shark, drug smuggler, and a suspect in two homicides. Perhaps Mr. Roberts borrowed money from Florio and couldn't repay him or a drug deal went bad, and that's why his wife was killed."

"You're crazy," Christian said. "Vince didn't have anything to do with Allie's murder. Christ, we're friends."

"Did you know Florio was a mobster?" asked Wheeler.

"No, but I'm not surprised."

"I believe we're finished," said White. "Mr. Roberts has answered enough of your questions. I was informed that Mr. Roberts's passport was found on the boat. I'd like it returned so he can go home and bury his wife, unless you plan to charge him."

Wheeler whispered into Drake's ear, and Drake nodded. Wheeler tossed his pen on the papers. "He can have his passport and leave the Bahamas under one condition: that he agrees to a polygraph test."

"I need to consult with my client," said White. After the agents and Drake left the room, White turned to Christian. "If you refuse the lie detector test, they might hold you here for a long time. Since you're innocent of your wife's murder, I suggest you take it."

Christian chewed a nail in thought for a moment. "What if I fail?"

"First of all, a polygraph is inadmissible in a court. It can't hurt you at trial since stress can cause false readings. If you fail the test, the police might consider you a suspect and keep probing, so refusing or failing the test puts you in the same situation. To keep you here, they might charge you. I can set hearings and a judge might free you, but that takes time. Take the test and pass it, and you can leave right away. But Christian, as your lawyer, I must warn you. If you killed your wife, you shouldn't take the polygraph."

"I told you. I didn't shoot her." Christian scowled. "Tell them I'll take their friggin' test."

CHAPTER FIVE

Wheeler sat alone in Drake's office and tapped a pen on the desk, waiting for Ralph to return with coffee. Two years earlier, he had quit smoking, but he still woke every morning longing for a cigarette to go with the beverage. To get over the habit, he played with pens, clicking, tapping, and chewing on them, but they made a piss-poor substitute for good old tobacco and nicotine.

His thoughts drifted to Christian Roberts and yesterday's interview. The mug shot hadn't done him justice. Wheeler's ex-wife would have called Roberts a heartbreaker, the type women fell for and men envied. He had large blue eyes, shaggy sun-bleached locks, straight pearly whites, and his tan, unblemished skin looked like he'd skipped puberty. And he had all the style and attitude that came with his looks. *This pretty boy had probably seen more ass than a toilet seat.*

Furthermore, Roberts was tall, six two, and about 175 pounds of lean muscle. To the untrained eye, his willowy frame looked harmless, but Wheeler knew from past experience that tangling one-on-one with someone like him would be a mistake.

Wheeler reflected on the interview. He had talked to thousands of witnesses and suspects and was skilled in reading body language, but Roberts was a puzzle, hard to read. He had answered the questions without hesitation and with reasonable explanations. He never squirmed in his seat, crossed his arms, stuttered, or shifted his eyes. Roberts's testimony was perfect, hence the problem. It was too perfect.

At the appropriate times, Roberts displayed remorse that he might have saved his wife if he had heard the other boat and irritation when Ralph asked if his marriage had problems. What Roberts didn't reveal concerned Wheeler.

Most people sweat and are nervous when put in the hot seat and questioned by the FBI, even when innocent, but that cold fish was calm and collected with an air that the interview was a game. Roberts's most notable flaw was his lack of either rage or disgust when his wife's killers were mentioned. He also didn't request or demand that authorities catch the killers, a common response from a grieving husband. Wheeler figured he had either misread Roberts or he was one great liar and guilty. The polygraph taking place now would, hopefully, reveal the truth.

Ralph entered the office and placed a cup of coffee on the desk in front of Wheeler. "They're still at it?" he asked and took a sip from his own cup.

"That polygraph operator is good, takes his time. I'm just glad he was available to fly out of Miami. I'd like to get off this rock."

Ralph chuckled. "I bet Roberts feels the same way about now."

Wheeler picked up the cup and slouched back in the chair, getting comfortable. "I have no problem letting him go, as long as he honestly passes the test."

"He doesn't strike me as a sociopath with no sense of right and wrong."

"Sociopaths come in all shapes. Look at Ted Bundy, charming, good-looking law student. Nobody would have guessed he murdered all those women." He had just taken a sip when the polygraph operator, a chubby man with thick glasses, stepped into the office.

Wheeler sat up and asked, "Well?"

The operator tilted his head and raised an eyebrow. "I'm not sure about that guy. I went through the questions twice and gave him time to relax between sessions but got mixed results."

"What about when you asked if he killed his wife?" Ralph said.

"He said no. The first time measured a lie, second time, he told the truth, but his guilt might come from his failure to save her, and he feels responsible. I asked if he knew the killers, and he definitely lied both times. He knows who did it. I asked if he was there when she was shot and died, and that also triggered two different responses."

"Son of a gun," Wheeler said and leaped up from chair. "I knew that young man was holding back when I questioned him."

"If he knew the killers," said Ralph, "we can rule out strangers and a theft gone bad. Maybe Florio's men did murder her, and Roberts is afraid to talk. That would add up."

"Could be," said the operator, "or you can chalk this whole test up to rattled nerves."

"Bull," said Wheeler. "A bomb could explode, and that kid wouldn't blink."

"Regardless, Agent Wheeler," said the operator, "I'm sorry, but with the subject's varied responses, the polygraph is a wash. It's inconclusive."

"Did I hear correctly?" White said as he and Sergeant Drake entered the office. "The polygraph was inconclusive?"

"I'm afraid so," said the operator.

White smiled and turned to Drake. "That means my client is free to go. Sergeant Drake, could you retrieve him from the interrogation room and give him his passport? I'm sure Mr. Roberts would like to be on the first flight home."

Sergeant Drake glanced at Wheeler with uncertainty.

Wheeler shook his head with disgust. "Let him go, Drake. If he's back in Florida, we can keep an eye on him, and if anything new develops, I'll extradite his butt back to Nassau."

Drake left the office and returned in minutes with Christian Roberts. The lanky blond tapped his passport against his chin and leaned against the doorjamb with a smug, schoolboy expression. "I hear your test was a flop and I can go."

Irritated, Wheeler marched up to Roberts and glared into his eyes. "You can drop that cocky grin. You failed the polygraph. You know lying to the police is a crime and carries a one-year sentence.

The guys in prison would love to get their hands on someone like you."

"Is that supposed to frighten me?" Roberts straightened to his full stature and looked down his perfect nose at Wheeler. "Your piddly-ass threats don't hold a candle to my demons. Besides, you need proof I lied. It doesn't appear you have it today."

"But I will get it," Wheeler seethed. "I'll prove you killed her."

Roberts's shoulders tensed and his eyes had an if-looks-could-kill stare, but then White interceded.

"Good day, gentlemen," White said, nudging his large body between Wheeler and Roberts and coaxing his client out the doorway before anymore was said. "Let's go, Christian."

Roberts gave Wheeler one last frosty glance and swaggered through the police station with his attorney toddling behind.

"Lawyers," Wheeler grumbled under his breath. *White's so fat he could sell shade.* He turned back to Ralph and Sergeant Drake. "That kid has a temper, a bad one. With his wife trapped for weeks on a boat with him, maybe he lost it and killed her. I need to get that strutting peacock alone and pluck some feathers."

"Dave, we should have charged him," said Ralph.

"With what, being a smart-ass?" said Wheeler, "Without solid evidence, a judge would toss the case at a hearing."

Sergeant Drake massaged his thin mustache in thought. "I wonder what Roberts meant by demons?"

In the backseat of a taxi, Christian sat beside his mother as they drove down the coastal road toward Millionaire Airport on Nassau. Frank had arranged for a private jet to fly them to Sarasota. Frank would remain behind for the hearing to release Allie's body and would accompany her casket back to Florida. Christian had argued with Frank and White, saying he should stay with her, but they convinced him that he needed to get out of the Bahamas while the getting was good. The FBI agents could change their minds and have Drake arrest him.

Christian solemnly gazed out the taxi window at the rocky beaches and slate waters sprinkled with small whitecaps. The landscape was fast fading to black with night's approach. His nervous mother made idle conversation. He forced a small grin to reassure her, but preferred not to divulge his thoughts.

His mind was a void, past crying, caring, or feeling. His soul and life rested in a dark Bahamian morgue, and he was stumbling blindly, clueless of direction. To function, he moved to robot mode again, like on the boat ride to Nassau, like during the FBI interview. *Just get through it*, he told himself. *Get home, deal with the funeral, and when finally alone, decide.* So far, this plan was his only one.

The cab passed the ruins of an old fort, and several miles later, arrived at the small private airport. He and his mother walked through the building, and the two pilots met them. One of the pilots carried and stowed their bags. On the landing strip, Christian, his mother, and the pilots climbed aboard an eight-seat Lear. As the jet took off, Christian pressed his head against the window and said good-bye to the dark ocean and twinkling island lights.

The jet soon landed at the Sarasota-Bradenton airport and taxied to Dolphin, a hub for small jets and private planes. Christian and his mother exited the aircraft and walked across the pavement.

"Christian, I think you should come home with me," his mother said.

"The farm is my home. Juan is waiting for me in the parking lot." In the terminal, Christian and his mother went through customs. The agent barely glanced at their passports and never asked to check their bags.

Outside, his mother stood by a taxi and made one last plea. "You shouldn't be alone, and Juan and his mother live a long way down the drive from your house. I know you, Christian, and you're very withdrawn and barely eating. You're not okay."

"Yeah, I'm not. My wife just died. I need to be around my horses now." He planted a kiss on her cheek. "I'll call you tomorrow about the funeral."

"You and those damn horses—just like your father." She huffed and climbed into the taxi. "Siesta Key," she said to the cabby as Christian closed the car door.

He wandered into the small parking lot and saw his SUV with Juan standing beside it. The short Mexican hurried to him. After three weeks away, the reunion should have been happy, but instead of smiles, Juan's eyes watered with tears. "I'm so sorry, Mr. Roberts. I'm so sorry. I will truly miss her. So will the horses."

Christian cleared his throat. "We'll all miss her."

Neither spoke on the forty-minute ride from Sarasota to the horse farm in Myakka City. Christian drove and appreciated Juan's silence. The horse trainer seemed to sense his needs. He drove through the farm gates and passed the house and barn. Only when Christian pulled up to the caretaker's house at the back of the property and Juan emerged from the SUV, did Juan speak up. "Mr. Roberts, Christian," he said, rarely using his first name. "If you need to talk, if you need anything, I am here."

"Thanks, Juan." Christian turned the SUV around and stared back down the drive toward the empty house, but stopped at the barn. He switched off the headlights, killed the engine, and stepped out. Across the open pastures, a crisp autumn wind blew against his face. The evening sky was moonless, cloudless, and lacked the glow of city lights, bringing out millions of stars. Their radiance cast the horse pastures in silver, grays, and shadows. Inside the dark barn, he heard the low nickering of the old bay stallion.

"Yes, Chris, I'm home," he answered, his father having given the same name to the horse and his son. A second horse whinnied excitedly, recognizing Christian's voice.

A horse's sound is as distinctive as its color, and although Christian couldn't see the horses, he knew the high-pitched whinny came from Mystery, the red stud colt in the third stall. He strolled down the aisle into the pitch-black stable and stopped at the colt's stall.

"Hey, Mystery," he said. Mystery was the horse's nickname, but he had been registered as Clever Chris. Breaking several track records, the handsome chestnut was most likely the fastest horse on the planet and had made Christian wealthy, besides bringing Allie into his life. The colt lowered his head into Christian's arms.

His eyes adjusting to the dark, Christian massaged the white star and strip on the colt's forehead and scratched behind his ear. After a few minutes, Mystery pulled away and anxiously looked toward the open doorway. He whinnied again.

"She's not coming, Mystery," he said. "It's just me, just me now."

The next morning Christian stirred to the stallion's nickering and the bang of feed buckets being tossed against the stall boards by hungry, impatient horses. He lay still for a moment and felt the hay beneath him. A blue horse blanket covered him, but he had no memory of retrieving it the previous night. He pushed the blanket aside, staggered to his feet, and saw Juan at the end of the barn, holding two feed buckets. Christian shook the straw from his hair and brushed off his clothing before stepping from the hay room into the aisle.

Juan shut a stall door and noticed him. "I'm sorry the horses woke you."

Christian reached down and petted the curled back of a tabby barn cat that rubbed against his legs. "I couldn't face that house," he explained.

"Your mother phoned me last night when she could not reach you at home. I called her back and said I found you sleeping in the barn with your boys, and you were fine."

"She's—ah—"

"She is a worried mother."

Christian bit his lip and nodded, thinking his response would have differed. "Thanks for the blanket," he said and strolled to his SUV, still parked in front of the barn. He pulled up the drive and entered the small ranch house he had shared with Allie. Everywhere, memories smacked him in the face. To deal with them, he skipped the usual coffee and fixed a hefty cocktail of rum and Coke. He took a few sips, trying to decide if he should tackle unpleasant tasks or get totally wasted.

After gulping down half the drink, he found the courage to make the agonizing call to Allie's parents, who lived twenty-five miles away in Arcadia. Frank had already informed them of their daughter's death and given them the details.

George, Allie's father, was a thin, quiet man, wrinkled, and tanned like a raisin from the weather and hard work. He was a mechanic and owned a small ranch with a few head of cattle. Allie's mother, Maggie, bartended part time at a steakhouse and was a robust blond who always had a joke on her lips and usually a cigarette or a beer in hand. They were simple country folks who struggled to make ends meet. When Christian married Allie, they were thrilled, Maggie boasting at the wedding that her new son-in-law and his millions would give their daughter a better life. Allie had been mortified, apologizing that her mother had had too much to drink. Christian laughed and told her, "But it's true, Allie. I am going to take care of you."

As the phone rang, Christian wondered how Allie's parents felt now. Their beautiful daughter was dead because her husband had taken her out to sea and failed to take care of her.

George answered the phone. "Chris, I'm glad you called." His voice was low and drained. "Your stepdad has been keeping us informed. It's a terrible thing, just terrible. Maggie and I are still in shock."

Christian agreed and retold the story that led to Allie's death. "I'm so sorry, George. I should've been there to protect her."

"But you'd probably be dead too. Allie wouldn't of wanted that. She really loved you. I just hope they catch the bastards who did it."

"I'm sure the Bahamian cops will find them."

"Speaking of cops, some guy named Wheeler called. Said he was with the FBI. He wanted to know if you and Allie got along, if you treated her right or ever had any knock-down, drag-out fights. He really got in my craw. Told him I ain't never seen two people get along better than you and Allie, and I hung up on him."

Goddamn Wheeler, Christian thought but masked his anger. "He's just doing his job. They have to ask those questions to rule me out as a suspect." He changed the subject and talked about the funeral. Since Allie had no will, Christian gave George the option of making the arrangements for his daughter, but Christian would pay for everything: casket, memorial at a church or funeral home, flowers, cemetery plot, and headstone. If Maggie and George weren't up to it, Christian's mother was willing to step in.

Christian already knew his mother's plan. They had briefly discussed it in the Bahamas. Angie wanted Allie's memorial to be at a plush funeral home in Sarasota and her remains buried in one of its stately cemeteries. His mother had scoffed when Christian mentioned cremation and scattering Allie's ashes at the farm, a place she had loved and where she would always be with him, but funerals were for the living, a ritual to lessen the pain.

"Thank you, Chris," said George. "Our minister told me and Maggie that you had the right as Allie's husband to bury her where you saw fit. Maggie will be pleased that the services can be held in our little church in Arcadia, and our girl will rest at a graveyard down the road. Her mother can visit as often as she likes, keep fresh flowers on the plot."

"That sounds fine, George. Let me know if I can do anything," Christian said, ending the call. *Parents aren't supposed to bury their children.*

Eight o'clock in the morning, and Christian had already finished his first cocktail. He made another, reclined in the desk chair, and called his mother. He told her that Allie's parents would make the funeral arrangements, and Allie would be buried in Arcadia.

"That redneck cattle town," Angie said, irritated. "They'll have the service in some crummy church and place your wife in a weed-infested cemetery. How could you do that, Christian, leave it up to them? Allie deserved better."

"I don't think Allie cares," he said.

"Well, I do. She was my daughter-in-law, and I want her to have the best. Call George back and tell him you've changed your mind."

Christian had kept his cool when dealing with his mother, who had turned into a demanding royal pain. They normally had a great relationship, talked easily, and she stayed out of his life. Only one other time had she gone off like this, when he was ten and she had dragged him from his father and horse farm home in Ocala and filed for divorce. Stressed and unsure how to deal with her sulking son who increasingly got into fights at his new school, she had become overbearing. It was happening again.

After finishing two strong cocktails, however, he was ready to end the nagging. "Mother, I'm not calling George back, and I don't give a shit if Allie's funeral is not up to your standards," he said with a raised voice. "I was with Allie three years and we were married only six months. She was with her parents a lot longer. If making the burial arrangements helps them with their grief, that's what I want. I know you're frazzled, but I've had my fill of your needy crap."

There was a long silence. "All right, Christian."

He hung up, feeling vindicated, but it quickly turned to shame. He had never cussed out his mother. *Allie's death changed her, but it's also changed me.* He no longer saw himself as level-headed, capable, and smart enough to handle anything life dished out. He now felt confused and cursed, his life so shattered that he could not begin to pick up the pieces. He walked into the kitchen and filled his glass with ice and rum but left out the Coke. *Plan two, get drunk.*

CHAPTER SIX

Christian's head throbbed, his joints and muscles ached, and his stomach felt like a furnace. The pain was self-inflicted, the result of using rum to drown his misery. For five days he had gone to the barn and gotten toasted. His drinking buddy had become Chris, the old stallion, who helped him slurp down the big tumbler of rum and Coke. Juan's frowns conveyed his disapproval of giving a horse alcohol, but he never said a word. At sundown, Christian would leave the stallion's stall and stagger back to the house, where he passed out on the couch, unable to face a barren bed. Rosa, Juan's mother, provided him with meals, but most of the food ended up feeding the nightly visitors in the raccoon clan. Christian hadn't eaten at all on the previous day.

He now tried to stand erect with dignity and concentrate on the minister's words, but doing so was grueling. His mind kept drifting, and in the small, claustrophobic church choked with the fragrance of flowers, he felt queasy. Could he make it through the ceremony without retching or collapsing?

He glanced around the crowded church and saw white; the walls, ceiling, and the casket covered with a huge bouquet of white roses. The large windows filled the space with bright sunlight that increased the pounding in his head. He fumbled for his sunglasses in his black suit pocket and covered his eyes. Thankfully, most people believed his bloodshot eyes were the result of tears rather than a hangover. His mother squeezed his hand, and he realized that the minister had finished a prayer and Christian was up next.

Days earlier, Allie's parents had called and asked him to speak at the funeral service. Intoxicated, he had agreed, but now he regretted it. He had risen this morning at dawn, made a pot of coffee to sober up, and had sat down at the kitchen table with a legal pad. Hours later, dozens of crumbled balls of yellow paper that contained his notes about Allie littered the floor. With time running out and unable to find the right words, he gave up. He showered, dressed, and left for Arcadia, deciding to wing his speech.

As Christian made his way to the podium at the front of the church, he heard a baby whine in the back, a few coughs, and the rustle of feet and clothing as the crowd of a hundred or so became seated. Allie knew a lot of people, besides having a huge family scattered around the state. They were all there.

At the podium, he uneasily removed the sunglasses as a hush settled over the room and then pin-drop-hearing silence. He gazed out at the faces of mostly strangers, their eyes judging, questioning, wondering; who was this boat guy from pompous Sarasota, a sportie, the midstate term for an outsider, this jerk that came to the country, married their girl, and got her killed?

Since Allie's death, Christian had lost track of his lies, but the time had come for some truth. He nervously cleared his throat and said, "I tried to write a good speech about Allie, but couldn't, so I'm sorry, sorry I took her out on my boat and didn't protect her, sorry we're here today to bury her." He gripped the podium to stop his shaking hands. He swallowed hard before continuing. "What can I say about Allie? You all knew her. She was beautiful, bright, fun, and the most fearless person I've ever met. She loved her horses, loved nature and the outdoors. She loved her alligator. She liked to kid around and laugh. Her laugh—" Hearing a woman moan, he lowered his head and gathered his wits. He looked back up. "Her laugh made my day. Allie was my best friend. She was my partner, my lover, my whole life. When I was with her, nothing else mattered. Now that she's gone, nothing else matters. I'm not sure how to go on." Stinging tears blurred his vision, and he tasted their salt on his trembling lips. He sniffled and realized he was crying.

"She . . . she—" On the verge of blubbering, he shook his head. "I can't," he muttered. "I'm sorry, but I can't do this." He stepped from podium and returned to his seat.

"You did good," his mother whispered into his ear.

Only a mother praises her son's failures. And again, he had failed Allie, had not done her justice with his lousy speech. She was so much more, a tigress who had saved his life, not once but twice. She wasn't afraid of anything. *But then, cowards usually have longer lives.*

Frank, George, and several of Allie's relatives carried the casket from the church to an awaiting black hearse. Christian, his mother, and mother-in-law walked behind the coffin. The crowd filed out behind them. Outside, Christian inhaled the fresh air and felt better, but then he had to face these people individually with hugs, hand-shakes, and nods, along with solemn words of thanks for coming as they expressed their regrets. *Get through it; just get through it.*

The crowd eventually broke up and strolled to vehicles for the procession to the cemetery. Christian, his mother, and Frank climbed into one of the two black limos parked behind the hearse. On the drive to the graveyard, his mother and Frank chatted quietly about the service. Christian gazed through the barbwire fences at the pastures and cattle. He felt stupefied, his mind refusing to grasp that he was burying the love of his life today. *And tomorrow, there's nothing, nothing worth living for.*

The limo entered the cemetery and stopped near the gravesite. Christian, Angie, and Frank left the limo and waited for the people to arrive and assemble at the grave.

Frank pulled Christian aside. "I called you several times but couldn't leave a message. Your phone or recorder must be broken."

"The recorder's unplugged, too many people calling me, but I saw your number on the caller ID and thought it was Mom. I didn't want to deal with her."

"Damn it, Christian, she's concerned about you."

"Believe me, I get it, Frank."

"I'm not going to go into that now," Frank said. "I was trying to reach you because Milford White phoned, said the Bahamian police received the court order to release your boat, and it had to be moved from the straw market docks. I told White to find a marina where the damaged bow and fiberglass could be fixed and the boat cleaned up. The repairs are nearly finished, and White found a slip at Atlantis, but he needs to be reimbursed. He's also wondering if you want the boat back in Florida. If so, should he hire a licensed captain to do the job?"

"Tell White to take that damn boat out and sink it."

"Christian, I know about your five-day drinking binge in the barn, and I understand you're in pain, but it's time to man up and get your act together," Frank said firmly. "Now, I need answers on this sailboat."

Frank must've asked Juan to keep tabs on me. Christian wearily rubbed his forehead. "I know I've been screwing up and owe you and Mom. I couldn't have gone through this without your help," he said. "Tell White I'll come to Nassau next week. I'll settle up the bills and bring the boat back myself. Give me something to do." Out of the corner of his eye, he saw two men in dark suits, standing beyond the crowd. One was taking pictures. "Those pricks, I can't believe them."

"What is it?" Frank asked.

"I'll handle this." Christian stormed off to confront the men. "What are you doing here?" he growled at the FBI agents.

McKenna focused the camera on Christian and snapped his picture.

Wheeler held his smiling jaw. "We like to take pictures at a murder victim's funeral. It's amazing how many times the killer is captured on film."

"The killer isn't here."

"How do you seem to know, Mr. Roberts?" asked Wheeler. Christian crossed his arms and refused to answer.

Wheeler surveyed the crowd. "Speaking of killers, I don't see your friend, Florio."

"Vince sent flowers," said Christian. "Now I think you should go."

"I think you need to talk to us," McKenna said. Christian only glared at them.

"He's looking at us like we're a jar of jalapeños, Ralph. He knows if he opens up and swallows some today, we'll burn his ass tomorrow," said Wheeler. "Son, I understand your reluctance to talk without a lawyer, but what strikes me odd is your lack of interest in this case. Most husbands question us, ask how the case is going, if we have any new leads, or if we're any closer to finding the murderer. But you, you don't seem to care. That leads me to believe you're either guilty or know who is."

"Fine," said Christian. "Any fucking new leads?"

"You definitely cuss like a real sailor." Wheeler chuckled. "But as a matter of fact, we do have new evidence. We did a more thorough test on your wife's revolver. Apparently, when *you* wiped it clean, you missed the bullets in the chamber. We lifted a nice bloody print, your print. You can explain how it got there when you loaded the gun, but the blood—that's a problem. It isn't yours or your wife's. Kinda blows some holes in your story. Son, you need to give it up and tell me whose blood is on that bullet."

"Agent Wheeler, I'm not your son, and I have nothing to say."

Lil Lenny, Allie's lanky cousin, and Big Lenny, her stout uncle, came up alongside Christian. "Chris, are these guys giving you trouble?" Big Lenny asked, puffed up and looking like an annoyed bear.

"They're FBI, keeping me informed on Allie's murder investigation."

Big Lenny nodded toward the people gathered at the gravesite. "Well, we're all waiting for you to start the service."

"They were just leaving," said Christian.

"Yeah, we have to get back to Miami," said Wheeler. "Christian, I'll see you around." The two agents sauntered to their car.

As Christian walked to the gravesite, his thoughts weren't on the funeral service, but the blood and bullet. With the gunpowder residue on Allie's hand, he had kept the revolver, so it appeared she had a shootout with pirates, but now realized his decision was a mistake. *I should've tossed the damn gun overboard with the rest of the stuff. What else did I screw up?*

The week following the funeral, Christian took Frank's advice and stopped drinking. He put on a mask to hide his sorrow and went back to the get-through-it mode, preparing to bring *Hank's Dream* back from Nassau. At a marine store, he purchased a new GPS, radio, and other gear for the sailboat. He also replaced his cell phone, laptop computer, and credit cards.

He had many friends in the sailing community, and several would gladly accompany him on the voyage from the Bahamas to Sarasota. Another sailor on board would make the trip easier, but being stuck on a boat and forced to make friendly conversation for days would be unbearable given his mood. He decided to go it alone.

He looked over the sea charts to plot the course, but was unsure if he should sail to the Florida Keys and make the run up the west coast to Sarasota, the same route he and Allie had taken four weeks earlier, or go through Lake Okeechobee and motor up the Intracoastal Waterway. He rolled up the chart and chose to let weather dictate his path.

With a large duffel bag filled with equipment, he boarded a commercial flight. In Nassau he took a taxi to Milford White's office to pay him for additional services and the fees incurred on the boat. He also needed the sloop hatch and motor keys the police had confiscated during the investigation.

"Come in, Christian," White said when Christian entered the lawyer's small office. "I'm sure you'd like to get to your boat, but we need to talk about the case."

Christian dropped the duffel bag next to the chair and sat down. "Wheeler already told me about the bloody print found on a bullet in the revolver. The son of a bitch showed up at my wife's funeral."

"That's terrible, no decency," White said with a frown. "Wheeler was probably hoping to catch you off guard and get a reaction. You didn't get rattled and try to explain this bullet?"

"If he made that long trip for a reaction, he was disappointed. I didn't say a word about the case or bullet."

"That's good, but this bloody print is bad news, proves you're more involved than you let on and had someone's blood on your hand when you loaded the weapon."

"How much trouble am I in?"

"Hard to say," White said, settling his bulk back in his large chair. "I believe they are still trying to decide if you're a conspirator in the murder or a victim, defending your wife. Either way, they can't move forward until they find the person who matches the DNA in the blood. At least they're now looking for a third party. Drake has been checking hospitals for gunshot wounds." White leaned forward. "Christian, it's time to tell me exactly what happened on your boat and whose blood is on that bullet."

"I've told you what you need to know."

"The authorities are convinced you know who shot your wife, and so am I. And when asked if you knew your wife's killers, you also failed that question on the polygraph. Now they have this bullet, further evidence you probably weren't diving, but were there during the gunfire. I can't defend you properly without the truth."

Christian stood and pulled his checkbook from his back pocket. "Can I get the bills and the keys for my boat? I want to get out of here before Drake learns I'm here, or I'll have to face the same shit, questions about the damn bullet."

"I'm not the enemy. I'm here to help." White reached into a drawer and tossed a set of keys on his desk. "My secretary has the paperwork on the bills. You can give her a check. One more thing, the FBI got the test results back on the blue paint scrapings taken off your boat's damaged bow. It's old marine paint, lead-based, and made in a Mexican factory, and apparently rare in the Bahamas. Most of our boat paint comes from the US. The Bahamian and US Coast Guard have been alerted and are searching for a damaged blue boat."

"I hope they find it. Get the cops off my back." Christian shoved the keys into his jeans pocket and left White's office.

At the marina on Paradise Island, Christian located his sloop docked in front of a seawall with a dock running alongside. He checked out the bow, hull, and cockpit and was more than satisfied with the repairs. *Hank's Dream* looked new. A fresh coat of paint concealed the fiberglass work done on the gunshot blasts and crushed bow. Opening the hatch, he did a quick inspection of the cabin. It was immaculate, scrubbed clean and polished. All traces of blood, broken dishes, and scattered clothing were gone. He set down his bag and looked inside the cabinets. Everything was neat and orderly, not a pot out of place. In the berth, the bed had a new bedspread, and even his clothes in the drawers were washed and folded. *Amazing, it's like it never happened. God, I'd give anything if that were only true.*

He hurried topside, concerned that by going through customs at the airport, a red flag had been placed on his passport, alerting the authorities of his whereabouts. Drake might decide to hold him this time. He started the motor, cast off the dock lines, backed the sloop out, and headed into the bay.

Since Allie's death, he had dreaded going back to his boat, dreaded the harrowing memories and crippling guilt when he stepped aboard, but as *Hank's Dream* reached the open water under raised sails, a peace washed over his soul like a soothing bath that removed the dirt and anxiety. Instead of dwelling on the horror of the recent past, he felt a rekindling of love for the boat and quiet empty sea. Out here, he was free, free of the troubled stares, condolences, or nagging questions; free of worried mothers or looking over his shoulder for cops; free of concerned friends and employees who watched his every move. Alone and out here, he could finally think clearly and reflect. *How did this happen? How did I lose her?*

CHAPTER SEVEN

Christian glanced back over the stern. No boats followed in the sloop's wake, and Nassau was a speck on the blue horizon. He was leaving the Bahamas for home. The rigging creaked with the strain of full sails, and waves whooshed beneath the thrusting bow. The familiar sounds, along with the rise and fall of the deck, comforted Christian like a rocking cradle consoles a baby. He settled into the cockpit behind the wheel and reminisced about the beginning of the voyage, the last for Allie.

On the horse farm, he and Allie had planned the trip since buying the sloop, but had waited until the end of October, when daily thunderstorms, tropical depressions, and hurricanes no longer threatened. The breezy warm days and cool nights of fall would replace the summer's heat, high humidity, and morning calms with no wind. They said good-bye to Juan and Rosa and the horses, even though Allie found it hard to leave her four-legged babies for a lengthy vacation.

They had driven into downtown Sarasota and parked at Marina Jack on the bay. In a dock slip, *Hank's Dream* awaited, forty-seven feet of sleek and beautiful, often jokingly referred to as Christian's mistress. They loaded the sloop with food, clothing, and supplies. Allie armed herself with magazines and travel books on places they would visit in the Caribbean.

"Allie, you don't need those books. I know where we're going and what's there." He had spent most of his life on the water, an experienced sailor, diver, fisherman, and surfer. He had visited the Keys and Bahamas numerous times and had seen a good portion of the Caribbean, but this big maritime venture was new for Allie, a horse trainer raised in the center of the state. Not that she was ill prepared. She had learned to snorkel, fish, and handle the sloop, and right before they left, had received her PADI card, proving she had completed scuba diving lessons.

But Allie had never seen the crystal-clear water and reefs of the Caribbean or the exotic island ports and people. With money and the ideal vessel, Christian planned to show her the trip of a lifetime. *So ironic,* he thought now.

"Christian, I'm sure you know every bar and fishing hole on these islands," she said and stashed the literature in a cubbyhole, "but there might be other things I'd like to do."

They left Sarasota and sailed south along the Florida west coast. With the wind at their back, Christian launched the spinnaker, and they rode the large swells and made good time. After a few days, they docked in Key West, also called the "Conch Republic" since its secession from the United States. The little rustic town overflowed with people who were there for Fantasy Fest, a huge Halloween blowout.

Christian and Allie walked the old narrow streets lined with Victorian buildings that held the gift shops, restaurants, and bars. On a crowded street corner, they watched the outrageous parade of cross-dressing gays and transsexuals. During the day, they feasted on the local cuisine and shopped. At night they partied hard in the crowded bars. Sloppy Joe's, Hemingway's old hangout, became their favorite.

After four days, the Halloween bash was over. They strolled down the streets ankle deep with party litter and visited the small museum of the *Atocha,* a Spanish galleon laden with silver and gold that sank in 1622 during a hurricane. Mel Fisher had discovered the shipwreck off the Keys. In the museum gift shop, Christian spent several grand on a Spanish coin made into a pendant. Allie's eyes sparkled when he placed the chain around her neck. "Something in memory of our trip," he said. When Allie died, he had placed the pendant around his own neck, a memory of her.

They sailed out of Key West and traveled up the Florida Straits, stopping overnight in Marathon. After Key Largo, they ran up the Florida coast, skipping Miami but they put in at Fort Lauderdale to refuel and buy more supplies. They then ventured the hundred miles across open water to the Grand Bahamas. They docked at Freeport, went through customs, and spent several days dining, touring the island, and visited a casino at night. For Christian, the casino quickly got old. Chips, cards, and slot machines were not his thing, although he was a gambler.

A few years back, he had risked everything, including his life, on Clever Chris, a Thoroughbred nicknamed Mystery. The red colt was a gift from his ill father, but there were problems. Mystery was a clone, illegally registered, and couldn't be raced, plus there was a substantial debt for the cloning still owed on the horse. At the time, Christian was content with renting out small boats on Sarasota Bay, but his easygoing life changed when he promised his dying father he would somehow raise the money and race the colt.

Naïvely, Christian entered the underworld of horse racing, with its crooked trainers, wealthy sheiks, and loan sharks. Despite his statement to the FBI, he met Vince Florio when the mobster gave Christian a hefty loan on Mystery. With his failure to repay Vince on time, he didn't have much of a choice: either run drugs off the coast for Vince or die. On top of those troubles, an ex-girlfriend, a psycho with a thing for arson, preferred to kill him rather than lose him.

Thankfully, he had met Allie. She trained his colt, and more so, kept him from going insane. She was unaware, of course, that Christian faced jail if caught racing the illegal colt or smuggling the mobster's drugs. During a hurricane, he saved Vince's life and was cleared of the debt. He raced Mystery and the gamble paid off. Christian walked away wealthy. Seven months later, he was in the Bahamas, with the perfect girl, on the perfect boat, enjoying the perfect vacation, a true believer in happy endings.

What a fool! What a damn fool I was! There are no guarantees.

Christian set aside his reflection of the past. He trimmed the sheets, put the sloop on autopilot, and went below. In the galley, he set a course for Bimini, a tiny island fifty miles off Florida. Initially, he planned to travel day and night to reach US waters, but in a hurry to leave Nassau, he had failed to check out the boat. Fuel was low, meaning no diesel for speed or to run the compressor and charge the batteries. He also had little food on board. He could still make the straight run, relying on wind and eating canned beans, but a night docked in Bimini shouldn't be bad. No one would know him. He'd be just another sea bum, as Allie liked to call him, touring the islands.

Fatigue also played a factor in a nonstop voyage to the States. The downside of sobriety was sleeplessness, tossing and turning all night. When finally asleep, he was jerked awake and covered in sweat from horrific dreams. It was draining. During the day, he was jump-out-of-his-skin anxious or annoyed with everyone, including himself, but he made a pathetic drunk. Prior to Allie's funeral, he had gone to the barn, guzzled down the rum, and sobbed into the stallion's mane. At sundown he stumbled back to the house and passed out on the couch. In the morning, he faced a miserable hangover, but at least he slept soundly.

In a lower cabinet he retrieved a bottle of rum and a small can of pineapple juice. He combined the two in a plastic cup and winced with the first warm sip. *Sucks, needs ice.* On the wall he glanced at a picture of Allie and himself after the boat purchase. He stared at her image. "Look at me, Allie. I'm a screwed-up mess. I should just end it, jump off this damn boat and drown."

He made his way topside and mumbled, "Yeah, yeah, I can hear you now." His voice became high pitched, mimicking her. "What a stupid idea, Christian. You're too good a swimmer to drown." He sighed. "No fucking pity. That's you. But why, Allie, why for once didn't you listen to me? You'd still be alive, and I wouldn't be alone." Even though she was gone, it felt reassuring to talk to her.

He sat on the bench behind the wheel and took another swallow of his cocktail. It was beginning to taste better. He eased back and propped his feet up on the console. "Okay, I'm here, nothing but ocean for miles, and I'm supposed to sort things out."

He drifted back to when he and Allie had sailed out of Freeport, heading south to skirt the Abaco chain of islands. He recalled the conversation with Allie. "We're done with civilization; no more towns, marinas, and people. It's anchoring near a deserted island and living off the sea. Are you up for it?"

"Aye, Captain," she said cheerfully. "I'm happy anywhere, as long as you're with me."

"Ditto," he said and kissed her cheek.

And she was happy, little-girl excited. She was captivated with the Caribbean waters, brilliant turquoises to a deep blue close to black. When taking her diving course, she dove in Sarasota Bay and the green Gulf of Mexico, but both were usually so murky in summer that a diver could barely see his hand in front of the mask. In the Caribbean, though, the waters were as clear as air, with more than hundred feet of visibility, and the reefs hosted delicate corals and colorful fish. It was like entering a silent fantasy world.

On her first dive, she had bubbled to the surface and spat out her regulator mouthpiece. "It's like flying, Christian," she said, breathless as a kid at a circus. "It's like a flying dream."

He could relate, remembering his first dive and drifting over the underwater terrain with the weightlessness of a bird.

After each dive, they discussed the things they had seen. "I love those paper-thin bushes," she said, her wide coffee-brown eyes gazing at him and her full lips made for kissing, smiling.

"That's fan coral," he explained. "It's actually an animal, not a plant." She had taught him about horses, racing, and country life, and he was teaching her about the sea. The lessons had a payback; her enthusiasm was contagious. After hooking up with Allie, he had never known a minute of regret, and there on his boat with his soul mate, he was happy, too, the happiest in his life.

His blissful memories of the start of the voyage ended, and Christian recalled his last scuba dive in the Bahamas, the dive that began the disastrous roller coaster of events. They had sailed beyond Abaco and were in the Berry Islands, a little stirrup chain that bordered the Grand Banks. Allie was stretched out on the cockpit bench in a bikini with her new floppy hat bought at the Freeport straw market. She was reading a booklet on the Berries while he steered the sloop past the sparsely populated little keys with their occasional shack or dwelling.

She pushed up the hat brim and looked at him. "Did you know the Berry Islands have the largest shark population in the Bahamas?"

"They won't hurt you, unless you splash around and act like bait." He took a sip of iced tea.

"So you keep saying, but those reef sharks and their darting around make me wish I had eyes in the back of my head, and I'm not about to pet a big nurse shark, like you do."

"Fair enough," he said. "I'd be crazy to get on some of those horses you ride."

She went back to reading. "God, Christian, a twenty-foot hammerhead was spotted at the southern end of Great Harbour near Shark Creek."

"Twenty feet," he said and whistled. "I won't be petting that baby. Besides, we've already passed Great Harbour."

In the late afternoon, Christian dropped anchor off a tiny remote key. He hadn't even bothered to look up its name. He pulled out his dive tank and gear from the aft hatch and asked, "Any preference on dinner?"

"I'm ready for a burger."

"Doubt I'll find any golden arches down there," he said and strapped on the dive pack.

Allie rolled her eyes. "Funny, real funny, Christian, I'm taking a shower while you're gone."

He spit into his mask to prevent the glass from fogging before he placed it over his face and stepped off the stern with a mess bag and Hawaiian sling, a spear that worked like a slingshot. At a depth of thirty-five feet, he quickly reached the bottom and took a compass reading. The seaweed swayed in the undercurrent and told him which way to go. At the start of a dive, it was wiser to swim against the current, so the return trip was effortless, gliding with the flow.

She wants a hamburger, he thought and swam along, but he had a feeling of being followed. Glancing over his shoulder, he saw the five-foot silver fish that trailed several yards beyond his fins. *Hey, buddy, come to check me out?* Barracudas were one inquisitive fish.

Christian disregarded the great barracuda that were as common as coral on a reef and treated the fish like a lagging dive partner. Despite a fierce reputation, they were generally harmless, but they could be a pain when spearfishing. He had lost his share of nice fish dinners to 'cudas that zeroed in like fighter jets and snatched up a speared fish before a diver retrieved it. Even angling topside, he had reeled in grouper only to find a fish head on his hook, a barracuda having taken the rest.

Off the reef, he spotted a queen conch resting on the flat bottom between blades of sea grass. He placed the melon-size snail with a pink underbelly into his bag. *Sorry, buddy, no fish dinner for you.* He looked around, but the 'cuda was gone.

Within ten minutes, Christian found three more conchs, enough for their meal that night. He checked the regulator gage for air— half a tank remaining. With a quick compass reading, he switched directions and headed back to his anchored sailboat. His thoughts were on preparing the conch. *Conch chowder, conch seviche, but breaded and fried conch is like a burger.*

With the current, he moved at a good clip. In the distance, he saw the reef and his buddy, the barracuda, but he wasn't alone. Between two large coral heads, several barracudas cruised in a wide circle, like vultures. Out of curiosity, Christian departed from his invisible path created by the compass and swam to them.

Ah, damn, who did this to you? He frowned and gazed at the long, gray body that resembled a small submarine as it tumbled and rolled lifelessly on the sandy seafloor. Christian, using his own frame for scale, figured the dead shark was twice his length, making it longer than twelve feet. The spotted patches on its back and sides confirmed the species, a tiger, one of the top predators in the Bahamas. No wonder the barracudas were leery and hadn't rushed in.

Christian hovered over the perfectly designed creature, magnificent even in death. The cause of its demise was obvious. The shark's dorsal fin, side fins, and tail had been sliced clean off. *Bastards! What a waste of a gorgeous fish.* A tiger shark that large had only one enemy— man. He sucked in a slow, deep breath and ran his hand across the sandpaperlike skin and down its long, slender body. After several minutes, he swam off, leaving the shark to the scavengers.

He swam to his sloop, enraged at the fishermen who had killed the shark, the exporter who would ship its fins to Hong Kong, and the Chinese who created the demand for shark fin soup. Sharks were senselessly being wiped out, but until that moment, the travesty had not affected him or entered his water world. He reached his sloop and surfaced near the stern. Holding the ladder, he removed his fins and tossed them on deck and pushed the mask to the top of his head.

Allie gazed down from the boat, wearing a white shirt and matching shorts. Her strawberry blond hair was tied back in a wet ponytail that hung off her shoulder. "So, what's for dinner?" She smiled, but he couldn't return the grin.

"Conch," he said quietly. He handed her the mess bag and climbed aboard.

Allie inspected the four large shells. "You're cleaning these slimy suckers."

He slipped out of the dive pack, and using a jug of fresh water, he rinsed his body of the saltwater. He shook the droplets from his hair and began washing his scuba gear.

Allie set the bag down and watched him while he stowed the gear in silence. After a few minutes, she finally asked, "What's wrong?"

He straightened and stared down at her. "I'm fucking pissed off, Allie. Came across a dead tiger shark, a twelve footer, but some asshole had cut off its fins, probably a goddamn long-liner."

"They took the fins? Why would they do that?"

He swept his hair back in frustration. "The fins are used in a Chinese soup that's supposed to bring good luck, long life, a hard dick, or whatever bullshit myth they can come up with. Because of that fucking soup, sharks are being hunted into extinction."

"That's terrible."

His eyes narrowed, scrutinizing her sincerity. "Allie, you don't care about sharks. You're like most people who believe they're dangerous, and the sooner they're gone, the better. But remove the top predator from an ecosystem, and that colorful reef you're enjoying will disappear."

He sidestepped her and snatched his sunglasses off the helm and slipped them on. "Sharks have been around four hundred fifty million years, longer than the dinosaurs. They've survived despite the mass extinctions of other animals, but they sure as hell won't survive us, a bunch of out-of-control, hairless apes obliterating every wild animal on the planet. In ten more years, one-third of all shark species will be gone, but who the fuck cares?" He slammed the aft hatch shut.

"That's enough, Christian," she ordered. "You're working yourself up over something that's out of your control. The only thing you'll accomplish is a ruined evening."

"I'm sorry I'm ranting." He slumped on the bench. "It's just I've known sharks were in trouble and ignored it. But seeing and touching that dead shark—" He stared across the pristine water. "That really hit home, Allie. We're destroying this planet, and sharks have now fallen into the crosshairs. When we have kids, I always figured I'd take them diving and teach them to appreciate and respect those great fish. That won't happen now. What do I tell our kids? That my generation sat back and let some greedy scumbags annihilate the sharks?"

She massaged his shoulder. "It is sad, wrong, and frustrating, but I don't have the answers. I might not share your passion for sharks, but I care about all creatures. Only a barbarian feels indifference when an animal goes extinct."

"Yeah," he said with a weighty sigh and picked up the bag of conch. "If we want dinner before dark, I'd better clean these." He placed a conch shell near the stern ladder for easy cleanup. With his dive knife, he punctured the second spiral, severing the conch's muscle from its shell. The gray snail slid out. He cut and peeled off the snail's tough skin and pounded the rubbery white meat with the knife handle, tenderizing it.

"How are you going to cook them?"

"I'm making conch burgers, of course."

An hour later, Christian kicked back on the breezy deck and stared at the western sky's intense pinks, orange, and gold laced with ribbons of lavender clouds. Allie sat cross-legged nearby, head down, consumed in reading her laptop computer.

He took the last bite of his burger. "Allie, give that machine a rest. You're missing the sunset, and we might catch a green burst." He had told her about the rare phenomena that sometimes occurred when the sun vanished into the horizon and a flash of bright green filled the sky. The cause was said to be a falling star. He had only seen the green once.

"I'm researching shark fin soup. Did you know the fins are practically tasteless and have no food value? Chicken or ham stock is added for flavoring, and the soup is extremely expensive. Despite all the myths, Chinese eat it for the prestige. The fin demand has risen in the last ten years because of the growing middle class in China." She looked back at the screen. "It's outrageous. It says that up to a hundred million sharks are killed every year for that lousy soup, and forty percent of the population has already disappeared."

"I know," he said and tossed up his hands. "Why do you think I got so pissed? I watched a TV show that filmed sharks being finned in the Pacific. A Taiwanese fishing boat was hauling in blues. The crew hacked off their fins and kicked them back alive, leaving the poor sharks struggling without fins in the bloody water. God, it was cruel." He huffed. "In Taiwan, they showed thousands upon thousands of fins drying in the sun on rooftops. I couldn't watch anymore and turned off the tube."

She closed the laptop and leaned her head against his chest. "That's truly horrible. It's bad enough animals are disappearing because of global warming or loss of habitat, but to wipe out a species for a worthless soup. How can people be so ignorant and selfish?"

"Yeah, we're *supposed* to be the most intelligent creature, yet unlike other animals, we destroy our own environment. We're like a friggin' virus. We take over, consume, and kill everything."

"You're right, Christian. What kind of place are we leaving for our kids?"

He placed his arm around her shoulder and kissed her forehead. They gazed at the last sliver of the dying sun that disappeared into the dark waves. A dazzling burst of brilliant green replaced the golden horizon. He jolted forward. "Do you see it, Allie? Do ya see the green?"

"Wow, I do. It's incredible."

"Make a wish, quick." Within ten seconds the green was gone. "What did you wish for?"

She wrapped her arms around his waist and hugged him. "That your sharks will be saved."

In the middle of the night, a noise caused Christian to stir in the forward berth. He listened to the gentle lapping of waves against the hull and felt the slight rolling motion of his anchored sailboat. Reassured, he nuzzled a pillow and reached for Allie, but the bed was empty. He sat up abruptly and looked around the dark cabin.

Beyond the doorway, a galley light created a dim glow down the companionway. He then heard the clicking of the computer printer making copies. He glanced at his watch, three o'clock. He left the berth and found Allie in the galley booth, staring at her laptop, unaware of him. "What are you doing up?"

She jerked her head, startled. "Jesus, Christian, you prowl around this boat like a damn cat." She took a sip from a coffee mug. "I couldn't sleep, all your talk about sharks. Now I'm concerned. I wanted to learn more about finning and if anything is being done to stop it."

"So, what'd ya find?" He slumped down into the booth across

from her, scratched his head, and yawned.

"Christian, it's such bullshit; the more I read, the more furious I get. Only the Bahamas and some little island in the Pacific have passed laws to protect sharks. The oceanic white tip is nearly gone, even in our own Gulf of Mexico. Tiger sharks and scalloped hammerheads have been depleted by ninety-seven percent."

"That's because sharks are like us," he said. "They mature slowly and give birth to only a few pups. They can't handle commercial fishing like other fish that grow fast and produce hundreds of offspring."

"That's right." She slid some printouts to him. "I Googled your tiger shark. It takes a tiger fifteen years to mature sexually, and they breed only every three years, having up to forty babies. That's twelve or so a year, not many for a fish."

He examined the papers. "Fifteen years, so that big tiger was probably close to my age. Did you know scientists still don't know exactly how long sharks live?"

"Even if people don't care about sharks, they should care about this." She shoved more papers at him. "Off our Atlantic coast, the cow-nosed rays have multiplied, since the tigers and hammerhead that eat them are gone. These rays eat scallops and clams. And guess what? This year's harvest of bay scallops and clams was the lowest on record. And there's more. Sharks keep the grouper population in check, which protects the parrot fish. Parrot fish eat and clean the algae off coral. Without sharks, the parrot fish will disappear, along with the reefs. Too much algae kills the coral. There goes the nursery for thousands of fish."

"I know, Allie. Without sharks, the whole ecosystem suffers."

She pushed the hair off her forehead and glanced down at the screen. "It says the bull, dusky, and smooth hammerheads are in even more trouble. Their numbers are down by ninety-nine percent. This is a crisis. I can't believe our government is sitting on its ass and doing nothing."

"That's because the commercial fishermen have a strong lobby in Congress."

She smiled. "How'd you get so smart and know all this?"

"I read about things I care about." He rose from the booth and stepped behind her. Wrapping his arms around her, he softly nuzzled and kissed her neck. "Let's go to bed. Like you said, no sense getting upset when there's no fix."

She pushed him away and growled. "Christian, that's unacceptable."

"Fine," he mumbled, realizing she was really fuming. When angry like this, she turned into a pit bull that wouldn't let go. Any jockey could testify she became a tyrant if her horses were mishandled. She had embraced sharks and was bent on helping them.

Glumly, he slumped back into the booth. *I pulled the cork on this, and now she's preoccupied with nothing else.* He could not lure her into bed, and if he left and went back to sleep himself, he would look like a jerk. His only alternative was talking it out.

"Okay, Allie. What do you want me to do, donate money, join a cause? It doesn't do any good. For decades, people campaigned to stop whale hunting and passed international laws, but it hasn't stopped the Japanese. They still harvest them, calling the crap research. Now you're talking about the Chinese. Hell, those suckers with their fucked-up fetishes and culture are the reason countless species are facing extinction. They're a billion strong and rich. They don't give a shit what foreigners think."

He took a sip of her lukewarm coffee. "On top of that, we're talking about a rather unpopular creature. The public will get behind whales, rhinos, polar bears, and tigers because they won't take your leg off at the local beach, but sharks are feared and hated. People don't give a rat's ass about saving them. Even if and when they do, it'll be too late."

"There has to be a way to stop the slaughter," she said with melancholy.

"You figure out the way, and I'll do it."

CHAPTER EIGHT

As Christian reached the halfway point between Bimini and Nassau, he thought about his last day with Allie, the last time he held her, made love to her; the last time he was mentally sound and a decent, happy guy. Every detail of that day was burned into his memory, like the crisp clear morning in New York on 9/11.

He had woke with Allie clutched in his arms, her back snuggled against him. He stared at the light that streamed though the portholes and filled the berth. Normally, he rose at dawn and was underway by that time of day, but they had slept in. The night before, they talked about sharks, but then the subject turned to kids. Allie said it was time. She wanted to have his baby. They returned to the berth, and the discussion was consummated with the act. For an hour he made love to his petite wife, but he felt different, a little ecstatic. Without birth control, procreation, rather than pleasure, had become the goal.

He looked at the time, nine o'clock. An early start was no longer an option. He thought about holding, nurturing, playing with his child. *It is time. I want to be a father.* Despite the passionate predawn workout and lack of sleep, he became aroused. He nipped Allie's neck and rubbed against her until she relented. Half asleep, she parted her legs, and he mounted her, his desire for her never wavering. Twenty minutes later, he collapsed beside her and panted to catch his breath.

Allie gazed at him with a pleased smile. "Where do you find the energy?"

"Not much else to do on a boat, and having a sexy crewmate helps." He chuckled and climbed off the bed.

"You have the cutest chuckle, like a naughty little boy's."

He slipped into a pair of cutoffs. "Well, this naughty boy will make you breakfast."

An hour later, Christian stood on the gusty deck under a cloudless sky. Overnight, a front had moved in and the fall air felt nippy. He hoisted anchor and turned the bow into the wind. "Allie, we're getting underway," he called into the cabin. "Is everything secured?"

"We're good," she answered.

Christian unfurled the main sail and turned the sloop so the luffing sail tightened and filled with the breeze. *Hank's Dream* lunged forward and glided through the translucent water. He shut down the noisy diesel engine, and the stillness was immediate. The only sound was the whistling wind and ruffling sheets. He gazed ahead at blue atop blue and inhaled the salty air. No other vessel existed on the vast horizon. He savored the oceanic peace and isolation from mankind. He would have been content to never step ashore again.

A half hour later, Allie joined him on the deck, wearing a white shirt over her pink bikini. "What's the next port of call, Captain?"

He glanced at his watch and raised his eyebrows. "Should've started sooner."

"That's your fault, wanting to fool around."

"I was just doing my duty—have to keep my wife satisfied." He smiled.

"Sure, blame it on me, when we both know you're the one with the insatiable appetite."

"Anyway, we'll be coming up on Chub Cay, the end of the Berries, and then we'll cross the Tongue of the Ocean. It's a six-thousand-foot-deep underwater canyon that runs through the Bahamas. The wind and chop should pick up. We'll be heeled over and really moving."

"Can't wait," she said with a twinkle in her eyes.

Like himself, Allie was an adrenaline junkie, the more risk and thrill, the better. He loved to ride out a stormy sea or play with sharks. She was a daredevil on horseback and liked to fool with her backyard alligator. Between the two of them, life was rarely boring, and for him, her brazen and unfazed zeal for life had been the attraction.

"The Tongue is thirty to forty miles across," he said. "If we go southeast, we'll hit Nassau. It has a cool old fort and the Atlantis theme park with great aquariums and water rides, but mostly Nassau is a tourist trap. Been there, done it, and prefer to skip it. I'd rather go southwest to Andros Island."

"What's on Andros?"

"Never been there."

She scrunched up her small nose with a frown. "I thought you'd seen all the Bahamian islands."

"Hardly," he said. "There are seven hundred and a couple thousand cays. I'd be an old man if I'd seen them all. I've been to Freeport, Nassau, and Bimini numerous times, and a pilot friend and I took his little plane down to Great Exuma and went diving, but that's it."

"So we don't know what to expect on this island?"

"I did some research. Andros is the biggest island in the Bahamas and has the world's third largest barrier reef, with a sheer wall that drops thousands of feet. I can't wait to dive that black coral." He grinned. "But mainly I want to check out the blue holes, underwater cave systems in the ocean. There are also freshwater blue holes inland. The island has rivers, subtropical forests, and swamps with tons of orchids and wildlife. Andros supplies most of the drinking water for the Bahamas. It's also been called the bonefish capital of the world. It'll be awesome. You'll love it, Allie."

"What about the towns, grocery stores? We're down to a few Cokes, and after lunch, we'll be out of bread."

Christian scratched the back of his head. "I didn't bother looking up that stuff."

"Typical sea bum," she said and rubbed his back. "Guess I'd better get online." She walked toward the cabin hatch.

"You'll end up spending all morning on that computer."

"I won't be long," she said with a singsongy voice, and disappeared into the cabin.

"Yeah, right," he grumbled. "I should accidentally kick that laptop overboard."

Allie surfaced an hour later when Chub Cay was in their sights. She sauntered toward him with a glass of iced tea. "If we're in for rough water during lunch, I'll make peanut butter and jelly sandwiches ahead of time."

"Good idea," he said and took a swig of tea as she started back to the galley. "Hey, what did you find out about Andros?"

"You wanted to get away from people? I think this is your island. From what I read, Andros is over a hundred miles long, but it's sparsely populated. It has three towns with only three hotels and restaurants listed on the Internet." She became serious. "I also got sidetracked on an article in the Bahamian newspaper. On North Andros, a seafood export company was harvesting thirty thousand sea cucumbers daily and shipping them to Hong Kong, but because the number of sea cucumbers has dwindled to five thousand, the company was considering the export of shark fins."

Christian frowned. "Are they?"

"There were rumors they're taking fins illegally. The Bahamian government just outlawed commercial shark fishing, and long-lining was banned over twenty years ago, so the tiger shark you found yesterday must've been caught in the ocean, and its body drifted into the Berries."

"No way. That shark was in good shape. It was killed recently and right here."

"Maybe a sport fisherman caught it on a charter boat."

"No fisherman or charter is going to drag a twelve-foot, five-hundred pound tiger aboard for the fins. Besides, where would they sell them? It all points to a long-liner. They have the boat, equipment, and men to pull a huge shark aboard. I'm betting they're fishing these waters because the pickings are easy. They dry the fins on board and unload them at the exporter on Andros. It all adds up."

"But it's illegal."

"Look around, Allie. Who's going to stop them? There's not another boat in sight. And to a poor Bahamian or long-liner, those fins are worth a fortune."

"I don't want to get into it again, too depressing. I'll make the sandwiches."

They passed Chub Cay and its surrounding pale-blue waters and turned southwest for the blue-black waters of the Tongue. Allie stood behind Christian and kneaded his neck and shoulders. He tossed back his head and closed his eyes. "Jeez, that feels good."

"When do you think we'll reach Andros?"

"I'm hoping before sundown," he murmured, enjoying the massage. "I hate sailing at night into unknown waters with all these uncharted reefs."

"Christian, we're coming up on another boat."

At the southwest tip of Chub Cay, a large blue trawler was less than a mile away, moored in shallow water near the deepwater drop off. "Looks like a commercial fishing boat. Take over," he said, yielding the wheel to her. He scrambled below for binoculars. Returning topside, he stared through the lenses at the distant boat. "Son of a bitch," he said. "It is a long-liner. They've stopped to haul in their catch. They're probably the ones who killed the tiger shark."

"Maybe they don't know it's illegal to long-line in the Bahamas."

"Bullshit! They know. They're breaking the law and don't fucking care. Keep us on this heading." He stared through the binoculars as the sloop grew closer. "I see four, no, five men on board, Jesus, they just hauled in a small shark."

"Maybe we should radio the cops."

"I haven't seen a Coast Guard or cop boat since we entered the Bahamas. The ocean's only several miles away, and those suckers will be long gone by the time the law shows up, and then there's no way to prove the sharks were taken in the Bahamas."

"Okay, we're getting close. What do you plan to do?"

"I'll know when we get there."

"Damn it, Christian, I've heard that before."

She left the helm, darted into the cabin, and returned with her forty-four-caliber revolver. She flipped the barrel open, making sure it was loaded, and slipped the weapon into a small cubbyhole next to the wheel.

He gave her a sideward frown. "Allie, we're not going to war. I'll probably just cuss them out."

"Right," she grumbled. "I know your temper and have seen what your venting leads to. I want some backup in case there's trouble."

"Whatever," he said, and started the motor. He turned the bow close to the wind and freed the sheets. "This is no time for sailing." The flapping main furled up within the mast, and the jib automatically rolled around the forestay. He pushed the throttle forward, and they motored within shouting distance of the rust-stained, fifty-foot trawler, close in length to his sloop. He saw the men—black haired and dark skinned, Hispanic looking and dressed in tattered, faded clothing. He noticed the boat's origin, Mexico, written on the bow.

For half a second, Christian felt guilty, cruising up in his shiny, expensive sloop to harass the impoverished fishermen, but then he saw the small hammerhead on the line. It thrashed wildly as it left the water on the trawler's starboard side. "That shark is protected here," he shouted to the men. "You have to release it."

The men looked at him as if he were crazy, but continued working. One man operated the noisy motorized winch that hauled in the long-line rope. A big guy used a gaff and pulled the hammerhead onto the open deck where two more men with knives leaned over the squirming fish. A fifth man with a mustache and a beer gut stood at the helm in the shade, overseeing the operation. He was obviously the captain.

"Hey, let it go," Christian yelled, edging the throttle back so his sailboat idled nearby. "You're breaking Bahamian law. It's illegal to catch sharks with a long-line."

The two men with knives straightened. The captain left the covered helm mid-boat and stepped to the trawler's side. "*No comprende,*" he yelled back.

"I'm calling the cops, turning you and your boat in," said Christian.

"Fuck off, Americana," the captain said and swirled his finger in the air, signaling to his men to continue.

Christian watched helplessly, hyperventilating with rage as the men stripped the shark of its fins, unhooked it, and kicked the blood-soaked fish back into the water. "Goddamn it. Take the helm, Allie," he snapped. He rushed to the aft hatch and snatched out his fins, mask with attached snorkel, and a leg sheath holding a large dive knife.

"Christian, what are you doing?"

He strapped the knife onto his lower leg. "Once I'm in the water, back the boat off a hundred yards. These assholes aren't going to be happy, and I don't want you hurt."

"Christian?"

"I can't stand by and do nothing," he said and stepped into the fins. "You want to save sharks? It starts now."

She grabbed his arm and kissed him. "Be careful."

He nodded, put on the mask, and leaped off the stern.

The bubbles cleared, and Christian saw that the depth was twenty-five feet, not too deep. He surfaced, blowing water out of the snorkel to clear it, and swam away from his boat in the direction of the trawler. Ahead he heard the angry yells of its crew, and behind him, the sloop's propellers engaged as his sailboat pulled away.

In the clear water he scrutinized the long-line, made of heavy rope. Attached to the rope every several yards were leader lines with a large baited hook. He wondered about the rope's length. Some fishermen were known to spew sixty miles of deadly line, thus the term long-liner. Besides grouper, tuna, and other commercial fish, their by-catch included everything from sharks to endangered sea turtles.

He took a deep breath and followed the moving rope down and noticed its speed had increased, the wrench working at full capacity. The men must have guessed his intentions. Hooks baited with chunks of fish zipped passed him. In the distance, he saw the next casualty, a gentle nurse shark. The six-foot, brownish-gray shark was clearly exhausted. It barely moved while being dragged upside down through the water.

Christian took out his knife and waited for the towed fish to approach. A few feet in front of the shark, he grabbed the rope that would hold him in place near the fish. He cut the leader line, and the nurse shark floated free, but sank toward the bottom with only its gills functioning. For a moment Christian feared he was too late, but soon the nurse's long graceful tail swayed back and forth. The shark righted itself and sluggishly swam away.

Christian surfaced and inhaled a huge breath of air, good for another three minutes. Topside, he heard the men cursing at him in Spanish and broken English. He submerged ten feet and met the next shark, another nurse, smaller than the first, but with more fight. It obviously had been hooked recently. With the fish stressed and struggling, he had difficulty cutting the line without getting bitten. Even a nurse will chomp down defensively and inflict a serious wound with its tiny teeth. Once liberated, the nurse shark took off in a hurry.

Before jumping off his boat, Christian had considered severing the long-line, but doing so would not save the sharks. Attached to the rope and each other, they would end up starving or suffocating. With the short leader line attached to a hook that eventually rusts and falls out, they stood a good chance of surviving the ordeal. He came across a few small black-tip reef sharks. They were so exhausted he had no trouble setting them free.

Christian spotted the next fish, but it wasn't a shark. *Okay, the pricks can have this one,* he thought, looking at the large red grouper. Plenty of laws were on the books that protected grouper, requiring a specific size and season. These fish weren't threatened, and when the men stopped the winch to remove the fish, Christian would get extra precious minutes to free other sharks.

He quickly gulped down another breath, kicked his fins, and sped downward, passing empty hooks. The next long-line victim caused Christian to pause, his heart skipping a beat. *Shit!* His eyes widened as he stared at the eight-foot, stout, gray shark with a broad, flat snout. It was a bull. Of all species, this was the one to fear.

He saw the white underbelly and male sex organs, and details about bull sharks flashed through his mind. The males had a higher testosterone level than an elephant, creating one belligerent fish. They could also live in fresh water and entered rivers and lakes. Since the extremely aggressive fish came in contact with more people, bulls held the record each year for attacking and killing the most people. The book *Jaws* was based on true events in New England when a shark traveled up river in the early 1900s and went on a killing spree. The guilty shark was more likely a bull than a great white and should have had the starring role in the movie.

As the shark grew closer, common sense came into play, and Christian thought about skipping this one, especially seeing its sharp, serrated teeth gnaw on the rope. Like a mad feline, the bull arched its body and swatted its tail, telltale shark signs it was pissed. It jerked its head in search of something to maul. *Screw the risk. I can do it. I can save him.*

The line stopped moving, with the men taking the grouper off. This was Christian's best shot. He held his knife out and raced up to the shark. As he cut the line, the bull lunged at his arm. With the heel of his hand, he hit the shark's blunt nose and pushed it back. The shark curled for a second attack, but then it must have grasped the realization that it was free. It darted past Christian so close that its rough skin scraped his shoulder and its tail smacked his face, and he had to readjust his mask.

The experience of shoving off a maneater threw Christian's adrenaline into overdrive. The tension depleted his oxygen, and his lungs burned. He shuddered and glimpsed his shaky hands, making sure he still held his knife. *What a rush!* After the shark disappeared, he headed up for air.

When Christian broke the surface, he heard a loud bang, and the nearby water erupted with sprinkles. It took him a second to register—gunfire. *These assholes are shooting at me.* He swirled around and faced the trawler twenty yards away. The captain held a shotgun. He pumped it and took a second bead on Christian.

Jesus! Christian dove down several feet and rapidly kicked his fins, making a beeline toward his sloop. The underwater acoustics emitted the motor sound of an approaching boat. Through the transparent water, he saw the white hull of his sailboat pass overhead. It was moving at full throttle toward the trawler.

Damn it, Allie. What are you doing? He rushed upward. He should have known she wouldn't listen to him and stay away when someone was taking potshots at her husband.

He hit the surface and shoved up the mask. "Allie, Allie," he shouted at the sloop, but it remained on a collision course with the trawler. "Allie, stop!" She either didn't hear him or was ignoring him. He raced through the water and then heard a crunching sound. He stopped and looked up. His speeding sailboat had slammed into the trawler's rear end. Seconds later, he heard a brief exchange of gunfire, five, maybe six shots. He tried to see Allie on the deck, but he was low in the water and still too far away. "Allie," he screamed several times, but got no response.

The trawler pulled away, detaching the two boats from one another, and took off at a speed that his sloop could never match. His sailboat sat still with the motor idling. He ripped off his mask and raced across the water to his sloop. He reached the stern, puffing more out of fear than exertion. He tore off his fins and sprang up the ladder. On the deck behind the helm, she lay on her side with the forty-four still clutched in her hand.

"My God, Allie," he yelled and collapsed to his knees beside her. He saw the gunshot wound to her chest and the blood that pooled beneath her, soaking her white shirt, bathing suit, and long hair. He grabbed a towel off the bench and applied pressure to her wound to stanch the bleeding. "Allie, please—please be okay."

Her eyes opened a crack, and she gazed up at him. "Christian? You're okay then?"

"Yes, Allie." He blinked back tears and swallowed a strangling knot in his throat. "Just hang on, Allie, you'll be fine. I'll radio for a chopper and get you to a hospital," he said, trying desperately to push down the panic. He started to leave for the cabin to make the call for help.

"Hold me, Christian," she gasped. "I'm so cold."

He sat down and cradled her in his arms. "Okay, Allie. I'm here. I have you." He buried his face into her hair and lost his composure. "I'm so sorry," he cried. "I'm sorry. This is my fault—freeing some damn fish."

"I'm glad you saved those sharks," she said between heavy breaths. "That's why I love you. Few men would risk their life for an animal."

"It was stupid and foolish," he said, whimpering.

"No, it was right." She reached up, swept his hair out of his watery eyes, and cupped his cheek. "My beautiful, beautiful Christian, don't let this change you. Save the sharks. Do it for me."

"I will, Allie, I promise. We'll save them together."

She winced and gritted her teeth. "Christian? Christian?"

"I'm here, Allie. I'm right here."

She gasped several times and her hand dropped like a rock from his face. Her brown eyes were open and fixed, and her body was dolllimp and still, with no breathing or heartbeat.

"No, no, no, don't leave me, Allie!" He scrambled back to his knees, tilted her head, and gave her mouth-to-mouth resuscitation. After twenty minutes of frantic CPR to start her heart, he fell back against the bulkhead and panted. Staring at her in a daze, all hope slipped away and reality set in. She was gone.

"Noooooo!" He bellowed so loud that the strain made his vocal cords raw. So shattered he couldn't breathe. He heard the hackling caws before he saw the black-headed seagull that circled overhead. He curled around Allie's small body and dissolved into a broken, blubbering heap. "I love you, Allie, and didn't tell you," he moaned. "I didn't even tell you." Never in his life had he experienced such immediate and total devastation.

Through the blinding tears, he glimpsed the revolver a tempting arm's length away. It seemed to say, *End it. End it, Christian. There's nothing left to live for.* He sat up slowly and took hold of the weapon. He caressed its hard, bluish steel and placed the barrel to his temple.

CHAPTER NINE

Enough, Christian thought, his eyes watering when recalling Allie's death and his near suicide attempt. For sanity's sake, he longed to forget that day, but nightly the tragic memory played like a horror flick in his dreams. He sniffled and shook his head, shaking off the past, and he focused on the present. Ahead on the endless blue horizon lay the island of Bimini.

In the late afternoon, Christian's sloop cruised past the moored sailboats in the harbor as he searched for a place to dock and refuel. He pulled in at an upscale marina and hotel a few blocks north of the little weather-beaten bars and restaurants that made up the onestreet downtown. Unlike Freeport and Nassau, Bimini was small, quaint, and quiet. A person could stand in the center of the road and see ocean on both sides. There were no big, flashy hotels and casinos, so no herds of tourists. The people visiting the island usually were sport fishermen or divers, Christian's kind of people. The harbormaster met him on the dock, checked his passport, and asked the length of his stay.

"Just overnight," Christian told him.

After refueling and hooking up electric to recharge the boat batteries, he took a shower and put on jeans and a long-sleeve black shirt. Allie had loved him in black, calling him a sex god, with his blond hair. He tucked in the shirt and rolled up the sleeves, not feeling sexy. He left the sloop and wandered down the main drag into the heart of town with dinner in mind.

At a roadside stand, he bought six conch fritters on a paper plate from a large Bahamian woman. Munching on the food while walking, he continued to the pint-size Compleat Angler Hotel, a two-story historical landmark with a cozy bar. He strolled through the courtyard of tropical plants and bougainvillea vines covered with hot pink flowers and entered the lobby. The wooden walls and antique furniture made him think he had stepped back in time. The hotel, like Sloppy Joe's bar in Key West, was another of Ernest Hemingway's hangouts. Christian felt a kinship with the author, since they both obviously loved the sea, fishing, and rustic hideaway bars with laid-back patrons and strong rum drinks. The sitting room off the lobby was filled with old black-and-white photos of Hemingway standing beside a thousand-pound trophy marlin. Christian gazed at the writer in a picture. *We may still have another thing in common.* Hemingway had taken a shotgun and killed himself.

To the left of the hotel desk, he walked into the dark, cool lounge and sat down on a bar stool. With only two other customers, the chatty black bartender fixed him a cocktail and asked about his trip, boat, the weather, and so on. Talking to him, Christian almost felt normal.

"You should stick around," the bartender said. "In a few hours we're having a little festival in the courtyard, a band playing Caribbean music. The locals come out and dance. It's fun."

"Sounds better than sitting alone on my boat tonight," Christian said, pushing his empty glass toward the bartender for a refill.

At sundown, the stools and tables filled with Bahamians and a dozen or so white tourists, including two nice-looking girls in their twenties. They sat down on either side of Christian and quickly let him know they were from Ohio and very available. They mentioned their disappointment in Bimini as a vacation destination because it had no action. But for the same reason, Christian loved the island.

"Where're you from, Christian?" one asked with a flirting smile.

"Florida, I'm just passing through on my sloop."

"A sailboat? We'd love to see it," said the other girl and placed her hand on his shoulder and ran her fingers through his hair, sending a clear message. They weren't interested in seeing a boat.

He was accustomed to the come-on. Like hummingbirds buzzing

a flower, women had been drawn to him all his life. Normally, he handled their approach with cool confidence, but not this time. He felt trapped and uncomfortable. Maybe the depression threw him off his game. He squirmed and tried to respond without being rude. It suddenly occurred to him that, like them, he was single. For years he could say, "I'm with someone," and halt the maneuvers of an engrossed woman. It was no longer true. He had no one, no girlfriend or wife, and was back on the meat market.

The slight rum buzz loosened his resolve. A night with those two was tempting. He then thought about Allie. That was his problem, he still belonged to her.

"Maybe another time," he said to the girls. He dropped a hefty tip on the bar and strolled outside into the noisy, jammed courtyard.

Off in the shadows, he leaned against a pillar and watched the party. The band consisted of four black men who played reggae with a fast beat. The crowd of mostly locals danced to the rhythm, while others stood around, drinking and laughing.

Christian felt conflicted, unsure if he should stay and have another drink or return to his quiet sloop and turn in. His indecision was terminated when a skinny Bahamian kid of about fifteen approached.

"Mister," the kid whispered, "you want to get high, good coke?"

"How much?" Christian asked.

"Forty dollars a gram."

I'm so fucked up. What can it hurt? He dug out his wallet and slipped the boy two twenties. The kid started to walk off. "Wait a minute. Where are you going?"

"Down here," the kid said and pointed to a narrow alley. "I'll be right back."

"Yeah, right, I'll go with you," Christian said. *I might look like a dumb tourist, but wasn't born yesterday.* He followed the kid down the alley that led to the western side of the island. The alley ended at a north-southbound road that separated the beach from small slummy homes crammed only a few feet apart. He and the boy walked north along the windy, deserted road made up of crushed shells. The slight glow of distant streetlights helped prevent a misstep in the numerous potholes.

After a block, they came to a dingy pink home surrounded by rubble and an old wooden boat on blocks. The front yard was foot-deep in weeds except for a sandy path that led to the house. "I have to go in there," the kid said.

"All right, I'll wait here." Christian leaned against a waist-high concrete wall that held back storm tidal surges. He watched the kid disappear into the house and turned into the relentless sea breeze that played tug-of-war with his hair. He stared out at the stars that littered the black sky like diamonds and at the dark ocean, unknowing and eternal.

A few minutes passed and then ten. After fifteen, he knew he'd been had. The average person would blow off forty dollars and walk away from the dodgy section of Bimini, but Christian fumed. Already angry with life, he never considered his welfare or the wisdom of his next move. He plodded down the path to the house and fist pounded the door.

A short black man in his thirties wearing a brightly colored African chemise with bell-shaped sleeves opened the door. "Hello," he said, his grin exposing a gold tooth that matched the dozen chains about his neck.

"Where is he?" Christian stormed. "Where's the fucking kid that came in here?" Without waiting for a response or invitation, he stepped past the man, partially inside, ready to shake his money out of the little thief. The faintly lit room reeked of pot and cigarettes, and the smoke distorted his vision. Through the haze he saw eight black men sitting on a couch and chairs, staring at a small TV, but no kid. Several of the men rose to confront him. In his frame of mind with a liquor buzz, Christian didn't care if there were a hundred. "The kid ripped me off," he growled. "Where is he?"

The short man waved to the men, bidding them return to their seats, and said to Christian, "I'm sorry the boy stole from you. He ran through my house and left by the back door. Tell me what he took, and I'll repay you."

Christian calmed and felt ridiculous, making a scene over forty lousy dollars. Obviously, the boy needed the money more than he did. "Don't worry about it. I overreacted. I'll get out of your hair." He started to back out of the door.

"No, no, I can't have an American thinking bad of our little island. Come in and let me make it up to you. My name is Jerry, and you're?"

"Christian," he said. "Look, it was only a few bucks for a gram of coke." He rubbed his forehead. "I'm kinda going through a rough time, and the kid probably did me a favor. I shouldn't be doing drugs."

Jerry closed the door behind him. "Christian, bad times are when a man needs drugs. They make you forget your problems." He stepped into a little kitchen off the living room and pulled out a chair from under an old wooden table. "Sit and relax. You're among friends." He called to a huge man in the group. "Joseph, fix our American a drink."

For a second, Christian's instincts stirred and he considered declining, sensing something squirrelly about the overly affable Bahamian named Jerry. Against his better judgment, he sat down. Jerry reached across a dish-cluttered counter and retrieved a tiny triangular baggie of white powder from a cookie jar. At the table he slid a small facial mirror in front of Christian and tapped cocaine on it. With a razor blade, he made a three-inch line of powder and handed Christian a short straw.

"There you are," Jerry said and joined Christian at the table. Joseph set a large glass of pineapple juice and rum in front of him.

"Yeah, here I am," Christian said with a sigh. "Screw it." He placed the straw in his nose, leaned over, and snorted up the coke. In minutes he felt better, talkative, and even a little happy. In between bumps of cocaine and gulps from the potent cocktail, he took tokes from a small glass pipe that smoldered with outrageously strong weed. All inhibitions left, and Christian kicked back with his new buddies.

"You're good looking, well dressed, and it sounds like you have a nice boat," Jerry said, and passed him the pipe. "What kind of worries could *you* have?"

Christian took a hit of pot. "My wife—" He coughed slightly, exhaling the smoke. "She died recently."

"I'm so sorry. You must have friends with you, helping you through this."

"No, I'm trying to get my sloop back to the States—stopped for the night to refuel at the marina up the street."

Christian was so toasted he didn't pay much attention to the questions. The drugs and rum kept coming all night. He was scarcely aware of the two young black women who removed his clothing and pleasured him on the couch as Jerry chuckled.

Semiconscious, Christian panted with the fondling. He slowly opened his eyes and gained a foggy perceptive of his surroundings. He was nude, breathless, and lying in a sweaty tangle of silk sheets on a large bed. A window air conditioner rattled noisily nearby. A black woman slept with her arm draped over his chest. A second woman massaged his erection and then climbed on and straddled him.

"Come on, baby, you can do it again," she whispered and rocked him back and forth, encouraging his climax.

Disorientated, he tried to comply and strained to release his depleted seed. After several minutes, his mind cleared enough to think and speak. "No, stop. I don't want to do this." He tried to remove the women and sit up, but the room was spinning, his head pounded, and he felt kitten weak.

The woman slipped off him and shook the other woman awake. "Violet, you better get Jerry. Tell him his pretty white boy is coming out of it."

Christian gazed at a broken blind that allowed light to filter into the dim room. "What time is it?" He rubbed his face and was startled, feeling the bristles of a slight beard. "How long have I been here?"

She giggled. "Two days, and for a white boy, you are quite a stud."

"Two days?" Christian exclaimed. "Shit, where are my clothes? I gotta get to my boat." He managed to sit up and swing his legs off the bed, but couldn't rise, too dizzy and feeble. "God, I've never felt this bad," he said, hunched over and holding his head.

Several minutes later, Jerry came into the room. "Here, Christian," he said and handed him a cup. "It'll get rid of the headache and make you feel better."

Christian took a sip and tasted rum along with a chalky bitter substance. "What—" He cleared his throat. "What is it?"

"Rum and a little medicine," said Jerry. "Drink up."

Desperate to feel better, he finished the drink and lay back down. He was too frail and sick to argue or even stand, much less walk to the marina. "But my boat," he mumbled.

"I found your sailboat and paid the dockage fees. You don't need to worry about it. Just rest now." Jerry turned to the two women sitting on the bed. "Shania, you and Violet give him a break. He's worn out." He left the room.

"Why would he pay for my boat?" Christian asked them and settled back on the bed.

"Jerry's rich," said Violet. "He owns jewelry stores throughout the Bahamas. They're a front for the drugs. And Jerry likes you, baby. Says you're intense and exotic, besides gorgeous. He wants to keep you."

"Keep me?" Christian said, alarmed and tried to rise again, but couldn't. The drink concoction deadened his pain but also immobilized him. He felt drowsy and fought to stay conscious. "What did he give me?" he murmured, struggling to lift his head off the pillow. "What's going on?"

"Don't fight it, baby," Shania said while leaning over him and stroking his forehead. "No one will hurt you. Jerry likes to watch. He pays us to have sex with men, especially pretty ones like you."

The conversation was Christian's last lucid memory. With no concept of time, he floated in and out of awareness, having vague flashes of the bitter-tasting drugs, the helpless feelings when being stimulated to arousal, and the women who sexually tag teamed him. And there were the glimpses of Jerry watching with his gold tooth glinting through his grin.

"That's it," Vince Florio growled. He slammed the phone down on the bar after hearing the recorded message for the umpteenth time. He wandered to the picture window in his Longboat Key house and stared out at Sarasota Bay. "Something's happened to him."

"Maybe the kid's in a place where his cell don't pick up," said Sal, Vince's right hand man who straddled the bar stool with his huge frame.

"Bullshit, I've left messages for four days, and he knows better than to *ignore* my calls. Plus, the little Mexican that runs his horse farm says Christian has been moody, depressed. He drank himself silly prior to his wife's funeral. Christian's mother has also been calling the farm, worried. The last person to see him was the Nassau lawyer, five days ago when he lit out on his sailboat."

Sal took a sip from the rock glass of bourbon. "Boss, you sure this kid is worth all the aggravation? I mean the skinny pissant's been trouble from the start. He might have the same attitude and spunk as your wife and maybe resembles your son if he'd grown, but they're both dead, and this kid is a sorry replacement. Hell, he's not even related."

"Christian is the best thing that's happened to me in a long time. He saved my life, and more important, he gave it new meaning. I care about him, Sal. Now I want him found. Put a trace on his cell."

The sound of breaking waves woke Christian. He lifted his face out of the white sand and saw he was lying on an empty stretch of beach. After a few minutes, he managed to gather his strength and sit up. He tried to recall the last several days, but everything was fuzzy, including the way he wound up on this shoreline. *What the hell did they give me, the date-rape drug, Quaaludes? Maybe mixed with Viagra to keep me hard and horny?* He had a hazy memory of the bedroom, the sex with the women, and Jerry. *They must've grown tired of their white boy and dumped me.*

Shaky, frail, and nauseated, he grabbed a nearby rock and hoisted himself to a stand, every inch of his body sore and hurting. He felt like prime rib ground into hamburger. Once on his feet, he quickly bent over and vomited. He straightened, wiped his mouth, and felt slightly better. He looked up and down the rocky beach, surveying his surroundings and getting his bearings. A few cottages rested a block to his right, and more buildings of the town were left and south. Behind him, short shrubs and weeds covered a vacant lot that rose up from the shore. With a low-hanging sun over the western ocean, he concluded it was late afternoon.

Before setting off, he buttoned his open shirt and zipped up the fly of his jeans and located his sandals lying nearby. In his back pocket, he found his wallet and, surprisingly, it still contained his cash and credit cards. He ruffled the sand from his hair and brushed off his clothes. He crawled up the steep bank to the lot, figuring he would come upon the main road. On Bimini, it was impossible to be lost.

He found the road and trudged down it, a scruffy, aching mess. His parched mouth, dry throat, and fierce headache were the result of a hangover and dehydration. With a queasy stomach, he wondered when he had last eaten. *Guess this is what they call hitting rock bottom.*

"I asked for this shit," he grumbled, refusing to feel victimized. He had angrily banged on the pink house door, looking for drugs, trouble—anything to squelch the grief. *Could've been worse. Two chicks molesting me is better than eight guys beating me senseless.*

After a mile, he came upon the marina and hotel. He ambled down the dock and was relieved when he saw *Hank's Dream,* his home away from home. Once on board, he planned to drink a gallon of water and then strip out of his dirty clothes for a shower. He could barely stand his own stench. As he stepped onto the sloop, he saw the open cabin hatch. "Shit!" he said, his first thought a thief. He leaped down the three steps, and a man's voice responded from the galley.

"About time you got back."

"Damn it, Vince," Christian said with relief. "Thought I'd been robbed. I was fixin' to tackle someone."

Vince sat in the booth and stared out the porthole with his fingers curled around a glass of ice and scotch. Nearby, a cigar smoldered in an ashtray. The middle-aged Italian looked up at Christian. The smile beneath his mustache dissolved quickly, becoming a furrowed brow of disapproval. "Christ, what happened to you? You look like shit."

"Feel like it too." He poured a large glass of water and inhaled it in one long gulp. He wiped his whiskery chin and mouth with the back of his hand. "How'd you find me? No one knew I was in Bimini."

"A word of advice, toss the cell phone if you don't want to be found. The signal led me to the island and finding your boat was no problem, but finding you—I got here yesterday and spent all day asking around. Finally, put some pressure on the locals."

Vince's pressure—no wonder Jerry cut me loose and discarded me on that beach. Christian refilled his water glass and eased down in the booth across from Vince. "Long story short, I got hooked up with a drug pusher on the other side of the island. Turned out he was a kinky little bastard, a voyeur—got his rocks off watching me have sex with two black chicks. The son of a bitch had me so wasted, I don't remember most of it. As soon as I get my act together, I'm going to find him and beat the crap out of him."

"I oughta beat the crap out of you, fooling with drugs," Vince scolded and puffed angrily on his cigar.

Christian chewed his lip and stared at the table thinking, *Vince, the big-time drug lord, is telling me I need to stay straight. Talk about calling the kettle black.* A thousand wisecracks came to mind, but instead, he kept quiet. He had too much respect for Vince to give him grief.

Vince breathed a heavy sigh and ran his hand over the pattern baldness on his head. "Getting wasted is not the answer, Christian. When my son died, my wife went down that road and killed herself with an overdose. I don't want that happening to you. I understand your pain—been there. It took everything I had to keep going after I buried my family. You got people worried, including me."

Christian drank the water and shrugged. "There's nothing to worry about. I'm good, really. Sure, I'm upset about my wife, and maybe I've been drinking a little too much and wanted to score some drugs for the night, but I'm okay."

"Look me in the eye," Vince said sternly, "and tell me you're okay, Christian."

Christian focused on Vince and his hard, dark-eyed stare. Lying to cops and everyone else came easy, but he and Vince had no secrets between them. Their friendship went far beyond a barbeque handshake. "I'm—ah—" His gaze drifted to the table.

"That's what I thought," Vince said. "I know you're hurting, but I promise things will get better, although you might not believe it now. Just remember I'm here for ya." He stood, stepped to Christian, and clapped his shoulder affectionately. "Go clean up, and we'll grab a bite at this joint."

Christian took a long hot shower, shaved, and popped some aspirin. He and Vince strolled to the marina restaurant and ate grouper sandwiches and fries. With food in his belly, Christian began to feel human again. After dinner, they returned to the sloop and leaned back in the open cockpit under the moonlight. Vince sipped on a two-finger nightcap, and Christian drank water, swearing off hard liquor for a while.

He told Vince the truth, how Allie had died, starting with finding the dead tiger shark, to his stupid move jumping off his boat to free sharks, to Allie being shot to death by the Mexican long-liners.

"I got her killed, Vince. The whole damn thing was my fault," Christian said, shaking his head. "When she died, I put a gun to my head. I should've pulled the trigger."

Vince listened quietly throughout his story, but now he leaned forward and glared. "You should've pulled the trigger? You goddamn young fool. It's those Mexicans that need a bullet to the head." He took the last swallow from his drink. "When I get back, I'll put Sal and his crew on it. They'll hunt down that trawler and take care of those bastards."

"Sal won't find them."

"You underestimate that fat Italian. He'll—"

"Vince, they're already dead. I killed them and sank their boat."

CHAPTER TEN

On the long stretch of barren beach, Sammy trudged through the sugar-white sand. The ten-year-old Bahamian boy carried his homemade fishing spear, a broom handle with three prawn spikes attached, and an old paint pail that contained his worn-out mask. His plan was to catch dinner and be home before his mother, who worked as a hotel maid on the island.

As he walked to his favorite fishing hole, he envisioned his pride when he showed her the conch, crab, or fish in the pail. She always rubbed his head and called him the man of the house, providing supper for her and his two little sisters. She usually cooked the seafood into a spicy stew consisting of tomatoes, tomato paste, onions, green peppers, corn, and, sometimes, diced potatoes with a dash of salt, Tabasco, and Pickapeppa sauce, all served over rice. Even when he came home empty-handed, he still got a smile and kiss. "There's always tomorrow, Sammy," she'd say, "and plenty of fish in the sea."

He reached the cove surrounded by layers of black rocks that sagged into the sea and became a reef. The water was calm there and lacked the rough surf and strong currents of the open beaches. He set the pail down on the sand, put on his mask, and picked up his crude spear. He waded into the water, carefully scrutinizing the bottom so he didn't step on a stonefish or ray. When the water was thigh deep, he lowered his mask, took the plunge, and swam head down, holding his breath. Three feet off the rocks, he investigated the crevices and hoped to spot another hognose snapper like the one he had speared the day before. On his way to deeper water, he saw several fish he had come to know, the six-foot green moray eel that made its home beneath a coral head, the large barracuda who occasionally followed him, and the two tan nurse sharks resting under a ledge. It was like visiting good friends.

The depth became fifteen feet, and he swam on the surface, staring down through the mask. Staying on the bottom would have required too much effort, traveling back and forth for air.

He saw nothing of size that would feed his family. He considered spearing some little yellowtail snappers and an equally small spotted Bahamian grouper but, instead, he swam out, farther out than he had ventured before. He had nearly given up when he saw huge antennas on the sandy floor, protruding from a rock shelf. With feelers a yard long, the spiny lobster had to be a monster.

Excited, Sammy inhaled a large gulp of air, raced down, and peered under the shelf. Sure enough, the crustacean was enormous, the biggest he had ever seen. He aimed for the lobster's head, a kill shot, and thrust the spear with all his strength. The lobster's backward tail propulsion was so powerful it jerked the spear out of Sammy's hand. He scrambled, grabbed the spear again, and carefully pulled the lobster from the rocks. Thankfully, the spear held and the lobster was dead. Bringing the flailing creature to shore would have been a job.

He surfaced and screamed, "Oh, Mama, oh, Mama, thank you, God, thank you." He swam toward shore, his arm aching from holding his heavy prize above the water so the barracuda wouldn't steal it. He thought about his mother's shock and awe. The lobster's body was nearly three feet, not counting its feeling antennae, and was enough to feed twelve people. In one piece, only half would fit in his pail.

He came ashore outside the cove, his smile stretching from ear to ear. He set the spear and lobster down and did a little dance on the sand, whooping and howling at the sun. He pictured the whole village coming out, congratulating him, and taking photos of his record-breaking catch as he walked down the dirt road to his house.

After ten minutes, he calmed down and realized the trip home would be long and strenuous. Besides his gear, the crawfish weighed more than ten pounds. He sprinted up the beach for his pail, but noticed something white that floated in the surf. It looked like a shoe. This was his lucky day. Maybe he would come across the other one and have a pair. He shuffled out and plucked it from the waves. Turning the shoe over, he screeched in terror and dropped it.

With a slight slap on his back, Dave Wheeler glanced up from his desk at Joe's smiling face. Joe was another youngster in the department, like his partner, Ralph.

"Great job, Dave," said Joe. "I can't believe you found that blood and fingerprint. We got this guy now."

"No witnesses, but it should be enough for a conviction," said Wheeler. Joe rattled on about the case. *He's like a dripping faucet,* Wheeler thought, *I can hear him, but can't shut him off.*

Wheeler had solved the case of the murdered girls who had been raped and stabbed, but as feared, the evidence had come with a fourth victim, a twenty-year-old girl. The crime matched the MOs of the other three. Her body was discovered in a Fort Lauderdale parking garage in broad daylight. Knowing the approximate time of death, he had collected and logged the parking stubs with that time stamp and hoped the killer had driven into the garage and not walked. It was a big break. Larry Holt, a truck driver who delivered produce for a large grocery store chain, had left his fingerprint and a slight smudge of blood on a ticket stub when he drove out of the garage. A rush was put on the DNA, and it confirmed the blood belonged to the victim. Since Holt traveled the state, it explained why the murders had occurred in different cities.

Wheeler had pulled Holt's record and mug shot. He was a tall, burly guy, early thirties, and looked like he shaved with a blowtorch. He had been arrested three times for assault on women, twice on an ex-girlfriend, and once for striking his mother, but he had only one conviction.

Holt lived with his mother in Fort Lauderdale, and after Wheeler questioned her, she said Larry was on the road, out of town, but she was unsure where. She stated her son had borrowed her car to pay an insurance bill downtown on the day in question. The insurance company was a block from the parking garage, and Holt was in the insurance office just prior to the time of the murder. A forensic team went over the mother's car and found additional blood belonging to the girl on the turn signal lever. The case was a slam-dunk, and an APB was put out on Holt.

Wheeler and Ralph had visited the grocery warehouse where semitrailer delivery trucks were kept. The manager said that the previous week, Holt made a delivery in Jupiter and disappeared, leaving his half-filled truck behind a store. He went missing on the same day the mother was interviewed. Wheeler concluded she had tipped him off.

"Dave, when Holt is brought in, do you think I can sit in on the interrogation?" asked Joe.

Wheeler had tuned out the rookie's yakking and was grateful when his phone rang. "Excuse me," he said, and answered it, "Wheeler."

"Hello, Agent Wheeler. This is Sergeant Drake, Bahamas. We found something of interest."

Wheeler leaned forward. "Something concerning the Roberts case?"

"Possibly," said Drake. "A boy was fishing on Chub Cay and found a white sneaker, but the shoe contained the remains of a foot. At first we considered it an accidental drowning, some drunk tripped off a dock, a fisherman fell out his boat and the scavengers ate the body, but so far, no one has been reported missing. The coroner estimated the death occurred several weeks ago, around the time Allie Roberts was murdered. Furthermore, when the area waters were searched for more remains, they found three small chunks of blue wood. To me the color is identical to the paint scraping taken from the damaged bow of Roberts's sloop. I was hoping your lab could confirm this."

"No problem," said Wheeler. "Send me a piece of the wood and the foot. If the paint matches the paint on the sloop, and the

DNA on the bullet matches the foot, we'll have enough to charge Christian Roberts."

After the call from Drake, Wheeler dug out the Roberts file. Busy with other cases, he had shelved it since going to Allie's funeral in Arcadia. That trip had proved fruitless. He had hoped to catch Christian Roberts distraught and off guard, plus the untimely intrusion of the FBI at the grave site was meant to enrage him. Without his lawyer, he might have slipped up and made an incriminating statement. Unfortunately, Roberts didn't bite. He was incensed but controlled his temper.

Wheeler gazed at Roberts's mug shot. *This kid is no dummy and doesn't rattle. Getting him to fess up will be like prying open a clam with a movie ticket.*

He ruled out a confession and would have to rely on evidence for a conviction. As the case took shape, Wheeler began to believe that Roberts hadn't killed his wife, but he did murder someone. His print on the bullet and the unidentified blood proved there had been a third party. Now there was this new development, the floating foot and chunks of blue wood. If it matched the blood and paint found on the sloop, he could close this case. The evidence would prove a boat crash and a confrontation at sea that resulted in the third party's murder; the motive: revenge for his dead wife. The hypothesis would explain Roberts's conflicting lies on the polygraph test along with his lack of cooperation and his indifference if his wife's murderer was captured. Roberts had already killed the guy. The scenario made sense and the pieces fit.

Wheeler was determined to take the swagger out of that hotshot with an arrest, but he also started to commiserate with Roberts. *If someone shot my girl, I'd be tempted to kill the murderer too.*

In the forward berth, Christian was roused from a deep slumber, hearing the thump of heavy footsteps on the dock planks and the loud voices of boaters as they climbed aboard a cabin cruiser in the adjacent slip. He covered his head with a pillow, trying to drown out the noise, but when the boat's deafening diesel motor turned over, he sat up, giving up on sleeping in. *I hate staying at marinas.*

He climbed out of bed, ambled into the galley, and turned on the coffeepot. Vince probably still snoozed in his quiet hotel room off the marina, since they had talked until late. Christian sat down in the booth, sipped from a mug, and thought about their conversation. He confessed the murders and told Vince about the events following Allie's death. Oddly, an Italian mobster was the only person he trusted with the truth.

The roaring cabin cruiser and its boisterous party motored out. With the Bimini marina tranquil again, he took his coffee and went topside to the breezy deck. A few older fishermen carrying poles said good morning as they strolled down the dock toward a skiff. After giving them a nod, he gazed at the deck where Allie's lifeless body had laid. Her blood was gone, scrubbed clean in Nassau, but the memory came back like a recurring nightmare.

He had picked up the forty-four revolver and held the barrel to his temple. Before pulling the trigger, he stared at her small frame, once strong and beautiful. Her last words thundered in his head. "Save the sharks. Do it for me." It was a ridiculous request with an impossible goal. What could he do, one single guy? No way could he stop the world from wiping out sharks. He lowered the weapon and realized he couldn't cop out and had to try to save them.

"Fine, Allie, I'll do this stupid thing for you, but I wonder if you really wanted to save sharks or me. You probably knew I'd feel like killing myself." He was grief stricken, but also annoyed. Her dying wish had trumped his suicide.

He mustered the gumption and rose. Half-crazed and in a fog, he had to snap out of it and make decisions. He noticed the sloop's idling motor. Allie must have put it in neutral after ramming the trawler, thinking of him. If she hadn't, he would be swimming like crazy, chasing his motoring sloop around the Bahamas.

He scooped her up, opting to place her on their bed before calling the authorities and heading for Chub Cay, the closest port. She felt sparrow light in his arms. He kissed her cheek and stepped toward the cabin but froze in astonishment. "Motherfuckers," he growled. Standing with a full view of the surrounding waters, he saw the blue trawler, sitting stationary a mile or so off the port bow. He hadn't looked for it or even considered a pursuit. His sloop, even under full sail and throttle, was too slow and could never overtake the trawler with its larger diesel. He had figured they were long gone, yet there they were, the men who had killed Allie and devastated his life.

He hyperventilated with rage. With his narrowed eyes fixed on the motionless trawler, he questioned why they were tempting fate by not moving. They had just murdered a woman. Perhaps the trawler's prop was damaged when the sloop rammed its stern and the high-speed acceleration finished it, or maybe they failed to detach the long-line in time and the props became tangled in the rope and froze up. In any case, Christian had a small window of time to get to them and avenge Allie's death.

His stepfather had once told him, "When a person no longer values his own life, he values other lives even less. They are the worst of murderers, the cop killers." Christian fit the profile. He didn't care if he died while taking out those men.

He hurriedly carried Allie's body into the berth and placed her on the bed. He kissed her forehead and sniffled back tears. "I'm going to get these bastards, Allie. I promise you." He covered her delicate frame with a sheet and stepped to a dresser. In the bottom drawer, he rummaged through the clothing and found the box of bullets for the revolver. He raced back up on deck, picked up the gun, and flipped open the cylinder. Allie had squeezed off four rounds. He reloaded the empty chambers and crammed a handful of extra ammo into the front pocket of his cutoffs.

Before getting underway, he needed to check his own boat. He scampered across the top of the sloop, past the rigging and mast. At the bow, he dropped to his stomach and inspected the hull. Sure enough, the sloop was damaged from hitting the trawler at full speed. The fiberglass was crushed and a cavity the size of a small watermelon existed in the hull. Luckily, the breach was a few feet above the waterline, and she was still seaworthy. He patted her deck. "Okay, girl," he said to the boat, "let's go waste those fuckers."

He rushed back to the helm, pushed the throttle forward, and swung the sloop around, taking deadly aim at the trawler. Travel time, he figured, was roughly fifteen minutes to the target. He had no plan, just to come on fast and blast everything in sight.

As *Hank's Dream* surged through the waves, Christian stared through the binoculars. He saw two men on the deck, and one pointed at his sloop. "That's right, assholes. I'm coming for you," he growled. Two more men emerged from the aft hatch. But their numbers kept coming up four. Where was the fifth guy? Allie was a good shot. Maybe in the gunfire exchange she had wounded or killed him.

He lowered the binoculars and thought, *One against four.* In a fistfight he might be in trouble, but there was the saying that a gun makes all men equal. Allie's Smith & Wesson was double action and held more rounds than the shotgun, which also had to be pumped. At a distance the shotgun was more accurate, but Christian's strategy was a close-range shootout, giving him a slight advantage. Of course, the men might have more than one weapon.

He turned the wheel, putting the sloop on intercept course, and picked up the revolver. A strong breeze tousled his locks and small whitecaps sprouted like mushrooms on the waves. Under a cloudless sky, his bare shoulders were bathed in warmth. He gazed out at the sea painted in a thousand shades of blue and inhaled the cool, dry air. It was a perfect day for sailing, not killing and dying.

As his sloop drew closer, he watched the panicked men dash about the deck. The revolver suddenly felt heavy, the grip moist from his sweaty palm. He breathed harder with the building tension. Could he do this? Could he take a life? He had no qualms about blasting the chubby captain with the shotgun, but the others, what if they surrendered? For a split second he considered a citizen's arrest.

Screw 'em. They're all guilty. They didn't stop him from shooting Allie, he thought, arguing with his conscience.

A shotgun blast ended his squabble of scruples. The pellets zipped past his head and sprayed the inner cockpit behind him. He dove to the deck and out of view. His eyes thinned to daggers, and he rolled to his back. Holding the revolver close to his chest, he seethed, "All right, you fuckers, game on."

He peeked over the side railing. The trawler was less than thirty yards away, and the pot-bellied captain was mid-center, with the shotgun pressed to his shoulder, obviously looking for Christian or his dead body.

No, shithead, you missed me. The sailboat motored into close range, and Christian eased the revolver up, took a bead on the captain, and fired.

The bullet struck the captain's leg. He screamed something in Spanish and hobbled to the forward cabin. Christian fired again but missed his wounded prey. Staying low by the helm, Christian reached up and pulled the throttle back, placing the sloop in neutral. His sailboat glided up and lightly bumped the trawler's starboard side. He poked his head up, but there was not a soul in sight. Instead of a quick shootout, it had become a game of cat and mouse. *But when it's over, will I be the cat or a dead mouse?*

He grabbed the sailboat's dock line and leaped onto the trawler's stern. The iodine smell of spoiling fish gagged him. He hastily looked around, pointing the revolver, before he squatted and tied his sloop to an aft cleat. Behind him, he heard wood squeak with footsteps, and he spun on the balls of his feet. A thin Hispanic man rushed him, wielding a machete over his head. Christian fell to his backside and fired into the man's chest. The machete stuck in the wooden deck inches from Christian's face, and the man collapsed beside him.

Face-to-face with the dead man's open dark eyes, Christian swallowed hard and trembled from head to toe. Horrified, he couldn't move for several moments. He felt the warm sensation of the victim's blood on his hands. *Get up, goddamn it! Get up!*

He gathered his limbs and scrambled to his feet. He glanced at the corpse and shuddered. He turned away, blocking out the image, the near-death experience, and the fact that he had just killed a man. There was no time to mull over the incident.

With his gun arm extended, he crept low along the boat railing. The fight-or-flight hormone had kicked in, and his adrenaline and senses were on high alert. Every sound, smell, and movement seemed amplified. Under a canvas, he slunk past the long-line winch and rollers and around large buckets containing wrapped ropes and baited hooks. He edged past the fish-gutting table and a stack of plastic bins, whipping the weapon around them, but he saw no one. The trawler seemed like a ghost ship, freakishly quiet and frightening.

He took a deep breath to calm himself and proceeded to the midsection of the boat. On the open-air deck, he cautiously lifted a floor hatch and saw only their catch, layered with ice. Overhead, a clothesline held more than a hundred shark fins that dried in the sun. One dorsal fin was huge, *the tiger shark*. His bare feet stuck to the fish slime on the deck, but he noticed a fresh blood trail that led to the forward cabin. *That's where they're hiding.*

He heard the creaking of the cabin door and ducked behind a shipping box for cover. The door opened a crack and a shotgun barrel partially appeared. Not hesitating, Christian jumped out and fired three rounds into the flimsy wooden door. The shotgun barrel fell in the doorway, followed by a heavy thud. A long, agonizing minute of silence ensued.

He wondered if he should take the risk, rush the door, and grab the shotgun or leave it as bait for his next victim. Before he could decide, he saw the weapon moving, obviously being retrieved by someone inside. Without hesitation, he unloaded the remaining rounds into the door. He pressed his back against a bulkhead as his sweaty hands groped in his pocket for more ammo. He fumbled with the bullets and managed to reload the empty chambers. He waited and listened. No movement, moaning, or voices. The only sound was his heavy breathing and the overhead cries of the lone seagull.

A six-foot gaff pole lay nearby. He grabbed it and inched closer to the cabin entrance. Standing off to one side, he used the gaff to open the door slowly. Immediately, a shotgun blast peppered the wood. If he had entered, he'd be dead. He slipped around the cabin to the port side, crept up the narrow railing, and peeked through a porthole into the galley.

A man hid around a corner for cover and aimed the shotgun at the door. He saw Christian, and for a split second, they stared at one another. The man swung the barrel as Christian squeezed the trigger. The revolver shattered the porthole glass and sent his adversary falling backward against the wall, where he crumbled.

Christian watched him. He didn't move and neither did anything else. It was eerie, dark, and still inside. He hurried back to the open deck and cautiously stepped into the cabin. The portly captain lay beyond the hatch, a bullet hole in his forehead. Christian sidestepped him and checked the other guy against the wall. He, too, was dead.

He picked up the shotgun and glanced around the meager galley. Between the sink and a rusted metal table, he saw a blanket that covered a third body on the floor. He squatted, pulled the blanket back, and checked the corpse. The dried blood on the man's shirt meant he had died earlier. *The missing deckhand, the fifth guy, Allie got him. There's one more.*

Christian held out the revolver and opened two storage hatches and a closet. Past the small stove, he faced a tight companionway that led to the berths. "Hombre," he called down the corridor, "*Ven aquí*—come here, come out."

With no answer, he pressed his back against the wall and edged sideways like a crab down the hallway, but winced with each mincing step that caused the wooden floor to creak. He came to a closed door. With its overwhelming stench of human waste and chlorine fumes, it had to be the head.

As Christian turned the handle to check inside, the door flung open. The force hit his hand and knocked the revolver from his grasp. Before he could reach down and recover it, a man built like a bull charged out, brandishing a large dagger. He swung the knife, and Christian jumped back, the blade nearly slicing his gut. Instantly, he popped the guy in the nose and left eye. For a second, the man reeled from the blows, giving Christian time to lunge and grab the man's wrist that held the knife.

In the narrow hallway they grappled body against body over control of the blade. Christian repeatedly slammed the man's wrist against the wall. Finally, the man lost his grip and the dagger fell at their feet.

The physical conflict had Christian at a disadvantage, too slender and lacking the mass and weight of his opponent. In a fight, he normally jabbed fast and hard with his long reach, while dancing around an adversary and staying out of striking range, but in the small space, Christian couldn't move. The stout Mexican was more wrestler than boxer, grabbing for him instead of striking. The guy clearly wanted to pin and throttle Christian.

Christian hammered his opponent's stomach and face with little effect. The man kept coming. He seized Christian's arm and flung him against the wall. Stunned, he tried to rise, but felt a huge arm wrapping around his throat. The large man stood behind Christian and held him restrained in a sleeper hold. Christian elbowed the man's ribs and thrashed wildly, trying to break free, but it was hopeless. He was finished.

As a diver, Christian could hold his breath longer than the average person, so he inhaled deeply, closed his eyes, and went as limp as a cornered possum. The man released him, and he toppled to the floor. Believing Christian unconscious, the guy stepped over his body to retrieve his knife.

Christian hoped his instincts were right, that the fisherman would prefer to carve someone up than suffocate him. When the man leaned over, Christian scurried backward up the companionway and grabbed the revolver. The man drew back and threw his dagger as Christian discharged the weapon. Lying on his back, he saw the blade lodged in the wall above his head and then noticed the blood seeping into the man's shirt.

The man still stood, blinking in disbelief while staring down at Christian. He touched his stomach and looked down at his bloody hand. He cursed in Spanish and stepped toward him. Christian fired again and again until the large Mexican finally tumbled over and landed at Christian's feet.

Christian coughed and puffed for air. Getting to his hands and knees, he fought the urge to throw up. He managed to rise, grasping his weapon, and stagger to the berths. He did a final search of the trawler and found no others. He stepped over the big man's body in the companionway and slumped into a galley chair at the table.

It was over. He had killed four men and survived with only a few bruises and a smarting neck. Coming off his adrenaline high, he felt traumatized and couldn't stop shaking while he gazed at the sprawled corpses in the cabin. Their open eyes and gaping mouths were frozen in silent anguish. Blood splattered the walls, soaked their ragged clothes, and flowed back and forth across the floorboard with the gentle rocking of the trawler. The ghastly scene resembled a slaughterhouse for humans.

Christian stared at the revolver on the table and couldn't believe he was capable of methodically hunting down and murdering each man. He glared at the dead captain. "You caused this," he snarled. "Were those fins really worth it?" He abruptly rose from the chair. *I don't have time to dwell. I need to focus and get through it.*

He considered the consequences. This was not justifiable homicide and far from self-defense. Manslaughter would even be a stretch. He might convince the authorities he was out of his mind with sorrow and then face second-degree murder charges. He rolled his eyes. *I planned it, came onto their boat, and deliberately killed them: first-degree murder.* In Florida, he could get the death sentence. At the time, he had no clue about Bahamian law, but was sure he would at least spend his life in prison.

"The truth will set you free" is bullshit. A lot of criminals were their own worst enemy, spilling their guts to the cops. His stepfather and

Vince had instilled in him, "You get in trouble, keep your mouth shut, especially if you're guilty."

His brain switched gears to how to beat the rap and come out unscathed. He studied the scenario—five men and a wife all shot to death, and him the only survivor. Getting rid of the long-liners would be no problem. The Caribbean was a great place for wrongdoing, with few or no witnesses and the capacity to sink evidence. For hundreds of years, the deadly reefs had chewed up and swallowed countless boats, starting with the earliest galleons. The tropical weather also played a factor. A glorious morning with calm seas could turn violent in the afternoon with thunderstorms having hurricane-strength gusts. The mysterious Devil's Triangle was famous for fouling up compasses and equipment, sending boats and planes on one-way trips to a watery hell. The Caribbean was a graveyard of ships and skeletons with any number of explanations for the trawler and crew's disappearance.

He rubbed his jaw, wondering how to justify Allie's death and his shot-up sloop. Pirates came to mind. Although not publicized like their notorious African counterparts, modern-day pirates did operate in these waters but kept a low profile by not kidnapping and ransoming their victims. Expensive boats had been found abandoned and adrift at sea, stripped of all valuables. Even a Sarasota doctor and his wife vanished while sailing here. Their ransacked sloop was recovered, but their bodies were never found.

With the scheme forming, he walked out on the trawler deck and surveyed the surrounding waters. Not a boat in sight. Fortunately, it was midweek and lacked the sport fishermen and dive boats that were prevalent on weekends.

Behind him, he saw the fringes of Chub Cay, nearly four miles off. Beyond the light-blue shallows lay the black-blue waters of the Tongue, a deep underwater canyon, a perfect place to sink a boat. He walked to the stern, oddly thinking that growing up in the tropical weather had rubbed off, a happy-go-lucky sailor in the morning, a deadly storm by the afternoon. He lifted his first

victim to a sitting position and dragged him into the galley with
the others. He grabbed the revolver, and with a padlock hanging
on the hatch, he locked the door. A floating corpse with a bullet
in it was asking for trouble.

He scampered to the bow and gathered up a rope for towing and
dove off the trawler. He was covered with blood, most of it Allie's
and his first victim's, but splatter from the others might also have
been on him and his feet. In the water, he washed the revolver and
his body and stripped out of his cutoffs, letting them drift away so
his sloop would not be contaminated with the wrong blood. He
swam back to his sloop, tied the trawler's towline to a stern cleat,
and released the bowline that had been tied to the trawler.

Christian scurried back to the helm and steered *Hank's Dream*
southward. The rope became taut, pulling the heavy trawler to deep
water. With the strain, his sailboat slugged along at only a few knots.
If the trawler was operational, he could have used it and towed his
sailboat, and reached the Tongue faster. Nervous, he chewed his
nails and scanned the horizon for another boater or plane. A sloop
towing a trawler would not go unnoticed. He knew there was no
such thing as a perfect crime and had heard on average, a criminal
makes twenty-five mistakes that can get him convicted, and offenders
might think and fix five of them. Christian hoped to beat those odds,
and his mind raced with the blunders he had made or would make.

Several miles and a half hour later, he reached the deep water
and stopped. He had considered many ways to scuttle the trawler:
shooting or chopping a hole in its hull, reversing the bilge pumps, or
pulling the scupper or drains. Doing one or all of them and it might
still take an hour for the trawler to sink. He didn't have explosives,
but he had the next best thing.

He dragged a dive tank out of the aft hatch, pulled the trawler
alongside his sailboat, and holding the tank, he hopped aboard the
fishing boat. He positioned the tank against the rear engine hatch.
He dove off the trawler and rinsed his feet and body again, removing
any evidence before climbing back on his sailboat. He untied the two

boats and steered a safe distance away from the trawler. He took one last look around and aimed the revolver at the pressurized dive tank.

Like Jaws, *baby.* In the movie, the great white had been terminated when the police captain shot a dive tank lodged in the shark's mouth. The great white blew up, end of story. It was ironic and only fitting the shark-killing trawler be taken out the same way. He pulled the trigger, and the tank exploded with a tremendous bang. Debris flew into the air, and the boat's stern was obliterated. He set down the weapon and watched the trawler sink beneath the waves. *Sharks; it had started and ended with them in mind.*

CHAPTER ELEVEN

Last night on the sloop, Christian had told Vince how he killed the four Mexican long-liners and scuttled their trawler. Wanting to distance himself from Chub Cay, the murder scene, and floating debris that consisted of a few buckets and chunks of blue wood, he had headed for Nassau on New Providence to report Allie's death.

Ten miles from the island and still in deep water, he had ransacked his sloop and tossed everything of value overboard; phones, cameras, computers, binoculars, radio, GPS, TV, and Allie's purse, jewelry box, and scuba gear. He kept his diving gear to make his story work, that he had been diving when she was killed. The worst part was removing her rings, the wedding and engagement ring, and tossing them into the drink. "The diamond caught the light and glittered all the way down," he had said to Vince. "It was like watching the sparkle go out of my life."

He removed the pendant of the Spanish doubloon from Allie's neck and placed it around his own. He had to save something. He also kept the revolver, since Allie probably had gunpowder residue on her hand, and he wanted the scenario to appear that she had a shootout with pirates. "That was a mistake, keeping the gun," he told Vince. "I wiped it clean of my prints, but forgot the bullets in the chamber. The first guy I killed nearly fell on me. We were eyeball to eyeball. His blood must've been on my hands when I reloaded."

Vince said, "I wouldn't worry. It's hard to prove a murder if they don't know who or where the victim is."

Talking to Vince, telling him everything, had eased Christian's mind, like dropping an anchor of worries overboard. The mobster knew the law and how to manipulate and beat the system. Vince and Christian shared a rare bond that went beyond words or feelings. They had saved each other's lives. Vince would have drowned if Christian hadn't saved him. In turn, Vince came to Christian's aid when a Miami horse trainer and two Arabs kidnapped him over a horse deal and planned to bury him in the Everglades.

Christian's morning reflection ended in the Bimini harbor. He took his last sip from his coffee mug and went below to the galley for a refill. He felt his sloop rock when someone stepped on board.

"Anyone home?" called Vince.

"Yeah, I'm awake. It's pretty hard to sleep in; too much noise at a marina," he said as Vince entered the cabin. "Want some coffee?"

"Had some, room service." Vince dropped a brown bag on the booth table. "Brought you a sandwich, figured you might be hungry."

"Thanks." Christian sat down and opened the bag. "Reminds me I need to buy groceries before I head out. While I'm in town, I'm going find that little pusher and knock his gold tooth out."

Vince chuckled. "You remind me of myself at your age, always looking for trouble."

"Don't have to look. Trouble finds me." Christian took a bite of the egg salad sandwich.

"Forget the pusher. He ain't worth it. You're still in the Bahamas, and if you get arrested for assault, you may never see daylight. They're lookin' for an excuse to charge you. Look at it this way, at least you got laid."

"Laid? It felt more like rape." Christian set the sandwich down and nodded with a deep, heavy sigh. "But I suppose you're right. I'm already in hot water—don't need to add more to the pot."

Vince settled back in the booth across from Christian, pulled out a cigar from his shirt pocket, and lit it. "I've been thinking about what you told me last night. Your wife asked you to save sharks before she died. That goal stopped you from blowing your brains out. Have you given it much thought?"

"Yeah, I think about blowing my brains out every day." Christian smirked. "But if you're referring to saving sharks, it hasn't crossed my mind." He shook his locks in discouragement. "It's ludicrous, Vince. They can't be saved, and even if I took on the cause, I have no clue where to start."

"Christian, you're smart, capable, and no slouch. Put a plan in place, and I'll help you."

Christian furrowed his eyebrows and smiled. "Since when do you care about sharks?"

"Don't give a shit about those bloodthirsty fish, but I care about saving you. Like I said, I've seen people go downhill after a tragedy, turning into dopers, drunks, even suicides. Whether you know it or not, you're on that path. It's far easier to quit, wallow in misery, and be a loser. It takes work and guts to pull yourself out of a hole and reclaim your life. Your wife gave you this cause to give you motivation, keep you from crashing and burning. Let's follow her lead."

Christian and Vince restocked the sloop with food, and in the afternoon, they sailed out of Bimini. Although Christian had intended to take the voyage home alone, he was glad Vince wanted to come along. Since his near-death experience on Tampa Bay, Vince had somewhat retired from the mob. The illegal activity was no longer worth the risk and money, plus he had already made his fortune.

Christian sat behind the helm and gazed ahead at the vast and empty blue ocean while Vince reclined on the side bench in Allie's old spot, head on a cushion, with closed eyes. Christian was unsure if Vince was awake or dozing. "I've been thinking about this plan to save sharks."

"What'd ya come up with?" Vince murmured.

"Those long-liners were a long ways from home, too far to cart the fins back to Mexico or Central America. Allie found an article on the Internet about a seafood exporter on northern Andros. There were rumors they were dealing with shark fins. Andros was just to the south when Allie and I had the run-in with the long-liners. It all adds up. The Mexicans were selling their fins to that exporter."

Vince lifted his head and looked at him. "What's your point?"

Christian pointed to the eastern horizon. "Andros is right over there, Vince. You get rid of a long-liner, but there's always another poor fisherman to replace him. The exporters make the real money, shipping the fins to Hong Kong. Without them, long-liners have no place to sell their fins, and it saves a lot of sharks. Maybe I should start there. We could be in Andros this evening."

Vince sat up and swung his legs off the bench, facing Christian. "So we sail to Andros, and you find the export company. What then?"

"I'm going to burn the fucker to the ground."

Hank's Dream stole into northern Andros in the middle of the night, moving through the ebony waters like an apparition, without sails and lights. Christian cut the engine before the sound was within earshot of the island and allowed the sloop to drift in on the evening tide. He dropped anchor fifty yards offshore of Mastic Point and the export warehouse.

On the trip over, he and Vince had discussed the arson. For it to be done right, Vince had said, someone should come in days ahead, get the layout, and check the security at a building before torching it, but Christian pointed out that it meant docking at a marina in Nicholls Town, producing a passport, and exposing themselves to witnesses. Two white tourists would stand out in the little settlement. With the FBI's sights on them, neither one could afford to become a suspect. The final plan was to slip in and out from the water without anyone knowing they had been there.

In preparation, Christian disconnected the sloop's GPS, and Vince removed the batteries from their cell phones. Christian found a pair of bolt cutters and a can of black spray paint, for a message, and placed the items in a mesh dive bag. He siphoned gas from his sloop's tank and half filled two plastic containers and then attached them and the bag to a five-foot tow rope. He also wrapped a lighter in a waterproof baggy and placed it in his pants pocket. In the aft hatch, he took out a mask, snorkel, fins, and dive gloves, to conceal fingerprints that might survive the fire. All was ready.

Christian slipped on a black t-shirt and gazed at the scattered dim lights on Andros. "Guess this is it," he said quietly, because voices carried on the water.

"I'd go with you, but I'm not much of a swimmer."

"You can't swim at all, Vince." He studied the distance and time it would take to go ashore, set the fire, and return to his sloop. "Once you see the flames, I should be back within a half hour. If it's longer, I got caught, so haul ass."

"Haul ass in a sailboat? That's a joke. Too bad we're not in a submarine; hit a target and disappear."

"Like Captain Nemo and the *Nautilus*." He smiled. "Jules Verne probably created the first environmentalist to care about the sea, and Nemo became a terrorist—ramming and sinking ships because his wife had died in a war. I have some things in common with him."

"The only thing I remember is Kirk Douglas fighting a big ass squid in the old movie. Anyway, how am I supposed to find you in the dark without running lights?"

Christian held up his wrist, showing Vince the compass with glowing indicators. "I'll find you." He donned the diving gloves and stepped into his fins.

Vince lowered the gas containers and mesh bag, using the rope. "Ya know I usually pay people to do this shit. But here I am, risking my skin for of all things, fish. If Sal and the boys knew, they'd think I'd gone nuts."

"You're in good company. Everyone thinks I've lost it." Christian descended the stern ladder. "I'm going to break in and make sure they have shark fins before I torch the place." He lowered his mask and quietly slipped into the water.

Vince handed him the rope and whispered, "Good hunting."

Christian gave him a thumbs-up and snorkeled toward the warehouse lights while dragging the bag and floating gas containers. He reached the small wharf and saw a fishing trawler tied in an outsider slip. Swimming around the boat to the dock, he found an old wooden ladder that went up several feet. He took off his fins and climbed up. On the dock near the ladder he left his snorkeling gear and hauled up the gas and bag with the rope. He carried the items down the pier, sneaking low in the shadows. He reached the shell-strewn parking lot behind the warehouse.

A high fence of tin sheets encircled the front and sides of the building for privacy and kept trespassers out from the road, but apparently no one anticipated an intruder from the sea. The place was wide open. Two outside lights burned from the roof corners of the warehouse.

He scampered across the lot and around a white panel van to a building back door. The low glow of the crescent moon helped conceal his movement. Stacked fish crates lined the outside walls, and off to one side were several drying tables with wire-mesh tops. He examined the small padlock on the door. *Piece of cake.*

He set down the gas tanks and took the bolt cutter out of the bag. As he started to sever the lock, a shadow raced out from behind the crates and passed his feet. Startled, he bound backward and nearly lost his footing. "Jesus," he muttered, and glared at the orange cat. He regained his composure, cut the lock, and stepped inside.

The warehouse was dimly lit by only one buzzing fluorescent light near the front. The place had the putrid smell of rotting seafood and diesel fuel. He crept past tables used for fish cleaning and inspected the empty crates. In a walk-in freezer, he found filleted fish and whole sea cucumbers. He walked back into the center of the warehouse. Gloved hands on his hips, he stood, frustrated, not finding shark fins, and trying to decide his next move. The wire tables outside suggested shark fins, the tables used to dry them, but maybe they were for the sea cucumbers. He had no clue how sea slugs were cured. He wanted solid proof of fins before he destroyed the place.

He glanced at two doors at the front of the building. One had to be the office. Possibly the shark fins had been shipped out, but there should be a record. He walked to the door, planning to rifle through the files for receipts and shipping orders, but the second door and its padlock caught his attention. *Why lock a room within an already secured warehouse unless there was something to hide?*

He snapped the door lock with the cutters. Using the lighter to see in the dark room, he peeked inside. Bagged and dried sea cumbers sat in boxes, ready for shipping. Beyond them, he came to several round fruit baskets that sat on the floor. Each was filled with sun-bleached shark fins, their size determining the basket they were in. *I knew it. Knew these bastards were dealing in fins. Okay, then.*

With confirmation, he went to work. He retrieved one of the gas containers and doused the fin baskets in the room and the wooden crates throughout the warehouse. He then noticed several large drums used to store the diesel fuel for the trawler. *Perfect. They're making this damn easy.*

With his second container, he made a gasoline trail from the warehouse drums to the dock. He returned to the building and tossed the plastic containers inside, knowing they would melt in the fire. He grabbed a newspaper out of a trash bin and hurried back to the dock. He glanced around for a place to leave his graffiti and spotted the trawler. Back in the water with the can of paint, he sprayed his warning on the trawler's hull that faced the sea.

He climbed up the ladder, lit the newspaper, and tossed it on the gas trail. He ran down the dock, his mind and heart also racing. The blaze lit up the lot by the time he returned to the ladder and his snorkeling gear. In the security of the dark water, he put on his fins and mask and swam toward his sloop with the bag containing the bolt cutter and paint.

Several yards out, he heard the explosion when the fire reached the gas drums. He stopped midstroke and treaded water, watching the fire incinerate the warehouse. The sea surface shimmered and glowed, mirroring the inferno. Black smoke billowed upward and blocked out the stars. The orange-and-yellow flames resembled monstrous fingers that clawed at the crescent moon. It was terrible and beautiful.

As he watched, he felt a reprieve from guilt and grief. He had done something for Allie, and her death took on new meaning. She had given nature an avenger.

CHAPTER TWELVE

Sergeant Drake and his forensic officer sat in the small twin-engine police plane. They had flown out of Nassau, and after a short flight, landed at the San Andros airport in the northern section of the island. An officer from Nicholls Town met them with a car, and they drove a few miles outside of town to Mastic Point. They pulled up to the charred remains of the warehouse that had housed Lunar Wholesale Seafood.

The local police listed the fire as accidental, bad electrical wiring, a carelessly tossed cigarette, or a boat battery sparked when in contact with something flammable. But the company owner had been beside himself, claiming arson. Unhappy with the small police department on Andros, he wanted experts brought in. To appease him, Drake had flown over to investigate the fire.

Drake and three Nicholls Town policemen stood on the shell lot and watched the forensic officer dig through the burnt rubble of beams and tin sheets that had been the roof and sides of the building. A blue compact car pulled in, and a stocky white man climbed out. His bald head and determined face were red from sun or anger as he marched toward them.

"Here he comes," commented one of the officers. "Mr. McGee, the owner of Lunar."

"You find anything?" asked McGee.

Drake offered his hand. "Mr. McGee, I'm Sergeant Drake from Nassau."

"Yeah, yeah," said McGee, brushing off the handshake and turning toward the remains of his building. "Like I told these cops, this was goddamn arson. Someone set the fire, and I got a pretty good idea who."

"Who do you think did it?"

"Near as I can tell nothing was stolen, outboard, computer, anything of value was left in the building to burn, so it had to be one of those goddamn out-of-towners that protested and picketed my business last year," growled McGee. "That damn article in the *Tribune* said I considered exporting shark fins to Hong Kong, and all hell broke loose. I got threatening e-mails, and then some of those goddamn environmentalists showed up here, carrying signs. Sons of bitches got the government to shut down commercial shark fishing, but they obviously still weren't happy. They had to burn my building. I was barely staying afloat exporting the damn sea cucumbers."

"Did you or any of your employees see anyone suspicious before the fire?"

"No, sir," one of the officers answered for McGee. "We interviewed the employees and everyone living nearby. No one saw any strangers here or in town."

"Mr. McGee, did you save the threatening e-mails, get their names?"

"Hell, yes. They were in my office." He nodded toward the smoldering building. "A lot of good they do me now. First a trawler goes missing three weeks ago, and now this shit."

Drake turned around and looked at the docks and white trawler. "What color was the missing trawler?"

"Blue, why?" asked McGee.

"We found some blue chunks of wood floating near Chub Cay along with the remains of a body. I'll need the names of the missing crew. Is there any way to get their DNA?"

"Jesus Christ," grumbled McGee. "The captain and his deckhands were Mexican and lived aboard. Any DNA they might've left was in the warehouse."

The forensic officer walked to them and held up a baggie containing a charred padlock. "I found this near the rear of the building, and it's been cut."

"That's the padlock for the back door," said McGee. "I knew this was arson."

"Sergeant Drake, you need to see this," yelled an officer from a small police skiff that had been searching the water for evidence. His boat was on the portside of the trawler that faced the ocean.

Drake, his forensic officer, the three local policemen, and McGee hurried down the dock. "What did you find?" Drake called.

The officer in the skiff pointed at the trawler. "Someone left a message on the hull in black spray paint. It says Stop Selling Shark Fins, and it's signed Captain Nemo."

At a South Beach restaurant, Dave Wheeler enjoyed a leisurely dinner of rib eye steak and baked potato with his eighteen-year-old daughter, Tracy. It was a rare treat, getting together. He had a demanding caseload, and she was preoccupied with her first year of college and a new boyfriend.

She poured more dressing on her Cobb salad. "It's just not fair, Dad. I'm a college student and an adult, but Mother still has me on a curfew, like I'm a kid. I have to be in at eleven o'clock on weekdays and two on weekends. It's ridiculous. Can you talk to her?"

Talk to my ex-wife? She's so narrow-minded she can see through a keyhole with both eyes. He put down his fork. "I'd rather not, Tracy, but those restrictions don't seem unreasonable. While you're living under her roof, she makes the rules."

"I should get my own apartment," said Tracy.

"That means paying rent and utilities. It means an after-school job, because I can't help you out. I'm already covering your tuition and car insurance. You'd better think it through. Freedom comes with a price." The music from his cell phone played. He looked at the caller ID, Drake in Nassau. He put the cell back in his pocket.

"I suppose that concerns work."

"I've been helping the Bahamas with a murder case."

They finished dinner, and he walked her to her Nissan. "I'll think about the job," she said and then gave him kiss on the cheek. After she left, he strolled to his car. Instead of going home to his empty apartment, he drove to his FBI office and returned Sergeant Drake's call.

Drake told him about an arson case he was investigating on Andros. A warehouse belonging to Lunar Wholesale Seafood had been burned to the ground. A message had been left by the guilty party protesting the owner's plans to export shark fins to China.

"Using Captain Nemo, that's imaginative," said Wheeler. "In *Twenty Thousand Leagues Under the Sea*, Nemo was somewhat of an ocean environmentalist and was disgusted with mankind, sank ships with his submarine. Offhand, I don't think your arsonist is a local. His profile suggests he's a young white male, educated, and a sci-fi buff. They tend to be creative. He's also a romantic, wants to change the world. I'd start with visitors to Andros, passenger lists on planes and boats. That's all I can help you with, Drake. I don't have time to take on your arson case."

"I understand, but I'm calling because the warehouse owner said he's also missing a blue trawler and its crew of five men. It disappeared about the same time that Allie Roberts was murdered. The foot and blue wood chunks that were found off Chub Cay might have come from that trawler. I was hoping you had the test results back on the wood and the foot, and they could be tied to the Roberts case."

"They're back. I planned to call you in the morning with the good and bad news," said Wheeler. "The good news: the paint scraping taken from the sloop and the blue wood chunks are a match, same paint, same manufacturer. The bad news: the DNA from the foot and the blood on the bullet casing taken from the forty-four came from different men. Any chance of getting the missing crew's DNA?"

"I don't think so. Any DNA from those men was on the trawler or in the warehouse. On top of that, they had recently arrived from Mexico. All the information the export owner had on the crew and trawler was in the warehouse office. Contact numbers, the Mexican port they came from, everything was destroyed in the fire. The owner can't even remember their full names."

"That's too bad," said Wheeler. "We need a victim that matches the blood on the bullet to charge Christian Roberts."

"But the paint, it proves that the sloop and the fishing trawler had a run-in at sea."

"Proves nothing if you don't have the paint from the trawler. Roberts could've hit another blue boat, and for all you know, that trawler and its crew are sitting in a Mexican port."

"The exporter says no. They were making good money and had no intention of leaving the Bahamas."

"Despite what the owner thinks, you need hard evidence and are a long way from making a case. Without the crew's DNA and trawler paint, you can't link Christian Roberts to them. Furthermore, if the trawler foundered in a storm, Roberts's sloop could've hit the floating debris. No DNA from its crew, and you have no proof of foul play."

"That's disheartening," said Drake.

"Keep digging, Sergeant, we'll eventually connect the dots. Evidence is like a shoe. Too big and loose, it'll trip you up in court, and too small, it pinches and hurts a case. The evidence has to fit just right."

Drake chuckled. "Shoes, very colorful, Agent Wheeler."

Wheeler tapped a pen against his lips in thought. "Getting back to this arson, the export owner was suspected of selling shark fins?"

"That is the rumor, and the arsonist must've believed it with his message."

"Is *Hank's Dream* still docked in Nassau?"

"The sloop left over a week ago. Customs notified me that Mr. Roberts had flown into Nassau, so I drove to the marina to speak with him. When I arrived, he and his sailboat were gone. His passport next showed up in Bimini, but he left the island a few days ago. I assume he is back in Florida."

"Interesting," said Wheeler. "He was sailing in the area when the Andros warehouse was torched. I'll pull a trace on his cell phone."

"Do you think he might be Captain Nemo?"

"He's already facing possible charges for his wife's homicide. It'd take a lot of balls to add arson to the list."

After the call with Drake, Wheeler shuffled through the papers in the Roberts file and found the computer printouts about sharks that had been scattered in the sloop's cabin. More and more, things pointed toward those fish. Roberts was a diver, and the printouts proved he was a shark enthusiast. The missing long-line trawler might have been illegally harvesting sharks, and the seafood company was burned for exporting the fins. Roberts, the floating foot, the trawler, and now the warehouse, all were in the same area of the Bahamas and at the same time. Wheeler did not believe in coincidences.

He located the printouts and began rereading them. He initially had dismissed the papers, thinking the couple were interested in sharks and came to the Bahamas to see them. He studied the information on several shark species, but moving on, he noticed a trend. The printouts weren't about sharks, but their worldwide demise as a result of a Chinese soup made of shark fins. He then found the substantiating evidence. Two papers contained a small article taken from a Bahamian newspaper. It revealed that Lunar Wholesale Seafood planned to export shark fins to Hong Kong, once the owner received the permits. The article also mentioned the rumors that the company was already shipping fins illegally. "Christian, my boy, you knew about the export company on Andros, and you were in the area. Ties you to the arson."

He leaned back, thinking about the possible chain of events. Roberts comes across the trawler and sees the crew bringing in sharks. He tries to stop them, and there's a shootout, resulting in gunshot blasts to the sloop and a dead wife. Roberts retaliates, murders the crew, getting the blood on a bullet when he reloads the forty-four, and then he sinks the trawler, hiding the crime. That scenario explained the evidence and implies he staged a pirate raid. It also would explain Roberts's behavior, tight-lipped, the hiring of a defense attorney, and his lies in the polygraph test. He knew who had killed his wife. He also perfectly fits the profile of the arsonist, but was he capable of slaying five men?

Wheeler reflected on Roberts's eyes, soft as a calm, blue sea but hard as sapphires when enraged. He had the temper to kill and the smarts to accomplish it unscathed. Like a switchblade, he was sharp, lean, and strong, and when provoked, he was as deadly as the opened blade. No doubt he could have murdered those fishermen. His farewell kiss to the Bahamas had been burning the warehouse. *Motive and opportunity, it's starting to fit like a comfortable shoe.*

Offshore of Andros Island, Christian found his sloop in the dark, using the compass. He climbed up the stern ladder, ripped off his mask, and tossed it, his fins, and dive bag into a corner of the deck.

Vince stared at the distant flames that consumed the export company. "Jesus, that place went up like a tinderbox."

"Yeah, we need to get the hell out of here." Christian cranked up the engine while raising the sails. He veered the sloop west, making a beeline for the Florida coast. Five miles from Andros, they could still see the glow on the black horizon.

"Are you happy now?" Vince asked.

"Don't think I'll ever be happy, but I'm satisfied. Glad I did it."

"Well, I actually feel pretty good about this. I've committed a lot of crimes, but this arson is a first, destroying something to better the world." He laughed. "It proves I'm not a total self-absorbed bastard."

They voyaged through the night, but a few hours before dawn, the sloop encountered pounding rain, strong gusts, and rough seas. A tropical low was rare that late in the year. In a foul-weather jacket, Christian stood on the tilted deck behind the helm and enjoyed riding out the huge storm swells. Vince, unfortunately, did not share his exhilaration. He was hunkered down in the cabin, stomach churning with his head over a bucket.

At daybreak, the storm broke and the sky was the color of newly minted gold. Vince crawled from the cabin midmorning looking pale and green. He collapsed on the side bench, grumbling, "Sailing is crap."

"I told you to come up on the deck last night. Sitting in a closed rolling cabin during a storm is only asking to be sick."

"Yeah, come up here and get blown overboard. No thanks. Already been there, done that with you and nearly fuckin' drowned."

"Last night's squall was hardly a hurricane." Christian looked at the GPS. "In a few hours, we should be off Florida. I'll put in at Lauderdale and get our passports stamped. You can catch a plane or rent a car and be back in Sarasota by the late afternoon."

Vince huffed. "What, leave you and miss all this fun?"

"It's no problem. I can bring the boat back by myself."

"I'm not concerned about your sailing ability. I don't think you should be alone."

"Worried I might sail off the deep end?" Christian grumbled. He appreciated that people cared about him but felt smothered. Everyone he knew, every place he went, he was analyzed. He started to regret confiding in Vince.

"Let's see, you've been drinking, drugging, and putting guns to your head or killing long-liners and burning down warehouses. I'm just curious about what you'll do next."

Christian threw up his hands with aggravation. "I'm not going to commit suicide, Vince. Allie wanted me to save sharks, and I'm sticking to that goal."

"No matter what you do, you won't get your life back. When you realize that—"

"I understand. Allie's gone. My life's in the toilet. When I'm finished with this cause, then you better worry." Christian spun the wheel hard to the north. The sails snapped in the shifting wind and the boom moved to the port side.

With the deck slanting to the other side, Vince grabbed a railing to keep his balance. "What are you doing?"

"Changing course. You want to stay and babysit? I'll make it easier for you. We'll pull in at Stuart and take the Intracoastal back to Sarasota. It's a boring damn trip but calm."

For the rest of the day they traveled offshore, leaving Fort

Lauderdale and West Palm Beach in their wake. Toward evening, they sailed through a wide pass and arrived at Stuart, a town located mid-state on the coast and went through customs. Exhausted from the twenty-four-hour straight run, they spent the night at a marina.

The next morning they motored down the St. Lucie Canal. As Christian predicted, the trip was monotonous with an endless view of cattle pastures on either side. They stopped in Indiantown for a quick lunch, and in late afternoon they reached the locks that would open up to Lake Okeechobee.

Christian maneuvered his sloop into the lock, joining other boats and their owners. Holding ropes attached to the lock, they steadied the sloop, and it became a little hectic, preventing the jammed boats from bumping as the water level dropped to the level of the lake. When the lock opened, they entered the massive lake.

Okeechobee sits on the northern edge of the Everglades and is the largest body of water within the United States, forty miles long and twenty-four across, but shallow with a hard rock and clay bottom. A sloop with a deep-water shaft like *Hank's Dream* could run aground, and with no tides to lift and free a sailboat, it could be a problem.

Rather than take a risk and travel straight across, Christian motored to a deepwater canal that hugged the southern shore. It was a longer but surer trip. Ten miles past Port Mayaca and in the middle of nowhere, he dropped anchor at sundown, deciding to get a fresh start in the morning.

After cruising still waters, Vince had completely recovered from the nausea. He sat on the bench and sipped his scotch. "Do you know what day this is?"

"Don't know, don't care," Christian said as he rerigged a saltwater fishing pole with a freshwater setup.

"It's Thursday, Thanksgiving. Instead of having a nice dinner with your family, you're stuck with me. We should've bought some turkey in Indiantown."

"Thanksgiving, really? If it makes you feel better, I prefer being here with you. My mother's been driving me crazy." He reached in the tackle box and dug out a plastic worm. "I don't care about the turkey, but I wish I'd picked up some night crawlers at that last stop. Would have been better than this lousy artificial."

"What'da ya think you'll catch?" Vince asked.

Christian threaded a plastic worm through the hook, making it weedless so it would not snag the water lilies. "Maybe a bass, some speckled perch or catfish. I'd be content with a couple of bluegills for dinner."

"Bluegills, those dinky fish—you'd better catch more than a couple."

"Vince, this is Okeechobee, not some northern mud hole. The bluegills here grow a foot long and can weigh several pounds."

As the sun descended into the vast watery horizon of cattails, Christian repeatedly cast out the line and reeled in, jerking the bait across the bottom. Instead of catching bluegills, Christian caught several shell crackers, a panfish with a black dot behind its gills. He gutted and removed the fish head and fins, and descaled them. Rather than fillet the fish, he left them whole. He dipped them in flour and fried them in oil. Using canned vegetables, he made tomato gravy for the grits and spiced black-eyed peas with cayenne, ham, and onions. He fixed a plate and set it before Vince in the galley booth.

Vince skeptically poked at the food and shook his head. "What a lousy Thanksgiving. You expect me to eat this shit?"

"It's what we eat in the South," Christian said and fixed his own plate. "If you don't like it, I'll boil you a hot dog."

Vince tried the fish and grinned. "These shell crackers taste like bass, hardly fishy." He dug in and sampled the other dishes. "Damn, Christian, this is good. I can't believe I'm eatin' and likin' grits." After finishing the meal, he leaned back and gazed at Christian. "You're a great provider, cook, and not to mention easy on the eyes. If you were a girl, I'd marry ya."

Christian smiled. "Sorry, Vince, I like you, but you're not my type."

"Where did you learn to fish and cook?"

"My grandparents. My grandfather and I used to fish every Saturday, and my grandmother—what a character—she taught me to cook. She'd always say—" Christian's voice rose two octaves, mimicking his grandmother. " 'Chrissie, boys need learn to cook, same as girls.'" He chuckled. "Heck, if I had the ingredients on board, I could've made us a badass key lime pie. I will miss them this Thanksgiving."

"And your parents, what did they teach ya?"

Christian set his fork down and said softly, "That nothing lasts, not a home, a marriage, not even a life. Guess I'd forgotten that lesson."

A gunshot blast erupted near the sloop. Vince ducked in the booth, and Christian jumped up and raced topside onto the dark deck. Two men wearing spotlights on their head were in a small aluminum skiff, several yards off the sloop. One held a rifle and steered the outboard. The other stood at the bow and held a harpoon gig and a line attached to a large wounded alligator that rolled and thrashed in the water between the two boats.

"You motherfuckers," Christian shouted at them. "It's not gator season."

"Fuck off," hollered the man steering as his partner pulled the alligator toward their boat.

"Come over here," Christian yelled, "so I can kick your sorry asses."

Vince came up on deck. "What's going on?"

Christian ignored Vince and shouted at the men, "Come on, you white-trash bastards. Don't have the balls to face me?"

Shot in the head at close range, the dead alligator was dragged into the men's skiff as Christian kept ranting. He stepped up on the railing and teetered on diving into the lake. "I should drag you out of that fucking boat and drown you pieces of shit."

"Christian, back off," Vince yelled.

The men stared up as if a lunatic hovered over them. "Let's get out of here," said one with panic. They gunned the outboard and took off.

"Goddamn poachers," Christian grumbled and watched the skiff disappear into the blackness. "They're lucky I didn't have a gun." He stepped down on the deck.

"What's the hell's the matter with you?" Vince growled. "You hear a gunshot and rush to it. Then you pick a fight with armed men, yet you want me to believe you're okay? If you had a gun, would you have shot them over an alligator?"

Christian was taken aback with Vince's perspective. Was he suicidal or had he become so depraved that murder was an afterthought? He sat down on the bench, pulled up his legs, and hugged them. "I don't know, Vince. Don't know if I would've shot them or was hoping they'd shoot me. I'm not sure who I am anymore."

CHAPTER THIRTEEN

Vince sat on the deck and relished the cool breeze off the immense lake as Christian guided the sloop down the canal that bordered the southern edge of Okeechobee. The water was pond still and the voyage peaceful, except when a speeding pleasure craft raced past and created a wake that rocked the sailboat. Like the previous night when confronting the alligator poachers, Christian again lashed out, cursing at the inconsiderate boaters. At one point, he chucked his Coke can at some reckless teenagers and hit their skiff.

The young man Vince had known was gone. His Southern composure and charm along with the lazy smile had been replaced with brooding and a temper matching nitro in a horse wagon, never knowing when he'd explode. Christian had been dealt a bad hand. He was angry and confused, unsure of his next move. Should he place a bet and stay in the game or fold? Life was like poker with winners and losers, a card game of chance and luck. Vince had learned that fact all too well.

After the Andros arson, Christian had been upbeat for a few days, but it had cost some poor slob a warehouse. Now on the Intracoastal, he was increasingly sullen while staring off into his own little dark world. When the sloop was anchored for the evening and they hit the berths, Vince heard Christian's erratic sleep, the tossing, calling, and jerking awake from nightmares. He rambled about the shadowy sloop, and Vince detected soft whimpers and sniffles coming from the deck. The kid also had no appetite, ate a fraction of his food. He was devastated over the loss of his wife, and worse, he blamed himself for her death. To add to his problems, he probably suffered from post-traumatic stress, like a war vet, after killing the four long-liners on the trawler.

Vince was terribly fond of Christian, but before Vince's eyes, the young man was falling apart. Helping him with his cause, Vince hoped to bring Christian back from the edge. With power, money, and criminal moxie, Vince's offer was valid. Increasingly, though, he was growing concerned and having his doubts. Would saving his sharks save Christian?

On the canal, a thirty-eight-foot Scarab motored past the sloop. "Hey, Christian, that kinda looks like my old speedboat, the one you sank." Vince chuckled.

Christian glanced at the Scarab and said solemnly, "Kinda."

The old Christian would have given me grief, claiming it wasn't his fault the Scarab had sunk. I miss him. With his Scarab in mind, Vince recalled how Christian had come into his life. He started out as a typical pigeon who wanted to borrow a couple hundred grand for a racehorse. Vince gave him the loan, knowing he couldn't repay it.

Vince had moved his operation to Sarasota and needed a native familiar with boats and the local waters for picking up drugs offshore. Christian fit the bill for the do-or-die job. For additional leverage, Vince threatened Christian's family and girl, expecting total cooperation, but he had underestimated the kid.

On the Scarab's maiden voyage, Vince, Sal, and three of his men had loaded up on the speedboat for a nice evening cruise, not realizing the blond punk at the helm was fuming about the threats and had plans of his own. On the dark bays, Christian took them on a ride through hell, pushing the Scarab to its maximum speed. He powered down only when the Scarab nearly collided with a giant freighter coming into Tampa Bay from the gulf.

Talk about guts, Christian had stood grinning at five soaking wet and shaken mobsters who wanted to rip his heart out. With his hand on the throttle, he gave Vince the ultimatum; keep his loved ones out of their deal, or he'd flip the Scarab and take them all out. His cold, blue eyes held little doubt he'd follow through. Vince agreed, having little choice, but when safely back on land, he wondered if this nervy kid should be killed or admired.

As it turned out, Vince could not help liking Christian. He was bold and bright like polished brass and had a noble quality, a refreshing break from Vince's underworld of rats. Among Sal and the guys, they joked that the boss had adopted the slinky Southerner. It was no joke now. Vince's boy was in trouble.

The sloop left Okeechobee and entered the locks at Moor Haven, the western side of the lake, and followed another long, wearisome canal that was lined with mostly pastures. Christian said the canal would finally end in Fort Myers.

"Can't believe there're so many damn cows in Florida," Vince said, glancing at a herd that grazed along the canal.

"Cattle are the state's second largest export behind oranges," Christian commented.

"Really? Guess a cracker would know. Say, why do they call you crackers?"

"Came from the old days, when cattle were driven across the state by the men cracking long whips. It's said you could hear a cracker coming from the sound."

"I thought it had ta do with eatin' saltines. So, smarty-pants, what's the next biggest export after oranges and cows?"

Christian gave him a bothersome glance. "Tropical fish."

"Never heard that. Where's all this fish at?"

"Vince, I appreciate that you're trying to chat me up, but I'm sorry. I'm not into it. In a few hours we'll hit Fort Myers and should be back in Sarasota tomorrow. What I want to know is how long do you plan to keep an eye on me once we're home?"

"What makes you think I'll have ya watched?"

"I know you. You've been staring at me like I'm Wallenda on a tightrope."

Vince chuckled. "Yeah, guess you do know me." He stood and walked to the helm. "These plans of yours, runnin' around and savin' sharks, they're all well and good, but are they enough? I normally don't hold with shrinks, but after this trip, I think you need one. And you're right about me. I'll be damned if I'll sit back and let you self-destruct."

Christian shoved his sunglasses to top of his head, exposing his wide, frustrated eyes. "A shrink, really, Vince?"

"I mean it. Get help, or I'll sic Sal and the boys on you. They'll camp out on your doorstep, and you won't be able to breathe."

Irritated, Christian covered his mouth, glaring at Vince. He took a breath and said, "Man, don't do this to me. Just leave me alone and give me time to ride this out. I know I have issues, but a shrink isn't going to help."

"You have issues, all right, more than *National Geographic*. Christian, I've been with you for days and know what depression looks like. You're sick with it." He patted Christian's shoulder. "When we get back, you make an appointment with a doctor. There're all kinds of new drugs that'll make you feel better."

"So, I'm supposed to pop antidepressants and pour my heart out to a stranger. Vince, I don't need it. Really, I'm okay."

"My wife told me she was okay the same day she killed herself."

In the quiet farmhouse, Christian jotted down the information on the psychiatrist and ended the phone call with his mother. He sat down on the couch and stared at the number of Dr. Mary Jane Edwards. His mother said she came highly recommended.

A few days earlier, he and Vince had returned to Sarasota by way of the Intracoastal Waterway. Alone, he would have entered the gulf at Fort Myers and sailed up the coast, but Vince wasn't fond of rough water. Instead, they motored slowly past seawalls dotted with homes and docked boats, more boring than the cows, and sailed only briefly through the small intermittent bays. The only thing that brought a smile to Christian's face was when they reached south Sarasota County and were greeted by Beggar, a well-known bottlenose dolphin. For nearly a mile, the friendly dolphin stayed with the sloop, half the time swimming backward in hopes of a fish handout.

Christian and Vince arrived at Marina Jack off downtown Sarasota, and after cleaning and unloading the sloop, Christian figured he would get another headache out of the way and visit his mother. Juan had left Christian's SUV in the parking lot, and before driving to his horse farm thirty miles away, Christian headed for Siesta Key. In his mother's home, he mentioned he was still feeling down and considering a psychiatrist. His mother's maternal need to help went into overdrive. She was elated he was seeking therapy. She said she would check around for the best doctor in the field and get back with him.

At the farm, he now picked up his cell phone to make the appointment. *This is so absurd. A neurotic mother and psychopathic gangster are telling me I need the head doctor.* He was grateful, at least, that the psychiatrist was a woman. Most women adored him, were putty in his hands, but men could be iffy. Some took one glance and instantly disliked him, the upside and downside of having good looks.

Grudgingly, he called the doctor and spoke to the receptionist, the whole time shaking his head. Vince had ragged his ass throughout the trip and then made good on his threats when they got back. On the road in front of the farm sat a black Cadillac containing Vince's men. *Sure I have problems, but I'm dealing with a lot of shit. My wife died. I murdered four men, and the FBI is breathing down my neck, yet I'm supposed to act normal. Why can't he give me a break?*

He rose from the couch and looked out the window at the Cadillac. "This is not only annoying, but embarrassing," he grumbled, wondering what his neighbors must think about a big black car with thugs who watched his house day and night. He strolled outside and down the driveway to the road.

In the car, Sal filled the driver seat, his tar-black head down, reading a newspaper. Like Vince, Sal was a middle-aged Italian from Brooklyn but huge, twice Christian's weight, and he used his size like an intimidating weapon. An average-built guy Christian didn't know sat in the passenger seat. He nudged Sal as Christian approached.

Sal glanced up from the paper and grinned. "Hey, kid, see you're still kickin'."

"Sorry to disappoint you, Sal." Christian leaned over and rested his arms on the open car window. "Tell Vince I made an appointment with a shrink for Thursday, so he can back off, and you can leave."

"No can do. Boss's orders, gotta keep an eye on ya. Vince tells me you got some screws loose and might off yourself."

"You think sitting out here will stop me?" Christian huffed. "I can blow my brains out in the house or hang myself in the barn."

"A piece of advice, kid," he advised, "use the gun. Strangling ain't no picnic; takes too long."

"Gee, thanks, I'll keep it in mind." Christian straightened and started to leave.

"Hey, kid, one other thing. You attempt suicide, you'd better damn well do it right, 'cause if I find ya still alive, I'll finish ya off myself, and I promise it won't be pleasant." Sal laughed. "That way, Vince can stop frettin' over your worthless ass."

"I have a suggestion for you," Christian sniped. "Eat a mint, Sal. Your breath alone can take me out." He walked back to the house thinking, *Yeah, the tub of lard would love to see me gone.*

Sal never hid that he disliked Christian and disapproved of his friendship with Vince. He always called him the kid, a pompous pissant, or worse with his laughing, threatening jabs. Under orders from Vince, Sal had saved Christian in the Everglades, but their relationship remained contentious. Of course, Christian hadn't helped matters, dishing out the same mockery that left Sal smile-less. *But who knows, if that fat Italian puts me out of my misery, he might be my only real friend.*

Over the next several days, Christian researched shark fins on the Internet. He first checked out the *legal* options to save the fish. He could write letters to politicians asking for laws to protect sharks or send out fliers to Chinese restaurants, requesting they take shark fin soup off their menus. He could also join a shark saver group, donate money, and buy its t-shirt. None of those options appealed to him or had the instant gratification of burning down a seafood export company.

The movement to save sharks was slowly gaining ground. Hawaii, Oregon, and Washington State had outlawed the sale of fins. California had joined them, its law taking effect the next year. A few small island countries such as the Bahamas had taken steps to protect their sharks, creating sanctuaries off their coast and banning commercial shark fishing.

Some celebrities also embraced the movement. NBA all-star Yao Ming had pledged to stop eating shark fin soup, but his statements were largely unreported in the Chinese press. Chef Gordon Ramsay did a TV show about the evils of shark finning, and the late naturalist, Steve Irwin, was reported to walk out of a Chinese restaurant if shark fin soup was on the menu. As a kid, Christian loved Irwin and never missed his show, *The Crocodile Hunter*. He related to the Australian when he excitedly held up an ugly reptile and said, "Look at this beauty." Christian recalled being devastated when his hero was killed in a freak accident involving a stingray. Irwin was fearless, passionate, and irreplaceable. With Irwin's death, wildlife around the world took a hit, losing a friend and ally.

After days of research, Christian concluded that by the time the international community stepped up to save sharks, one-third of all species would be extinct. China was the worst offender; fifty percent of fins were consumed there. They would probably stop only with the death of the last shark. Other animals were also critically endangered because of the China demand: rhinos for their horn, elephants for their tusks, tigers for their bones and teeth, Asian black bears for their livers, and the list of species went on and on.

Even in Florida, the native soft shell turtle had been threatened because of the Chinese fetish for its meat. Another was mullet, the fish schools at one point becoming scarce in the local waters, since their roe was a delicacy in China. Thousands upon thousands of gutted fish bodies had floated and covered the area bays until Florida finally passed a net ban and ended the travesty.

China wasn't solely to blame. Throughout the world, Chinese people and their ridiculous traditions committed mayhem on wildlife, the US close to the top of the list of offending countries. Christian felt discrimination played no part against a race and its culture. The battle was about conservation and saving the ocean environment and sharks. He didn't care if the enemy was yellow, black, or white.

Resentfully, Christian dragged himself to his SUV on Thursday and drove to Sarasota for his appointment with the psychiatrist. He found Dr. Edwards's office in a building complex off US 41 near Sarasota Memorial Hospital.

"Christian Roberts," he told the receptionist. "I have a two o'-clock appointment."

She handed him a clipboard containing umpteen papers that he had to fill out. He sat down and jotted down his life history, medical information, and reasons he was there. *This is such bullshit.*

After completing the paperwork, he was escorted into Edwards's office and left to wait. He walked around the room, taking in a plush couch and chairs, and the rich wooden walls with oil paintings and bookshelves. Alongside the large desk, a serving table held a brewing pot of coffee, the aroma filling the air-conditioned room.

Dr. Edwards entered holding the clipboard. Her overweight, big-boned body looked awkward in the gray suit jacket and skirt. Judging from her age, she had ten years on him. Her drab brown hair hung shoulder length around her homely face with lackluster green eyes. Christian's first thought was wondering if she had ever been laid.

"Take a seat, Mr. Roberts," she said, smiling. "Would you like some coffee or a soda?"

"No, I'm good." He sat down on the couch, leaned back, and crossed his legs and arms, displaying closed-minded body language.

She poured herself a cup and took a chair across from him with a coffee table between them. She read the papers. "I see you recently lost your wife. Maybe we should start there."

"Let's not," he said. "Look, this wasn't my idea. I'm only here to get certain people off my back."

"That's not unusual. Many clients seek therapy because someone is concerned and has urged them to get help. May I call you Christian?"

He flipped up his hand, not caring.

She looked back at the information. "Christian, you've listed that you have trouble sleeping and have a loss of appetite, but you failed to fill in the blanks about abusing alcohol and drugs. Have you been intoxicated or high on drugs?"

"Yeah, fill in the spaces—done it all."

She marked the paper. "Are you high now?"

"No." He stood and started pacing. "Listen, my wife died and I'm pissed," he growled. "Losing sleep, not eating, getting wasted— that's rather fucking typical, I believe."

"You agitate easily. Have you noticed an increase in these mood swings?"

He stopped pacing and stared at her.

"Christian, you're exhibiting signs of clinical depression. It's not to be taken lightly. You also left the question blank about suicide. Have you had thoughts of taking your life?"

Every fucking day, he realized and sat back down on the couch. "I told you. I'm not answering your questions or doing this. As far as I'm concerned, depression is anger without the enthusiasm."

"That's somewhat true." She grinned. "But you need to treat it."

"Maybe I like my anger," he spouted off. "Maybe it's the only feeling I have left. And maybe I don't want some shrink picking my brain and doping me up with artificial happiness." He closed his eyes and inhaled a slow, deep breath. *To control my goddamn mood swing.* "Doctor Edwards," he said, calmer, "I'll make you a deal. Put me down for the appointments, and I'll pay for them, but I'm not coming back here. Then I won't be lying to these *concerned* people, and we won't be wasting each other's time."

"I can't do that." She went to her desk and returned with a paper and pen and handed it to him. "If you don't plan to follow up, I'd like you to sign this."

"What is it?" he asked and scanned the sheet.

"It's a suicide contract, stating you refused psychotherapy. When you kill yourself, I don't want your grieving relatives to file an incompetency suit against me."

He was stunned. She really believed he'd do it. Coming from a doctor, it was unsettling. A few seconds later, he grasped that the contract was a scare tactic, meant to manipulate and frighten him into getting help. *Two can play this game, bitch,* he thought. *She wants to screw with my head. See how she likes it when I screw with hers.* He scribbled his name on the contract and gave it back to her. "Here you go, Mary Jane. I can call you Mary Jane, right?"

She looked at him strangely and nodded.

He sighed deeply and leaned across the coffee table for closer contact while his gaze penetrated hers. "I have a confession, Mary Jane," he said softly. "I have trouble talking about personal stuff with a stranger. Guess I'm a little insecure. Suppose we get out of here, and I buy you a drink. The Five O'clock Club is just around the corner. It's a nice quiet bar, and we can get to know each other. I'm sure your significant other won't mind."

"I don't have a husband or boyfriend," she said and nervously shuffled the papers.

"Me either, not anymore," he said above a whisper. "I'm pretty lonely." He chewed his lip, lowered his head, and his locks drifted into his eyes, giving her his lost-little-boy look. "You're right about me. I need help. I'm confused, miserable. At times I feel trapped in a hopeless situation, and the only way out is to die. I need a friend, someone I can lean on and confide in. I'm just not comfortable here with this doctor business. What do ya say? Will you go with me?"

He continued to entice her with his sappy song, and after ten minutes, she fell for it, breathing a little hard, her eyes saucer-size orbs. He sensed she would follow him anywhere, do anything for him, that she longed to hold and comfort him, a vulnerable, good-looking guy in need of a hug.

"Oh, Christian," she sighed. She suddenly stood and stepped back, staring as though he were a panther that stalked her.

She straightened her suit and shook off the jitters, collecting herself. "Wow, you're good," she said, catching her breath. "I never met a man with such a gift. You open up those big hypnotic-blue eyes, chew your pouty lip, and use that silky-soft voice. The seduction is incredible, Christian. I imagine most women fall apart under your spell and find you irresistible."

"But not you." He flicked his hair from his eyes and settled against the couch.

She returned to the chair. "I'd be a liar or without a pulse," she scoffed, "if I said I wasn't attracted to you. You're captivating, intelligent, extremely handsome, and when you turn up the heat, very sensuous. But mostly you're the typical bad boy, complex, uncontrollable, and a challenge to understand. That James Dean persona drives women crazy."

"So, I'm a bad boy, a lousy cliché." He shook his head in disgust. "You don't know me, don't know what I'm about, and I really hate being told I'm a foregone conclusion."

"You're right. I don't know you. As I said, you're complex, but I do see the anger that's driving you. If it's not controlled, it'll drive you off a cliff, and what a waste that would be."

He chewed a fingernail, haunted by her words. After a minute, he brushed off her comments and managed an anxious grin. "Talking to you, I do need a drink," he mumbled. "Let's go to the bar. It's only fair I get to analyze you."

She smiled. "I'd love to go and pick your brain, as you call it, but I can't. I'd be breaking the doctor code of ethics if I socialized with a client, and although it's tempting, you're not worth the loss of my license or being charged with a crime."

"Mary Jane, I'm brokenhearted," he joked.

"Okay, okay, I tried to scare you with the suicide contract so you'd continue therapy. You saw through it, pushed back, and exposed my weakness, had my heart in my throat. I'd say we're even with jerking each other's chains. But, seriously, Christian, you do need treatment. Without it, your life is at risk. And you're bright enough to know when you're hearing the truth." She glanced at her watch. "We still have a half hour."

"Fine," he said with a shrug. "Give me your best therapy spiel."

She rattled off the signs of clinical depression and talked about breathing exercises to reduce his stress and control his anger. She handed him a sheet of instructions. She added a list of local grievance groups that met weekly and wrote out a prescription for Zoloft, an antidepressant.

At the end of the session, she said, "I wish you'd reconsider and make another appointment. When you were coming on to me and said you felt trapped in a hopeless situation and the only way out was to die, you weren't making it up. That part came from your heart. I could help you."

"I'll think about it."

They walked into the reception room. He started to leave when an urge hit him, and he turned back. "Screw your ethics and license, Mary Jane." In front of the receptionist and a waiting female patient, he took her into his arms and kissed her full on the lips. He pulled back slowly and released her. "Had to. I was a jerk in there, and you were a good sport about it."

Startled, she stared at him, her cheeks flushed, her eyes the size of golf balls. She finally became unflustered. "Thank you, Christian." She grinned. "You've made my day, probably my year, with that kiss."

He strolled out of the office, thinking he liked Mary Jane. She was no beauty, but was good-natured and smart. He had known plenty of pretty airheads and found them tiresome, a waste of time. He was actually wishing he could hang out with her as a friend, not a doctor.

• • •

Outside the building, he put on his Ray-Bans and walked to a trash bin. He crumpled up the paperwork and tossed it in. He might fit the mold for clinical depression, but he refused to go down the medical path for treatment. *Like I need groups, pills, and to learn how to breathe. What I really need now is that drink.*

Since the Bimini escapade and hitting rock bottom, he had been sober, but after the therapy session, only a rum and Coke could drown his anxiety. *Jesus, I really am broken. I want to save sharks, but I'm wondering if I'll even be around.*

He drove out to Siesta Key, feeling whipped with the growing stress. He frequently thought about taking his life, but it didn't concern him. He was strong, levelheaded, and no matter how down in the dumps he became, he could control the suicidal impulse. Now a doctor had told him different. He chewed a nail, a habit he had quit when he had married Allie, but short nails had become the least of his problems.

He pulled up to the Beach Club, one of his drinking holes during his single days. He sat down on a bar stool and didn't recognize anyone, including the bartender. Most of the customers were tourists or retirees. He glanced at his watch. Four o'clock on a Thursday, what did he expect? Any locals he might know would be in after five and work.

He nursed a tall rum and Coke, wondering why he had come here. He certainly wasn't looking for company. He heard laughter when some guys entered, but he ignored them and stayed focused on his drink.

"Chris, Chris Roberts," one of guys yelled. "Where you been, man?"

Christian glanced up and saw Skip, an old high school classmate. He and Skip had surfed many a wave and partied hard. Skip had the same red sunburnt face, long body, and short legs, along with straggly blond hair, although the strands were even thinner. "Hey, Skip," he said, standing and offered his hand.

"Screw that. Give me a hug, you lanky son of a bitch." Skip

embraced him and stepped back. "Damn, you haven't changed; still the fuckin' babe magnet." He introduced Christian to his two friends, Todd and Jim. Todd was pudgy with a round, acne-pocked face that resembled a cratered moon. His frizzy brown hair looked like he practiced electrical socket poking. Jim was rope thin with scruffy long hair and a beard.

Skip put his hand on Christian's shoulder and turned to his friends. "Boys, you are looking at surfing royalty. This son of a bitch can ride a tsunami."

Christian smiled. "Still love to exaggerate, Skip."

"Hey, I ain't shittin' 'em. Chris, remember when we skipped school our senior year and drove like maniacs across the state to catch that hurricane?" He glanced at his friends. "Here I was, sittin' on the east coast in the blowing wind and rain with tons of other surfers, and we're starin' out at waves the size of skyscrapers. And there's my boy, Chris, all alone, ridin' those huge, gray mothers. The sucker had more balls than a bowling alley." He glanced up at Christian. "Takin' on that outrageous surf, I figured you for insane."

Just coming from a shrink, Christian flinched at the mention of insanity. "I remember that trip. The last wave caught me in the curl and pounded me, broke my board in half, and slammed me into the bottom. I nearly drowned. Came home with all kinds of scrapes and bruises."

"Yeah, you got hammered, but you sure were awesome," Skip said and took a swig from his beer.

"What are you doing now?" Christian asked.

"Same old shit, working construction, but it's slow. How about you? Last I saw you was on St. Armands Circle, and you were with a long-legged brunette." Skip raised his eyebrows to his buddies. "You dudes, you should've seen this chick hangin' on Chris. The two of them could've doubled for a young Brangelina."

Todd frowned. "Who?"

"Brad Pitt and Angelina Jolie," Skip said, annoyed. "You live in a damn cave?"

Christian took the last swallow of his drink. "That must've been over three years ago when I had a boat rental business. I broke up with her. Turned out she was a little psycho."

"You dumped that babe? Unbelievable. What have you been doing since?"

"My father gave me some racehorses. I met a girl, a horse trainer, and moved to a farm in Myakka. I still live there with the horses."

"And what about the girl?" Skip grinned.

"I married her."

"No shit, you got married?"

Christian rubbed his jaw. "I was. She passed away about a month ago."

Skip frowned. "Oh, man, that sucks. I'm so sorry."

"It's okay. I'm dealing with it."

Skip called to the bartender. "Give my man here another drink."

"Thanks, Skip," said Christian, "but I should get going. We'll hook up another time."

"No way. Listen, I got a great idea. Todd and I and another dude are drivin' to Lauderdale tomorrow and catchin' a plane the next morning for Costa Rica. I got a free place to stay a block from the beach. Surfing, man, fucking surfin' the Pacific. You gotta come. It'll be awesome, like old times."

"I've heard about those waves that come from New Zealand. By the time they hit Costa Rica and its lava bottom, they're consistent and well-groomed. It sounds great, but I just came back from a trip and have some catching up at home. Besides, I haven't been on a board in years."

"Bro, it's like bike ridin'. And what are ya gonna do in Myakka, sit in the sticks and pet nags? We'll only be gone ten days, and I can tell you're down. You need this. Plus, you've been talkin' about surfing the Pacific since I've known you. This is your chance. Get 'er done before you're too old."

Christian's cell phone chimed. He stepped aside and answered it. "Hi, Mom."

"Christian, I'm reminding you about dinner Monday night and

am also wondering how your appointment went with Dr. Edwards."

She's wondering if I went. "It was fine. She's nice. But Monday night, we're supposed to have dinner?"

"It's your birthday. We'll have lobster and steak, your favorite, and you can tell me about your therapy."

Tell her what, that Edwards says I'm suicidal but I'm refusing treatment? I'd rather have a tooth pulled than face that dinner. He glanced at Skip who gave him the thumbs up. "Mom, I'm sorry, but I've already made plans for my birthday. I'm going to Costa Rica."

CHAPTER FOURTEEN

Friday morning, Christian packed his carry-on bag, feeling good for the first time in a long time. He was looking forward to the Costa Rican trip with Skip, Todd, and some older guy named Wade. Being with Skip was a trip in itself. The guy was a hoot, always up and never hid his admiration for Christian, the previous night a case in point.

In the past, Skip had been the voice of reason when Christian lost his temper and wanted to mix it up with some jerk. Skip would step in, calm him down, and tell him the asshole wasn't worth it. Christian needed someone like that now.

Once as close as brothers, the two had drifted apart when their lives went in different directions. Christian saw how it happened. He grew up and lost interest in bar hopping, surfing, and scoring with chicks. He moved on to wanting a business, a home, and one girl. Skip, though, was the same as the day he left high school. He worked just enough to get by, searching for the next party, lay, and perfect wave.

Before zipping up the bag, Christian did a final inspection: clothes, shaving kit, camera, and most importantly, his passport. He folded up the printout of the plane ticket from the Internet and slipped it into his wallet. Anything he forgot, he could buy over there. He now waited for Skip and the others to arrive.

Initially, the men were going to drive to Lauderdale in Skip's old van, but quickly the plan changed when they saw Christian's roomy new SUV in the bar parking lot. They decided to meet at the horse farm, leave their cars, and Christian would drive over. He had made the journey many times, pulling a trailer of Thoroughbreds back and forth from the Miami tracks. Fort Lauderdale airport was just up the road.

Early that morning, Christian had told Juan he was off to Costa Rica and would be back in ten days. Christian also called Vince and said he was doing great, the visit with the shrink had gone well, and he was going on a surfing vacation with friends, so Vince could take the pressure off and pull his watchdogs. His cheerful, optimistic tone must have been convincing. Five minutes later, the black car parked on the road drove away. He hoped Vince wouldn't reconsider and send Sal after him. In his black suit and white shirt, he would stand out like a beached killer whale while he watched Christian surf. A mobster shadowing him would be hard to explain.

Outside, he put his bag in the SUV and felt a twinge of excitement at the coming adventure. He then remembered his shortcomings. Mary Jane had warned him that with clinical depression, he would experience extreme highs and lows. *Damn it, I refuse to be an emotional cripple. I can beat this shit. I'm going to have fun if it kills me.*

He heard a car on the shell driveway. A rusted, dented Toyota pulled up and the man rolled down the window, and asked, "You Chris?"

"Yeah, you must be Wade. Park your car off in the yard so the driveway's clear for the feed trucks."

Wade nodded, pulled up onto the lawn, and climbed out. "Jesus, you live a long ways out." He gazed at the pastures and horses. "But you have a beautiful place."

"It's nice, but takes upkeep, not to mention the long ride. Don't want to come home on gas fumes needing milk."

"Yeah, that could be a problem." Wade chuckled. "So, Skip still isn't here?"

"Punctuality has never been his strong point. I have Cokes in the house, if you'd like one."

"Sure," said Wade. They walked into the ranch-style house, and Christian handed Wade a soda. Skip had said Wade was a cool old hippie and sailing bum. He looked the part, appearing to be in his sixties, about six feet tall, and in good shape, except for a slight potbelly. He had a weathered face and a salt-and-pepper mustache, goatee, and thinning hair pulled back into a dinky ponytail.

Wade leaned against the counter and viewed the barn. "Skip tells me you're old surfing pals and you're also a sailor. Have a boat?"

"I have a forty-seven-foot Catalina at Marina Jack." As soon as the words left his mouth, he regretted them.

Wade raised his eyebrows. "Forty-seven-foot, wow, that's nice, and Marina Jack is pricey. You must've done well with these horses."

"I did all right." Since coming into his millions, Christian had learned that people treated the wealthy differently. They either labeled him a snob or became suck-ups and moochers, expecting him to pick up all the tabs. Christian, therefore, played down his money, not wanting the hassle of a rich-guy role. He would rather fit in as an average Joe. He heard Skip's van outside. "I think they're here. We can get going."

Christian, Skip, Todd, and Wade loaded up the SUV and started the two-hundred-mile journey using the back roads. They would travel seventy-five miles east on S.R. 70 and then pick up the rarely used Highway 27 in the center of the state and head south to Fort Lauderdale.

From the start, it was a party. In the backseat, Todd rolled joints and Skip made cocktails. Wade talked about Costa Rica, having been there a dozen times. For the others, the country would be a first. As designated driver, Christian passed on the pot and drinks, planning to get high at the motel. Jokes were in overflow. Wade started to tell one, but began laughing halfway through. His infectious laughter had everyone roaring before the punch line. There were also the stories containing the three S's: surfing, sailing, and sex. Christian was content to listen and smile. The three-hour trip flew by fast.

In Lauderdale, Wade directed Christian to the motel. "This place is only a few miles from the airport, and there's a great barbeque place next door."

Christian pulled into a cracker-box-orange motel that sat a few feet off the busy four-lane highway. If star ratings could be in the minus category, this one would make the list. He could only imagine the condition of the rooms.

"This is perfect," Skip said as they climbed out of the SUV.

"There's even a pool," said Todd.

They're either stoned or I have become a snob, Christian thought. He considered suggesting a nicer place, but refrained. After all, sleazy motels were part of the adventure.

They checked in, and Skip and Todd, coworkers and best buddies, shared a room with two double beds. Christian and Wade, the latecomers to the trip, did the same. Christian, in a matter of hours, had grown to like the old guy. He had led an interesting, carefree life of travel, women, and boats. He was Skip thirty years in the future.

Christian opened the door of his motel room and coughed at the strong smell of disinfectant mixed with mold. He set his bag down on the old terrazzo floors with skimpy throw rugs and gazed at the cracked-plaster walls and faded curtains and bedspreads. The bathroom had a dripping faucet in a rust-stained sink and see-through towels. A dead roach floated in the toilet.

Wade came in. "What do you think?"

Christian stepped to the open door for fresh air and leaned against the frame. "It's fine, Wade."

Wade sat down on the bed and chuckled. "Bullshit. It's a dump. Skip told me you grew up on Siesta Key and your dad's a lawyer. You have a nice ride, boat, and horse farm, and judging from that look on your face, I'm guessing this place is not up to your standards. Where we're going won't be much better. I'm just letting you know before you get on the plane."

"I appreciate the warning, but I knew what I signed up for with Skip. To clarify things, my dad was a struggling horse trainer. As a kid, I didn't have two pennies to rub together. My stepfather is the lawyer. I left home at eighteen and lived in seedy apartments during college, and then I roughed it out on the bay in an old

Morgan. I scraped by, renting out boats and giving sailing lessons. So, yeah, I have money now, but I'm not the rich spoiled brat you think I am."

"Hey, never thought you were a brat; spoiled, maybe. Well, good. I didn't want you to be disappointed on this trip."

"I won't be." Christian glanced at the bed Wade sat on. "I just hope I don't get lice off those bedspreads."

"Oh, shit!" Wade said, jumping to his feet.

After settling in, the foursome walked next door to Freddy's Bar-B-Q. They sunk their teeth into huge pulled-pork sandwiches, succulent and cheap. Dinner and the strong cocktails were excellent. The rest of the night, they sat around the tiny pool and drank, with only Todd and Skip taking a dip. At eleven, Wade went back to the room to sleep. Todd and Skip followed an hour later.

Christian slipped into the shadowy room and stared at Wade in the other bed, snoring like an outboard motor. The day with the guys had been great, but Christian was now alone with only his tormented thoughts for company. He undressed and stretched out on the sheets, but sleep was impossible. After a half hour of wall staring, he put on his jeans. Barefoot and shirtless, he walked out to the pool. He reclined in a lounge chair and gazed at the stars, recalling his admission to Mary Jane. "Trapped in a hopeless situation and the only way out is to die." The truth of the words rang in his head. He did feel cornered with no escape from the pain. In the course of a day, he had gone from an optimistic high to a bleak low. *Allie, you told me to save sharks. That's hopeless. I'm hopeless. Damn, damn you for making me stay here.*

Christian was unsure how many hours had passed when he felt a hand on his shoulder, shaking him awake.

"Come on, Chris," said Wade. "Come back to the room. The bugs will eat you alive out here."

Christian sat up. "I must've fallen asleep."

"I hope my snoring didn't chase you out."

"No, I have problems I'm trying to work out. Sometimes I can't sleep. Other days I can barely get out of bed." Christian stood and they started back to the room.

"I lost two wives. They up and divorced me, but I guess that can't compare to having a young wife die. You're hurting and angry, but there's no door to bang on, no one to cuss out. I can't imagine."

Christian stopped walking and stared at him.

"Something else Skip mentioned about you."

The next morning, Christian took a shower, and unsurprisingly, there was no hot water. The gang loaded up in his SUV and hit the McDonald's drive-through on the way to the Fort Lauderdale airport. A few hours later they sat in the back of a Spirit jet flying over the Caribbean toward Costa Rica. Skip, always thinking ahead, had purchased a bottle of vodka in the duty-free shop prior to boarding. With Bloody Mary mix from the flight attendant, they made their own cocktails and saved a few bucks.

Halfway through the nearly three-hour trip, they had a good buzz from the strong drinks. Impersonating a flight attendant, Skip borrowed the stewardess's apron, wearing it over his t-shirt and shorts. With her cap on his scraggly mop, he walked up the aisle taking drink orders from the other passengers. The expressions on their puzzled faces were hilarious and had everyone in the back of the plane, including the flight attendant, howling. Spirit was a small, unconventional airline. On a bigger carrier, Skip might have been in trouble for his prank.

Around noon, they landed in the mountainous airport outside of San Jose and went through Customs. Wade dickered with several cab drivers until one agreed to take them into town for a reasonable price. A half hour later and in the heart of San Jose, they arrived at the Royal Dutch Hotel & Casino. The hotel building was several stories high and faced a side street of warehouses and loading docks. The dining room, bar, and small casino were across from the lobby. The rooms were filled with bargain-basement furniture and a snowy TV with no English stations. Again, the bathroom had flimsy towels and no hot water. Despite the grand name, the place was hardly befitting royalty.

After dropping their luggage in the rooms, they walked the crowded streets of San José in the cool mountain temperature. Christian found the prices comparable to those in the US. The money was easy to figure out: 5,000 Costa Rican colones equaled ten dollars. At nightfall, Wade took the group to a huge pink hotel called the Del Ray near a quaint city park.

"This is the hottest place in town," Wade told Christian, Skip, and Todd as they entered the lobby. The ground floor consisted of room after room of various bars, each filled with gorgeous young women that outnumbered the men five to one. Bug-eye excited, Skip and Todd chatted with the Costa Rican girls, called *ticas*. The ones from Nicaragua were called *nicas*. With Spanish and Indian blood, the girls had tawny skin, silky black hair, and stunning dark eyes. The male patrons were mostly older white Americans.

Christian ordered a drink and leaned against the bar. Wade stood nearby and talked to a silver-haired man who had retired in the States and moved to Costa Rica. The man said he had a beautiful eighteen-year-old *tica* who was in love with him and waiting at home.

Christian chuckled to himself. *You mean she loves your money. Is he that delusional?* He looked at the rest of the old fools, all traveling here for the same dream of having a young woman want them.

Several women approached Christian, and he politely declined, even when they offered to pay for his drink. Word must have spread that he was not interested, because eventually the women left him alone.

Todd rushed up to Christian and Wade and nodded toward a *tica* in a red dress, sitting at the end of the bar. She tossed back her long, shimmering hair and batted her eyes at Todd. "I think she likes me."

Christian nearly choked on his cocktail, restraining a laugh. "Go for it, Todd," he said in earnest. "Buy her a drink." After Todd left, he turned to Wade. "I couldn't burst his bubble and tell him they're all prostitutes. He'll find out soon enough. I just hope he uses a condom."

"The girls here are clean and always have protection," said Wade. "They actually have to carry a license that shows they've been tested monthly. Maybe you should go upstairs with one—might take your mind off those problems that kept you up last night."

Christian glanced around the room. "They're pretty and I don't mind paying, but—" He looked back at Wade. "I still love my wife."

The next morning, Christian and Wade met Skip and Todd in the downstairs restaurant for breakfast.

"What happened to you two last night?" Skip asked Christian and Wade. "We looked around and you were gone."

"We skipped out early," said Christian. He turned to Todd. "How'd you make out with the girl in the red dress?"

"Shit, she turned out to be a hooker."

They all laughed. After breakfast, they took a cab to the bus station. Amazingly, the bus ticket was only four dollars for a two-hour ride to the town of Jacó. The roomy and air-conditioned bus was even more of a surprise. With the low price, Christian had expected a crowded clunker, crying kids, and crates of chickens.

On the winding mountain road, Christian stared out the window at the jungle and the occasional cattle pasture with rows of tightly packed small trees serving as fencing. In the occasional villages, neat little houses were landscaped with palm, banana, and mango trees, along with flowering hibiscus bushes and bougainvillea vines, the same flora grown at home. Among his co-travelers, he alone appreciated the scenery. Skip and Todd slept, hungover after a long night. Wade also dozed, either from age or boredom.

The bus drove through a canopy of trees where Christian saw a dozen varieties of orchids. *Allie would have loved this.* He realized the date. Had she lived and they continued their voyage through the Caribbean, they would probably be enjoying Costa Rica together now. He closed his eyes. *That's damn depressing.*

The bus pulled into Jacó, which was sandwiched between the Pacific and a mountain range. The main drag was a short block from the beach and lined with gift shops, restaurants, and bars. From the bus station, they took a cab through a neighborhood of small lots with nice houses and duplexes. Most were enclosed with brick or wrought-iron walls or high chain-link fencing. Many of the windows were barred. In minutes they arrived at Harry's house, their place to stay. Wade explained that he and Harry went way back to their high school days in Sarasota.

"Hey, Harry," Wade shouted as they stood on the shady sidewalk before a locked iron gate.

Harry came out carrying a ring of keys and stepped around a flea-bitten Rottweiler. "Shit, Wade, you back again?" he mumbled. He ambled through a small courtyard that contained tropical foliage, buckets of junk, mesh hammocks, and paint-chipped patio furniture, along with an old Harley chained to a palm tree. In front of the garage, a banged-up silver Jeep and blue car sat on the driveway.

Christian's first impression of Harry was his height, four feet ten a stretch. A baseball cap rested on his dark, graying hair, and with brown eyes, a mustache, and a goatee, he resembled a shorter version of Wade. As a baby, Harry had come with his parents to the US from Spain, and they had been circus performers based in Sarasota.

Harry yawned and unlocked the gate. "I heard you'd died, Wade."

"Not yet," Wade said with a chuckle. "Three heart attacks, but I'm still here." In the courtyard, he gave Harry a hug and then introduced Skip, Todd, and Christian, who had squatted to stroke the dog.

"Jesus, looks like you brought half of Sarasota with you," Harry said to Wade. "Well, you can have your old bedroom, but two of your friends will have to share a double bed in the spare room, and one can sleep on the couch."

"I'll take the couch," Christian said. "By the way, your Rottie is a sweetheart."

"Bitch is worthless," said Harry. "Been robbed three times. The bastards probably step over her when they smash in the front door. They'll steal you fucking blind around here."

Christian straightened and understood why each residence looked like a fortress.

Harry stared up, taking notice of Christian. "Christ, who's this tall motherfucker?"

"Chris is a hot dog surfer," Skip said with a grin. "He can ride any wave or woman."

Harry's eyes narrowed. "Your hot dog better not think about riding my *tica* when she visits, or I'll fuck up his pretty face."

Always the attitude with these short dickheads. They love to bust my chops. Christian pushed his sunglasses up to the top of his head and picked up his bag. "Harry, I have no intention of touching your girl, but if it's going to be an issue, point me to the closest hotel."

"Relax, Chris," said Wade. "Harry's just screwing with you. He's like an old woman, loves to give grief. Ignore him."

"Fuck you, Wade," said Harry. "Well, come on in. I have some beer." The others walked in, but Christian remained by the gate. In the doorway, Harry turned and grinned. "You too, Hot Dog, get your butt in here."

Christian realized he needed to lighten up, that Harry was just messing with him. When the front door closed, the living room became as dark as a cave, because of the heavy-curtained windows. The three-bedroom, one-bath home was a mix of worn furniture and wood statues. Off the living room was a small kitchen with broken cabinets and messy counters. Outside, a Jacuzzi sat in the grassless backyard among the dead leaves from a giant rubber tree. It was definitely a bachelor pad.

Harry handed out the beer and dropped a bag of weed on the coffee table alongside a clay pipe. Its handle featured a couple having sex. Skip and Todd sat on a quilt-covered couch, and Todd filled the pipe, lit it, and passed it around. Harry reclined in a La-Z-Boy chair that faced a large TV. Christian and Wade took up regular chairs.

Christian quietly sipped his beer as the guys laughed and talked about their surfing plans. When the pipe reached Christian, he inhaled a few tokes but failed to get the uplifting high. Feeling the need for some alone time, he stepped outside to the courtyard. At a wrought iron and glass table, he eased into a chair and petted the dog. He heard loud squawking overhead and spotted three blue-and-gold macaws flying south. To see the beautiful birds would normally have been a treat, but he sighed. Playing the part of a merry traveler while bottling up his real emotions was grueling, and worse, the guys knew he was faking and miserable. He was a subdued and overly sensitive downer. *I should never have come.*

He heard the front door open and the jingle of keys. "Hey, Hot Dog," Harry said, "Wade and I are going to town for more beer and food. Why don't you come with us?"

Friendly now; no doubt they told him about my recent loss. Christian rose and put on his smile. "Sure."

Christian and Wade climbed into the old, covered Jeep, and Harry drove a few blocks to town. Instead of going to a grocery store, he parked on the street behind a battered pickup with its bed loaded with fish and ice. He talked in Spanish to the truck owner, a local fisherman, and asked about his day's catch, eventually selecting several dolphin fillets.

"Do you have shark?" Christian asked the man as he paid for the dolphin.

"No shark, no more, they gone," the fisherman responded in broken English.

Christian nodded, confirming what he had learned on the Internet. Ten years earlier, the Costa Rican waters had teamed with sharks. Cocos Island off the coast held witness to a rare world event when thousands of scalloped hammerheads gathered in schools and circled the islands. The scientists guessed they came to breed. The studies showed the schools had dwindled to a fraction of their original size as a result of overfishing for shark fins. As a last-ditch effort, the Costa Rican government made Cocos Island a shark sanctuary and banned long-lining in the area, in hopes of saving the species. Only time would tell if the sharks could recover or if it was too little, too late.

The threesome next drove to a liquor store, and Christian and Wade split the bill for beer and bottles of rum, vodka, and mixers. They returned to the house, and Harry marinated the fish fillets in Italian dressing and then grilled them to perfection. The fish was served with rice and beans, the ethnic staple in Central America.

Curious, Christian asked Harry about his line of work. He obviously didn't lack for anything. He was vague, saying he did a little of this and that. As evening approached, Christian had his answer with the steady stream of people who visited the house and sampled lines of cocaine on a dresser in Harry's bedroom.

My luck is running, Christian thought skeptically. *Like Bimini, I'm hanging with another pusher.*

Among the customers, Christian met a classy blond real estate agent in heels who drove a Lexus. Next to arrive was a young *tica* with an eight-month-old baby on her hip, both dressed in shabby clothing and in need of a bath. A hooker, she propositioned Christian and his friends until Wade ran her off. Four white guys Christian's age followed. Tourists from the States, they had come for the water sports, women, and drugs, and not necessarily in that order. Skip learned the lowdown on surfing conditions from them. Three Costa Rican men arrived, and the small living room was jammed with people going and coming from Harry's bedroom.

After a few hours, Christian gave in and snorted several lines. The coke was pure; it hadn't been cut with speed that hampered sleep, destroyed an appetite, and caused a wired, fried effect. The nose candy was also cheap, twenty dollars a gram. On the buzz, he felt more energized, sociable, and talkative. Living here year round, he could easily become addicted.

After a while, he stepped out of the noisy, congested house and into the seclusion of the night. He stared up at the tree branches that rustled in the humid ocean breeze. He then noticed Wade sitting alone at the patio table.

Christian eased into a chair and joined him. "You're missing a good party in there."

"Hell, I've been to enough parties to fill three lifetimes." Wade smiled. "But what's your excuse for ducking out? That hot realtor can't keep her eyes off you, wants to take you home and jump your bones."

"I've noticed. I'm just not—" Christian chewed his lip.

"Not ready yet. I know, you still love your wife."

"I got messed up and slept with two chicks not long ago and still feel guilty as sin, like I betrayed my wife's memory." He glanced at the front door, hearing Skip laugh. "Besides, I've never been much of a party animal like Skip. Always went along to get along, but it was never my thing. I'm a boring guy, Wade. My idea of a good time is hanging out on my boat or farm and enjoying nature and the quiet."

"That doesn't make you boring, just smart. Why did you come on this trip, when you knew it would be one big party?"

"I figured a new place, new faces, and doing some surfing, I might get my act together. Losing my wife has really screwed up my head."

"Have you thought about getting help?"

Christian chuckled. "Yeah, I went to a shrink, and she made me sign a damn contract holding her blameless when I killed myself."

Wade leaned toward him and frowned. "Suicide, Chris? How worried should I be?"

Damn cocaine, loosening lips that sink trips. Christian took a seething breath, angry at himself for yapping away without thinking. "I'm fine, Wade, no need to worry. I should've never told you that shit. Do me a favor and don't tell the guys. They already tiptoe around me and treat me like their problem child."

"I won't tell them if you promise not to cut your wrists while we're here. I can't afford another heart attack."

"You're on." Christian smiled. "Actually, my wife, Allie, must've known I'd fall apart. Right before she died, she asked me to do something. That goal has kept me going, kept me alive."

"What did she want you to do?"

Christian chuckled at the improbable. "It's pretty crazy. She asked me to save the sharks."

Before crashing on the couch, Christian talked to Wade for hours about sharks, explaining their demise because of the Chinese demand for fin soup. Wade, an old sailor and sea lover, was unaware of the plight of sharks and became so outraged that Christian feared he might keel over with another heart attack.

"How are you going to save them?" Wade asked.

"Good question." Christian enjoyed the camaraderie with a fellow shark lover but wasn't stupid enough to admit he had already taken steps in the Bahamas by torching a business and killing longliners. The confession could come back later and bite him. He liked Wade, but Vince was the only person he trusted with that information.

Early the next morning Christian woke with the Rottweiler licking his face. He made a cup of instant coffee and drank it in the outside courtyard. Back inside, he roused Skip and Todd in the spare bedroom and asked if they wanted to hit the beach. A half hour later, the threesome, dressed in trunks and t-shirts, were hiking down the sidewalk toward town and the surf, leaving Harry and Wade still asleep. They stopped at Dunkin' Donuts for more coffee and strolled to the coast. In front of an open-aired beach bar, they stood under coconut palms and gazed across an expansive gray beach at the surf. The waves weren't big, maybe six feet, but there was a wide span of calm water between each breaker, making it perfect for surfing. They rented surfboards from a vendor and soon rode the swells of the cold Pacific.

At noon Harry and Wade arrived at the bar, and Christian and his pals took a break from surfing and joined them for lunch and drinks. Christian leaned his board against a tree and grabbed his shirt from a branch. Before he slipped in the patio bar, Harry asked how he got the small scar below his ribs.

"I was shot," Christian said. His four pals looked startled and appeared to want the details. "A crazy ex-girlfriend. She wasn't happy that I'd left her."

"Holy shit," said Harry. "I've pissed off some women, but none of them tried to kill me. What happened? Is she in jail?"

"She's dead. Allie stepped in and shot her with a spear gun before she could finish me off."

"Must be why you married Allie," said Wade.

"Yeah, one of many reasons," said Christian. Talking about Allie, he felt the rise of heart-wrenching distress. When she was alive, he had risen every morning knowing he loved her, taking that love for granted. Only with her death did he fully appreciate the depth of his feelings. Life was unbearable without her. The thrill of the earlier surfing flowed out of him like a receding tide. "Sorry, I don't want to talk about this." He slumped down in a chair at the table.

Wade reached over, patted Christian's back, and changed the subject. "Well, did the surf live up to your expectation, boys?" he asked.

Within a half hour, more people clustered around them, since Harry was well known and popular. A man with a silver crew cut strolled to their table. "Wade, I didn't know you were here. I heard you'd died."

"Who started that damn rumor?" Wade grumbled. Everyone grinned.

Outside the bar, Christian drank his cocktail while chatting with a man on a sorrel mare. A *tica* wandered past, peddling shell necklaces. All took place against a backdrop of an endless beach and misty jungle mountains that rose out of a dark blue ocean.

For the next several days, Christian's ritual became surfing in the morning with Skip and Todd, drinking in the bar in the afternoon with Harry and Wade, and partying at night with a mixed bag of Harry's friends. Life was easy in the beautiful remote section of the world. With no meddling mothers, gangster friends, and FBI, no shrinks or reminders of Allie, and no pressure to fulfill the goal of saving sharks, Christian began to relax and feel better. He slept sounder, had fewer nightmares, and found himself devouring his meals. He was tempted to stay forever.

CHAPTER FIFTEEN

Late morning, Christian sat on his surfboard in the ocean and looked up and down the barren coastline. He was the only one in the water. A half hour earlier, Skip and Todd had complained about the small waves and left for a relaxing day of drinking in the beach bar. Harry's Jeep was now in the parking lot.

Time to pack it in. Christian caught a wave and rode it to shore. With the board under his arm, he trudged through the loose sand toward the guys. Midway on the wide beach, he came upon a lone sunbather, a young Costa Rican woman reclined on a towel. "Morning," he said in passing.

She sat up. "You, good surfer. I buy you drink at bar."

Christian stared at her breasts that spilled out of the skimpy bikini and smiled. "Thanks, but not today." He had grown accustomed to the prostitutes' daily propositions. Although beautiful and tempting, they struck out with him, still upset with himself with his indiscretion in Bimini. He had strayed and lion-size guilt gnawed at his gut for betraying Allie, only dead weeks. Jerry and the two black hookers might have drugged him, made him unaware of the sex, but he had gone off half-cocked, looking for trouble. He put himself in the situation. *I can be such a dumbass.*

He ambled up to the bar and saw his four friends sitting at a table on the open-air patio. Two other men were among the group. All eyes stared toward the surf, fixed on the girl.

"What did she say to you?" Todd called.

Christian leaned his surfboard against a tree. "She wanted to buy me a drink."

"You lucky fucking dog," said Todd. "She didn't say shit to me. I suppose you turned her down?"

Christian shrugged and moseyed into the bar. He ordered a Bloody Mary from the barkeeper before pulling up a chair and joining the six men. The girl's well-endowed breasts remained the subject of conversation.

"Todd, forget her," said Skip. "You're blowing all your money on these chicks, and I'm not lending you any to get home."

"Chris," said Wade, "I'd like you to meet Ned and Jimmy. They're originally from the States, but they work here now as charter captains."

"Barely working, you mean," Ned said, shaking Christian's hand. "Damn Taiwanese long-liners have wiped out everything that swims, every damn fish being shipped to Asia."

"Long-liners?" asked Christian.

"Yeah, a slew of them," said Ned, "Puntarenas up the coast is lined with export companies, and it's the hub for the foreign fleet. Panama and Belize lets those sneaky bastards fly their flags. One look at Caldera Port with those boats, and a sport fisherman loses his lunch."

"It's not likely to end," said Harry. "China has a grip on this country. They paid to fix the roads and built the new soccer stadium. I also heard they bought five hundred brand-new cars for the Costa Rican police force."

Christian asked Ned, "What effect has the fishing had on the shark population?"

Wade cleared his throat and lifted his eyebrows when glancing at Christian.

"Hell, haven't caught a shark in years," said Ned. "With the fin demand in China, sharks have probably been hit the hardest, especially the scalloped hammerhead. Used to be thousands schooled around Cocos Island, but not anymore."

"I read they banned long-lining around those islands and made it a shark sanctuary," said Christian.

"They did," said Ned, "but outside the sanctuary, the trawlers are as thick as thieves. Every shark has to run the gauntlet, coming and going from Coco. Most of the big sharks are gone. Now they're working on the babies, the three-and four-footers. Hammerheads are doomed."

Jimmy added his two cents. "Well, the government did pass a law saying the fins have to be attached to sharks when the trawlers come to port. A Taiwanese boat captain was busted and fined thirty-six thousand for trying to offload sharks without their fins. Because of the crackdown, there's talk that the foreign fleet might move its operation to Nicaragua."

"And good riddance," said Ned, "but God knows if the fish will recover in time to save my business. People from all over used to come here for the great fishing. These days, I take a charter out, and half the time it's a sightseeing trip. Lousy slant-eyed bastards, they've cleaned out their side of the ocean, and now they're doing it here. "

Christian turned to Harry. "How far is Puntarenas from Jacó?"

"Roughly thirty miles north," said Harry, "but given these mountain roads, it's about an hour's drive."

"I'd like to check it out, do some sightseeing," said Christian. "I'll pay for gas and the use of your Jeep plus your time as a guide and an interpreter."

Harry grinned. "Got nothin' going on tomorrow."

At ten o'clock the next morning, Christian, Wade, and Harry loaded up in the Jeep for Puntarenas. Skip and Todd remained behind, preferring to surf. On the first part of the northern trek, the old Jeep traversed the two-lane highway with the coast on the left and mountainous jungle on the right. Normally, Christian would have been enthralled with the scenery, but his mind churned with longliners, seafood exporters, and the madness to save sharks.

Halfway through the trip, they came upon a long bridge over a deep gorge and the Tarcoles River. "Wanna stop and see the crocs?" Harry asked.

"Yeah," said Christian.

After crossing the bridge, they pulled off the road and parked behind a tour bus. Its occupants with their cameras had unloaded and were walking across the bridge to see the crocodiles. Christian followed the group as Harry and Wade, uninterested, waited at the Jeep.

Halfway across the bridge, Christian looked over the railing. Hundreds of yards down, he gazed at the sandy-colored reptiles that rested on the riverbank. A man and two women stopped near him and also looked below.

"Jesus, they're huge," said the man. "If I fell off this bridge, those man-eaters would make short work of me."

Idiot, the fall would kill you, Christian felt like saying. *And those crocs are no more dangerous than an alligator.* He knew the Costa Rican and Florida crocodiles were the same species, known to be shy and didn't have the deadly temperament of their cousins, Nile crocodiles in Africa and Australian saltwater crocs. *Allie would've liked to see these. She loved Al.* He smiled, reflecting on her soaking up the sun in the backyard with Al, the ten-foot bull alligator. *What kind of woman hangs out with a gator? God, she was weird.* His feel-good moment was short lived. His friend and lover was not only gone but irreplaceable.

He plodded back to the Jeep. "Let's go."

The men arrived in the town of Puntarenas and followed the coastal road to Sandpoint, a narrow strip of land that jetted out into the Pacific. Miles across the water were the mountains of the Nicoya Peninsula. They drove along a public beach dotted with the occasional bar or restaurant. The other side of the road was a jumble of small, ragged hotels, shops, and more eateries.

"You guys wanna grab a bite and a beer?" asked Harry.

"I'm ready," said Wade. "Anything to get out of this bouncing Jeep."

Harry pulled into an open bar on the beach side, and they piled out. Christian looked up and down the road. "Where are the trawlers and export businesses?"

Harry pointed inland. "Caldera Port is on the other side of the peninsula, several blocks down the street, but there's nothing to see. Walls run along the road, blocking out the view of the water. Can't even see the boats and warehouses."

"You go ahead and have lunch," said Christian. "I want to check it out."

"That place isn't for sightseers, so be careful."

"I'll be all right," said Christian. "Be back in a few." He strolled down the street and entered a ghettoish neighborhood of small, block houses, their yards spewed with weeds, nets, and fish crates. On the other side of the peninsula, he reached the port road similar to a wide, trashed alley lined with deteriorating storefronts. The area was like the toilet at a rundown gas station that no one wanted to use or clean. Opposite the stores, a high wall ran the length of the street, concealing the waterfront, seafood exporters, and the docked boats. The barriers varied in material from company to company, some portions painted concrete block, while others consisted of old tin sheets. If the walls were there for security, why not use a fence? It seemed more like they wanted to keep the operation private and out of sight.

Christian walked several blocks and came to an open lot, a break between the wall and two exporters. Trash and knee-high weeds filled the lot, and beyond were a few dry-docked boats resting in the shade of mangroves. He wandered through the lot to the rocky shore and stared out over a partially collapsed seawall. Blue-and-white trawlers were docked or moored behind the warehouses. The boats ranged in size from small, twenty-foot fishing boats up to large trawlers. He counted fifteen. Given his limited view, the empty dock slips from trawlers out at sea, and the length of the port, he figured the fishing fleet was substantial, each boat spewing miles of deadly long-lines. No wonder the fish had been depleted and sharks were in trouble. Ned, the charter captain, had said the sight would make a sport fisherman sick. Christian did feel ill and angry. This wasn't fishing. It was ocean rape.

He started back to meet Harry and Wade at the bar. A block

away, he saw a paneled refrigerated truck that had backed into the driveway of an open gate. Hoping for a glimpse of the export business behind the green wall, he hustled to the gate. Three Costa Rican men were loading Styrofoam shipping boxes into the truck as a uniformed guard stood nearby. The men ignored him as if he were a nosey tourist peering between the truck and wall.

Their attitude changed when he asked about buying shark fins.

The guard growled in Spanish and waved, motioning for him to leave.

Christian defensively opened his arms and came up with a spur-of-the-moment lie. "My girlfriend's Chinese, and she wanted to make fin soup for my birthday."

The guard, not buying his bullshit, kept yelling in Spanish. The men stopped loading boxes and stepped to the front of the truck. With fists cocked on their hips and hostile sneers, they resembled a pack of pissed-off Dobermans, and he had stumbled into their junkyard.

Christian moved away before a push became a scuffle. *They sure are fucking touchy about shark fins.*

Across the road, a skinny preteen boy straddled a rusty bike. "Señor," he called to Christian, "you want fish? Come, I take you."

Christian followed him as he rode his bike to the next street corner. Under the canopy of a small tree, a man stood at an improvised table of a board resting atop two wooden crates. On the table he skinned a thirty-inch eel. A nearby bucket held more of the silvery eels.

The boy dropped his bike in the dirt. "This my uncle. He sell you fish."

Christian tried to restrain a grin, but unsuccessfully. "Ah, no thanks, not in the market for eels. I'm looking for shark fins."

The boy translated the English into Spanish for his uncle. The uncle reached in the bucket and grabbed another of the snakelike fish. *"No las tengo,"* he muttered, gutting it. *"No tengo aletas tiburónes."*

The boy explained, "He says no shark fins."

"Does he know where I can buy some? Which warehouse carries them?" Again, the boy translated his words into Spanish.

The uncle frowned and lowered the knife, his eyes sizing up Christian. His retort to his nephew was harsh. The boy translated, "My uncle says go. You look for trouble, not fins."

They got my number. This probing would've gone better with a Chinese face. Caldera Port probably had its share of meddling Americans and environmentalists who wanted to shut down the fin trade. As he thanked the boy, he noticed the three Costa Rican men had left the panel truck and were hustling toward him. One carried a baseball bat, and the others held three-foot-long lead pipes. *Oh, shit,* he thought, and felt the hairs rise on the back of his neck.

"American," yelled the man with the bat as the trio approached. "What you want here?"

Christian backed to the middle of the street. "I told you. I was looking to buy fresh fish."

"*Aletas tiburónes*," the uncle grumbled to the men.

"Shark fins are dried," the man snarled and thumped the bat end against his palm. "You Americans come here to put a poor fisherman out of work. We are tired of your kind." The uncle packed up his eels and left with the boy as the men formed a half circle around Christian, forcing him farther down the narrow side street.

"I'm going, I'm going," Christian said, stepping backward to stay out of striking range of their weapons. Fighting off three men would be difficult enough, but three holding clubs? He was better off making a run for it, but a glance over his shoulder revealed his entrapment. Three more men hustled toward him from the opposite end of the street. With connecting buildings on both sides, he was cornered with no one to see, hear, or help him. He searched his pocket for his cell phone, but remembered he had left it at Harry's house, wanting no trace of his visit to the port.

"I don't want trouble," Christian said, hoping to talk his way out.

"Too late, you find it," said the English-speaking man with the bat.

As the six men closed in, Christian, in a panic, looked for a shield and grabbed a fish crate from a stack near a doorway. The men raised their clubs and stepped to him. He lunged at the closest man and swung the crate, knocking him down, but then felt a blow to the back of his head.

At the cabana, Wade and Harry sat at a table with an ocean view and were finishing their lunch of rice, beans, slaw, and grilled fish. The waiter approached with the third round of beers.

"I wonder what happened to Hot Dog," Harry said and took a sip from the bottle.

"Yeah, Chris should've been back by now." Wade glanced at his watch. "It's going on an hour."

"He's an oddball, so damn tight lipped and withdrawn. And he makes the rest of us look like onions, attracts chicks like flies, yet he hasn't touched any of them. Wade, I'm starting to think that boy is queer. He's pretty enough to be a fag."

"Chris isn't gay," Wade said, annoyed. "He's hurting over the loss of his wife and isn't ready for a fling. I feel sorry for him."

"You feel sorry for—?" Harry coughed in disbelief. "Shit, that sucker has it all; young, tall, good-looking, and he's got money. Have you noticed his Rolex?"

"Well, I'm getting worried about him. Let's pay up and get out of here."

Harry swallowed the last of his beer and set the bottle down. "Yeah, that port isn't exactly a tourist destination. Those fishermen can be pricks. Last year they poured gasoline on an outsider who was asking about shark fins. Luckily they were stopped before setting him on fire."

"Damn it, Harry!" Wade jumped out of his seat. "Wish I'd know that. Chris is into saving sharks and came to Puntarenas to get the scoop on fins. Should've never let him go off alone." He threw some money on the table.

"Fuck, no one told me," Harry said while hurrying to the Jeep. Driving down the main drag of Caldera port, they passed a side street that was more like an alley.

"Stop, stop!" Wade yelled. "There's something going on down

there." Harry backed up the Jeep, and half a block away, they saw a body crouched on the road. Six men stood around it and watched one man kick the downed victim.

"It's Chris," said Wade. Harry whipped the Jeep down the side street. "There're six of them. Us old farts are going to get our asses handed to us."

"Not necessarily." Harry stopped the Jeep thirty feet from Chris and the men. He reached under his seat and pulled out a 9mm. Like a short version of John Wayne swinging off his horse before a shootout, Harry stepped from the Jeep, gun in hand, and confronted the men, shouting in Spanish. When one man yelled back in defiance, Harry fired over their heads. The men scattered and raced up the street.

Wade stared at Harry, too astonished for words.

"Standard stuff for a pusher," Harry said as they hustled to Christian.

Wade rolled Christian over and held his bloody head. "We need to call the cops and get him to a hospital."

"No cops, no hospital," Christian gasped and struggled to rise. "Just get me out of here."

"Agreed. Don't need the police in my life," said Harry. "We'll take him back to Jacó. There's a walk-in clinic near my house. Let's move before someone calls in the gunfire."

Harry pulled the Jeep alongside Christian, and the two sixty-year-old guys managed to get him to his feet and into the vehicle. Christian held his ribs and curled up on the backseat. Harry dug out a blanket from the back and covered him. "In case we're stopped. All that blood would take some explaining." He and Wade hopped in and they sped off.

Harry drove through town and off the peninsula, careful not to exceed the speed limit. "Once we're out of town and back on the highway, I'll find a place to pull over," he said. "There're towels in the back that can be used as bandages."

Wade turned in the passenger seat and looked at Christian. "What happened?"

"Don't know," Christian said, flinching and holding his side. "Tried to buy shark fins, and they jumped me."

On an empty stretch of highway, they came to a lone gas station surrounded by jungle and a few small dwellings. Harry pulled up to a gas pump and quickly refueled, and Wade found a water faucet and wet a towel. Pulling back the front seat, he leaned over Christian and pressed the towel against a deep, bloody gash on Christian's left cheek.

"Damn, they nearly took out your eye. You definitely need stitches." Wade shook his head. "Harry said at the bar they're prickly about outsiders asking about fins. I heard that and freaked, knew you'd gotten yourself in trouble."

Christian halfheartedly nodded. "Mention shark fins and that port is like stepping on a bed of red ants, coming from nowhere and attacking. I know some Spanish from my Mexican horse trainer and caught a few words like 'vamos oceano.' I think they planned to kill me and dump my body in the ocean."

Christian reclined on Harry's worn couch and held an ice pack against his swollen cheek and black eye. Half his body was bruised and hurting. Several days earlier, he had learned the hard way to be smarter and more cautious. With tempers running hot on both sides of the shark fin issue, this was no game but a war with faceless enemies, men loading fish crates, a man cleaning eels, even a boy on a bike possibly setting him up.

Harry and Wade had rushed him back to Jacó and taken him to a walk-in clinic. After x-rays and an exam, the doctor diagnosed he had a few cracked ribs, a mild concussion, and needed seven stitches for the cheek cut and several more for the blow to the back of his head. Christian had been lucky.

The front door opened and light flooded the dark living room as Harry walked in. "You're awake," he said. "So how's the Hot Dog this morning?"

"Not too hot," Christian murmured.

Harry leaned over and studied him. "Yeah, your pretty face is all fucked up, but before long, you'll be breaking hearts again. Well, you missed saying good-bye to your surfing buddies. I just dropped them off at the bus depot, and they're on their way back to Sarasota. Now you're stuck with us old guys."

"Prefer being stuck with you and Wade. Todd and Skip are okay in small doses, but after this trip—" He sighed. "Let's just say they lack a maturity chip."

Harry huffed and collapsed in his stuffed chair. "Hey, Wade and I might be old, but it doesn't mean we grew up. Speaking of Wade, is that son of a bitch still sleeping? Wade!" he shouted toward the front bedroom. "Get your lazy ass up."

Wade stepped out of the bedroom. "I was up. I was up, just getting dressed." He walked to Christian. "How's the face? Need more ice?"

"Wade, you've turned into a fucking nursemaid with that kid," grumbled Harry.

"Thanks, Wade," said Christian, "but I'm good. Just got some ice from the fridge, but getting up and down is a killer, with these ribs."

Wade nodded. "Yeah, cracked ribs can hurt for six to eight weeks."

"What are your plans, Hot Dog," asked Harry. "Heading back to Sarasota once you're healed enough to travel?"

Christian grimaced with pain when he sat up. "That's the plan, but before I leave, I intend to pay Puntarenas another visit."

"You barely got out of there alive," said Harry, "and you're going back? You're fucking nuts."

"So I've been told."

Over the next ten days, Christian rested on the couch or hobbled around the house and patio. His constant companion was Harry's Rottweiler that never left his side. The stitches came out and the bruises that covered his body slowly healed. His mind remained focused on revisiting the port. This time he wouldn't be a tourist.

Since arriving in Costa Rica, he had suffered with bouts of depression. Beaten and hurting, he half expected to sink deeper into a demoralizing wad of self-pity, but instead, the thrashing had been a wake-up call. With the surfing and partying, he had grown indifferent to the goal of saving sharks. Now he was back on track, incensed, determined, and fully committed. The port had become his next target.

The first seeds of his plan had germinated when he lay bloody in the Jeep on the way back to Jacó. As he entered the clinic with Harry and Wade's support, he had said, "I don't want my name or this incident connected with Puntarenas. Tell them I'm Joe Blow and took a tumble down a cliff a few miles from here." With his fabricated story, he was already taking precautions, knowing he would go back and wreak havoc, this time with a double motive of avenging sharks and himself.

Recuperated enough, Christian began to strategize, but realized he needed help. Wade and Harry were the perfect conspirators. Wade had been outraged when learning about the demise of the sharks, and with a failing heart, he had nothing to lose. He might be up for one last adventure with a worthy cause. With Harry, it was all about money. He lived modestly and risked jail nightly when selling his $20 grams of cocaine.

Christian sat the two men down on the living room couch and asked if they would like to each make a hundred thousand dollars.

Harry nudged Wade. "Told ya he had money. Who do you want me to kill, Hot Dog?"

"No one," said Christian. "Buy a boat and equipment for me and do some driving."

"What's this about, Chris?" asked Wade.

"I want to put a dent in the fin trade at Puntarenas. Plan to torch the long-line trawlers and exporters. You in or out?"

"Jesus, you are nuts," said Harry, "but for a hundred grand, I'm in."

Wade rubbed his jaw, conflict in his eyes. "You'll be putting some poor people out of business, innocent people who didn't hurt you."

"If they're wiping out sharks and destroying the ocean environment, they're not innocent. It comes down to choice; hurt the livelihood of some fishermen or bring attention to a horrific crime, the extinction of a species. I choose the sharks. There will always be plenty of fishermen."

"Damn," Wade said, gazing at the floor. "All right, count me in."

In the days ahead, Wade and Christian filled empty beer bottles with gas and oil and stuffed a rag in the top, turning the bottles into Molotov cocktails. Christian carefully wiped the fingerprints off each bottle, put them into a box, and stored them in the garage. With Christian's shopping list, Harry visited the surrounding towns. At one marina, he purchased a green tarp and a two-man raft that automatically inflated with the tug on the cord. At another, he bought a twenty-five-horsepower outboard motor and a gas tank. In a dive shop, he bought a knife, dive gloves, and snorkeling gear and picked up a straw hat from a street vendor. To be extra cautious, he paid cash for everything.

Christian had two major concerns. The first was leaving a money trail in Costa Rica when he paid Harry and Wade. During the trip from the Bahamas, Vince had suggested that Christian transfer funds into a Cayman account, saying, "You never know if you might have to run, and cops will have difficulty following that dough." But wiring more than $200,000 into a little Jacó bank might draw unwanted attention.

Christian's second worry involved devising a solid alibi when Caldera went up in smoke. At the port, the three dockworkers, the guard, the eel-cleaning uncle, and even the boy on the bike could finger the blond American who asked about fins and was beaten. With plenty of motive to burn the place down, Christian couldn't afford to become a suspect, especially with the FBI already watching him.

Harry solved both problems. "We'll drive to Panama and get your passport stamped so you'll have an alibi when the port is torched. While there, you can wire the money into a Panamanian bank and pay us. Say it's for a land purchase."

"But how do I return to Costa Rica and do the deed without having my passport stamped again?" asked Christian.

"You'll see." Harry grinned.

Predawn Tuesday morning, Christian gave the plan the test run. The deflated raft was strapped to the top of the Jeep. The outboard motor, its gas tank, the snorkeling gear, and the green tarp were placed in the back.

"Leave your cell phones in the house," Christian said. "Their signals can be traced."

The men loaded up in the old silver Jeep, and Harry drove north on the jungle highway. Five miles south of Puntarenas, they left the highway and traveled down a dirt road near the small coastal town of Corralillo. On a desolate beach, they inflated the raft, attached the outboard, and launched the small boat. Wade climbed in the back to steer the motor. Christian put on a straw hat to conceal his blond hair and waded out, pushing the raft to deeper water.

"Have fun," Harry called, standing on the beach.

Wade cranked up the outboard, and Christian hopped in. They cruised up the coast to Puntarenas and were soon skirting a large sightseeing ferry docked at the farthest point of the peninsula. They entered the port waterway and glided over the green surface with the occasional blue-purple oil slicks and floating trash. Most marinas and ports smelled of salt and sea, but this one reeked of death, decaying fish, rotten seaweed, and gasoline fumes. The view from the water revealed a vast armada of vessels, some docked, some moored offshore, and ranging in size, but all with the sole purpose of reaping sea life until life ran out. *Mankind,* Christian thought, *the scourge of the planet. Will we ever exist in harmony with nature?*

They scoped out the back of the export warehouses with their loading docks and equipment. The fishermen, guards, and dockworkers paid no attention to them. Christian recognized the vacant weedy lot with dry-docked boats that he had walked through earlier. Using it as a reference point, he counted the waterfront warehouses down until they came to the one where the paneled truck had been loaded with shipping containers. "There it is, the export company with the green wall," he said. "That's where those pricks work. It's the first one that goes."

They motored up the length of the port, Christian making mental notes of the prime targets, the big foreign trawlers and export companies, and then they headed back. They spotted Harry's Jeep hidden in the foliage beyond the beach and pulled in. The whole excursion had taken only two hours.

"How'd it go?" Harry called and walked to the beached raft.

"Easy pickin'," said Christian.

Wade unhooked the gas line from the outboard motor. "We're doing this tonight? With no moon, it'll be pitch-black. How will we find Harry and the Jeep on a long, dark beach?"

"Flashlights. We'll signal each other," Christian said. "I once smuggled drugs in from the Gulf for a mobster. Used a strobe light so the freighter knew when to drop the goods overboard. That'll work here."

"Damn, Hot Dog," said Harry. "All this time, I had you figured for a fresh-faced, dumb blond."

"Used to be naïve, Harry," Christian said and unscrewed the motor clamps from the raft. "But I went into horse racing and got my hands dirty. When you nearly die, you wise up. Having a mob boss for a friend also helps." He lifted the motor off and held it upright on the shore. "How did you think a dumb blond got rich?"

"You're full of surprises, Chris," said Wade. "We're seeing a whole new you. Hey, Harry, did you find a place to stash the raft?"

Harry pointed toward his Jeep that was parked on the dirt road near the dense foliage. "Other side of the Jeep. No one will spot it in those woods, and I hacked off some palm fronds for extra cover."

Despite the pain in his cracked ribs, Christian was stronger and in better shape than his older companions, so he did the heavy lifting and carried the outboard to the jungle. Harry brought the gas tank, and Wade dragged the raft. They placed the snorkeling gear, gloves, and dive knife in the raft and covered it, the tank, and the motor with the green tarp, further piling on the cut fronds to conceal it.

Harry glanced at his watch. "Ten o'clock, we're running ahead of schedule. After we pick up your gear at the house, we should make the Panama border around two."

They raced back to Harry's house in Jacó. Christian loaded the box of Molotov cocktails into the back of the Jeep and stacked his and Wade's carry-on luggage on top. The Rottweiler hovered at Christian's side, perhaps sensing he was leaving.

Harry held up a long-handled lighter and two flashlights. "Put in new batteries," he said, and stowed them.

When Wade added a small cooler with drinks, he said, "Man, it stinks of gasoline in here. I hope we don't get stopped."

"That box isn't going to be with us long," said Harry. "I got a perfect place to hide it outside Jacó."

"Wade's got a point." Christian grabbed an empty gas can out of the garage and then saw something he had nearly forgotten. He picked up a can of red spray paint and set it and the gas in the backseat. "Anyone sticks his nose in the Jeep, we can explain the smell."

"What's the paint for?" asked Harry. "Plan on spraying a trawler while you're there?"

"Something like that."

"We need to get going," said Harry. "Panama is roughly a hundred and twenty miles, but some of those roads are a bitch."

Christian squatted and massaged the dog's ears and neck. "Good-bye, girl, wish I could take you with me."

"Come on, Hot Dog," Harry said and eased into the driver's seat. "Kiss your girlfriend good-bye, and let's go." Christian petted the dog one last time and climbed into the back. Wade took the passenger seat. As they drove out of Jacó, Christian glanced down the street at the beach bar he had visited daily after surfing. He knew he would never see that little piece of paradise again.

CHAPTER SIXTEEN

"Damn shame you're going to trash that outboard and raft," Harry said to Christian as he steered the Jeep toward Panama. "I could re-sell it and make some decent fucking money."

Christian sat in the back and stared at row after row of palm trees. Sadly, the lush jungle had been replaced with commercial tree plantations in southern Costa Rica. Earlier, they had stopped and stashed the box of Molotov cocktails and the gas can in some bushes outside of Jacó. Harry started up again, whining about wanting the raft and outboard motor.

Christian cleared his throat. "It's evidence, Harry. A witness might see two men in a raft during the fire. Cops will be searching for the arsonists. If they pull us over and see the raft and motor, the nightmare begins. We're suspects with illegally stamped passports. I'm picked out of a lineup as the American who asked about fins and was beaten. There's the fucking motive. I'm not taking the risk so you can make a few grand."

"Chris makes sense," said Wade.

"Bullshit. He's overly cautious," said Harry.

"Maybe," said Christian, "but I'm considering everything that can go wrong. You've been damn lucky, selling the coke out of your house. One pissed-off customer running his mouth to the law, and you're busted."

"Speaking of coke," Wade said and dug a tiny bag of white powder out of his shirt pocket. "Anyone want a bump?" He rolled a dollar bill into a makeshift straw.

At two o'clock, they reached Panama and the border town of

Paso Canoas and drove down the rutty road lined with shabby souvenir shops and crowds of people looking for a bargain. Harry pulled into a dirt lot between a food vendor shack and an outdoor cabana restaurant, and parked the Jeep between two cars. A man approached and Harry paid him for the parking space.

"Grab your gear," Harry said. "Customs is a block up the street." They walked up the road, and Harry pointed to a narrow grass median with another dirt road and small houses on the other side. "We're standing in Panama, and the road and houses over there are in Costa Rica."

Christian finally understood. There was no fence, not even a small hedge that separated the two countries. People walked back and forth at will, nothing and no one stopping them. They reached the little Customs office stationed in the center between the two roads. Throngs of people walked around and passed it. Inside, the three men filled out declaration papers, and a female agent checked the contents of Christian's and Wade's bags. Back outside, they got in line at a teller window. The man glanced at Christian and stamped his passport.

The trio continued up the road to the bus depot and bought tickets for the city of David. The whole area screamed of poverty, with its decrepit buildings and trash-littered streets. The meagerly dressed people milled around, waiting for buses. Christian shared a bench with a woman holding a red rooster in her lap.

After ten minutes, the men boarded the crowded bus to David. Christian managed to get a window seat and reflected on his bus rides through the two Central American countries. Costa Rica was modern, clean, and a true tourist destination, with pristine jungle mountains and small concrete-block homes that were nicely land-scaped with fruit trees and gardens. Panama was Third World, with an impoverished economy. Like nasty scabs on the landscape, hovels of tin shacks sat along the road and cluttered the hillsides.

The Panamanians stared at Christian as an oddity, a blond American who used the public transportation system. Wade and

Harry did not garner a second glance, blending in because of their dark hair and eyes.

The bus stopped numerous times, picking up and dropping off passengers, so the trip to the bustling city of David took forty minutes. After collecting their bags, they hiked down the fractured sidewalk lined with vendors under makeshift canopies. Their tables held produce and exotic fruit. Christian stopped in front of an unconscious man sprawled across the walkway, unsure if he was drunk, injured, or dead. Wade, Harry, and the others sidestepped and ignored him. Christian raised an eyebrow and moved on, strolling past the run-down storefronts.

The threesome came to a four-decker hotel and went in. Amazingly, it was nice. Clean tile floors, a crystal chandelier, mahogany walls and a desk adorned the lobby. A staircase befitting a southern mansion led to the upstairs rooms. When checking in, Christian purposely used his credit card. He and Wade quickly dropped their bags and cell phones in their spacious rooms. They found Harry downstairs at the restaurant bar off the lobby, holding a beer. "Okay, Hot Dog," he said, "you got your alibi."

Christian, concerned with time, suggested they take a taxi back to the border rather than the slow bus. They were soon in Paso Canoas, back in the Jeep, and heading north on the Costa Rican highway. It was five in the evening, and Christian hoped to be in the raft and off Puntarenas around midnight.

However, no plan is complete without glitches. Halfway through the trip, they had left the straight, smooth highway of palm plantations and cattle pastures and were back on the mountainous road that snaked through the jungle.

"Goddamn it," said Harry. "The fucking Jeep is overheating with all this traveling and climbing these mountains. I've got to pull over."

They stopped at a bridge with a rocky ravine and small stream. Harry popped the hood so the engine would cool. Christian grabbed the small drink cooler and carefully climbed down to the stream, knowing Costa Rica had a multitude of venomous snake species. He filled the cooler with water for the radiator and smiled, spotting a teddy bear-size sloth clinging to a tree.

Shortly, they were on the road again, but had to stop an hour later at an isolated gas station and small store nestled in the jungle and repeat the process of letting the old Jeep engine cool.

As Harry and Wade stood at the Jeep talking, Christian wandered to a roadside picnic table under some huge trees. He sat down and munched on a burrito purchased at the store. He heard a bird squawk overhead and looked up. On the orchid- and bromeliad-covered branches, he saw the black toucan with its large colorful beak. His delight of seeing the bird dissolved, though, when he remembered what he was doing, why he was there. *Allie, did you have destroying a port in mind when you asked me to save sharks?*

Strangely, the toucan squawked again and bobbed its head up and down. Ruffling its feathers, it stared down at him, almost expectantly. "Okay, then." He heard the bang of the Jeep hood, and Harry waved him over. They were ready to go again.

Christian checked his watch, ten after midnight, as the Jeep turned off the main highway and traveled down the sandy road toward the coast. The men had stopped and picked up the box of the gas-filled beer bottles they'd hidden in the shrubs.

They parked and used flashlights to locate the raft and motor. From the jungle to the shore took several trips, carting the boat, motor, its tank, Molotov cocktails, and snorkeling gear, along with the long-handled lighter, dive knife, flashlight, and paint can. Once again, Christian wore the straw hat to hide his distinctive blond hair that could stand out like a beacon, even in a dark harbor.

"Don't get busted, and if you do, don't mention my name." Harry chuckled while Christian treaded water and waves, guiding the raft out with Wade at its stern.

"Sure thing, Harry," called Christian. "We ought to be back in an hour and a half." When the water was waist deep, he climbed into the raft. Wade started the outboard and steered the raft to calmer water before heading north along the coast.

"I guess we're really doing this," Wade called over the noisy motor.

Christian nodded and leaned back against the raft, staring at the distant city lights of Puntarenas. Their reflection in the water took on the effect of two cities, one upright, the other upside down.

"I'm nervous as all get out, but you're calm, like you've done this before," Wade said.

I have. Christian smiled a response, a real, unfaked smile. The earlier surfing and carousing couldn't compare to the contentment he felt at this moment. Saving sharks gave his life meaning and filled the void. *I get off on this. Guess that makes me a sick fuck,* he thought while Wade veered the inflatable north.

"Costa Rica? What the devil is he doing down there?" Dave Wheeler said, munching on a burger and studying the computer screen on his desk. Christian Roberts's passport had been red flagged at the Fort Lauderdale airport and showed he had boarded a Spirit jet bound for San Jose, Costa Rica.

Ralph sat nearby, a box salad in front of him. "Think he's running?" he asked. "When he came back from the Bahamas, he moved a million dollars from the States into a Cayman account." He stuffed a sliced tomato into his mouth.

"Naw, he's got deep roots in Sarasota and has no reason to run, at least not yet. Drake hasn't come up with a victim that matches the DNA on the bullet casing. We have only circumstantial evidence, not enough to win a case."

"We can always hope for a confession."

"That kid's too savvy. He was raised by a lawyer and is buddies with a mobster. They taught him to keep his mouth shut. He'll never spill his guts." Wheeler dug into the small bag for the last of his fries. "Damn takeouts. Never enough ketchup."

"If he's not likely to fess up, why are we bothering with another trip to Sarasota?"

"Because enough time's gone by for him to forget his earlier statements. We rehash them, and he might slip up and get caught in a lie. I also want to question him about the new evidence, bring up the computer printouts about sharks found on his sloop, especially the one about the exporter on Andros that was torched. Why he was in Bimini with Vince Florio and the reason their cell phones were disconnected. Also I'd like to check the GPS on his sloop, see where it's been. The arson on Andros occurred within the timeline it would take a sailboat to cruise from Bimini to Andros, plus Roberts perfectly fits the profile of Captain Nemo. I want to know if he's a sci-fi fan."

"You're going to give him a heads-up and reveal that evidence?"

"It's iffy, but in this case I'm hoping he'll freak, knowing what we have, and stumble on his explanations." Wheeler crumpled the fast-food wrappers into a ball and tossed them into a trash can several yards away.

"Good shot," said Ralph. "You quit smoking. Now, give up that greasy fried food, and you'll live longer."

"First of all, I quit smoking because it got expensive and I was tired of the bitching and trying to find a place to light up. It had nothing to do with my well-being. As for the fast food, I'm working at clogging my arteries and making my heart work overtime. Good health is merely the slowest possible rate at which a person can die. I don't want to feel ridiculous when I'm old and lying in a hospital bed dying of nothing."

Ralph closed the lid on his salad. "Guess that's one way of looking at it, but for your own good—"

"Lay off, Ralph. Next, you'll be saying I shouldn't drink. Let me be clear, the vice-free turn my stomach. They're boring pains in the asses that think they've taken the moral high ground and have the right to preach to the rest of us who are trying to have fun. Those jogging, tea-toting, grass-eating vegans drop dead every day. It's a roll of the dice on who gets to live longer, so quit harping before you really piss me off."

Ralph took a breath and changed the subject. "When Roberts returns to the States, we're paying him a visit then?"

"That's the plan. I'd also like to drop in on Vince Florio, get his version on why he was in Bimini with Roberts. Between the two of them, we could get mixed accounts."

"I'll contact Customs in Costa Rica so they'll inform us when Roberts checks out."

Wheeler rubbed his jaw. "I'm curious about why Roberts went there. Call one of our agents who works Sarasota and have him drive out to the horse farm in Myakka and question the employees. They probably know."

"Good idea."

"I've been over this case and the evidence a hundred times, and I'm getting a bad feeling. Unless Roberts does something stupid, he might beat an arrest."

"This is the stupidest thing I've ever done," Wade said and maneuvered the raft toward Caldera port. "If we get caught for arson in a foreign country, we'll be spending the rest of our days in a shithole prison."

Christian sat in the bow and looked back at him. "What days, Wade? You've said you're one blink away from another heart attack, and I have nothing to live for except this. We're both fucked. But if you wanna back out, I'll drop you off at the ferry dock and do it myself."

"No, I'll do it. At least I'll go out with a bang." At the harbor entrance, Wade throttled down and the motor ran just above an idle. The raft slowly traveled up the center of the waterway. Fishing boats came and went at all hours, so the sound of a boat motor was commonplace.

Christian pointed to a forty-foot trawler docked at a warehouse. He swiped his thumb across his throat, motioning to Wade to cut the engine. In the dark water and shadows, they sat in silence and stared off the starboard side at the dimly lit buildings and boats. The harbor was deserted and quiet.

Christian slipped on his fins and mask. "I'll be back in a minute," he whispered. He grabbed the paint can and carefully slid overboard. He took a large gulp of air, and to avoid ripples, he swam underwater. He resurfaced at the trawler's port side. On the hull above the waterline, he sprayed his message Stop Finning Sharks—Capt. Nemo.

Christian swam back to the raft and climbed aboard. Wade started the outboard, and they motored to their first target, the export warehouse with the men who had beaten Christian. Kneeling in the raft bow, he put on gloves and lit the rag in a Molotov cocktail. He threw the bottle against the building and the port lit up. Hastily, he tossed a few more onto the decks of two long-line trawlers. Wade gunned the outboard and steered toward open water as Christian, like a demon bringing hell to Earth, threw the fire bombs at the passing boats, docks, and warehouses. In the raft's wake he heard screams, shouts, sirens, and intermittent explosions from stored chemicals and fuel. The smell of decaying fish was replaced with the acrid odor of smoke and fumes. Within fifteen minutes, the deed was over, and they reached the safety of the Pacific. Christian gazed back at the inferno. At least eight buildings and more than a dozen fishing boats burned.

The raft leaped and crashed hard in the waves as it raced southward along the coast. "Shit, that was unbelievable!" Wade said.

Christian's eyes sparkled with the reflection of the distant flames and he smiled, admiring Nemo's work. Forty-foot plumes rose like fireworks into the black sky. He closed his eyes and nodded. With his efforts, he hoped the fish in these waters would get a reprieve, and that his guilt would wither to ashes.

They cruised offshore the dark beach until they saw the blinking light from Harry's flashlight. Christian turned his flashlight off and on to answer the signal. The two men beached the raft, and Wade stepped out.

Harry rushed out of the shadows. "How'd it go? How'd it go?"

"It was unreal, Harry," said Wade. "I've never been so freaked out in my life, but Chris was as calm as you please."

"Hey, my adrenaline was pumping," Christian said and pushed the raft out to knee-deep water. "I'll be back shortly." He hopped in the raft and fired up the outboard. He cruised a hundred yards offshore, put on his fins and mask, and slit the rubber sides of the raft with the dive knife. With the motor and his weight, the raft sank quickly beneath him, all evidence disappearing into the deep water. He swam back to Wade and Harry on the beach. Christian quickly changed into dry clothes, and the men piled into the Jeep. Back on the highway, they headed south for the long trip to Panama.

The sun was rising over the distant mountains when Christian and his two companions crossed the border. Harry motored through the town of Paso Canoas and found another long-term parking lot. Once again, Harry paid the attendant, and the three strolled past the customs office and caught a taxi for David.

They arrived at the hotel, and Christian stared at the souvenir shop across the street that had just opened its doors. "I'm going to check out that store."

"You're shopping?" Harry asked, shaking his head. "We'll be in the restaurant, having breakfast."

Christian hiked across the street and entered the store that carried mostly t-shirts, beaded jewelry, straw hats, and drastically reduced brand-name perfumes and colognes. With Christmas approaching, he pulled out a credit card and bought Opium for his mother and cologne for his stepfather. He walked back across the street and into the hotel. In the sparsely occupied restaurant, he sat down with Wade and Harry.

"So what'd you buy?" Wade asked as Christian placed the small bag on the table.

"Christmas gifts for my parents, but really I wanted to use my credit card, confirm I was here."

"Shit, Hot Dog," said Harry, "you sure are worried about this alibi. There's no fucking way you can be connected to Puntarenas."

"Let's hope not."

They ordered breakfast of fried eggs and ham. The excitement and the anxiety of last night began to fade like shadows with the dawn and left them quietly pondering the arson.

"I still can't believe we pulled it off," Wade mumbled and set his coffee cup down. "Craziest thing, craziest damn thing I've ever done."

"Kinda wish I'd been there," said Harry.

Christian laid his napkin on the plate of half-eaten food and rose. He dropped a twenty on the table, having learned that Panama used US currency. "Breakfast is on me. I'm beat and hitting the sack. I'll catch up with you all at dinner."

"Iris Hotel is up the street and has a great bar. Mostly gringos hang out there," Harry said. "We'll celebrate tonight."

Christian left the restaurant and lumbered up the stairs to his room. The night prior to the arson, he barely slept because of his growing tension. Last night, he didn't sleep at all. Only Wade had dozed in the Jeep on the trip back to Panama. In his room he stripped out of his clothes and took a lukewarm shower, finding no hot water again. He collapsed on the bed and closed his eyes, but so overtired, he remained awake. He envisioned the burning boats and warehouses at the harbor, the sirens and cries of men. He recalled the smell of smoke that overpowered the other aromas. *New images, new nightmares to torment me.*

He recalled his nightly dreams. They were always the same, terrifying, full of panic and despair: holding Allie as she took her last breath, the struggle with the Mexican on the trawler, his strong arm choking him, and then the corpses scattered about, their bodies going into rigor with horrified stares and twisted open mouths. And the blood, always the blood, everywhere and coming to life like a python that slithered up and suffocated him. Finally, there was the black-headed gull, the only witness to it all. It circled overhead, its caws turning into accusations that his actions had killed his wife.

With Andros and now Puntarenas behind me, maybe I'll start dreaming about fire. It would be a nice break from the damn blood and bird. He rolled to his side and clutched a pillow. He had felt good about torching the port, but it was over. Safe in a hotel in a different country with the stress gone, he had time to reflect on his misdeeds. *Am I justified, destroying one thing to save another? Or have I become a monster?*

Christian woke to his chiming cell phone on the dresser. He glanced at his watch. Six o'clock in the evening. He dragged himself out bed and recognized Wade's cell number. "Hey," he muttered.

"You up?" asked Wade.

"I am now." He rubbed his eyes and caught a yawn with his fist.

"Harry and I are downstairs in the restaurant. Get dressed and meet us for dinner. We need to talk, Chris." Wade didn't sound like his usual upbeat self.

"Okay, be there in ten. Order me an iced tea." He closed the phone, walked into the bathroom, and splashed water on his face. In the mirror, his reflection frowned at him. His boyish looks were gone. The cheek cut that had required stitches was still surrounded with dark bruises from the beating, and he hadn't shaved in weeks, so he sported an unkempt blond beard. His windswept hair was nearing shoulder length, after no haircut in months. He looked older, rough, like a hardened criminal who belonged in prison.

He left the look, not caring about his appearance. He dressed in jeans and a blue t-shirt. Slipping into his sandals, he headed downstairs to meet Harry and Wade.

Wade and Harry sat in the near-empty restaurant at an isolated table, out of earshot of the others diners. "Here he comes," Wade said and watched the young man stroll into the dining room. With a slinking lean frame and effortless spring in his long stride, he seemed part cat.

In the last several weeks, Wade had grown close to Christian. They were both native Floridians, disgusted with the growth, and shared the same passion for sea and sail. Like Christian, Wade got along famously with women, whereas some men considered him a jerk. Both Christian and Wade were also equally outraged over the extinction of sharks. Christian was a man of few words, especially in a crowd, but when he did speak, he revealed his intellect and wit. Wade liked him; thought he knew and understood him. He saw through the forced smiles to conceal his grief, but now Wade wasn't so sure. His perception and admiration for Christian was vanishing.

Christian approached the table and eased into a chair. "What's good?"

"Fuck what's good," Harry growled low. "Have you turned on the TV in your room and seen the news? It's all about Puntarenas."

"Of course it is." Christian casually opened the menu and glanced at the items.

Harry shoved Christian's menu down and glared. "Well, what's this shit about Captain Nemo? They reported this Nemo also left a similar message about shark finning in the Bahamas after an export company was torched. They mentioned a missing long-line trawler with a crew of five that might also be the work of Nemo. They're saying he's a dangerous eco-terrorist and probably a murderer. You want to explain, Hot Dog?"

The waitress approached their table, and all talk ceased. "Fish sandwich and fries," Christian said and handed her the menu. He took a sip of his tea, his manner cooler than the ice in the glass. After the waitress left, he leaned back and gazed at them, his eyes seeming to grasp their insides. "What do you want me to say, Harry, that I'm a sick son of a bitch, and Puntarenas wasn't my first rodeo? Probably won't be my last?"

"No wonder you were so damned worried about an alibi," Harry grumbled.

"My God, Chris," Wade said, startled. "I thought this was about revenge for the beating and maybe saving a few sharks, but it goes beyond that. Did you have something to do with that trawler? Did you kill those fishermen in the Bahamas?"

Christian rubbed the bristles on his jaw. "Yeah, I killed them," he said nonchalantly, "after they shot my wife. Now you have the whole story and know I have nothing to lose by killing again." He leaned forward, his blue eyes taking on a soulless stare. "So am I going to have a problem with you two?"

Wade and Harry were stunned into silence.

"Good." Christian went on. "Tomorrow we'll go to a bank. I'll pay you off, and we'll go our separate ways. I don't take betrayal well, so for your sake, I suggest you forget me and this conversation."

Wade glanced at Harry, obviously thinking the same thing. For weeks, they had slept, drank, and joked with the quiet, laid-back surfer, but had never really known him. After the beating, a different Chris emerged, calculating and determined as he plotted the attack on the port and carried out the arson with nerves of steel. Confronted about the murders, he now revealed a dark side. He was not only deadly, but apparently proficient, capable of taking out five men in one sweep. Wade recalled that Christian was also unstable; a shrink had diagnosed him as suicidal. The young guy had been so smooth they never saw through his act, that they had harbored a killer.

Wade uneasily sipped his drink and set it down. "Come on, Chris," he said quietly. "You're with friends. We're not going to screw you over and tell anybody."

"Yeah," Harry agreed. "We'd only be fucking ourselves. Besides, sounds like you had good reason to kill them."

"Fine, just remember if you get busted and rat me out, I have friends, the kind you don't want to meet." He smiled with all the warmth of a blizzard.

Wade swallowed deeply. Christian had mentioned he had run drugs for the Mafia and was friends with a mob boss. He wasn't making idle threats. Getting in his face about his past had been a huge mistake. He and Harry had opened a can of worms and found a cobra. All the hints had been there, but Wade had failed to see them. He summoned a grin. "Jesus, lighten up, Chris. All this intimidation is going to give me my final heart attack. When you were beaten and down, we helped you, saved you from those assholes. We care about you. We're not about to rat you out."

Christian's penetrating stare diminished with a nod. "Okay, then."

The food arrived at the table, and he produced his beguiling smile. "This does look good. I'm starved."

Dr. Jekyll and Mr. Hyde.

After dinner, Christian followed Wade and Harry a few city blocks to the Iris Hotel, a paint-peeled, wooden two-story that looked ready to collapse. On the street, a narrow staircase led up to the small bar with an outside balcony overhanging the bustling sidewalk. Inside, the patrons were mostly white men in their golden years and largely from the States. Christian ordered a cocktail and paid a dollar, finding Panama far cheaper than Costa Rica. Harry and Wade's beers cost fifty cents.

Christian picked up his drink and stepped outside onto the balcony, leaving Wade and Harry sitting on stools inside the congested bar. After the confrontation in the restaurant, they were probably glad to be away from him. He leaned against the railing and stared at the city lights of David and below heard groups of people chatting in Spanish. Several teenagers clustered around a bench in the small city park opposite the hotel. Compact cars, mainly red taxis, raced up and down the street.

He sighed when hearing Wade's familiar laugh. He felt bad about the intimidation that had driven a stake into the heart of their camaraderie. Wade and Harry would never again look at him the same way. But arson was one thing, arrested for murder another.

Vince had told him, "Never trust friendship to keep a silence. Fear's the key, and your threats better be a step above the law's—a person prefers prison to getting whacked for snitching." If arrested, Wade and Harry might think twice about making a deal and telling the cops he was Nemo. Then again, the whole thing could backfire in Christian's face. Only time would tell.

In the restaurant, he had been surprised, learning the media had connected the dots so quickly. Nemo had struck in the Bahamas and now Costa Rica, but given the Internet, it wasn't a stretch. Google Captain Nemo, and the Andros arson was bound to pop up.

He smiled, feeling a little psyched. His goal, the thing that kept him moving forward and alive, was working. Destroying several trawlers and export companies in small countries wouldn't put a dent in helping sharks, but the criminal acts of a dangerous eco-terrorist drew the attention of the international press, and publicity, good or bad, was more effective than any bomb.

People would learn about the fin trade, and with sympathizers, laws might get passed that protected sharks. Christian knew his approach was controversial. After all, he wasn't much better than a sadistic Middle Eastern terrorist hoping to enlist followers. Most people would disapprove of his criminal methods and want him caught. A few animal lovers, environmentalists, and nuts might cheer Nemo on, but opinions didn't matter. He didn't matter. His only objective was to enlighten people and, he hoped, sway them to his cause. Of course, sharks were equally controversial. People either appreciated or hated them. The same was true of the character he emulated. The notorious Captain Nemo was arguably both hero and villain. He protested war, taking out ships, yet he cherished the sea. *Hell, all this controversy. I don't know if I'm right or wrong, sane or crazy, a good guy or bad. Or maybe I've become all those things.*

CHAPTER SEVENTEEN

At the *Washington Post*, Trish Stevenson sat at her desk and read the Associated Press wire for the third time. The article was short, less than five hundred words, and it described an arson in Puntarenas, Costa Rica. At the port, fourteen trawlers and nine export buildings had been torched and two fishermen suffered minor burns. Not huge news, but what intrigued Trish was the arsonist. He had scrawled graffiti on a surviving trawler, saying Stop Finning Sharks—Capt. Nemo. The previous month, a similar message had been left on Andros Island in the Bahamas, where another export company rumored to sell fins was burned. The company owner also blamed the arsonist for a missing trawler with a five-man crew. The authorities in both countries concluded the arsons were the work of one eco-terrorist, and he was possibly a murderer.

Jim, a reporter from three desks down, strolled into her cubicle. "What do you think, Trish?" He had brought the wire to her attention. Months earlier, she had written a story about the fin trade, responsible for the dwindling shark population. Their numbers reduced by forty percent in the last ten years.

"Interesting," she said, twirling her lengthy chestnut hair with a finger. He loomed over her shoulder, and she tried not to gag on his pungent cologne. Jim's sharing had nothing to do with professional courtesy. From day one, he had bombarded her with date requests that she politely rejected, not that he was bad looking. He was tall, lean with thick brown hair and hazel eyes, but he was so obnoxious and full of himself that it turned her off. She noticed he had once again removed his glasses before entering her space.

"If you follow up," he said, "I'd be happy to help with the research. We could put in some late hours. I'll buy the takeout."

She rose and slipped away from him. "Thanks, but I'm caught up with my backlog and don't need the help. If you'll excuse me, I need to talk to the editor about this story."

"Say, if you're not busy tonight—"

"I am," she interrupted. Polite rejections were wasted on the knucklehead.

Mary, an older coworker who sat at a desk across the aisle, had an ear-to-ear smirk between her round cheeks. She turned her head and watched a deflated Jim walk back to his desk. "What a jerk," she said. "He thinks he's God's gift to women, wants to get in the pants of every pretty new face. Honey, you're smart to give him the boot."

"If nothing else, he is persistent." Trish straightened her blouse and picked up the printout. *Am I still considered new after seven months?* She thought and walked to her editor's office.

Larry's office door was partially ajar, so she tapped lightly and stuck her head in. Larry James sat at his desk, focused on his computer. In his fifties with thinning hair, he was one sweet, patient guy with her. He did have a temper, though. She had seen him raging at other reporters.

"Come in," he said, never taking his attention off the screen.

"I hope I'm not interrupting."

He looked up and grinned. "Not at all, Trish. What is it?"

She placed the printout in front of him. "This came across my desk, and I'd like to pursue it, do a follow up to my shark fin story."

Larry leaned back and read the wire. "Waste of time," he said. "Our readers aren't interested in arsons that occur in dinky countries. No one was even killed."

"But a trawler and its crew are reported missing."

"That's the statement of some Bahamian exporter, not the police. They obviously have no proof the crew is dead. We'll look pretty stupid reporting it if the trawler shows up and everyone's fine.

Elections are coming up, and you're perfect for following a senator around and getting him to open up."

Trish was not giving up easily. "Mr. James, there was a great response to the fin story. People were upset that sharks were disappearing because of the Chinese fin soup. Now, apparently, this Captain Nemo is taking it seriously. He's breaking laws and putting himself on the line to save sharks."

"He's no better than those animal rights fanatics that burn down labs to save a bunny." He shook his head. "Amazingly, those same people have no problem wearing makeup and taking drugs when they're sick, all of which were tested on the bunnies and proven safe."

"There's no shortage of rabbits, but in ten years, according to researchers, one-third of all shark species will be extinct, and the stability of the ocean environment will be affected. This is a true cause. I'm rooting for Nemo, and I believe many of our readers will feel the same way."

"The tree huggers will love him, but the rest will think he's a crackpot who belongs behind bars." He thumbed his double chin and reread the printout. "It's a case of whether the end justifies the means, but controversy is the name of the game. Okay, write your article, but don't slant it. We don't need grief from the right wingers."

Trish nodded and took the printout. She hurried back to her desk with a smile.

Mary glanced at her. "You look like the cat that swallowed the canary. What are you working on?"

"One heck of a canary," Trish said and handed her the printout.

Mary shrugged. "If you say so, but I don't see it. That's a couple out of a million arsons in the world."

"The story isn't the arsons. It's Captain Nemo and his cause and messages. It's almost romantic, risking his life to help a species. I'm going to play him up as a hero."

Trish sat down and went to work with her first call to the Bahamas. After being put on hold and switched around to several divisions, she was finally talking to Sergeant Drake in Nassau, the officer leading the investigation into the Andros arson.

Drake informed her that there were no new leads and no witnesses, and any evidence had been lost in the fire. Mr. McGee, the export company owner, had made the statements to the press that the arson was the work of an eco-terrorist and also implicated him as a murderer because of the missing trawler and its crew. Drake couldn't validate the owner's claims. He did mention a foot in a shoe found floating off Chub Cay, but without the crew's DNA, the body part couldn't be tied to the men on the missing trawler.

"The trawler was from Mexico," said Drake. "It's conceivable the crew went home or the boat hit a reef or storm and sank. Transient fishermen are impossible to trace. Mr. McGee can't even remember their last names. All the information—their names, boat registration, even the town of origin—was in the company's office and lost in the fire. Fire destroys evidence and the ocean conceals it. I have both working against me."

"Let's talk about Captain Nemo and the message he left about shark finning," she said. "You have no suspects, no idea who he is?"

"Your FBI has profiled him as a young, white male, most likely American, with the money and means to commit these arsons. He used a boat and struck from the sea, avoiding customs and airfares. I know, since I questioned almost every tourist on Andros. Since our suspect is an idealist, fighting for the environment and using a science fiction character for an alias, he's educated, according to Agent Wheeler."

"The FBI?" she questioned. "I didn't think they handled arsons in other countries."

"The Miami field office and I are collaborating on an unsolved murder case, a US citizen killed in the Bahamas. We had a person of interest, and he happens to fit Captain Nemo's profile. He also might have a motive to destroy the trawler and commit the arsons, but at this time, it is only a theory with no solid evidence to support it."

"Who is the person?"

Drake was silent for a moment. "I'm not at liberty to say."

"Thank you for your time, Sergeant. Perhaps my article will shake things up and a witness will step forward."

"I can only hope."

Trish hung up and wasted no time getting to an Internet search on the murder of an American in the Bahamas that occurred close to the arson date. The articles popped up, and she read about the Allie Roberts murder that took place while a couple was vacationing on a sloop. The husband had sailed into Nassau, claiming thieves ransacked his boat and shot his wife. At that point, the Bahamian police considered him a person of interest. A second article stated he had been released and the case was still pending.

She found no other murders of US citizens during that time. "This has to be it," she mumbled and scrolled down the screen to a photo of the husband, Christian Roberts, taken outside the Nassau police station after he had struck a reporter. "Wow," she whispered. "Look at you!" She printed the picture and stepped to Mary's desk. "See this guy? He might be Captain Nemo."

Trish's coworker studied the photo. "My, my, my, that dreamboat belongs in the movies, instead of bopping around on the sea," said Mary. "If he's your superhero, does that make you Lois Lane?"

Wheeler sat in front of his computer, rehashing the Costa Rican arson on the screen. "Anything?" he asked when Ralph walked to his desk.

"They have nothing, no witnesses or evidence so far. I did learn Nemo's message was sprayed on another trawler and written in English, same as the Bahamas. At least we know why Roberts was in Costa Rica, still on his shark crusade."

Aggravated, Wheeler shoved the paperwork aside. "That damn kid is like a dead mackerel on a moonlit beach, all shiny and slippery, but rotten inside. All right, get back with the Costa Rican authorities and tell them we have a possible person of interest, that Roberts might be Captain Nemo, and send them his mug shot. Maybe someone saw him poking around the harbor before the arson. I'll pull his credit card statements and cell phone locations. Time to turn up the heat and fry this mackerel."

The next day, Wheeler reviewed Roberts's credit card statements and rubbed his temples with discouragement. No charges were made in Costa Rica, not a restaurant, hotel, or even a gas station bill. He must have used cash. The only charges were in David, Panama, checking into a hotel on the same day as the fire, more than 150 miles away, and early the following morning, he made a purchase in a gift shop, all great evidence for a defense attorney. His cell charges revealed he made a few calls to his horse farm from Jacó on the Pacific coast of Costa Rica, but with few cell towers, Wheeler couldn't pinpoint where Roberts had stayed and with whom.

Wheeler faxed Roberts's mug shot to the Jacó police and asked if they could check around. Someone in that little town must have seen the striking blond American and perhaps had knowledge of his trip to Puntarenas. To commit the crime, Roberts would have had to travel day and night to set up an alibi in the Panamanian hotel, get back in Costa Rica to carry out the arson, and then return to Panama to buy the gift. The scenario was thin, but possible. A bigger "if" was whether a jury would swallow it.

Even more disheartening, Ralph learned that Roberts's passport was stamped in Panama prior to the arson and showed he never left the country.

"He did it, Ralph," Wheeler said, irritated. "He's just damn good about covering his tracks. In both arsons, he had the opportunity, sailing near Andros and within driving distance of Puntarenas. And his motive, a vendetta against shark slayers, since Mexican long-liners more than likely killed his wife."

The phone rang on Wheeler's desk, and he answered with a growl, "Wheeler."

"Agent Wheeler, my name is Trish Stevenson. I'm a reporter for the *Washington Post*. I'm writing an article about the arsons that took place on Andros Island in the Bahamas and now in Costa Rica. There were messages left by Captain Nemo concerning shark fins."

"The FBI doesn't handle arsons in other countries."

"Yes, but Sergeant Drake in Nassau said you were assisting him with the unsolved murder of an American, Allie Roberts, and this case might be connected to the arson. You have a person of interest, Christian Roberts. Do you think he's Captain Nemo?"

Goddamn Drake and his diarrhea of the mouth. "Ms. Stevenson, the Bahamian police department asked us to assist with the Roberts murder. Early in the case, the husband was a person of interest and questioned. We have found no evidence linking Roberts to his wife's murder, the arson, or Captain Nemo."

"So you're disputing Drake's statement that there was speculation by your department that the murder and arson were connected, not to mention the missing trawler and crew? The only person of interest has been Mr. Roberts, who, I'm told, fits your profile of Nemo. According to the Bahamian paper, he claims that pirates killed his wife, but it could have been the long-liners on the trawler that murdered the wife, and Mr. Roberts retaliated, did away with them and the boat and then burned the export company, its place of origin. Sergeant Drake mentioned a theory, and I'm assuming that's it."

"Ms. Stevenson." He chuckled. "You have a vivid imagination, but you could drive a warship through your hypothesis and never scrape a fact. To my knowledge, Christian Roberts is not involved in any crimes. The murder is an ongoing investigation, and I can't comment further. Good day, Ms. Stevenson."

Wheeler hung up the phone. *Damn reporters, I'm more allergic to them than pollen.* How did she get all that information, put the pieces together, and arrive at the same conclusion he had? Drake was obviously a big help, divulging that the murder and arson had ties to the same person of interest. Wheeler had wanted to catch Roberts off guard when questioning him. Now Drake and this *Post* reporter would screw up the interview. Before long, Roberts would read about himself in the paper. Wheeler picked up the phone, planning to give Drake a piece of his mind, when Ralph stepped to his desk, grinning like a moonlit possum.

"Guess what," Ralph said. "I learned from Panama that Roberts flew out early this morning and he arrives in Lauderdale in a half hour. I've notified the airport authority, and they'll grab him at Customs. A squad car will bring him to the Dade County jail."

"Thank God," Wheeler said, putting the phone down. "The press called, and they're on to Roberts. At least now he'll be unprepared for questions concerning the arsons."

Ralph chuckled. "I also alerted Dade that Roberts was extremely dangerous and wanted for questioning in six murders, counting his wife's, as well as for arson. Doubt those officers will be gentle with our boy."

"Good thinking, Ralph. Roughed up and thrown in jail should scare the smarts out of him. He'll probably be distraught, believing it's over, and primed to break or blunder."

"Heck, didn't consider that. I figured questioning him here would save us a trip to Sarasota."

At ten in the morning, Christian sat in a small closed office at the Fort Lauderdale airport and faced the desk of a large Hispanic man wearing an airport security uniform. As soon as Christian had produced his passport in Customs, he was nabbed by two guards and brought here. His mind now raced. Had they discovered new evidence linking him to the murdered crew or did he screw up the arsons?

"Why am I being held?" he asked. "My papers are in order, and I didn't smuggle anything in from Panama."

"Don't know," said the guard, "just got the call to hold you."

Four Lauderdale police officers entered the office. "We'll take him," one said.

"Bullshit! You're not taking me anywhere!" Christian stood. "Am I being charged with something?"

Before Christian could blink, he was slammed face-first against the wall, the officers knocking the breath and fight out of him. They forced his arms behind his back, and he felt the handcuffs clamp tightly around his wrists. He was jerked back around and held by his upper arms. He licked his busted lip and tasted blood. They ushered him through the airport amid the stares of other passengers. The abuse left Christian shaken, the cops treating him like a dangerous felon. *But then again, I am.*

Outside, at the arrivals gate, he was placed into the back of a squad car. The two officers took the front seats, and one drove out of the airport. Several minutes into the ride, Christian collected himself and asked with an even tone, "Why am I being brought in?" When the officers failed to respond, he asked, "You can at least tell me where I'm going."

"County," said the driver.

End of the line. I'm busted. Christian tilted back his head and closed his eyes. *Rather be dead than spend the rest of my days in a cage.*

In the Fort Lauderdale police station, Wheeler flashed his FBI badge at the desk clerk. "You have our suspect, Christian Roberts." Ralph stood nearby holding a sizable file box with "Christian Roberts" written on its side.

The woman tapped the computer keys. "He was brought in an hour ago and is in a holding cell."

"Have a guard bring him to an interrogation room."

Twenty minutes later, Wheeler and Ralph entered the room with a two-way mirror for observation and recording. They found Roberts in handcuffs, sitting at a table. A police officer stood behind him.

Christian looked up. His startled eyes resembled a deer's caught in headlights. "Wheeler, what's going on?" he asked. "You know I didn't kill my wife. You know it." Wheeler saw his appearance had changed since the interview in the Bahamas. His hair was shoulder length and a beard masked his boyish looks. Yellowing and dark bruises covered half his face amid a small contusion on his cheek. Someone had apparently worked him over.

"Let's lose the handcuffs, and you can go, Officer," Wheeler said. "He'll be all right." He took a seat facing Roberts. Ralph set the box down on the table and made certain that Roberts saw his name on the huge file.

Christian glanced at the box as the cuffs were removed. He took a deep breath, lowered his head, and rubbed his wrists. "What do you want?" he asked softly. "Why am I here?"

"Christian, I don't believe you did kill your wife," Wheeler said, sympathetically, "but you're not innocent. We know you had a run-in with a trawler and its five-man crew. They were probably harvesting sharks and you tried to stop them. Things got out of hand and Allie was killed. Your rage and revenge is understandable. You want to tell me about it, son?"

Christian stared at his feet and remained silent.

"I notice you're not denying it," said Wheeler. *Come on, you little sucker, open up and spill your guts.*

"I didn't kill anyone."

"We know you did," said Ralph.

Christian lifted his head, bit his lip, and looked at Wheeler. His gaze shifted to Ralph, his eyes narrowing. *Son of a bitch!* Wheeler thought, seeing the return of confidence. *Lost him; he's on to us.*

Christian leaned back in the chair and massaged the beard stubble on his chin. "You have the evidence I killed those men, or are you just guessing?" Not waiting for a response, he chuckled and shook his head. "I'll give it to you, Wheeler. You had me going. I was freaking. Funny thing is when I was taken into custody no one could tell me the charges. I wasn't read my rights, fingerprinted, or photographed, pretty standard stuff with an arrest. Leads me to believe you're fishing and have nothing but speculation." He stood with a smug grin. "Sorry, but this fish isn't biting. I'm outta here."

"Sit down, Roberts," ordered Wheeler.

"What, no more Christian or *son?*" Christian asked, returning to the chair. "And just when I thought we were getting close."

"I liked you better when you were freaking out. For your information, you were read your rights in the Bahamas, and the Miranda rule still applies here, but we'll do it again." Wheeler rattled off his rights. "I suppose you want your lawyer now?"

"Naw, I don't think so."

Wheeler was surprised. A defense attorney could halt the interrogation, but Roberts was probably curious about his file, wanting to know what they had on him. His looks had not only changed since his last interview, but also his attitude. He was no longer stoic, suffering from the shock and death of his wife. He was a new animal, mentally tougher and focused, ready to take on the FBI alone.

Wheeler drilled him, first rehashing Roberts's earlier statements about his wife's murder. He asked the same question ten different ways but, unfortunately, Roberts answered consistently and even seemed bored.

After a few hours of getting nowhere, Wheeler moved on to new questions concerning the new evidence. "We took some blue paint scrapings off the damaged bow of your sailboat and learned the paint came from a Mexican factory. The same paint showed up on wood chunks floating off Chub Cay where a blue Mexican trawler was last reported fishing, and it's now missing. Given the time of your wife's death and the time you reached Nassau, you could have easily been in the Berries off Chub Cay and had a run-in with that trawler."

Christian leaned back. "Told ya, we were north of Nassau when Allie died, and I don't know how my sloop was damaged. Maybe I hit some floating debris when I sailed to Nassau and didn't notice. It was dark. I was upset."

"Did I mention the foot? Yeah, a foot in a shoe was also discovered near the chunks of wood. The decomposition puts the time of death of its owner around the same as your wife's and around the time the trawler disappeared. You do see how that ties you and your boat to the missing trawler?"

"No, I don't see," Christian said with irritation. "You want scenarios? The trawler rams my sloop and the crew kills my wife while I'm diving. Their hull is also damaged and they make it to Chub Cay before they sink. The sharks feasted—" He stopped in mid-sentence and stared at Wheeler like a light had come on. "The blue paint on my sloop and the wood chunks, do they match the trawler's paint?"

Damn him. Wheeler hesitated. "It's Mexican paint, so most likely the trawler had the same paint."

"Most likely, but no proof without the trawler." Christian's blue-eyed gaze had the glint of amusement, like he was winning this game. "Same with the foot, without the crew's DNA, it can't be matched to any DNA found on my sloop. Isn't that right, Wheeler?"

Wheeler straightened in his seat, not happy that the wiseass had found the weakness in the case and was now questioning him. Before Wheeler could respond, Ralph piped in.

"We don't have the crew's DNA or trawler paint yet, but we'll get it," Ralph said.

Christian glanced at Ralph and rolled his eyes. He turned to Wheeler. "What am I doing here, Wheeler? You have nothing that ties me or my boat to this missing trawler. For all you know, the trawler sank for a variety of reasons or it's docked in Mexico. And the foot probably belongs to a drunken fisherman. All you have are hunches and coincidences." He stood, his knuckles on his hips. "Unless you plan to arrest me, I'm leaving."

"You're not going anywhere," said Wheeler, "and I don't believe in coincidence."

Christian settled back into the chair and took a seething breath. "I know you can hold me for twenty-four hours without charging me, so I hope you're enjoying this."

"I am." Wheeler dug out another file from the box. "Let's talk about sharks. We found several computer printouts about sharks and the fin trade in the cabin of your sloop. Two pages were a Bahamian article concerning an export company on Andros Island that was rumored to sell shark fins. Did you read the article?"

"Nope, Allie was into the shark research. Check for prints, and you won't find mine on those papers."

"That doesn't mean she didn't tell you about it. The trawler came from the export company, and its warehouse was burned the same day you left Bimini. The distance and timeline matches. You sailed out of Bimini in the morning and arrived at Andros in the evening, in time to set the fire. "

"So now I'm an arsonist." Christian smiled. "Never knew I was so devious. Do you have any witnesses or evidence that proves I went to Andros?"

"I'll ask the questions. What were you doing on Bimini?"

"Getting fuel, did some drinking. By the way, I do have a witness who will testify I never set foot on Andros."

"You call Vince Florio a witness?" said Wheeler.

"You are keeping track. I'm impressed."

"Any reason you disconnected your cell phone when you left Bimini?"

"I didn't. The batteries went dead. Didn't notice until I reached Florida."

Wheeler questioned and requestioned Christian about Bimini, Vince Florio, the arson, and sharks. Christian danced around the questions and made snide remarks, but revealed nothing useful. He was relaxed and seemed to relish making a mockery of their case that lacked teeth. Meanwhile, Ralph paced the small room, growing irritated with Roberts and his pretentious, unflustered attitude.

Ralph bent down and growled into Roberts's face. "You like science fiction, Roberts? Ever read *Twenty Thousand Leagues under the Sea?*"

Christian chuckled. "Is that a crime now?"

"Answer the question," Ralph snapped.

"Guilty," Christian said and glanced at his watch. "After six hours, I know you've been dying to hear that. I love sci-fi and read the novel, along with millions of other people. I also saw the old movie with Kirk Douglas."

Ralph blurted, "Did you leave a message at the warehouse arson saying, 'Stop Selling Shark Fins,' and sign it Captain Nemo?"

"Sounds like a cool dude, but it wasn't me." Christian sat up, taking interest in the new interrogator. "What's your name again? You're such an afterthought, I forgot." Wheeler recognized that

Roberts had picked up on Ralph's irritation and was deliberately toying with him.

"Ralph," Wheeler said and waved his hand, motioning him to back down.

"That's it, Ralph," Christian said with a smirk. He laced his fingers under his chin and looked up at Wheeler's younger partner. "Ralphie, did you know that light travels faster than sound? That's why some people look smart until they speak, you, for an example. Let Wheeler do the asking. You're out of your depth here."

Ralph's face flushed, and he grimaced. "You cocky prick, I'm going to bring you down."

"Take it easy, Ralphie. I'm the one who is supposed to lose it here."

Ralph loosened his tie, slumped in a chair, and grumbled, "I'd love to take you outside and teach you a lesson."

In a nanosecond, Christian's smile dissolved, and his tone turned serious. "Let's go."

Ralph jumped up with clenched fists.

Wheeler interceded. "Ralph, take a break and get some air." Ralph glared at Christian and gritted his teeth, seething. He stomped to the door.

Christian's teasing smile returned. "Ralphie, I'm looking forward to that lesson."

After Ralph left, Wheeler turned to him. "You having fun?"

"Oh, yeah, I love sitting in a room for hours talking to you and that clown."

"Was your smart mouth the reason someone beat you up?"

"It would take more than one, Wheeler."

"So several took you on? Why?"

"As it happens, I took a tumble down a cliff, hiking in the mountains."

"You don't strike me as the clumsy type." Wheeler glanced at the papers. "This happened in Costa Rica? I see you made a few calls to your farm from Jacó."

"Damn, you *are* watching me."

"Where'd you stay in Jacó?"

"That's for me to know and you to find out."

Wheeler questioned him about Puntarenas, the arson in the port, and the message that Nemo had again left on a trawler.

"This Nemo gets around. Maybe you should be looking for some-one with a submarine instead of a sloop. As far as the Costa Rican arson, I was in Panama that night and saw it on the news the next morning. Check my passport and credit card statements. They'll prove I was nowhere near Puntarenas during that fire."

"Or you did a lot of driving." Wheeler placed a legal pad in front Roberts. "I'd like you to print Stop Finning Sharks and sign it Captain Nemo."

"Handwriting comparison?" Christian commented, and scribbled the message. "I'm telling you, Wheeler, you have the wrong guy." He slid the pad back to Wheeler.

"I'm looking at the right guy, Roberts, or maybe I should start calling you Nemo." He glanced at the writing. Roberts had purposely written in block letters, different from Nemo's messages. Disgusted, Wheeler rose from the table. Eleven hours of pressure and hard questions, and Roberts had not cracked or slipped up. The gamble had not paid off. He picked up the box.

"We're done?" Christian asked. "I can finally go?"

"I'm going, but you're not." Wheeler smiled. "Since you had such a good time playing with us, you can spend the night. It'll give you a taste of things to come." He started for the door.

"Wheeler, hope you enjoyed it. There won't be another sit-down."

Wheeler told the guard to return the prisoner to a cell. He and Ralph walked across the dark parking lot to their car. They had arrived at the police station late in the morning, and it was now going on eleven in the evening.

Ralph carried the box and looked at the asphalt. "I'm sorry, Dave. I should've never let that guy get to me."

"Yeah, some days you're the dog, and other days the tree."

"That interview sure was a waste of time."

"Not necessarily. Granted, Roberts is unshakable and knows what and what not to say, but he did reveal some insight about himself."

"Like what?" Ralph asked and placed the file box on the car trunk while he dug in his pocket for the keys.

"When a normal person is facing prison, he doesn't taunt the FBI. I originally thought Roberts was arrogant, but that isn't it. He just doesn't care. There's no tomorrow for him. After his cocky performance today, I don't think he's playing with a full deck and is possibly suicidal. Smart, dangerous, and unbalanced; that's a bad mix."

CHAPTER EIGHTEEN

Christian, rather than being returned to the small holding cell, was escorted to a large cell that held five men: three black youths, a middle-aged Hispanic, and one skinny white guy who was sprawled on the floor, stinking drunk. Christian found an isolated corner and sat down on the nasty concrete. Hugging his jeans, he lowered his head against his knees and closed his eyes, anticipating a long night.

He thought about the FBI interrogation. Sure it wasn't wise, going it alone without a defense attorney. A lawyer could have protected his rights, probably ended the cross-examination, and gotten Christian released. But lawyers complicate things, and Christian wanted to know what the FBI had in their files—evidence or witnesses that could bring him down.

A long grilling and one sleepless night in the tank were worth the reprieve of worry. Amazingly, Wheeler's hypothesis was dead-on and supported with a lot of circumstantial evidence, but nothing was watertight. Everything could be disputed in a trial. Christian's biggest foul-up and main concern was the blood on the bullet, if they found a victim to match its DNA. When Wheeler brought up the foot found off Chub Cay, Christian felt his heart sink, but luckily the foot didn't belong to Christian's first victim, whose blood had gotten on Christian's hands when he reloaded the revolver. *So far, so good.*

He reflected on Wheeler. The guy came across like a southern hick in a suit, an old bloodhound with his nose on a trail, but really he was more fox. He had determined Christian's motives, movement, and crimes, and knew he was Nemo, he just couldn't prove it, at least not yet. The man had earned Christian's respect. In the future, he needed to be extra cautious with Wheeler on his tail. Ralph, the younger agent, had not merited a second glance. He was a geek that played by the rules and didn't think outside the box.

Christian felt a slight kick on his leg and lifted his head.

"Hey, man, you got a cigarette?" asked the largest of the three black kids.

"Don't smoke."

"Yeah, you do. Give me one, or I'll fuck you up good."

With the threat, Christian analyzed his opponent. The kid looked about eighteen and was Christian's height but was built like a Clydesdale, with a thick neck, wide chest, and rippling muscles that tested the strength of his tank top. Christian's frame was lean but racehorse quick and agile. "You don't want to mess with me," he said, glancing up through his long strands of hair.

"Get your ass up, honky," the kid said, pounding his fist into his palm. His friends joined in and three hovered near Christian.

Christian rose and put his hands on his hips. "Kid, you don't know what attitude is until you've seen mine." He stepped toward the kid, posturing to prove he had bigger balls.

"Amigos, stay away from that hombre," called the Hispanic man. "I heard the guards say he murdered six people."

"That true, man?" asked the big kid.

"What do you think?" Christian glared into the kid's eyes, and the three moved away, giving him space. With his back against the wall, he slid down and rested his forehead against his knees again. *Murdered six people. No wonder the cops at the airport slammed me into the wall. FBI assholes.*

Wearing a bathrobe, Vince Florio reclined in a lounge chair by the pool, turned off his cell phone, and stared out at Sarasota Bay. In late December, the days were warm, in the mid-seventies, and the nights in the high fifties. He gazed up at the brilliant blue morning sky, with not a cloud in sight, unlike New York, where the heavens were a constant depressing gray.

He laid his cell on the side table and picked up the Bloody Mary. Taking a sip, he rehashed the call from Christian. He was back from his surfing trip and on Alligator Alley outside Miami, driving home.

With the waterfront view and Christian in mind, Vince thought about the night he nearly died. On Tampa Bay at the height of a hurricane, he had been thrown from a boat wreck. Injured and choking on saltwater, he lost all hope of surviving. Out of the huge waves, Christian appeared like a guardian angel. He grabbed Vince's life jacket and dragged him to shore, swimming nearly seven miles through the rough surf. *Why did he do it, risk his life, when he had every reason to let me drown? And how do I repay the unrepayable?*

Vince's savior now needed saving. Christian suffered from depression like Vince's wife, déjà vu all over again. After the crib death of their son, she had overdosed on pills and died. Vince failed her, a wife who had much in common with Christian. They both were striking, insolent blonds, and good actors, knew how to hide their emotions and despair. Vince feared they might yet share one final thing, dying young at their own hand. *I can't lose him too.*

He heard the sliding glass door close and turned from the bay. He raised his arm, shading his eyes from the sun, and saw Sal lumbering toward him with his three-hundred-pound frame. *Sal, more devoted than a dog, more trustworthy than a wife.* "How's the diet?"

Sal pulled up a chair and collapsed. "Fuck the diet. They wanted me to give up spaghetti."

"I just got off the horn with our boy. He's back from Costa Rica. Says he wants to come over and go fishing tomorrow."

"He's your boy, not mine. And he ain't interested in fishin'. Probably in another jam and wants to unload. Wonder what the little pissant's done now. I know you like the kid, but I still can't believe you got suckered into burning down that Bahamian warehouse. Shit, there wasn't even any profit in it."

Vince grinned. "Yeah, but it was fun." His smile faded and he turned to Sal. "And, Sal, I do like Christian. I think of him as a son. If something ever happened to me, I want you to watch his back."

Sal pulled out a cigar and lit it. "You're expecting trouble?"

"Word is my old associates got a beef. They're not happy with my retirement. Apparently, my connections dried up and went elsewhere. It's left a hole in their pocket."

"What's the plan?"

"Told them I'd come up after the holidays and have a sit-down. It's no big deal. Now about Christian—"

"Ah, Christ, I can barely stand the kid. He swaggers in with that smug look, and I just wanna pop him."

Vince glared at him. "Damn it, Sal, I ain't askin'."

"All right, all right," Sal grumbled. "For you, I'll try and keep the little shit healthy and out of trouble."

Early the next morning Christian's SUV pulled into the drive-way, and Vince opened the front door. As Christian strolled to the house, Vince frowned. "Jesus, what the hell happened? Someone used you as a punching bag?"

Christian hugged Vince, the Italian way of greeting, and smiled. "Yeah, I got into a scrap. Think this looks bad? You should've seen me a few weeks ago. I'll tell you about it on the water." With the FBI interested in both of them, Vince gave up checking the house for the pesky eavesdropping devices and conducted business outside.

"Well, lose the beard and get a haircut," Vince said as they walked through the living room.

"What, don't like my new disguise?"

"You look like a bum, and you'll be treated like one."

"Well, you're not gonna believe the week I've had. I should be home, recuperating, instead of here."

Sal's right. He's here to unload. On the dock behind the house, they climbed into Vince's twenty-nine-foot Grady White and cruised across the bay to a grass flat, a watery office where they discussed private matters. After anchoring, they stepped out in knee-deep shallows and waded with their poles. Christian told Vince about his time in Costa Rica, the beating in Puntarenas, and the subsequent arson at the port with Wade and Harry, followed by the trip to Panama to establish an alibi, and then being detained in the Lauderdale jail and interrogated by the FBI.

First, Vince questioned the wisdom of hiring the two older men for the arson when Christian had known them for only weeks. Vince then became miffed, learning that Christian had allowed the FBI to interrogate him without an attorney. "Are you nuts? Have a death wish?" he raged. "Or are you getting too brash for your own damn good? Maybe it's all three. Don't worry about what they have. When the FBI has a witness or concrete evidence, you'll know. They'll knock on your door and shove a warrant in your face. In the meantime, don't talk to them, and never without a lawyer." He shook his head with aggravation. "Christ, I thought I instilled that into you."

Throughout the morning, they cast their lines and talked, Vince giving his expert criminal advice to the amateur. During the process, they even managed to catch a few speckled trout. Toward noon, they waded to the boat.

"Christian, I've been giving your shark cause a lot of thought. It's one thing to go off half cocked and throw bottles of gas at trawlers and warehouses, but if you plan to pursue this, you need to be educated."

"What do you mean?"

"You should know how to handle all manner of weapons, how to throw a knife, make a bomb, pick a lock, and fine-tune your fighting skills, so when you're cornered in an alley with six men holding bats, you can defend yourself. You want to be Nemo, this eco-terrorist, you should be the best."

"A mob boot camp," Christian said with a smile. "And who's going to teach me?"

"Sal, for starters," said Vince as they climbed in the boat and pulled anchor.

"He hates me. Still hasn't gotten over that first boat ride in the Scarab."

Vince chuckled. "Well, you did scare the shit out of him, and that's hard to do. Tone down the lip and treat him nice. He'll warm up. You can learn a lot from that big lug."

They motored across the bay to New Pass and tied the boat to a seawall at the Salty Dog restaurant. They sat on the open deck, drinking cocktails. Vince ordered a blackened grouper sandwich, and Christian had the Buffalo wings, the hottest in town.

Vince took a sip of his scotch. "After the holidays, Sal and I are goin' to New York. Have some business I need to take care of. I think you should come with."

"New York in January?" Christian shuddered. "Vince, I've seen snow only twice in my life, and I hate big cities."

"You'll survive. New York is a good place to start your training."

"I'll consider it. A cold, crowded city with no sky. That's sure to cheer me up."

After the fishing trip with Vince, Christian shaved his beard and had his hair trimmed to collar length before visiting his mother. He stood in her living room and stared at the decorated tree and the wrapped gifts beneath. He felt the moisture growing in his eyes and held his mouth and nose, preventing a sniffle. The holidays were supposedly a joyous time, but with the recent death of a loved one, they were the worst. This was his first Christmas without Allie since he met her. At home in Florida, his depression and suicidal urges were his constant companions. He felt like a rowboat in a horrific storm, swamped and sinking, the dark clouds closing in, and with no one around to bail him out.

For the sake of his mother, stepfather, and grandparents, he managed to maintain without so much as a tear, but they weren't fooled. He heard their hushed voices in the kitchen and saw their concerned looks. He was on a stage and failing miserably with his really-I'm-okay act. The family sat down to a quiet turkey dinner, and after opening gifts, he couldn't wait to leave.

Alone on the farm he wasn't much better. The horses in the pasture, the alligator meandering through the lake, the house, especially the bedroom, everywhere held memories and visions of Allie's face. The temptation to drink until unconscious was overwhelming. He had told Vince he would think about the New York trip, but he knew now. He had to go.

CHAPTER NINETEEN

A few days after New Year's, Christian threw his luggage into his SUV. He told Juan he would be on the beach with a friend and was uncertain when he would return. The FBI had questioned Juan about his whereabouts in Costa Rica. This time, that wouldn't happen. No one except Vince and some of his men would know he went north. He drove to Vince's house on Longboat Key and parked his SUV in the drive for all the neighbors to see. One of Sal's men drove Christian, Vince, and Sal to the Sarasota-Bradenton airport and dropped them off at Dolphin, the small hub for private jets. Wearing sunglasses and a sweatshirt, Christian pulled up the hood to hide his hair and face before stepping out of the car.

Sal glanced at Christian. "Kid, you look like a damn bank robber."

"Really? I was aiming for celebrity." Christian grinned. "I caught a lot of shit after my last trip. The FBI dragged me in for questioning, and I spent a night in jail. I don't want to have to watch my back in New York."

Sal chuckled. "What a wuss. One night in the slammer ain't shit. Well, you better've remembered a disposable phone. Goddamn cells are like homing devices."

"Learned that too, getting pinpointed in Jacó," said Christian as they strolled into the airport building. "I picked up a disposable and a new warm jacket."

"Yeah, New York can freeze your nuts off."

Christian noticed that Sal was being civil, almost friendly. Obviously, Vince had had a word with him, too, wanting them to get along.

One of the pilots told Vince the jet was ready. After their bags were stored in a tail compartment, Vince, Sal, and Christian climbed aboard the Lear and sat down in large creamy leather seats with polished wood interior and tables. The jet taxied to the runway and took off in half the distance of a commercial jet.

After the Lear leveled off, Sal said, "Kid, the bar's up front. Why don't you act like a stewardess and fix us some drinks."

Christian made cocktails for Sal and Vince and grabbed a Coke for himself. He sat down at a small table facing Vince and asked, "Is this your jet?"

"Owning a jet is a waste of money and for stuffed shirts. The plane's a lease run through a corporation. Cost four grand a trip, but there're no ID checks, no security, and no passenger list, unless you leave the country. We can pop in and out of airports with no one knowing."

Several hours later, the jet landed at JFK. Christian stepped out under dreary, overcast skies, and a freezing air blast left him shivering. His teeth chattered, and he saw his breath on the wind. "Damn, it's frigging cold here," he said and hastily threw on his new leather jacket.

Sal laughed. "That jacket ain't gonna keep your skinny butt warm. Better do more shoppin'."

Outside the airport, they parted ways with Sal catching a cab bound for his home in Brooklyn, but he said he would see them tomorrow. Christian and Vince climbed in the back of a black Town Car that drove them toward Vince's home on the Upper West Side.

On the ride through the city, Christian traveled through the man-made canyons created by the tall buildings and stared at the crowded sidewalks and the bumper-to-bumper yellow cabs. The Town Car passed a fire truck parked with blinking lights on, and a fireman stood center street, cursing at a cabbie. While stuck in traffic, Christian looked at a horse-drawn buggy in the next lane. Amid the honking horns, sirens, and shouts, the bay gelding kept its head down, its eyes lacking spirit or life. The downtrodden creature was a far cry from his Thoroughbreds that would have broken their legs to escape this city. He could relate.

"What'd ya think of New York?" Vince asked.

"Don't think it's for me."

They arrived at Vince's home located on Eighty-Fifth between Broadway and Central Park. Christian looked up at the barren trees that lined the street and the three-story townhouses, all connected but separated by various colors of gray or brown block or red brick. "This is the fancy area?"

"Yeah," said Vince, "my little slice of New York, probably worth more than my waterfront home in Florida. Let's get inside before you freeze."

Christian stepped in and gazed at the hardwood floors and Oriental rugs. Off the foyer, the living room was furnished with a rich, velour couch, oversized cherry leather chairs, and antique tables. With walnut walls and heavy velvet curtains, the place had the feel and smell of dark old wool, warm, but cheerless. It was a big contrast from Vince's Florida home of light marble floors, bright floral rattans, and endless windows bringing sky and sea inside.

"We're on our own," Vince said, and led Christian upstairs to a spare bedroom. "I didn't bother calling in the housekeeper, since we're not going to be here long." He opened the bedroom door.

"Nice," Christian said, dropping his bag at the foot of a large canopy bed with carved wooden posts. Out the window, he glimpsed Central Park down the street. After settling in, they left for dinner, taking a taxi several blocks to a corner restaurant called Harry's on Ninety-Sixth. A waitress came to their table, and Christian ordered sweet tea.

She seemed confused. "Sweet tea?"

"Just bring him an iced tea and some sugar," said Vince. "I'll have a scotch on the rocks." He turned to Christian. "You're out of luck if you're expecting sweet tea, collards, or grits here. You're in the North, boy."

Over a pasta dinner, Vince said he would be busy with phone

calls and meetings the next day. "Why don't you get a map and take in the city? And Sal's right about your jacket. You need to pick up something warmer. The best deals are in the garment district."

Early the next morning, Christian dressed in everything warm he had, jeans, a t-shirt covered by a black cashmere sweater—a gift from Allie—and the thin brown jacket. He slipped on his sunglasses and skipped down the brownstone steps as eager as a kid on an adventure in the big city. *Everyone talks about New York. There must be something to it.*

He strolled east toward Central Park, deciding to see it first. On the sidewalk he passed people walking dogs, pushing strollers, or hurrying off to work. Being from the South, he smiled and nodded to those making eye contact with him but was met with somber glances and frowns. *Guess smiles here are as rare as sweet tea.*

In the park, he ambled down the empty paths that were surrounded by a bleak brown landscape. He sat down on a bench and crossed his arms, sticking his hands under his armpits for warmth, and watched several pigeons squabble over a bread crust. Beyond, a bum and his brown mutt slept bundled in a tattered blanket beneath a stark tree. He was not impressed with Central Park, but with spring leaves and flowers, he imagined it was probably beautiful. He loved the outdoors, but within twenty minutes, he was miserable. The bone-chilling weather drove him out of the park and into the closest store. At the register he bought a city map.

With a destination in mind, he headed for Broadway, one of the main streets through town. On the median between traffic lanes, he found the underground subway station. He had considered a cab, but using the subway was part of the journey. For several minutes he watched commuters come and go through an iron gate, but he couldn't find a sign with the prices or information on how to get on the subway. He approached an officer, a hefty black woman.

"I'm new here and have never ridden the subway," he said. "How do I get on?"

"Where do you want to go?"

He glanced at his map and pointed to the garment district, planning to buy a warmer jacket. "Here, I guess."

"Round trip will cost five dollars." She took him to a machine and helped him convert his cash into tokens. She explained where to switch trains and where to get off. "Think you got it?" she said, beaming at him.

"Yes, and thanks for your help," he said, appreciating her smile.

Christian walked through the gate and boarded the train. Nearly a half hour later, he got off but was surprised, finding himself in Chinatown. Referring to the map, he saw he'd gotten off at the wrong stop, but the garment district was within walking distance. He wandered the jam-packed sidewalks of mostly Asians and stepped around garbage bags piled knee deep on the curbs. In between the bags, street peddlers shouted at him as they stood near their card tables laden with merchandise, hoping to sell him a watch, t-shirt, or souvenir. He passed small jewelry and gift shops, an occasional Chinese restaurant, and open-air stores with low tables containing fresh produce or seafood, some fish species unfamiliar to him. At one of these stores, he stopped short and stared at the slender gray fish a few feet long that rested pathetically on the crushed ice. Despite their missing heads, fins, and tails, he recognized the baby sharks. Those fish, combined with his sadness and anger, made an unpalatable dish.

An old Chinese man wearing a fish gut-stained apron approached him. "You want fish? I help you. What you want?" he asked.

Christian pushed down his disgust and asked, "Do you have shark fins?"

The Chinese man stared at him and abruptly walked away, not answering his question. *Shit, just like Puntarenas. Touchy subject.*

Christian pressed on and entered the next seafood store. He saw more baby sharks, but no fins. He again inquired about shark fins and, again, he received the same cold treatment. He had a new agenda, buying a jacket forgotten. He stopped at every restaurant and examined the menus posted outside. Under soups, shark fin was not listed, but each had an inexplicit soup with no explanation of the contents, which was outrageously priced at as much as twenty dollars a cup. All other soups were only five dollars. Probably to avoid public ridicule and hide that the broth contained shark fins, each restaurant had come up with the various soup names such as Chang's Seafood Special or Seafood Delight.

In a Chinese grocery store, he finally found the fins for sale. Shelves from the floor to the ceiling held huge jars containing dried sea cucumbers, starfish, abalone, and thousands of seahorses. Seahorses, like sharks, were facing their own extinction, with the Chinese demand. Hundreds upon hundreds of dried shark fins filled the glass containers. They were lumped together according to size and price, starting at $175 a pound for a four-inch fin and going up to $800 a pound for those measuring two feet, coming from massive old sharks. He put on a tourist-face smile and stepped up to the little female clerk behind the counter.

"My five-year-old son loves sharks," he explained. "He'd go crazy if I came home with one of those fins. How much does one cost?"

The Chinese girl bought his bullshit and grinned. She went to the jars and scale. Christian picked out a small fin, and she weighed it. "Fourteen dollar," she said.

"I'll take it." He paid her, and she placed it in a brown bag.

He headed up the street to a small city park. In the center was a large statue of an Asian man in a long coat. Chinese men sat at picnic tables and played some sort of board game. Nearby, a group of musicians played traditional Chinese music as old people, children, and their mothers rested on benches, talking. He didn't hear one word of English.

Christian gazed out at the hundreds of Chinese and saw he was the only Caucasian. He took the fin from the bag and ran his finger over its smooth surface. It had belonged to a shark, one of a precious few born, and then the little shark beat the overwhelming odds and survived its first year. It had probably taken another four or five years to reach the size matching this fin. All that luck of survival, and it lost its life for a ridiculous myth. It died for prestige, greed, ignorance, and fourteen dollars.

He put the shark fin back in the bag and looked out in the park at the Chinese faces and listened to their chatter and laughter while wondering about the people who felt no remorse for wiping out sharks and countless other species.

Toward evening, Christian returned to Vince's home and opened the front door with a key that Vince had given him. Standing in the study doorway, he saw Vince at his desk, shuffling papers and appearing weary.

"Hey, Vince," Christian said, and strolled into the room. "Sorry I'm late."

Vince looked up and his face brightened. "Didn't hear you come in. You'd make a good burglar." He leaned back in the leather chair. "So you took in the city. Have any problems getting around?"

"None, but still don't see all the hype about New York, or it could be I'm just splitting hairs. This morning I visited Central Park and then rode the subway to Chinatown. That was interesting."

"The subway?" Vince said. "I haven't used it since I was your age. When I get done with this work, I'll take you around and show you the sights. We'll take in a museum and maybe catch an opera or a Broadway play."

Christian sat down in a chair opposite the desk. "An opera, Vince?" he said with a grin. "Don't get all sophisticated for my sake."

"I saw one once. My wife dragged me to it."

"What's with this work? I thought you retired."

"Me too," Vince said with a sigh, "but my old partners are pitching a fit. Want me back in, but enough of that. Did you buy anything?"

"Actually, I did." He retrieved the bag and placed the shark fin on the desk.

Vince examined it. "You bought this? I thought you wanted to *protect* these fish."

"I needed something to look at and hold, a reminder of what I'm doing and why. The Chinese grocery stores have thousands of fins. Maybe I should bring my fight here instead of burning down warehouses in insignificant countries. If I take out a few stores, it sends a message to the others and their customers. And we're talking New York. The publicity for Nemo's cause would be huge."

"Yeah, you're also talking about serious heat. You're already a person of interest in those arsons, and Wheeler is one hard-ass. If he believes you're Nemo, you'd better keep your head down."

"I don't care about that. All those fins—" He shook his head. "It's sickening, Vince. I'm taking out those stores, with or without your help."

"I can see that." Vince rose, stepped to a small bar, and fixed a drink. "You know how to pull it off? You can hardly motor up in a boat and toss a bottle of gas. Most stores have alarms, motion sensors, surveillance video, and shatterproof windows. And the fucking street cameras are everywhere. A tall blond in Chinatown sticks out like a sore thumb."

"I know. That's probably the reason I was beaten up in Puntarenas. I would have had less hassle with a Chinese face."

Vince sat down with his drink and thumbed his mustache in thought. "Okay," he finally said. "Tomorrow Sal and I are having lunch in Little Italy, meeting someone on another matter. You need to come along. Maybe I can get you that face." He took a sip of his cocktail and set it down. "Christian, my boy, your education in crime is about to begin."

The next day, Christian and Vince stepped to the curb in front of the townhouse and climbed into Sal's black car, unsurprisingly, another Cadillac. Sal drove them to Little Italy, a few blocks from Chinatown and stopped at a red brick restaurant with the name *Vince's* on the maroon awnings. "You own this place?" Christian asked.

"Hardly," said Vince. "It's been called *Vince's* since 1904. I'm old, but not that old." Leaving the car, he walked to an elderly man standing outside the restaurant. "Joseph, how ya doin'?"

"Oh, Mr. Florio, I'm fine, just fine, but the neighborhood—" Joseph said with a headshake. "Chinatown is closing in and the clothing shops are taking over. They even tried to limit the street space for the Feast of San Gennaro. It's terrible. Soon Little Italy will be gone." He held up his bag. "And you won't be able to buy a cannoli."

Vince offered up his palms. "Blame Giuliani; he chased out the good people who ran roughshod over the neighborhood and kept the trash from moving in."

As Sal, Vince, and the old man talked, Christian shuddered in the frigid weather and mumbled, "I'll meet you guys inside." He stepped into the small restaurant and saw a bar that faced several wooden tables in the dining room, its walls covered with celebrity photos.

"No goddamn pictures," ranted the Italian proprietor with a plug-ugly mug. He stood behind the register and faced a woman holding a camera and take-out menu. He snatched the flimsy paper menu from her hand. "Those cost money, and you're not ordering anything."

The woman stepped back. "I'm a writer and you, sir, have just made it into my next novel." With a huff, she brushed past Christian and went out the door.

"Bitch," the proprietor grumbled and then noticed Christian. "And what do you want?"

"Tony, he's with me," Vince said, stepping inside with Sal.

"Mr. Florio, I'm sorry. I didn't know," said Tony, suddenly obliging. "Welcome, welcome back, I have your table ready."

New Yorkers sure are friendly, Christian thought cynically. In his home state, they had gained the reputation for being uppity, impatient, and sometimes even rude, unlike other northerners. Putting prejudgements aside, he had arrived open-minded in this culture capital of the world, but so far, New Yorkers were running true to form.

Tony led them across the tiny white-tiled floor and seated them at the back table with a street view.

"Get the spaghetti, kid," Sal said. "It's got incredible gravy."

Halfway through lunch, Sal nodded toward the window. "There he is."

Christian saw a dark-blue Lexus pull up to the curb and a trim Chinese man in his thirties stepped from the car. Nicely dressed in a black coat and silk shirt, he entered the restaurant but didn't acknowledge the diners. He walked with purpose past the register toward the kitchen and disappeared.

Vince rose. "Finish your lunch, Christian. We'll be back in a few." Sal stuffed a forkful of spaghetti in his mouth and followed Vince. They also vanished around the corner. Twenty minutes later, the Chinese man reappeared. At the door, he hesitated and looked directly at Christian before stepping outside. He drove away in his car, and Vince and Sal returned to the table.

"Okay, you're meeting with him tomorrow at two," Vince said and handed Christian a scribbled-on napkin. "Here's the address. Give him your spiel and tell him what you need."

"Who is he?" Christian asked.

"Lee Chow, a head honcho in the Flying Dragons. It's a Chinese gang," Vince said. "We used to do a lot of business together."

"You're not coming?"

"Kid," said Sal, "you know the boss don't get involved."

Christian recalled that Sal had handled everything when Christian smuggled drugs from the Gulf for Vince. The only exception had been when Vince came along as an extra pair of hands during the hurricane.

"Christian, you're determined to do this. It's your deal," said Vince. "I'm just opening doors, but this time it'll be done professionally, no half-ass bottle tossing. Chow is somewhat of a jerk, but for the right money, he'll have one of his boys plant the bombs. You just need to plan and pay for it."

A bitter, drizzling rain fell when they finished lunch and stepped outside. Under the restaurant awning, Vince said, "Give Sal your driver's license. He'll get you a fake ID, new passport, and license.

That way you can skip town anonymously." Sal put Christian's license in his pocket, and the three men hustled to the Caddy. Vince settled into the backseat. "Sal, also contact our little squirrelly friend. I'm thinking a small plastic with a timer."

"He can handle that." Sal turned the ignition and grinned when glancing over his shoulder at Vince. "Just like old times, eh, boss?"

The following day the weather had become even colder with yesterday's rain. Christian left the townhouse and hustled down the icy sidewalk. Smatterings of snow flurries had gathered at the bases of trees, their branches decorated with icicles. He clutched his arms and grumbled, "God, I need to buy that damn jacket."

He reached Broadway, hailed a taxi, and communicated the address on the napkin to the Ethiopian driver. During the ride, he reflected on the previous night's discussion with Vince and Sal. Two Chinatown grocery stores that sold shark fins would be bombed in the wee morning hours, to avoid victims. Christian would be the go-to man, the backer and the brains, but would not participate in the event or be in town when the crime occurred. Christian disliked that part, saying he should be there and he'd look like a coward if he wasn't.

"Bullshit," Vince had growled. "I wasn't born yesterday. You get high off burning and bombing, but get over it and start using your head. This is your party, but you're not going. You need to distance yourself from Nemo's attack and have an airtight alibi to throw off the FBI."

In the end, Christian agreed. He realized he did get a satisfaction high when watching a building go up in flames. It was like hitting the home run that won the game, but more importantly, he felt the weight of guilt lift from his shoulders because he was doing it for Allie. Saving the sharks and oceans was secondary.

He glanced out the window and saw he was in Chinatown. When the taxi pulled up to a small, rundown shop that opened to the street, he questioned the driver.

"This is the address you gave me," said the cabbie. "That'll be thirty-three bucks."

Christian handed him two twenties. "Keep it," he said and climbed out onto the sidewalk. For a minute he stared into the shop, able to see its entire contents. One side held shelves of perfume boxes, and the other walls were covered with purses. Toward the back, two Chinese saleswomen, one old, one young, stood near a table of folded t-shirts. He saw no back door that led to an office or storage room and no Lee Chow. He rechecked the address, thinking one of the numbers was incorrectly jotted down.

The old woman walked to the storefront. "Come in, come in and get warm," she called and waved him in. "We have nice purses for your sweetheart, maybe some perfume."

He pushed his sunglasses to the top of his head and stepped inside, deciding to thoroughly check out the store before notifying Vince. "Don't have a girl," he said and meandered to the table. He unfolded a t-shirt and smiled, reading the caption that said "Don't piss me off. I'm running out of places to hide the bodies." Thinking it would make a good gift for Vince, he handed it to the old woman. "I'll take this one."

"No girl," said the old woman with a Chinese accent. "You need nice cologne, get one."

"Momma, I think he'd be more interested in a purse," said the young salesclerk.

"I'm not with anyone, but I do like girls," he said, making it clear he wasn't gay.

"Oh, I didn't mean—" she stuttered anxiously. "I mean I'm glad you like girls."

He glanced up from the shirts and smiled, taking notice of her. She was close to his age and resembled a china doll, with her porcelain skin, a petite frame, long shimmering black hair, tiny nose and mouth, and dark almond-shaped eyes. "Maybe I can buy a purse for my mother," he said, a sorry excuse to stay in the shop and talk to her. She was definitely pretty, and he knew with her nervousness, she liked him too.

"Come, I'll show you some purses."

He followed her midshop into a slight corner, barely visible from the street. He looked up at the hanging handbags and unhooked a brown leather one. Examining it, he felt foolish and muttered, "I never bought a purse before. What do you think? Is this a good one?"

"They're all garbage." She rehung the brown bag and pulled a small walkie-talkie from her pocket. "He's here," she whispered into the receiver. "We're coming down." She parted the merchandise and pressed against the wall, revealing a low trapdoor. "Hurry now, but watch your step. The stairs are steep."

"You . . . you work for Chow?" he asked a little surprised, ducking beneath the purses and slipping through the door.

"He's my brother," she said and closed the door behind him. She followed him down the shadowy narrow staircase, the wooden steps creaking with their weight. At the bottom was a dingy brick basement that appeared to be more than a century old. With its musty aroma, it smelled like it too. A crude bare bulb hung from the ceiling and gave enough light to see a display of hanging purses. Christian was ignorant about handbags, but he did know name brands. Seeing Chanel, Gucci, and Louis Vuitton on some of the bags, he figured they were illegal knockoffs.

"You made it," said a man's voice.

Christian turned and saw Lee Chow sitting on a stool. Behind him, two young Chinese men stood with hardcore looks and mean eyes. Both sported dragon tattoos on their arms. "Yeah, I made it," he said coolly, sensing hostility. This was no friendly get-together. He stepped to Chow and crossed his arms. "Thanks for the meeting."

"As a favor to our Italian friend, I will hear you out. He mentioned you'd pay well," said Chow. "What do you want?"

"I need to hire a man to plant two bombs in a few Chinatown grocery stores. The explosions should go off after hours, so no one will get hurt, not even the cleaning crews. I'm willing to pay fifty grand for the job."

"You want me to help you blow up my neighborhood?" Chow sneered and slid off the stool. "Why do you want to do such a thing?"

"Those stores carry thousands of shark fins for Chinese soup. Because of that soup, sharks are facing extinction. It's wrong. I want to send a message and stop it."

"So this isn't about insurance fraud, competition, or revenge? You're just a fanatic with an agenda, and you need someone to do your dirty work." Chow slowly meandered around Christian. "You're tan and speak with a slight southern accent. You're not from around here."

"I'm from Florida," said Christian.

"Florida," Chow said with a sardonic chuckle. "That's where old people go to die."

"And 9/11 terrorists learn to fly," Christian said, making it a poem.

"Yes, heat does breed scum." Lee stepped to Christian, and they were face-to-face. "Florida, you're lucky the Italian is your friend. You want to attack my city, culture, and people. I've killed others for less."

"I'm getting the feeling you're not interested in the job."

Chow nodded at his sister, who stood in the shadows behind Christian. "Lin, take this southern trash out before I change my mind and have Roy and Charlie do it."

Christian started up the flight of stairs with Lin following. Chow called after him, "By the way, Florida, I eat fin soup every day. Brings me good luck and makes my dick hard." The men cackled.

Christian hesitated on the steps.

"Keep moving," Lin whispered and touched his back, pressing him upward. "My brother is hoping to provoke you so he can hurt you."

At the store register, Christian dug out his wallet to pay for the t-shirt. "That didn't go over well," he said to Lin.

"What will you do now?"

He shrugged. "Take care of it myself. I wasn't big on hiring help in the first place."

Lin glanced around and whispered, "You can't. You just can't. The stores have surveillance cameras, and you stand out. After the bomb-ing, the videos will show you in both stores, and you'll be caught."

"The blast should take care of the cameras and tapes."

"But there will be witnesses who remember you in the stores, and there are also street cameras."

Christian chewed his lip with a curious half frown, half smile. "Why should you care?"

She pulled a *Washington Post* out from under the counter. "Have you read this today?" She pointed to an article on the second page titled "Captain Nemo Strikes Again."

Christian scanned the article that gave an account of the arsons in the Bahamas and Costa Rica and called Captain Nemo an eco-terrorist who left messages about his cause to save sharks. It mentioned Jules Verne's novel and his controversial Nemo character and listed shark statistics, proving the Chinese soup was causing their demise. The article was far from condemning, saying Nemo was taking a stand for wildlife, and it never mentioned the missing trawler and crew.

"You're him. You're Captain Nemo, aren't you?"

Christian raised his eyebrows. "Mind if I keep this paper?"

"I need to talk to you. Where do you go from here?"

"Uptown, Eighty-Fifth between Broadway and the park," he said.

"Good, we can't be seen together here." She looked around sus-piciously. "Meet me in an hour in front of the American Museum of Natural History by the statue facing Central Park."

With the paper and t-shirt bag in hand, Christian left the shop and caught a cab. He arrived at the massive stone-block museum with giant white pillars less than a mile from Vince's townhouse. Outside the entrance was a large bronze statue of an Indian standing alongside a white man mounted on a horse. Icicles hung from the statue and resembled large teeth biting out at the chill. Christian stood on the sidewalk stomping his feet and hugging his arms. He couldn't imagine dealing with such weather month after month.

He reflected on Lin, the Chinese girl, and wondered why she wanted to talk. He shuddered, wishing they had chosen to meet inside.

CHAPTER TWENTY

"A twist of fate," Lin mumbled and watched the blond Floridian slip into the cab. It sped away, blending with traffic. Her day had started like most others, picking up the *Washington Post* before work. A recent graduate of American University in DC, she still felt a connection to the capital and bought the *Post*. She had obtained her degree in environmental politics, but jobs were scarce, and she was forced to return to New York and her mother's shop. The four years away had been enlightening and changed her outlook on life.

Early that morning, she'd read the article about Captain Nemo and found herself admiring the mysterious man who wanted to save sharks, but she never dreamed she would meet him. Around noon, she was helping a customer pick out perfume when her brother and his two thugs, Charlie and Roy, entered the store.

Lee motioned her aside. "At two o'clock, a blond guy in his twenties will come in. Bring him downstairs."

She lifted a skeptical eyebrow. "Another pusher, Lee?" she asked. "I told you I'm done with your lousy gang. I'm not going to be a look-out, drug mule, or messenger anymore."

He grabbed her wrist and twisted until she cringed with pain. "My gang and business paid for your fucking education, and the only thing I got was a cunt sister. You'll do as I say."

"All right, all right, I'll bring him down." Lee released her, and she rubbed her aching wrist with teary eyes.

At two o'clock, the young blond man had wandered up to the store, and her mother went into sales-pitch mode, coaxing him inside. Lin knew he was the one that Lee wanted to see in the basement, but she felt paralyzed. This guy was so gorgeous she couldn't move. His lanky frame meandered through the shop as he occasionally flicked the locks out of his ocean-blue eyes, and his mentioning he was single made him even more attractive. At the table, he read a t-shirt caption and revealed a lady-killer smile. He handed the shirt to her mother and appeared to be finished shopping.

Lin managed to get her hormones in check and approached him, but stupidly blurted out that he'd be interested in purses. He assumed she thought he was a homosexual. With his pretty-boy face and slender build, he was probably a little defensive and explained he liked girls. She took him to the basement and listened to the discussion between him and Lee about bombing two grocery stores because they sold shark fins. Lee rejected the job, acting as if he cared about his neighborhood, which was a lie. Lee didn't care about anything or anyone and was not above destroying a local store. It was envy. Florida was everything he wasn't. Before any discussion, she saw it in her brother's eyes and knew Lee would not help him.

During their meeting, she made the correlation between the *Post* article and the blond. He had to be Captain Nemo, the daring man who had stepped up to save sharks.

Before leaving to meet him, she hurriedly brushed her hair, put on fresh makeup, and told her mother she was taking the rest of day off. She climbed into a cab and felt the nervousness in the pit of her stomach. Approaching the museum, she directed the cab to a side street to survey the visitors, making sure no one knew her. If Lee found out, it would be bad for her and Mr. Florida, regardless of his Italian connections. In the distance, he was easy to spot with his sun-bleached hair and standing half a head taller than the other tourists.

She pulled her hood up and walked to him, seeing that he was freezing. *Poor thing, out of his element,* she thought, *I'd give anything to warm him up.* She tapped his shoulder, and he whirled around. "Florida, you need a warmer coat."

"So I've been told," he said, quivering. "Let's go in. Your Yankee weather is about to do me in." He smiled. "By the way, it's Christian."

They hurried up the steps and entered the museum. In the lobby, he immediately strolled to the towering skeleton of a T. rex and looked up starry-eyed at the dinosaur. "Wouldn't it have been great to meet him?"

"No thanks." Lin migrated to his side and looked up into his heart-stopping blue eyes. "Why do you want to save sharks?"

Christian nodded at the dinosaur. "Don't want them ending up like him, extinct and a rack of bones in a museum."

"I believe in your cause, and I'm not alone. Most of the younger generation Chinese realize those old traditions have to stop. They're destroying what little wildlife is left. It's criminal."

"Your brother is obviously not one of them."

"My brother has no honor or principles. He rejected the job because he's always been a jealous asshole, and you're, well, you're nice looking."

They wandered through the museum and talked about sharks and the environment while taking in the exhibits. Some were the stuffed animals from various continents, and other displays were skeletons of prehistoric mammals and dinosaurs. Christian was engrossed, no doubt an animal lover, but when they entered the Hall of Ocean Life, he became unglued.

"Wow, check out this guy," he said gazing at a Megalodon shark. "Can you imagine swimming with him? It would have been great."

Lin grinned at his little-boy excitement. Besides his looks, Christian was fun, genuine, and interesting, yet a mystery. He revealed little about himself or his life in Florida. Lin had no secrets and told him about her tough life growing up in Chinatown as part of her brother's gang and then going to college, a move that altered her values.

After a while, he got around to asking. "So why did you want to talk to me?"

"I'll do the job, plant the bombs in the stores. If I get the fifty thousand, I'll be free of my brother and this city. And I care more about the environment than a dated culture. Any business, Chinese or not, should be blown up if they're selling shark fins."

He pushed his locks back and sighed, uncertainty showing in his eyes. "I can't let you do it, Lin. It's too dangerous. If you need money to get away, I'll give it to you."

"You're a pretty sweet guy, but, Christian, I want to do it. First off, you're not talking to some little Chinese girl who's lived a sheltered life. I used to run drugs for my brother, and that was far more dangerous than hiding a bomb in a store. I spent four years in college studying the environment, hoping I could make a difference. Now I've met a guy with a cause who is making a real difference. Our meeting was a twist of fate. We were destined to help each other."

"You remind me of someone," he said with soft anguish. "She was small, pretty, and fearless. God, she wasn't afraid of anything." He shook his head. "It killed her, Lin. She died helping me. If things go wrong, I can't have you on my conscience too."

"Nothing will go wrong. I can slip into those stores without notice. If you do it, you'll be caught." She took his hand, lacing her small fingers through his long ones. "And this world can't afford to lose Captain Nemo."

Christian entered Vince's home at eleven in the evening and heard the TV in the family room. He strolled in with his two shopping bags and saw Vince stretched out on the couch, watching a program. "Hi, Vince."

Vince sat up. "Where the hell you been? I was about to call Sal, have him go Chinatown to hunt down Chow. I was afraid you and that jerk might've got into it. I tried your cell a million times."

"Shit, I left it upstairs on the charger. Sorry about that."

Vince grabbed the remote and turned off the TV. "How did it go? Is Chow gonna find someone for the job?"

"It didn't go." Christian shrugged out of his new heavy-duty London Fog and plopped down in a large stuffed chair. "He wasn't too excited about me wanting to blow up his neighborhood. But I found someone else. We took in a museum, did some shopping, and had dinner. She helped me pick out some warmer clothes and a jacket."

Vince leaned forward. "She?"

"Yeah, I'm not too happy about that either. She's Chow's sister, but doesn't want him to know she's helping me. It turns out she's pretty tough and an environmentalist—thinks it's great I'm trying to save sharks."

Vince frowned. "Baloney. That girl got a glimpse of you and was smitten. She's doing it for you."

"That's not it. She's planting the bombs for the money, wants to leave town and get away from her brother. And she's into saving the environment."

"Yeah, yeah, Christian, wake up. You're a clever kid, but not the best terrorist. You need to start using your God-given gift. Men would kill for your looks, and you gotta know how you affect women. It's time you use that asset to your advantage."

"I know women like me, but I'm not a use-'em-and-lose-'em kind of guy."

"You slay me." Vince laughed. "You can burn, bomb, and murder, but you get a conscience when it comes to a girl's feelings. Look at James Bond. He has no problem seducing and using women with his charm and looks. They get him out of all sorts of jams."

"Bond is a chauvinistic pig."

"Maybe, but women love him. Think of yourself then as Charlie with his angels. You already got the Chinese girl."

Christian rolled his eyes. "I think you've seen too many movies and TV shows." He reached in one of his bags and pulled out two boxes of tea. "We stopped at a store and bought these. Think the explosives will fit inside?"

Vince examined the box. "Should work. Don't forget to wipe off your fingerprints in case the bomb is discovered or doesn't go off. Sal's picking everything up Tuesday, including your new ID. You'll fly out Thursday night, so we're thinking Friday. You need to tell your girl, see if that works for her."

"I bought her a disposable phone so we can stay in touch. I also bought you something." Christian tossed the t-shirt to Vince.

Vince held up the shirt, read the caption, and chuckled. "Very funny, but hiding bodies? I believe this shirt fits you too."

"That reminds me." Christian handed the *Washington Post* to Vince, pointing out the article.

"Well, well," said Vince. "Looks like the captain's gettin' famous."

Over the next several days Christian spent most of his time with Lin, but never in Chinatown. It was too risky. He couldn't afford to be spotted and filmed on the streets, and Lin had to avoid her brother and his gang members. With the right companion, he was enjoying New York. The food in the restaurants was incredible, and the glamorous nightclubs made Sarasota's look like nursing homes. With the museums, theaters, concerts, and stores, there was no lack of entertainment in New York, and Christian almost wished his visit were longer.

He and Lin strolled the city streets after taking in an Off-Broadway play, and she told him how she had once admired and loved her older brother, but that was before she went to college, before she crossed him. Christian grew angry, hearing that Chow bullied and hurt her.

"For his sake, your brother and I better not cross paths again. I have no tolerance for a useless fucker who harms women." He stopped walking and faced her. "If you're doing this job to get away from Lee, I already said I'd help you. I'll get someone else for the job."

"No, I'm doing it, and not just for money to get away or to help sharks." She stood on her toes and kissed his check. "Christian, I'm doing this mostly for you."

Vince was right, he thought. He took her hands. "Lin, there's something you need to know. That woman I said reminded me of you, the woman who died. She was my wife. I'm not ready, not sure I'll ever be ready for another relationship."

Lin nodded. "When you talked about her, I figured as much."

She looked down. "You're telling me this because you know how I feel about you."

"I'm sorry. I never meant to lead you on."

"Don't be sorry. You've kept your distance and have been straight from the start about your priorities. I just hope when this is over, we can remain friends."

"Absolutely."

Wednesday afternoon, Lin checked into a hotel on Broadway, fearing her brother was becoming suspicious and she might be followed. Sal had picked up the small plastic explosives the previous night. He met Lin and Christian in her room and explained the timer before packing the bombs in tea boxes. She had brought two sets of clothes to disguise her appearance between grocery stores. Everything was set.

After Sal left, she and Christian walked up the street to a corner deli and ate Moroccan sandwich wraps and soup. They returned to the room with a to-go dessert and kicked back on the bed, nibbling the éclairs and talking until late.

"I guess I need to go. I have an early flight and haven't even packed my bag yet," Christian said and started to rise off the bed.

"I don't want you to go," she said and ran her hand across his chest.

"Lin, I don't think my staying is a good idea. You're my friend, my partner in crime, but I can't make a commit—" She leaned over, covered his mouth with a kiss, and placed her other hand on the crotch of his jeans. After a long celibacy, he was instantly aroused.

"No commitment, I just want you," she whispered and unzipped his jeans. "Consider it part of my payment."

He had thought of sleeping with her. She was sexy sweet, but he had many issues. Foremost was betraying Allie's memory, and then there were Lin's feelings. Sleeping with her was crossing the friendship line. He gazed at her while panting with the stimulation. She was risking her life for him. The least he could do was make love to her. And who knew how many tomorrows there were?

"Okay, okay," he breathed and leaned back on the pillow. *Terrorist, murderer, arsonist—I'm far from a frigging priest.*

On Thursday Christian dozed periodically on the Delta jet, exhausted from the marathon in the hotel the previous night. Lin was insatiable. He barely caught his breath after each climax before she encouraged him again. It was great and, amazingly, he did not feel guilty afterward. *Maybe there's something to this James Bond shit, love 'em and leave 'em happy, satisfied, and loyal.*

After an hour layover in Atlanta, the commercial jet touched down in Sarasota. In New York he had purchased his plane ticket at JFK, using his new fake ID, compliments of Sal's underworld connection. Outside the airport, he stepped into a warm breeze and cloudless golden sunset. He closed his eyes and inhaled the humid air that quenched his dry mouth, nose, and lungs. In the parking lot, several Quaker parakeets chirped in a nearby palm tree. *Florida. I was born and raised here, and I plan to die here. You never realize how good home is until you go away.*

He caught a cab that drove him out to Longboat Key and Vince's home. After ten days, his SUV waited for him in the driveway. Vince was still in New York, but would return to Florida later that night in the private jet. The less he and Christian were seen together, the better—fewer witnesses.

Christian settled into his vehicle and drove to his horse farm in Myakka City. At the house, he unlocked the front door and saw Juan walking up from the barn.

"Mr. Roberts, you're back," said Juan. "Did you have a good time?"

"Yeah, it was relaxing." He grinned, inwardly thinking of Lin and that he was really dog tired. "Everything okay here, the horses?"

"All is fine, but I think your gelding misses you. He hasn't been ridden since—" Juan lowered his head.

"Since I left for the Bahamas with Allie. I know. I plan to start riding again. It's just taken a while for me to get my head back on straight. I need to get caught up on bills and phone calls. We'll talk tomorrow."

"Okay, Mr. Roberts. It is good to have you home."

"I agree a hundred percent." He opened the door and walked into the small farmhouse with his carry-on bag. In the bedroom, he placed the bag on the floor and stared at his wedding photo on a dresser. Allie had been so lovely and happy that day. He picked up the picture and whispered, "I'm sorry about Lin, Allie, but she's taking a real gamble for our cause. I had to sleep with her." He sighed. "Yeah, right. You're not buying it. Shit, you know I'm not perfect." He set the picture down, collapsed on the bed, and hugged a pillow, realizing he hadn't lain on their bed since her death. He had slept on the living room couch. A whiff of her perfume on the pillowcase caused his eyes to water, and he moaned softly, "Allie, I keep wishing this was all a bad dream and I'd wake up and find you next to me."

CHAPTER TWENTY-ONE

In the agency car, Wheeler sat in the passenger seat and reviewed his notes as Ralph drove toward the office. They had spent a long, annoying day in a rough area of Homestead, knocking on doors and quizzing relatives, friends, and neighbors of Angel Garcia. Several months earlier, he had been released from prison and matched the MO for several recent bank robberies. That was the job: search, and research, question and requestion. As far as action, Wheeler had not had to pull his weapon in ten years.

"They either don't know where he is or are not saying," said Ralph.

"I'm betting half of them know, especially the trash-mouth sister. I'd enjoy throwing her in jail more than her brother. Tomorrow I'll get an order for a phone tap and hope the sister pans out."

"What about the others?"

"Forget them." Wheeler closed his notepad and leaned back in the seat. "They're as useless as a Slinky, good for a smile only when they fall down some stairs."

Ralph chuckled.

Wheeler's cell phone chimed. "What now? I was hoping to go home early for a change." He glanced at the number and didn't recognize the caller. "Wheeler."

"Hey, Dave," said a soft-spoken man. "I was thinkin' we got off on the wrong foot. I'd like to make it up to you with dinner tonight."

"Who's this?"

"Christian," he said. "You know, your murderer and arsonist."

"Christian? Christian Roberts?" Wheeler said, taken aback. Ralph glanced over, appearing stunned.

"That's right," said Christian. "The last time we parted ways, we were both unhappy. You didn't get your confession, and I spent a night in jail. I happen to be in Miami looking at a car, and I have no plans this evening. Despite everything, I respect you, Dave. It's a bummer we're adversaries, but maybe we could pass the olive branch over steak and drinks."

"You're full of surprises." Wheeler chuckled, hiding his suspicion. "Fine, we'll meet you."

"No we, just you," said Christian. "I'd like to have a friendly chat without the dimwitted partner, and please, no wires or surveillance." He told Wheeler the time and restaurant. "And Dave, there's one more thing."

"What's that?"

"Wear your suit. This place has a dress code."

Wheeler put his cell back into his pocket. "That's a first, a potential suspect buying me dinner. He's up to something."

"When we get back, Fred can wire us for undercover."

"He said no wires, surveillance, or partner."

"Who cares what he wants? He might say something incriminating, and you need the wire."

Roberts has a point. Ralph can be a dimwit. "We questioned him for hours, Ralph. You should know he's too smart to implicate himself. I'm playing his game by his rules. I'm curious to see what he wants."

"At least bring your gun. He *is* a murderer and dangerous."

At seven o'clock Wheeler arrived in South Beach and pulled up to the swanky restaurant on A1A across from the ocean. The valet took his keys and handed him a ticket. The place was definitely out of his budget. He strolled inside and told the pretty hostess his name.

"Right this way, Mr. Wheeler," she said.

He followed her and in the distance he saw Roberts at a window table. His chin rested on his laced fingers, and he stared out at the dark ocean with a dejected gaze. He looked totally different from when Wheeler last saw him. The scruffy beard and facial bruises were gone, along with the jeans. His long windblown locks had been trimmed to a stylish collar length. In a pricy black suit, he could easily pass as a model in a men's magazine.

Wheeler and the hostess approached the table. "Mr. Roberts, your party has arrived," she said, staring at him like he was dessert, good enough to eat.

Christian turned from the view and flashed a smile more with his eyes than his mouth. "Thank you for coming, Dave." He rose and put out his hand.

"You clean up well," Wheeler said, shaking his hand and sitting down. "I was a little surprised you called. You said you'd never speak to me again."

"I had a change of heart." He glanced at Wheeler with eyes as clear as blue sky and yet unreadable.

"Does that mean you're ready to confess?"

"Confess to what?"

"You and I both know you're guilty."

"You digging, me denying; it's work. Let's enjoy the evening." The waiter approached the table, and Christian handed him a black American Express card. "Make sure my friend and I have the best." The waiter stared wide-eyed at the black card with unlimited credit that required a special invitation. "Yes, sir. Yes, sir, Mr. Roberts."

"What would you like to drink, Dave?" Christian asked.

"Scotch and water is fine."

"Make it a nineteen seventy-five Glenrothes or the oldest you have," Christian said to the waiter. "I'll have another martini, stirred." He smiled as if it were a private joke.

"You're down here to look at a car? It's a long ways to drive."

"Miami has the closest Ferrari dealership. They have a black one, a few years old, with only three hundred miles, but it's nearly the same price as a new one. Did you know there's a ten-year waiting list for a new Ferrari? It's ridiculous."

"Are you buying the car to impress the girls?"

"Come on, Dave."

Wheeler chuckled. "No, I guess not." He was amazed with Roberts's transformation and not just his cleaned-up look and expensive rags. He behaved like a polished, sophisticated gentleman. Wheeler realized he was dealing with a true chameleon.

Over drinks and a steak dinner, the best in Wheeler's memory, they talked about a variety of subjects: cars, boats, the economy, and Everglades restoration. Wheeler had known Roberts was bright, but he found the young man was a treasure trove of knowledge, well read, and interesting.

"When you come to Sarasota, we'll go sailing."

"What makes you think I'm going to Sarasota?" Wheeler asked. "It's not my area."

Christian's lips curled into a mischievous grin. "You're a hound that's caught the scent. I know you'll be visiting me. Besides, you think I'm the infamous Captain Nemo. How could you resist a boat ride with him?"

Wheeler chuckled. "I suppose that would be worthwhile."

They seemed like old friends, chatting over a dinner. Wheeler told him about his day, trying to get a lead on the bank robber. Roberts became engrossed, asking questions and trying to puzzle out the case. Wheeler was enjoying Roberts's company, but there was the job. Relaxed with a few martinis in him, Roberts might open up.

"You were in Costa Rica for quite a while. Must've been fun."

Christian wagged his finger and gave him a thought-we-weren't-going-to-go-there look. He nodded to the waiter, who promptly came to the table. "Dave, you want some dessert, an after-dinner drink?"

"No, I'm stuffed. Best scotch and steak I've ever had. Thanks."

The waiter brought the bill and Christian scribbled his name and the tip. The waiter looked at the bill. "Thank you, Mr. Roberts, please come again."

"Leave a good tip, and they don't forget your face," said Christian, "Guarantees great service next time."

They walked outside the restaurant into a strong wind blowing off the Atlantic. "So, are you going to buy the Ferrari?" Wheeler asked.

"You think I'll need a fast getaway car?"

"I do." Wheeler laughed. "I'm not sure what this dinner was about, but if you were hoping to change my opinion of you, it has. I like you, Christian, but I'm still going to arrest you."

"I'd buy you a whole restaurant if I thought it would get you off my back," Christian joked, "but I'm glad we did this. If not for the circumstances, I believe we could be friends." He gazed up at the stars and breathed deeply. "God, it's a glorious night, too nice to waste inside a hotel."

"Let's walk. I'm not in a hurry," said Wheeler. They crossed the street to the sidewalk that ran along a wide stretch of dark beach with the distant sound of crashing waves. "I know you didn't kill your wife, but you killed her murderer. Whether it was self-defense or pure revenge, I understand your motives. But those arsons—why, Christian?"

Christian stopped, leaned over the barrier, and placed his arms on the railing, and gazed out at the dark ocean. "Did you know that indifference is the most powerful force in the world, more powerful than hate, greed, or even love? Indifference doesn't take action against injustices, but allows—lets bad things happen, like the extinction of a species. Indifference is why this planet is in trouble." He turned to Wheeler. "Do you have any kids?" he asked. Several evening bicyclists, joggers, and strollers passed them on the sidewalk.

"I have an eighteen-year-old daughter who started college, but I'm divorced, and I don't see her as often as I'd like."

"A daughter, that's nice." He sighed and looked back at the watery black horizon that shimmered in the moonlight. "Right before Allie died, we were trying for kids. A son would've been great, but I was hoping for a daughter. I'm better with girls." He pulled himself up to his full height. "You wanted to know why this Captain Nemo burns boats and warehouses? He's taking on indifference, hoping to save the oceans for our children. He doesn't want to explain to them that he did nothing to prevent this tragedy."

"But it's wrong, Christian. Arson is against the law."

"Perhaps the law is wrong, and people who wipe out a species are committing the greater crime. Once sharks are gone, the ocean environment will collapse. It's a matter of perspective."

"Could be, but until the laws change, I have to enforce them," said Wheeler. "You keep going, and you'll be caught."

A young woman with shoulder-length dark hair approached, talking on her cell phone. Wheeler noticed she had an uncanny resemblance to his daughter. She walked past them, unaware of a large man who was trailing her. As the man rambled past, Wheeler took a long hard look at his bulldog mug. "Motherfucker," he murmured and pulled out his cell phone. "Christian, I gotta go."

He took up the pursuit, tagging behind the man while hectically making the 911 call. "This is Agent Wheeler, FBI," he said in a hushed voice to the dispatcher. "I need police backup. I just spotted Larry Holt, a suspect in four murders. He's walking north along the waterfront on A1A in South Beach, and I'm following him on foot." He glanced over his shoulder for an exact address and noticed Christian had disappeared.

Up ahead at a break in the barrier, the girl left the sidewalk and went down several steps that opened up to the unlit public beach. Holt followed her. Wheeler hurried to the stairway, realizing he couldn't wait for help. If he didn't act, Holt would be lost on the pitch-black coastline. He pulled the Beretta from his shoulder harness, skipped down the stairs, and saw Holt's huge shadow near a cluster of palm trees.

"Hold it!" he shouted and pointed his weapon at the suspect. "FBI. Put your hands up." Holt stopped in his tracks and turned as Wheeler cautiously moved closer. "I said hands in the air."

Instead of complying, Holt lunged at Wheeler. His Beretta discharged, missing Holt and fell into the sand. Unarmed, Wheeler found himself pitted against a bigger, stronger, and younger guy.

Wheeler punched Holt's face and then his gut, but it was like trying to knock down a brick wall with his fists. Holt wasn't fazed.
He retaliated with a hard blow to Wheeler's stomach that doubled
the agent over and sent him to his knees. He coughed and stared
up at the barrel of his own weapon, aimed at his head, and Holt's
sinister grin.

"Fucking pigs," Holt said and took a step closer to finish him off.

Your life is supposed to pass before your eyes when you face death,
but Wheeler could think only about his stupidity. All those years
of training, his instincts and smarts, and he had blown it, getting
within arm's reach of a killer. *Stupid!*

Out of the darkness, a slender shadow blindsided Holt, crashing
into him with a shoulder blow. As the huge guy went down, he fired
the Beretta. The bullet hit Wheeler's upper arm near the shoulder.
Lying in the sand, Wheeler managed to lift his head and saw Christian
on top of Holt, hammering at his eyes and nose. Holt knocked him
off like a mosquito and scrambled to his feet. Christian rolled to a
stand. They stood opposite each other, fists up, preparing to duke it
out. Holt swung several times but never connected with his quicker
target. Christian danced around the monster, ducking and jabbing
at Holt's bloody face. The fight seemed almost biblical, like David
attempting to bring down Goliath. With Christian's relentless assault,
Holt appeared to tire, staggering and puffing hard.

"You scrawny bastard," Holt said, panting for breath. "I'm gonna
take you out."

"Get in line, asshole," Christian said and leaped clear of Holt's
charge and grasp. In the distance, sirens blared with the approach
of police cars, and Christian glanced in their direction. He flew at
Holt and pummeled his apish face. Holt swung blindly.

"I don't have time to dick with you." Christian gave a quick kick
to the big man's balls, and Holt collapsed into a groaning, sweaty
heap. Christian pressed his knee into Holt's back while removing
his own tie and used it to bind the man's wrists behind his back. He
stood, found the Beretta in the sand, and pointed it at Holt. "Don't

move, asshole. I got no problem with blowing your head off." He sidestepped to Wheeler. "You all right, Dave?"

Wheeler sat on the ground and gripped his blood-soaked arm. "Yeah. I think he just winged me," he mumbled, feeling numb with shock.

Christian called to two teenage boys with skateboards who had been drawn to the scene by the gunfire. "Go hail down those cops. Tell them an officer's down and needs an ambulance." The kids raced up the steps to the street. Christian squatted near Wheeler and shook out the pain in his right hand. "They should be here soon."

Wheeler stared at Holt in astonishment. "Where'd you learn to fight?"

"High school, every frigging jock thinks you're after their girl. Got my ass kicked a few times before I took up boxing. Got pretty good." He stood and brushed the sand off his suit. "I hope that jerk isn't wanted for parking tickets."

"He raped and murdered four girls."

Christian lifted an eyebrow. "He's lucky. If I'd known, I would've used my tie on his throat." He handed Wheeler his weapon when the first squad car stopped on the street. "I'm taking off. Don't need this." He started to stroll away.

"Christian," Wheeler called. "Thanks, thanks a lot."

Christian gave him a nod and disappeared into the night.

Wheeler lay in the hospital bed with his shoulder and upper arm in bandages. The gunshot wound was not serious, a flesh wound, but the doctor insisted he stay overnight. Two detectives stood near his bed, wrapping up their questions and report.

On the ambulance ride, Wheeler had wrestled with the decision to name or not name Christian in the arrest of Larry Holt. In the end, he said for the record that an anonymous citizen had jumped in, knocked the gun out of Holt's hand, and wrestled him to the ground. Christian's testimony as a witness wasn't necessary, since Holt was going away for attempted murder of an FBI agent, and the murder of the four girls. With his fingerprint and his last victim's blood on the garage parking ticket, along with other evidence, the rape and murder cases were solid.

Ralph rushed into the room and brushed past the leaving detectives. "My God, Dave, I just heard you were shot. I first thought that Roberts had done it, and then I learned it was Larry Holt. What happened?"

"I got careless. After dinner, I spotted Holt on the oceanfront and thought I could handle him myself. I got too close and overconfident. The sucker rushed me. Before I knew it, he had my weapon and was pointing it at my head."

"Lucky someone tackled Holt and made the citizen's arrest."

"That someone was Roberts. I left him off the witness list because he has enough problems. He'll face his own courtroom some day. Besides, I owe him my life."

"Roberts saved you? That's unbelievable. Why do you think he did it?"

"I don't know. I think Christian was a decent guy, but losing his wife really screwed him up. Last time we dealt with a mouthy, scruffy sailor. Tonight he was a classy gentleman. Damn kid is as diverse as weather. One thing, he's a heck of a fighter. He pounced from the shadows, and Holt never knew what hit him. It explains how he could take out five fishermen on the trawler."

"I suppose he didn't say anything we could use."

"Nothing incriminating. Christian talked about Nemo in the third person. He explained Nemo's cause, and it does have some merit."

"It's Christian now. Dave, you sound like he's your buddy."

"Anyone who saves my life is my buddy. Too bad I have to put him away."

The next afternoon, Wheeler sat on the edge of his hospital bed, stiff and hurting. The painkillers were worthless, only made him sick to his stomach and drowsy. He had been released and was trying to get ready, using one hand to get his trousers on. Ralph would arrive any minute to give him a ride home. His daughter had visited and insisted she stay with him, at least the first week, helping out in between her classes. He hated infringing, but some high-quality time with her would be nice.

Ralph walked into the room holding a newspaper. "How are you feeling?" He looked grim, his lips pressed tightly together.

"I know that look, like a cat with the stepped-on tail. What is it?"

"You're not going to be happy." He handed Wheeler the paper. "Answers why your buddy wanted to treat you to dinner last night. He was looking for an alibi, and what's better than an FBI agent?"

Wheeler read the article in the *New York Times*. Nemo had struck again, but this time in New York City, bombing two Chinese grocery stores. A day prior to the attack, a *Washington Post* reporter, Trish Stevenson, had received a postcard with a picture of New York City saying, "Welcome to New York." The note on the back said, "Stop selling shark fins," and was signed Captain Nemo. The *Post* alerted the police, but with no date, time, or place for the terrorist attack, little could be done. Some authorities thought it was a prank, until the bombings occurred on the following night.

"I've been working on this all morning," said Ralph. "Pulled Roberts's credit card statements, checked passenger lists on airlines, and looked for anything that might put him up there. So far, nothing. I told New York that Roberts was a person of interest and sent his photo, prints, DNA, profile, and even a copy of his signature for a handwriting specialist to use on the postcard. Hopefully New York will find evidence, a witness, or a conspirator that proves he's Nemo and was behind the attack."

"Well, the little sucker has done it now," Wheeler said and tossed the paper on the bed. "He's been playing in small countries with inadequate police departments, but now he's facing US authorities."

"But he has a darned good alibi proving he was in Miami."

"He didn't need me, Ralph. He paid for dinner with a credit card and gave the waiter a large tip, so he wouldn't forget him. And there are other witnesses, a car dealer, hotel clerks, and he probably put all his expenses on a card. That dinner was payback for putting him in jail. He used me, knowing I'd choke on it. It's time to get a warrant and do a search of his home and vehicle. It might yield evidence that proves he visited New York and set up the bombing."

"I'll handle the warrant and him."

"Ralph, I know this guy irritates you, but try to be tactful. Think of it as saying 'nice doggie' until you can grab his collar and throw the mutt in a kennel."

In Chinatown, Charlie Wong leaned against a closed storefront on a dark side street and eyed a pair of white tourists who had finished dinner and were leaving a restaurant. Stupidly, they flaunted their money, the woman in a full-length mink and the man, a nice suit. Although his gang leader, Lee Chow, discouraged petty theft, those easy targets were begging for it. The woman chatted and the man laughed as they strolled down the street, unaware that Wong followed.

When they approached an alley, Wong made his move. He pulled his FNP-9 from his jacket pocket and rushed them. "In the alley," he growled and motioned with the pointed handgun.

"Don't hurt us. We'll give you everything," said the man. The couple raised their hands and shuffled into the alley past garbage bags and boxes.

"Wallet and purse," Wong said and gazed at the woman's coat. "And take off the mink." He crammed the wallet into his back pocket and took off running with the purse and fur bundled in his arm.

He jogged several blocks, but at an intersection, he was caught in the beaming headlights of a squad car. He darted down another alley, but the two officers left their car and pursued him on foot. As he passed an open dumpster, he tossed the purse, coat, and his gun inside. If he could reach the end of the alley, he could blend into the crowds that walked the main drag. He was nearly there, when flashing red lights on a second police car raced up, blocking the exit and his escape. He frantically tried to open the back doors of a few businesses that lined the alleyway, but all were locked.

"Don't move! Hands up!" one officer yelled as the four closed in.

Wong gave up and put his hands in the air. One officer shoved him against a wall, handcuffed him, and frisked him. He removed the man's wallet. Wong had forgotten he still had it.

"This doesn't look like you," the policeman commented. "Where's your ID?"

"That's Charlie Wong, a member of the Dragons," said another officer who strolled up holding the fur and purse. "Haven't see ya in a while, Charlie. Lucky we were in the area when the call came in, and you got greedy. Don't see too many Chinese men running down the street with mink coats." He held up Wong's bagged handgun. "Armed robbery, Charlie. You're going away for a long time."

Wong climbed into the back of squad car and was taken to the police station. He sat shackled to a desk while an officer filled out the report.

"I want to make a deal," Wong said to the officer. "I can ID Captain Nemo, the guy behind those Chinese grocery store bombings."

Christian returned home and prepared for the storm. Before going to Miami, he had trashed some of the evidence that could tie him to New York such as subway tokens, receipts, newspapers, an iPad, and even his clothes, afraid they might retain some northern pollen. But there were things he wanted to keep.

In a small plastic box he placed the fake passport and driver's license, the disposable phone, the small shark fin, his Cayman bank account information, and an old thirty-eight revolver that had belonged to his father. He sealed the container and walked down to the barn. He glanced at Mystery in his stall. The red stud was prone to kick and bite strangers.

"No cop in his right mind is going come in and mess with you," he said to Mystery. With a shovel he pushed aside the shavings in the horse's stall, dug a hole, and buried the box.

A few days later, the storm arrived in the driveway in the form of four FBI agents in unmarked cars, two Manatee County sheriff's deputies, a K-9 unit with a bomb-sniffing dog and his uniformed handler, along with a flatbed tow truck and its driver.

Out the window, Christian saw Agent Ralph McKenna leading the group to the front door. Christian opened the door before Ralph could knock. "I've been expecting you, Ralphie. Have your warrants?"

"Here," Ralph snarled and shoved the paperwork at Christian. "There's also a warrant to search your boat and take your vehicle."

Christian glanced at the papers and smiled. "Yeah, good idea, Ralphie, check those GPSs. Gee, I just heard about New York and this Captain Nemo fellow. It's too bad. Someone needs to put him away." He turned to the men who filled the house and were opening drawers and closets. "Ralphie, you or any of your guys care for coffee or a Coke? It's a long drive out here."

"It's Agent McKenna, and no one wants a drink," Ralph said, his temples pulsing. "Where were you last week?"

"Don't like me much, do ya?" Christian grinned. He strolled into the living room and parked himself in a large stuffed chair with one leg lazily slung over an armrest. He gazed up at Ralph. "How is my friend, Dave?"

"Answer my question. Where have you been since returning from Panama?"

"Ralphie, you're a boring guy and lousy at manipulation," Christian then said the magic words, "I think I'd rather speak to my lawyer."

Agents and police spent several hours at the house and barn and searched the workshop building used to restore boats. The officials took photos and vacuumed the rugs for hair and fibers and filled five boxes with Christian's clothes, a checkbook, passport, and every bill receipt and scrap of paper with a scribbled note. They also took his cell phone, luggage, and a newly purchased computer, all in the hope of finding a clue that connected him to New York. They questioned Juan and Rosa, who said that Christian had gone to the beach and stayed with a friend.

His SUV was loaded on the flatbed. Its GPS would show Christian had been at the farm, his mother's house, Longboat Key, and, lastly, Miami. Prior to the bombing date, Vince's neighbors would further validate the SUV was parked in the driveway and hadn't moved.

Christian figured if they found evidence in Florida or in New York, it would only mean the game was over. Because he did not care, his anxiety amounted to zilch. Better to piss on it and move on.

CHAPTER TWENTY-TWO

A week after the FBI house raid, Christian saddled Hunter, his red gelding, and led him out of the barn. The crisp, chilly weather in late January was perfect for a long morning gallop through the woods and countryside. His favorite mount hadn't seen a bridle in nearly four months. Since he was lying low at home, not having contact with Vince, he took the opportunity to put normality back in his life.

He still suffered with depression, but not so much during the day when he worked alongside Juan, grooming and caring for the horses, mowing, and toiling around the farm. The nights in the dark, lonely house was when he struggled. He had poured every drop of liquor down the sink, eliminating the temptation to drink. He tried reading books, watching TV, and going on online, but was too antsy and distracted to enjoy those activities. Every evening he had to convince himself to go on, and when finally asleep, he faced the ghastly nightmares of blood, seagulls, and death.

Outside the barn, Christian put his foot in the stirrup, but Hunter broke into a canter before Christian had settled into the saddle. "Easy, easy, boy," he said and reined him in. "You're itching to go? Maybe we can outrun my demons."

Held back on the drive, Hunter moved sideways in a choppy, halted lope to the back of the property. They reached the long straightaway lined with pine trees, and Christian turned the Thoroughbred loose. Like a rock in a slingshot, Hunter dug in, as though bursting once again out of a starting gate. He pounded the turf in a fast, hard pace.

On the exhilarating ride, Christian clung to the horse's mane and watched the trees zip by. *Maybe I'll be thrown and die. Wouldn't that be convenient?*

After a vigorous ride, Christian slowed Hunter to a gentle gallop and finally a walk when they entered the shady forest, so the gelding would cool down. They returned to the barn, and Juan was waiting to give Hunter a bath and rub down.

"Mr. Roberts," said Juan, "it is your life and your horse, but I was holding my breath, watching you. It is dangerous enough taking a horse that fast on a track, but in an open pasture—"

"Hold the lecture, Juan. I know it was crazy," Christian said, hopping off Hunter. Patting the horse's neck, he noticed a silver compact car parked near the house with a woman standing beside it. "Who's that?"

"I don't know her name. She arrived after you left the barn. I told her you could be gone hours, but she said she would wait."

"I don't recognize her," Christian said, watching the woman walk down the drive toward him and the barn. Strolling to meet her, he saw she was in her twenties and had large eyes, a small nose and mouth, and a hint of freckles on her cheeks, all framed in lengthy light-brown hair. She was dressed in a short skirt and heels that made her legs look like they stopped at her shoulders. He met her halfway between the house and barn. "Can I help you?"

"I hope so," she said, red lipstick outlining her smile. "I've come a long way to see you, and I must say I'm not disappointed. You're absolutely fearless on horseback."

He gazed at her, thinking that perhaps she was a horse buyer or a real estate agent interested in his property, but she did not appear to be a cop. One thing for sure, she sparked his interest. "I'm sorry, but who are you?"

"Oh, forgive me. I feel like I already know you, Christian," she said and extended her hand. "I'm Trish Stevenson. I work for the—"

"*Washington Post*," he grumbled, withdrawing from the handshake and cramming his hands in his jean pockets along with his desire for any future endeavors. "I know who you are and have nothing to say." He sidestepped her and marched toward the house.

"You've been following my articles, then, about shark fins, and you mailed me a postcard from New York." She tripped along the uneven ground, trying to keep pace with him. "Christian, I know you're Captain Nemo."

He halted and turned, catching her in the crosshairs of a hard stare. "I'm not Nemo, lady, and I didn't mail you any damn postcard. I've read your articles because the goddamn FBI is trying to frame me for those arsons and bombings when they should be looking for my wife's killer."

"The FBI has questioned you, then, about Captain Nemo and the attacks?"

"Yeah, they came here with a warrant, tore up my house, and took my vehicle," he growled. "I was in Miami having dinner with an FBI agent when those bombs went off in New York, and I was in Panama when the Costa Rican port burned. As if the harassment wasn't enough, now they're leaking my name to the press."

"Actually, Sergeant Drake in Nassau turned me on to you, said you were a person of interest. Agent Wheeler denied your involvement, but you just confirmed he lied," she said as they reached the house. "With a warrant, they must consider you a suspect."

Christian spun on his heels. "Christ, as if my life isn't already a fucking zoo, I have to deal with you. Are you planning to put my name in your next article?"

"Probably," she said. "Nemo needs a face, and your face will definitely sell papers."

"Just get the fuck off my place."

"Christian, it's going to come out you're a suspect, regardless of whether I write the story or not. You've read my articles and can tell I'm on your side. With your story, you can deny the allegations and explain your alibis. If Nemo goes to jail, the sharks lose. I don't want that."

"I'm telling you I'm not him," he said. "A story about me will hurt, not help, but your readers will be happy, learning the cops have fingered the eco-terrorist."

"Christian, don't you realize you have a following? The paper has been flooded with favorable responses, people thinking you're a hero, and your actions have made an impact. In light of the bombings, the New York City commissioners are taking a hard look at shark fins. There's talk they might impose a ban, outlawing fin sales in Chinatown. You've done this."

"Not me. Some guy named Nemo. I have nothing to say." He opened the side door to the house and started to step inside.

"Christian, there's a witness. He's willing to testify that you were in New York and plotted the bombings!"

Christian stopped dead in his tracks, his heartbeat in overdrive. He turned slowly. "A witness? Who is it?"

"I said I don't want Nemo in jail. Besides a story, I came here to warn you."

Christian tilted his head, studying her for a long moment. "I guess you'd better come in." In the kitchen he poured two glasses of Coke, and they settled on the living room couch. "How do you know there's a witness?" he asked.

"Jim, a reporter in my office, learned about the guy. Jim's a piece of work." She breathed. "To get the information, I had to go on a date with him. Anyway, Jim used to work for the *New York Times* and still has connections with NYPD. One of the cops tipped him off about the witness."

Christian stood and paced the room. "What's his name?"

Trish retrieved a notepad from her purse and read, "Charlie Wong, a Chinese gang member with the Flying Dragons. A few days ago, he was arrested for armed robbery in New York. For a lighter sentence, he made a deal in exchange for his testimony against you. He claimed a tall, blond Florida guy offered him fifty thousand to plant bombs in two Chinatown groceries. Yesterday Wong picked you out of a photo lineup. FBI must've sent them your mug shot. So far, this is hush, hush, to protect Wong."

Christian stared at the floor, thinking. *I'm fucked.* He glanced up at Trish. "Guess I am in your debt."

"You are. I had to go on that miserable date and fight to keep the jerk's hands off me." Trish wet her lips. "But I'm betting you could make up for it." She blushed and shook her head. "I mean . . . I mean I'm talking about you giving me your story."

"Sounds like blackmail," he said with a flirtatious grin that hid his fears. With Wong's testimony, the FBI had potentially solid evidence. He wondered if he had days, weeks, or a month before the FBI or a US Marshal came and hauled him away.

He stowed the meltdown inside and moved to acting mode, pouring on the charm. He could tell Trish arrived already carrying a torch for him. Better to fan that flame. Her inside track with the NYPD could be useful. He agreed to give her his story, but under the condition that she would hold off publishing it. He needed a few weeks to get his life in order. For an hour she took notes, and he lied through his teeth, discussing his alibis for the three terrorist attacks and the heart-wrenching details of his wife's murder. Concerning Wong picking out his photo, he said it was mistaken identity. He never met Wong or was in New York.

When the interview was over, he told Trish he would pick her up at her hotel for a night out in Sarasota. Whatever it meant was up to her.

He had never utilized his looks to exploit women, but he had seen the advantage with Lin and now Trish. Like Vince had said, he wasn't the best terrorist, but he could mesmerize the pants off most women while winning their devotion. Right or wrong, he needed them, and they wanted him.

After Trish left, he showered and shaved. His mind wasn't on the date, but on Charlie Wong. Vince needed to know about the new development. Christian dressed in jeans and a dark-blue pullover sweater. He climbed into the Mustang convertible, a rented car, while the FBI had his SUV. *I should've bought the Ferrari. Would've been nice having one last thrill. At the rate things are going, I might never drive again, sail a boat, or make love to a beautiful woman.* He shuddered and started the engine.

He had time before his date with Trish, so he cruised out to Longboat Key. Vince met him with raised eyebrows. "I thought we decided to keep our distance."

"Got a big problem," Christian said and strolled through the house and out to the backyard. On the windy seawall, he told Vince about the reporter who learned Charlie Wong had turned state's witness.

"Damn it," Vince said, "That fucking rat. All right, don't do anything crazy. The cops need to get their ducks in a row before they arrest you. Tomorrow, you hire the best criminal lawyer in Sarasota. You did get a solid alibi for New York?"

"Yeah, but one you might not approve of. Drove to Miami and had dinner with Agent Wheeler."

"You used an FBI agent for your alibi?" Vince's eyes blinked hard, conveying either disbelief or disapproval. "Jesus, you have balls, Christian."

"You said I needed a solid alibi."

"Yeah, but I didn't say you should piss off an FBI agent. Wheeler must've been irate when he learned about the bombings. Now you're socializing with the reporter that's covering the case? Christ! What am I going to do with you?"

"Hey, Bond was your idea."

"Dinner with the FBI and a reporter wasn't. You're walking a tight-rope made of dental floss. You should be running from these people instead of rubbing elbows. One slip of the tongue and you're screwed."

"I'm already screwed, and we both know it." Christian glanced at his watch. "I gotta run."

Christian drove to the Longboat Key Publix and bought steaks, lobsters, potatoes, a prepared Cobb salad, and drinks. In the check-out line, he grabbed a bouquet of flowers. Initially, he considered taking Trish to a waterfront restaurant, but January was the height of the tourist season in Sarasota. Every restaurant in town would be jam-packed. Even a reservation didn't guarantee a short wait.

He arrived at Marina Jack and carried the groceries to his docked sloop. On board he stowed the food in the refrigerator, put the flowers in a pitcher in the sink, and prepared *Hank's Dream* for possibly his last cruise with a beautiful woman. He returned to his car and drove to Trish's hotel near the airport. He found her room and knocked. She opened the door wearing a short cocktail dress and heels. Her hair hung in stylish loose curls. She was hardly prepared for boating.

"You look fantastic," he said, "but I guess I should've called and talked about tonight. I was thinking dinner on my sloop, and a sunset cruise, but that's okay. I know a good restaurant."

"No, give me a minute to change. Your idea sounds great. Besides, there's nothing more fitting than an evening on Nemo's boat."

He took a deep breath, tired of denying he was Nemo. After few minutes in the bathroom, she emerged in jeans, a knit shirt, and sneakers. Her hair was pulled into a ponytail.

"Ready," she said and grabbed a jacket.

They drove to the marina, and after boarding, Christian mixed up a batch of margaritas before getting underway. *Now I'll find out who she really is.* Take a girl out on a sailboat, and her true character comes out. The prima donnas sat back and never helped, too afraid to break a nail. The bitches constantly complained, starting with the wind messing up their hair. The insecure squealed with each swell of a wave, half the time huddling below in the cabin, and the fragile immediately became seasick.

As they prepared to set sail, Trish did not belong in any of those categories. She scampered across the deck and cast off the lines. He sailed north under the Ringling Bridge and up Sarasota Bay with the backdrop of a flaming pink-and-lavender horizon. A crisp wind had the sloop heeled over and moving at top speed as it tugged at their hair. She appeared to love every minute. Off an isolated mangrove shoal, Christian lowered the sails and dropped anchor. In the cabin, he prepared dinner, grilling the steaks and lobster and popping the potatoes in the microwave, while Trish set the table in the cabin, dished out salad, and refreshed their drinks.

She was not only attractive, but also smart, considerate, and adventurous; his type of girl. In another time and life, he would have pursued a relationship with her, but his world was chaotic and his freedom hung by a string. *No woman deserves to be dragged into my mess.*

After dinner, they sat on the deck. "I want to thank you for this evening. It far exceeded my expectations," Trish said as she gazed up at the stars.

"I was trying to make up for your lousy date with Jim."

"You did. I feel like I'm in a fairy tale with a textbook Prince Charming, but I also know you're dangerous, capable of arson, bombings, and maybe even murder."

"Are you afraid of me?"

"I wouldn't be here if I were." She slid closer to him. He wrapped her in his arms, and his soft, slow kiss ignited a long night of passion.

In his apartment, Wheeler sat in a stuffed chair and readjusted his arm sling as Ralph paced back and forth, ranting about Christian Roberts.

"We have him, Dave," Ralph said. "We have that son of a bitch now. I'll get an arrest warrant in place and haul him up to New York myself."

"Not yet," said Wheeler. "There's one witness, and not a very good one. Wong is a felon and gang member. Tell the New York detectives that Roberts has an alibi for the night of the bombing, but we have his passport. He's not going anywhere. We'll do a wait and see. Hopefully, they'll find a second witness or physical evidence confirming he visited New York. We'll work the Florida end with the evidence taken from his house. Ralph, let's not hop on a train, only to learn it's heading the wrong way."

Ralph flopped down in the chair, the wind out of his sails. "I really want him bad. I want to see his face when I clamp on the handcuffs."

"He must've gotten to you when you served those warrants."

"The condescending prick said I was boring and lousy at manipulation."

Wheeler chuckled. "You should know talking to him is like making a phone call and getting the answering machine. Instead of a response, you end up with aggravation. What about the witness the police found in Costa Rica?"

"It was looking good. A fisherman cleaning eels identified Roberts from the photo, said he was in Puntarenas a few weeks before the arson, trying to buy shark fins. He said six dockworkers with bats cornered Roberts in an alley and beat him up." Ralph shook his head. "When the police asked for the names of those guys, the fisherman recanted the whole story, either out of fear or loyalty. He probably realized he couldn't implicate Roberts without involving his neighbors in assault and battery on a tourist."

"Six thugs with bats; even Roberts couldn't hold his own against that. Now we know how he got the bruises he had when he came back from Panama."

"Want me to do a search on the hospitals down there to see if his name pops up?"

"Go ahead, but I doubt he used his real name. It's even more doubtful he told the doctor he was attacked in Puntarenas, but there's always a chance. It would prove he visited the harbor and got the layout. Besides saving sharks, the beating would have given him an additional motive for the arson."

After Ralph left, Wheeler reclined in the chair, feeling at odds with himself. The New York witness was a big break in the case.

Wong's testimony might send Christian to prison, but Wheeler wasn't pleased. How could he feel good about putting away a young man who had saved his life?

At midday, Christian was finally heading back to his farm. He and Trish had spent the night on his sloop and returned to the marina in time to pick up her luggage and check out of the hotel. He dropped her off at the airport for a late morning flight back to DC.

As he drove toward Myakka, the charmer was gone, along with thoughts of the date. His weariness was the only reminder of the all-night sex.

He chewed a nail and focused on his uncertain future. Given the New York witness and the impending arrest, he had a narrow window of time to make decisions. He had the money and could run, hiding from the law in some Third World country, or as Vince suggested, he could hire a criminal lawyer and take his chances in court. The last option, one that had nagged at him from the start, he preferred more than a lifetime in prison. He could kill himself.

He pulled into the long driveway at the farm and stopped. Climbing out of the car, he gazed at the pasture of horses. Whether on the run, in jail, or dead, he had not drawn up any provisions for them. He decided his horses would be his first priority. Frank, his stepfather, could set up a trust that made sure the horses stayed here under Juan's care. If he chose the last option, his remaining money would go to a wildlife charity. Thinking about his funeral soothed him. He would rest beside Allie.

He walked into the house, sat down at the desk, and called Frank. Without going into details, Christian made an appointment at Frank's office for the next day. His stepfather could also hook him up with a good criminal lawyer. He hung up and closed his eyes. *Frank is going to freak, wondering why I want a will and a trust for the horses, and when I ask him for a referral on a defense attorney, he'll know I'm in deep shit. Better take my chances and get a criminal lawyer out of the phone book.*

He rose from the desk chair and realized he had to retrieve the box hidden in the barn that held all his choices. In Mystery's stall, he dug up the plastic container that police had failed to find. In the hay room, he sat down on a bale, opened the box, and stared at the contents. He glanced at the fake license and passport in the name of Jeff Roads and the Cayman bank account information, money, and ID needed if he ran. He pushed aside the disposable phone and caressed the revolver, wondering about it as an alternative. Did he have the guts to off himself?

He eyed the small shark fin he had purchased in New York. He took it out and caressed the smooth, gray surface, noticing it was lightweight, barely significant, yet Allie had died and he had thrown away his life for these fins. Despite the terrorist attacks, he had not made much of an impact worldwide or accomplished his goal. Seventy-five million sharks were still slaughtered yearly, and forty percent of the population had already disappeared. The statistic ate at his gut like acid.

He toyed with the dried fin. *Maybe I've chosen the wrong targets.* The barbaric traditions and the ignorant, selfish people eating fins, they are the problem and should be stopped.

But was there time? And was he enough of a monster to pull off one last great terrorist attack, something so awful that the entire planet would take notice and halt the obliteration of sharks? *I belong in a mental hospital, prison, or the electric chair with what I'm considering.*

CHAPTER TWENTY-THREE

In her San Francisco apartment, Lin Chow rolled out of bed and walked to the kitchen to make tea. Since leaving New York, she felt like a free spirit, no longer under her brother's physical and financial control. She sat down on the pale-blue suede sofa with her mug and admired the recently purchased décor: the contemporary chrome lamps, a large abstract painting, and a five-piece Danish dining room set. There wasn't a shred of the tacky Chinese furnishings like those that cluttered her mother's home.

She reflected on the man who made her new start possible. "Christian, Christian," she said aloud. Saying his name caused her stomach to rise to her chest. Never had she fallen so fast and hard for someone. His appearance resembled a work of art, flawless, but after spending several precious days with him, she was more attracted to his complex personality.

In the museum, he initially had come across as country-boy sweet, almost an innocent in a big, cold city with his childlike enthusiasm and infectious smile. He hardly appeared to be a dangerous eco-terrorist. As she came to know him, she saw his serious, intellectual side and his brazen, hot-headed temper. On the crowded street, a large man rudely bumped into her, and Christian cussed him out. Lin interceded before the confrontation came to blows. He truly was Nemo: fiery, alluring, and mysterious. At times she glimpsed his sadness, the dark, forlorn gaze in his deep-blue eyes.

At the hotel on Broadway, Lin watched the beautiful but tragic man and longed to hold and have him. The passion of that last night would forever stay in her memory.

Her thoughts drifted to the following two days after Christian had left for Florida. For $50,000, she had planted the two bombs disguised as tea boxes in the grocery stores. The job had been quick and easy, no one was hurt, and with insurance, even the store owners recovered their losses. She thought she might have regrets, betraying her own race, but with a glance at the bay outside her window, all her misgivings disappeared. No one had the right to devastate the fragile ocean environment.

The cell phone in the bedroom chimed, and she hurried to answer it. Only one person had the number of the disposable phone. "Hello?"

"How's it goin'?" he said with his soft southern drawl.

She gulped down a breath to mask her excitement. "Christian, I was just thinking about you."

"Must be ESP," he said. "Are you doing okay?"

"I'm great. I love California, the weather and people. I rented an apartment with a view of San Francisco Bay, and I'm having fun decorating it. Tomorrow I'm picking up a new Toyota. Once I have wheels, I'll be looking for a job, maybe something in a clothing store."

"That sounds good, Lin. I'm happy for you. Actually, I was calling about another job, real easy, and it's not against the law."

"And I thought you called because you couldn't live without me."

"We did have fun sneaking around New York, and—the hotel. I'd like to see you again, but it's too risky, and my life is a little hectic now," he said with a weighty sigh.

She plopped down on the bed. "Okay, what's the job?"

"I need thirty large shark fins, preferably hammerheads. You'll have to visit several Chinese grocery stores and spread out your purchases so you don't draw attention. Overnight them to my mother's house on Siesta Key. On the return address use a phony marine name, so I can say it's a boat part. I'll give you a hundred grand plus expenses for the fins and shipping."

"Christian, you don't have to pay me. I'd do it for nothing, and besides, that's way too much."

"No, I want to pay you. Look, I have money."

"Well, California passed a law banning the sale of fins, but the law doesn't take effect until next year, so I doubt I'll have trouble buying the fins, but what will you do with them?"

"You don't want to know."

"It doesn't matter. You know I'd do anything for you." When he was quiet for half a minute, she kicked herself for sounding like a needy loser.

"I appreciate that, Lin, but I'd prefer you did this for sharks, not me."

"Of course, of course it's for the sharks. I'll take care of it tomorrow." She jotted down his mother's address. She noticed he sounded weary. "Christian, are you okay?"

"Just have a few worries, but I'm good. We'll catch up down the road. Thanks, Lin."

After the call, Lin curled up in the bed pillows. *He's not good.*

The next day she visited San Francisco's Chinatown and purchased the dried shark fins at four grocery stores. At five to eight hundred dollars a pound, they set her back nearly $6,000. She returned to her apartment and boxed up the fins, along with the receipt, so Christian could reimburse her. She wrote his mother's address on the top and a fake return, Oceanside Marina with a made-up address. She drove to a post office and mailed the fins, wondering why he wanted them.

After the phone call to Lin, Christian drove into Sarasota and arrived at his stepfather's law office near the courthouse for his appointment with Frank. In a comfy big chair across from Frank's desk, he sat down and gazed out the window at the tropical plants and water fountain while explaining he wanted a will and a trust for his horses. He looked back at Frank, expecting a knee-jerk reaction. He didn't have to wait long.

"What the devil is going on with you, Christian?" Frank asked. "You take off for Costa Rica, not telling us where you are or who you're with. Then you show up one night for Christmas, banged up with a cut on your cheek. You were so moody, we were afraid to ask what happened. Christ, you're too old for fights. Then we don't see or hear from you for over a month. You don't answer your phone or return your mother's calls when she leaves messages. She finally learned from Juan you were on the beach, right here in town. To add to her worries, she found out you never made another appointment with the psychiatrist, and now you want to make out a will."

"Frank, had I known you were going to give me grief, I would've gone to another lawyer," Christian fired back. "What I do is my business. If I've been avoiding you and Mom, it's because of all this bitching and treating me like a damn kid."

"You're acting like a kid, irresponsible and inconsiderate, with no regard for your mother's feelings. She's worried sick about you."

Christian pushed the bangs from his eyes and took an absorbing breath. "I'm sorry, but I'm not the same person I was. For Mom's sake, I'll try to stay more in touch."

"All right, let's drop it. Now why do you want a will?"

"Allie died unexpectedly with no will. The same might happen to me. I was looking at the horses and it came to mind. I want to make sure they don't end up in a bad home. I just need the paperwork."

"That's it? You're worried about the horses? Are you sure there's nothing else going on, like depression?"

"Sure, I'm depressed, but not enough to blow my brains out." For a second Christian thought about telling Frank his troubles, but changed his mind. *I don't need him on my back now. Soon enough my arrest will be in the newspapers.*

For the next hour, they worked on the will and a trust for the horses. Once everything was typed up, Christian would return the following day to sign the papers. He mentioned to Frank that he was expecting a boat part from California, but since he was in and out at the farm, he had it shipped to their house, a plausible reason.

"I'll tell you what. Bring the paperwork home," Christian said. "When I pick up the box, I'll sign the will and trust, and I'll stay for dinner. That should make Mom happy."

In the late afternoon, he left Frank's office and drove to City

Island and the bait shop near the New Pass Bridge. He purchased four dozen shrimp and headed to Vince's house.

"Want to go fishing?" Christian asked, holding up the bait bucket when Vince opened the door.

Vince's narrowed eyes stared at Christian. "Fine, grab the poles, tackle box, and a bag of ice while I get ready."

Vince changed from his dress pants and shirt to khaki Dockers and a loose sweater. By the time he walked to his boat, Christian had filled the ice cooler, dumped the shrimp in the bait well, set up the poles, and cast off all but one dock line. He stood at the helm with the twin motors running. Vince climbed aboard, griping, "Takes me at least a half hour to prepare to go out. You're ready before I change pants."

"Practice. I used to do this for a living, remember?" Christian cast off the last line and scrambled to the upper deck behind the controls. "You want to steer?"

"You do it. You got the practice." Vince waved his hand ahead. "Where are we goin'?" he asked, and eased into the first-mate seat alongside the helm.

"I think we'll try north Longboat and the bayside of the channel." Christian maneuvered the Grady White toward the open bay. "I added some weight to the poles. We'll go for mackerel, mangrove snapper, and maybe even hook some red grouper."

Vince gave him a sideward glance. "We're not here to fish. What's the scoop?"

Christian throttled back and slowed the boat to just above an idle. "I figure Nemo has just enough time to carry out one last attack. Once my face hits the papers, I won't be able to move around freely because of the publicity, and my arrest won't be long in coming."

"What are you planning?"

"Something unequivocal and terrible," said Christian, "an assault that stops the shark finning once and for all. I'm going to kill some people, Vince. I've thought long and hard about it, but given the choice between saving the sharks and sparing humans, it's a nobrainer for me. This planet already has too many people, but sharks—I have to do this."

"Oh, man, I have the feeling I'm gonna need a drink." Vince stood and placed his hand on Christian's shoulder. "Ya know I don't give a shit about the people, but give it up, Christian. Let some animal rights group save the sharks. Right now you're guilty of plotting the bombing of two stores. With a good lawyer, you're likely to be acquitted at trial if Wong is their only witness. Even if you're found guilty, you're facing ten, fifteen years max. With good behavior and no criminal record, you could be out in five. That's not a life sentence, but now you're talking about murder. Don't throw your life away."

"I don't have a life, Vince. You've been a great friend. I owe you a lot and appreciate the advice, but I'm going through with this."

At nine that night, Vince stood in his driveway with Christian, who held his bait bucket containing six puffer fish. He bid Vince good night, but his quick hug felt like good-bye. They had fished well past dark and caught a dozen snapper and two grouper. Christian released them, since they were undersize, but kept the inedible puffers.

The first few hours on the boat, Vince tried to discourage Christian from going through with his newest plan of attack. Whether it was his stubborn dedication to sharks or the fact that he was living under a shadow of doom, Christian remained unshakable. Ironically, Vince even appealed to Christian's humanity. He didn't want to kill innocent people.

"They're not innocent!" Christian had lashed out. "They're materialistic, uncaring bastards eating a soup they know is wiping out the ocean and sharks. And if they don't know, the ignorant pricks will soon get a lesson."

Vince sadly shook his head. "You've become a true fanatic." With depression from his wife's death, the trauma of murdering the longliners, the near-death beating in Costa Rica, or the strain from the

FBI and his impending arrest, one or all, Christian had snapped. He obviously didn't care about himself or anyone else, just his sharks.

For the latter part of the fishing trip, Vince had given up and shut up as Christian revealed his intentions. When the bait ran out, they motored back to the dock.

Christian drove away, and Vince walked back in his house. At the bar he fixed a drink and reflected on Christian's plan. It was brilliant. *The kid might just pull it off and save his sharks.*

Christian returned to his horse farm and put the fish in the refrigerator. He would deal with them tomorrow. He glanced at his watch, eleven o'clock at night, but still early there. Paranoid that the FBI had planted bugs in the house, he walked outside into the cool night air and vast pastures where any unfamiliar car could be seen for half a mile. He leaned against the board fence and placed a call with the disposable phone.

"Hey, Harry, how's it going?"

"Who's this?" Harry asked.

"It's the Hot Dog. I was wondering if you and Wade want to make some more money, this time no fireworks."

"Oh, fuck. Wade's dead, Chris. Died of that heart attack he was always talking about. He got that money and partied himself to death."

"Aw, shit," Christian said, feeling a sinking in his gut. "I really liked him."

"Yeah, he might've been an old bum and woman chaser, but everyone liked him. Funny thing is, he really took to you. After you left, he blew off everything you had done and said. He didn't take your intimidation seriously."

"Christ," Christian said and closed his eyes, "I acted like a real asshole."

"Don't worry about it. We cornered you and you freaked. Anyway, what's this job? I can always use more money."

CHAPTER TWENTY-FOUR

The following morning, Christian woke to the racket of a pair of sandhill cranes honking near his bedroom window. In the kitchen, he drank coffee and considered his next terrorist attack. *Damn, even Vince thinks I've turned into a heartless bastard and fanatic. Maybe I have.*

He left the house and walked out to the workshop he had built to restore boats in his spare time. A small Luzier sailboat sat on a trailer, its wooden hull sanded and ready for a new coat of varnish. When he and Allie returned from their trip, he had planned to finish the boat. It was another sore reminder of a life he once had.

The warehouse also acted as a garage to store a grown man's toys. He slid between the sailboat and tool bench, passing a ten-horse outboard motor and a dirt bike. At the back of the building, he stepped up on a three-wheeler's seat and removed his old yellow surfboard that hung from the rafters. He examined the board and mumbled, "Should work."

He recalled seeing numerous surfboards loading and unloading at the Panama and Costa Rican airports. A surfer bringing his own board into those countries was a common sight and would not attract attention.

He placed the surfboard on the workbench. With a power saw, he cut out a rectangular square in the top at the center. He removed enough of the inner Styrofoam to hollow out a smuggling space for thirty shark fins. Before leaving, he reinserted the cutout to make sure it fit flush. Once filled with the fins and touched up with a little fiberglass and paint, no one would know about the fins inside.

He walked back into the house for his next task. He took the pan of puffer fish out of the refrigerator and gutted them, but unlike other fish he had cleaned, he kept the entrails and ovaries and discarded the fish bodies. He put the tiny fish guts in a Ziploc bag and placed them in the refrigerator, wondering if there was enough. After burying the puffer fish in the garden, he loaded up his poles in the car and headed to town for another fishing expedition. Rather than using a boat, he waded in the grass flats off City Island. He caught some nice edible speckled trout, red fish, and mackerel, but released them and kept the puffers.

All his life, he had fished and made a habit of learning about each species. Strange now, his knowledge would be used for wrongdoing. He knew the female ovaries and entrails of all puffers, also known as blowfish, carried one of the deadliest poisons on the planet, stronger than arsenic, and comparable to cyanide and strychnine. A person ingesting it could die within the hour, plus the potency was not destroyed by cooking. With its fishy taste, it was perfect for shark fin soup.

Only the Japanese were crazy enough to eat puffer fish, calling it *fugu*. They claimed it gave them a high, but the fish flesh had to be cleaned and prepared by a specially trained and licensed chef. Even then, Christian recalled that over a twenty-year period, 3,000 people had been poisoned from eating *fugu*, and sixty percent had died. Rather impressive numbers for a little fish that anglers discarded.

At sunset he waded back to shore with eight puffers crammed into his floating bait bucket. He put them in the trunk and drove to Siesta Key and his mother's house, knowing Frank would be home at five thirty. He hoped to sign the papers, eat, grab his shipped box of shark fins, and be out of there in a few hours. When he pulled into the drive, he stared suspiciously at the silver Mercedes parked near the front door.

In wet cutoffs, sneakers, and an old stained t-shirt, he entered the house through the kitchen door and met his mother's frown.

"Christian, you're a mess," said his mother, "and I invited a guest for dinner."

"I was fishing and wasn't about to drive all the way home to change."

"I tried calling you all afternoon," she said, "but, of course, I can never reach you."

"Like I said, I was fishing."

"Well, take a shower and shave. There're some nice clothes in your old bedroom."

"No, Mom, I don't have time to clean up and entertain your friends all night." He saw the shipping box and the will and trust papers on the kitchen desk. He grabbed a pen and flipped through the various pages that required his signature. "Tell Frank I signed the papers. He can find someone in his office to fudge as witnesses." He picked up the box. "We'll do dinner another night."

"You can't go."

"What's the problem?" said Frank as he and a woman entered the kitchen.

Christian was floored and immediately agitated, seeing Mary Jane, his psychiatrist. "Ah, Jesus, you invited her? What is this, a goddamn intervention to see if I'm wacked? I'm outta here."

"Christian, don't you dare step out that door," his mother ordered. "We're very concerned about your behavior and wanting this will. Mary Jane was nice enough to come over to talk to you, but if you leave, I swear, Frank and I will have you committed."

"Pull that damn stunt," Christian said with a raised voice, "and you'll never see me again."

"Let's all calm down," said Frank. "I don't think threats are necessary or productive."

"I agree," said Mary Jane. "Christian, this won't take long, and it'll give your parents some peace of mind. No intervention, just you and me. We'll go out by the pool for a private chat. Come on."

"Fine, fine," he said with a disgusted headshake. "Let's get it over with." He carried the box out to the pool, placed it on a chair, and slipped out of his shoes and shirt. He dove into the pool to remove the sticky saltwater from fishing, but also to cool down mentally, not physically. After swimming one lap, he climbed out and took a towel from an outside cabinet.

Mary Jane sat in a lawn chair, waiting for him. "Tell me what is happening with you," she said. "I hear you're reclusive, irritable, and then you drop a bombshell and ask for a will."

"Yeah, I'm fucking irritated. Tends to piss me off when I'm ambushed with a shrink and then threatened into cooperating," he said while drying his torso. "Can they really put me away?" He covered his shoulders with the towel and sat down across from her.

"If you're a threat to yourself or others, they can Baker Act you, lock you in a mental facility for forty-eight hours. Christian, can't you see they're afraid for you? And, frankly, I'm also concerned. You haven't recovered from your wife's death, and your depression appears to be worsening. You've shut everyone out, even stopped visiting your grandparents, whom you dearly love."

"I'm tired of being analyzed and coddled, plus I've just been busy. I spent time in Costa Rica, trying to put my life back together. It helped. I'm not drinking or taking drugs, and I eat and sleep okay. I'm really doing better, Mary Jane."

"That's good, but why the will? It's a red flag that a clinically depressed person is contemplating suicide and doesn't plan to be around."

"Killing myself is nowhere near the top of my to-do list." He lowered his head and stared at his feet. "Had I known this damn will would cause so much grief, I would've forgotten about it. Truth is, I was thinking about my horses, wanted the best for them, in case something happened to me. Obviously, I wasn't thinking how it might look."

"I don't buy that, Christian. I'm sure you love your horses, but you're a young man who will outlive them. There's something else going on."

He stood and removed the towel. "Maybe there is, but suicide isn't it. I promise I'll make an appointment in a few weeks. We'll sit down, and you can repick my brain."

"We need to discuss your problems now."

"Not going to happen, Mary Jane." He placed his shoes and shirt on the box and picked it up. "Enjoy your dinner. My mother's a pain in the ass, but she is a good cook."

"You're not going in to say good-bye?"

"Still too irritated."

"Christian, call me if you need anything, anything at all."

"I'll keep that in mind." He left the screened pool enclosure, walked around the house, and climbed into the car. *Down the road, I might need Mary Jane for an insanity defense.*

Christian felt uncomfortable walking into a Sally Beauty Supply store. After searching what seemed like mile-long aisles with millions of products, he gave up and grabbed a hair dye box with a brunette on the cover. He strolled to the salesclerk at the register. "Is this hard to use?"

"It's for you?"

"Yeah."

"Why in the world would you dye your great blond hair?" the girl asked.

"I don't want it permanently brown, just something temporary that comes out easily in a day."

"Well, you don't want this." She picked up the hair dye and came out from behind the counter. "I'll show you." She walked through the store, and he followed. "I thought I recognized you. You're an actor, aren't you?"

"I've been called that." *But it wasn't a compliment.*

She stopped at the end of an aisle and removed a can of spray from the shelf. "Here, it's real simple. Spray it on and wash it out with shampoo. It comes in all colors, purple, orange, green, or brown." She gazed at him, a little starstruck. "So, the role, is it for a movie or TV?"

"A play, no cameras," he mumbled while reading the instructions on the can. "Thanks, this should work."

He left the store and drove home to transfer money from his Cayman account into a cashier's check to pay Harry for his role in the newest scheme. Using his fake ID, he had rented a different vehicle, an SUV, and booked a commercial flight from Tampa to San Jose, Costa Rica, leaving in a few days.

The day before, he had spent all day preparing the puffer fish, shark fins, and surfboard. Starting with the puffers, he cleaned the eight new fish and added their ovaries and entrails to the others, bringing the count up to fourteen. He spread them across a baking sheet and placed them into a 200-degree oven for eight hours. In his late teens, he had once used the same procedure to dehydrate psilocybin mushrooms to get a hallucinating high.

While waiting for the fish innards to bake, he worked in his cluttered warehouse on the dried shark fins. He drilled a hole up through the bottom and base of each fin, and carefully saved the excess powder so he could patch the fins and conceal the holes once filled with the dehydrated fish innards.

At times guilt crept in, and he felt like the mad Unabomber sending out his packages of death, but then he reflected on the millions of sharks that were senselessly killed every year. His anger and commitment quickly returned.

That evening, he put the dehydrated fish guts in a blender and ground them into a fine powder. He used a paper funnel and filled the fins with his poison. He mixed the excess gray fin dust with glue and vigilantly doctored each fin, so no trace of a hole could be seen. He put on gloves and wiped his fingerprints off each fin before putting it into a freezer baggie and stacking them in the surfboard cavity.

By midnight, he had repaired the surfboard with strips of new fiberglass, covering the rectangular hole that held the fins. His next job was a meticulous cleanup of the warehouse building and house, removing all traces of fins and fish. The following day he sanded the fiberglass patchwork and sprayed the entire board with a fast-drying coat of yellow paint. He was ready, but was the world ready for him and his deadly message?

•   •   •

In Costa Rica before sunrise, the cell phone on the living room coffee table started buzzing. Harry woke, but rather than get out of bed and answer the call, he buried his head under a pillow. It didn't help. He still heard the sound.

"Motherfucker," he growled. "Who the fuck is calling this early?" He crawled out of bed and staggered through the dark house. Nearing the phone, he tripped on his sleeping Rottweiler and scrambled, grabbing a chair to prevent a fall. He snatched up his cell and hit Talk, still cursing at the yipping dog. "Get the fuck out of my way, goddamn it."

"And good morning to you too," said Christian.

"Fuck, Hot Dog. What the time is it?"

"Your time, six thirty, I said I'd call today. You need to get moving. I'm boarding my flight and should be there in three hours. I'll meet you outside baggage claim with my surfboard. And, Harry, bring a knife."

"All right, all right, all right," Harry said. "See ya in a bit." After the call, Harry threw on clothes and put the dog outside, still peeved about Christian's early flight and the impending long drive through the mountains to pick him up at the San Jose airport.

"The shithead could've rented a car with all his money and saved me a long-ass trip," he said and climbed into his Jeep. "The overly cautious prick, too fucking worried about paperwork and someone remembering him."

At mid-morning, Harry pulled up to the airport and saw the lanky blond waiting on the curb. Wearing shades, a baseball cap, and holding a surfboard, he looked like the average tourist who visited Costa Rica for the waves. Looks could be deceiving, though, and Harry wondered about Christian's newest plot, since he didn't reveal anything over the phone.

"Hey, Harry," Christian said and placed his board on the Jeep roof rack. "Good seeing you. Hope you're up for some driving."

"Not sure seeing you again is good." Harry got out and helped Christian tie his board down. "I believe the cops are on to you. After you left, they showed up with your picture and questioned me and the people at the beach bar, asking if we knew ya or seen ya. Good thing I have a lot of friends, and everyone kept their mouth shut."

"Sorry about that," Christian said and both men climbed into the Jeep. "I've been on their radar since my wife died and the shit in the Bahamas. I made one damn mistake when here. I called my farm to check on the horses and say I'd be here longer. They traced my cell and learned I had stayed in Jacó. That's the trouble with experience, you don't get it until after you need it."

Harry drove out of the airport. "So, where are we going?"

"The Puntarenas harbor, but nothing criminal, just a fast delivery to an exporter, and I'll be back on a plane and out of your hair by midnight."

"Sounds good, as long as you're making it worth my while."

Nearing Puntarenas, they pulled off the highway and onto a deserted mountain road. Christian removed the items from his bag and went to work, radically changing his appearance. He sprayed his hair brown, put on a fake mustache, and darkened his eyebrows with a pencil liner. When finished with his disguise, he could pass for a Costa Rican. He next cut his surfboard open with Harry's knife and removed the shark fins.

Harry frowned. "Thought you were trying to save sharks?"

"Better you don't ask too many questions." Careful not to touch the fins, he dumped them into a garbage bag and stored them in the Jeep. He also wiped his fingerprints off the ruined surfboard, the knife, and everything used in his disguise before heaving them into the foliage off a cliff. They soon were on the main road and traveling west toward the port.

"You're being damn careful, as usual," Harry said while driving, "but if the cops suspect you of being Nemo, why in the devil take the risk of walking in and out of airports with cameras and going through customs?"

"I have a fake ID, and on camera, I might resemble Christian Roberts, but with sunglasses and a hat, the cops can't prove it. Actually the worrisome part is over. The fins and I got in without a hassle."

"You have it backward. Coming into Costa Rica is a walk in the park. They love tourists and don't bother them. Leaving and facing US Customs is the problem. They think everyone is a drug smuggler. Even with a fake passport, you're more likely to get busted on the return trip."

"Harry, once this job is done, it doesn't matter what happens to me."

Harry raised his eyebrows, but didn't bother to comment and embellish. He knew the kid was screwed up, half the time down in the dumps and the other half a little psycho. *With his looks and wealth, it's a damn shame.*

They arrived in Puntarenas and drove past the shell of three burned-out buildings, and beyond, several charred hulls, remnants of trawlers, rested in the waterway, all testaments to Christian's fiery rampage. "Enjoying the view?" Harry asked, gazing at the destruction.

"I am. I don't feel bad one damn bit. Pull into an alley. I need a fish crate for these fins."

On a side street, Harry stopped in front of a stack of empty crates. Christian hopped out and tossed a crate into the Jeep. Farther up the street, Harry parked in front of a stucco dwelling. They got out and Christian placed the fins in the crate so they appeared to have come off a fishing boat.

"What's next, Hot Dog?" Harry asked.

"Simple, we walk to the harbor road and tell the first locals we see that we found the fins and ask if they want them."

"Well, of course they'll want them," said Harry. "They're worth a lot of money. I got a better idea. Why don't we just sell them to an exporter?"

"Sure, and they'll want your name and the name of your boat for the receipt and will probably give you a check you'll have to worry about cashing. Trust me, Harry, the money isn't worth it. You don't want these fins coming back to you."

"That's bull. Once the exporter has them, who can say what fin came from who or where?"

"I'm counting on that, but I'm also not taking any chances." Christian walked toward the main drag, carrying the crate of fins.

Harry followed and was more curious than ever about the fins and Christian's plan. They came upon four men who sat under a shade tree. Harry spoke to them in Spanish, initially following Christian's instructions. He told them that he and his friend had found the fins on the road, but he relied on human greed to lie when he asked if any of them had lost the crate. An honest man trying to do right was more believable than a charitable idiot giving away a fortune in fins.

The closest man and obviously the quickest thinker jumped up and claimed the fins. He snatched the crate from Christian's hands. Only when Christian and Harry started to walk away did the man thank them. Halfway down the street, Harry explained to Christian exactly what he had said to the men. "I don't know what your deal is with those fins, but if that guy gets in trouble, it's his own damn fault for lying."

"Good thinking, Harry," Christian said. "We're done. Just get me back to San Jose and my evening flight. I need to hit a restroom along the way so I can wash this shit out of my hair. I have to be blond to match my passport."

"That's it?" Harry asked.

"Yep, except one last thing besides paying you." In the Jeep, Christian dug into his bag and handed Harry the cashier's check along with a white envelope. "Inside here is a postcard addressed to the US. I'd like you to mail it two weeks from now. And, Harry, don't mail it from Jacó or touch it. Your fingerprints will have the cops banging on your door."

"Two weeks from now is Valentine's Day. Mail is slow here. Your postcard won't reach the US for probably another two weeks."

"I know. I plan on having it arrive around the end of the month."

"For this kind of money, you didn't need to fly over here, put on a disguise, and do this. You could've shipped the fins, and I could've handled it, but maybe you don't trust me."

"Has nothing to do with trust. I didn't want to leave a paper trail from Florida to Costa Rica, plus packages get lost, stolen, and confiscated in the mail. There's also the time factor. I wanted it done quickly." Christian paused with a slow breath. "Besides, this is something I had to do myself."

At the offices of the *Washington Post*, Trish sat at her desk and reread her finished piece on Captain Nemo for what seemed like the hundredth time. The story was ready. It was only a matter of a short walk down the aisle and handing it, with Christian's photo, to her editor for publication, but she was having difficulty rising.

Her loyalty kept swaying back and forth between Christian and her job. She gazed at his picture, taken aboard the sloop. He stood at the helm in a dark blue sweater, the wind mussing his longish blond hair, with a backdrop of inky bay water and flaming sunset. The photo was gorgeous, one of the best she had ever taken, or maybe it was the subject.

Closing her eyes, she relived the memory, more like flashes in a bewitching dream, first him on the horse, both lean-muscled daredevils racing as one across the pasture. She then spoke to him and stared up into his incredibly blue eyes and, finally, they spent the evening on the sloop. She relived his seductive smiles and little-boy chuckles while he cooked dinner, followed by the tender kisses and crawling on top of her, making her his.

She had never met a man so close to a living fantasy. He was gorgeous with an outdoorsy nature, but Trish was more drawn to his intellect. He was laid-back, sweet, and interesting, yet beneath his pretense lay reckless tension, bleak and menacing, created from his devotion to a dead woman.

The thought of Christian in prison made her ill. Given his makeup, it would be like caging a wild bird; chance of survival not good. *The heck with the job, I can't do it to him. This story with his picture will only hurt him.* She shoved the article in a drawer and picked up the phone.

"Hey, how's the writing?" Christian said, obviously seeing the *Post* on his caller ID.

"I'm finished."

"I hope you didn't portray me as too much of a bad guy."

"No, it's actually favorable," said Trish. "It says you're a person of interest and police suspect you of being Captain Nemo, but it mentions your alibis for the arsons in the Bahamas and Costa Rica, and that you were in Miami during the New York bombings."

"I appreciate it. Are you calling to warn me that it's about to hit the newsstands?"

"Christian, I'm giving up the exclusive and holding off on the story. If and when you're arrested, I'll put it out, along with every other reporter. I don't feel right making your life miserable with the press camped on your doorstep."

"I don't know what to say, except thanks."

"You know you've ruined me? I used to be a hard-hitting journalist. Everything took a backseat when it came to my job. Now I'm a sap, staring at your picture and having pipe dreams."

"Sorry, I didn't mean to do that."

"Yes, you did. Let's be honest. I came to Florida to expose you and get a fabulous story. You went after me to stop it. You won."

"I suppose that was my initial agenda, but after knowing you, honestly, Trish, I wished we'd met under different circumstances. I had a great time with you on the sloop, something I rarely experience anymore. "

"Christian, I don't regret a thing. Being with you was like getting a first car and driving to Disney."

He chuckled. "No one's ever said that before."

"You apparently never dated a writer." She laughed. "But, seriously, I can't remember having a better time. I know your life is in shambles, but regardless, I like you, and hope we stay in touch."

"Count on it," he said. "If things work out and I get out of this mess, maybe you can give me a tour of DC."

"It's a date."

Several weeks after her phone call to Christian, Trish received a postcard from Costa Rica with a picture of a shark. The back inscription said, "A warning to the world: eat shark fins and die—Captain Nemo."

For an hour, she frantically called Christian, but he didn't answer his home or cell phone. With no choice, she gave the postcard to her editor who notified the police.

In the Miami diner, the cute young waitress approached Wheeler's table holding a pot of a fresh-brewed coffee. "Refill, Dave?"

"Sure," Wheeler said and pushed his cup closer.

"I'm going to miss you coming in here for your breakfast."

"Darlin', I'll miss you too, but I have had my fill of disability leave. I'm ready to get back to work." His cell phone chimed. He recognized Ralph's number. "What's up?"

"You're not going to believe this. You're just not going to believe this, Dave," said Ralph, his voice high pitched and anxious. "I just got word Roberts is at it again."

"Settle down, Ralph, and explain."

"Captain Nemo sent another postcard to the *Washington Post* reporter. It's postmarked Costa Rica, and said, 'A warning to the world: eat shark fins and die.' It can only mean he plans to bomb or burn restaurants that serve fin soup, but which restaurant and where?"

"It said a warning to the world, eat shark fins and die." Wheeler leaned back and thought about it. "I don't think he intends to blow anything up. This is a worldwide threat, and 'eat and die' most likely means poison. He's imitating the Tylenol scare when pills were laced with poison, causing the manufacturer to pull every bottle nationwide from the shelves. I'm betting he's tampered with the fins. I'd start with New York and have the fins removed from the Chinese stores and restaurants and then tested."

"The detectives up there are scrambling to get an arrest warrant in place for Roberts. They want him behind bars before the story hits the papers and warns him. Once the Manatee County Sheriff's Department has the warrant, they'll bring him in, maybe as early as today. I'm getting his case files together. I want to question him before he's shipped out of Florida. This is it. He's going down."

"I'll be in the office shortly." Wheeler stood and motioned to the waitress for his check. "I'll be coming along." He sighed, slipped his phone into a pocket, and rubbed his healed gunshot wound. *Christian, what are you doing? Have you stepped up your game? Gone to mass murder?*

After Wheeler arrived at the Miami FBI office, he and Ralph drove across the state to the Manatee County Sheriff's Department in Bradenton, a city north of Sarasota. Although Roberts's farm was directly east and closer to Sarasota, the location was a few miles within Manatee County. After his arrest, a US marshal would fly him to New York.

An hour later, the sheriff's department received the arrest warrant from the New York prosecutor. Wheeler and Ralph, along with four deputies in two squad cars, drove to Roberts's horse farm.

They banged on the house door, but no one answered. Juan, the Mexican farmhand, hurried up from the barn and unlocked the door. While the deputies did a search of the house, barn, caretaker house, and the small boat workshop, Wheeler and Ralph questioned Juan about Roberts's whereabouts.

"Señor Roberts left yesterday," said Juan. "He only said, 'Take care of my horses.' It was strange because he knows I always do so. He seemed very sad."

"He didn't say where he was going?" asked Wheeler.

"No, but perhaps he went to the Keys or is visiting his mother or Señor Vince."

Ralph asked, "Has he taken any trips, since I was here last with the search warrant? Returned to Costa Rica, maybe?"

"No, Mr. Roberts has been here every night," Juan said and gazed up at Wheeler. "Why do you do this to him? He is a kind, honest man and already suffers with the loss of his wife. They were so much in love."

Instead of the psychological thrill of the hunt, Wheeler felt disgusted, chasing Roberts down and locking him up. "All right, you're willing to testify in court that Roberts was here, and to your knowledge he never left town?"

"Sí, señor; my mother too," said Juan and pointed to a distant farmhouse. "The neighbor, also, will say the same. Two weeks ago Mr. Vic's cattle escaped on the road. Mr. Roberts helped him catch them. They spent nearly a week replacing the barbed wire on the fences."

Wheeler raised an eyebrow and glanced at Ralph. "That would've been the same date that the postcard was stamped and mailed from Costa Rica."

"Yeah, but he could've dropped it in a mailbox the night before, got on a plane, and been here by morning to catch cows," Ralph said.

"No," said Juan. "I can see Mr. Roberts's house from my home and his lights have come on every evening, and his car is here in the morning. Until yesterday, he has gone nowhere."

"That's all for now," Wheeler said to Juan. He and Ralph walked to their car. "With these witnesses and the fact that we have Roberts's passport, it's doubtful he went to Costa Rica and mailed the post-card. I'm also betting the postcard is like the last one and doesn't have his fingerprints."

"So he's got the money," said Ralph. "He hired someone to mail the card and commit the crime, just like the New York grocery stores."

"Until we find the person who helped him, there's not much of a case, only the sketchy New York witness."

A deputy walked up to them. "We searched the property. He's not here."

"All right," Wheeler said. "My partner and I will take the warrant and visit his mother and Mr. Florio's residence in Sarasota. Put out an APB on him, that he's a suspected terrorist, possibly dangerous and mentally unsound."

An hour later, Wheeler and Ralph arrived at Roberts's mother and stepfather's home on Siesta Key. When his parents saw the arrest warrant and learned of the accusations against Christian, his stepfather was speechless, and his mother cried hysterically. They obviously had no knowledge of Christian's crimes or where he was, but with their consent, Ralph did a quick search of their home.

At sundown Ralph pulled into Vince Florio's driveway and stared at the large waterfront home on the bay. "Maybe we should've called for backup."

"Unnecessary," Wheeler said and opened his passenger door. "Florio might be a mobster, but he's not stupid. He won't give us trouble." He walked to the front door with Ralph and pressed the bell.

Vince answered the door with a grin. "Agent Wheeler, it's been a while. You must've missed me, to drive this far, but maybe you didn't get the message I'm retired."

"I'm not here about you. I'm looking for your young friend, Christian Roberts." Wheeler retrieved the arrest warrant from his jacket pocket and handed it to Vince.

"Christian isn't here," Vince mumbled while reading the warrant in the doorway. He handed it back to Wheeler. "This warrant is bullshit. To my knowledge, Christian's never been to New York."

Ralph jumped in. "He was there mid-January, plotting the bombing of two Chinese grocery stores. We know he's Nemo. Now the *Washington Post* has received a second postcard from him, warning of another terrorist attack. We need to search your house."

"I don't think so," Vince said. "Your warrant doesn't mention my address. You'll have to get another warrant. Also, mid-January, Christian was here with me. Just ask my neighbors. They'll tell you his SUV was in my driveway for ten days. Put that in your notes,

Agent. I'm not fond of court appearances, but for him, I'll show up and give him an alibi."

"That's bull," said Ralph, "Lying to the FBI and harboring a fugitive is a crime. You'll go to jail with him."

Vince laughed. "Wheeler, Christian told me about your partner. Tell your boy he belongs back on his mother's tit and needs to grow some teeth before he threatens me."

"Ralph, wait in the car. I'd like to speak with Mr. Florio alone," said Wheeler.

Ralph huffed and walked to the car.

Wheeler turned back to Vince. "We've searched Christian's farm and his mother's home and can't find him. There's an APB out on him. You know it's better if he turns himself in rather than risk being shot by some nervous cop."

"If I see him, I'll tell him."

"That's not what I want. I'm a pretty good judge of character, and I believe Christian has suicidal tendencies. The Mexican at his farm said he seemed awfully sad yesterday, and I learned from his parents he drew up a will. With this newest postcard, he has to know it's over and we're coming for him. I'm worried, Vince. The kid saved my life. I like him. I know you do too. Do you have any idea where he might be?"

"Did ya know he also saved my ass, pulled me from the drink when I nearly drowned? So, sure, I care about him, but really, I haven't seen him in weeks and don't know where he is."

"Okay." Wheeler breathed deeply and turned to leave.

"Wait," said Vince. "Have you checked his sloop at Marina Jack? His wife died on that boat. If Christian plans to kill himself, he'll do it there."

"Thanks." Wheeler hotfooted to the car, and he and Ralph raced to Marina Jack on the bayfront off downtown Sarasota. They hustled down the dock, only to stare at the empty slip where *Hank's Dream* had been.

CHAPTER TWENTY-FIVE

Early in the morning, Chef Chin entered the large warehouse of the Beijing market. With a face that looked like he had stepped on rakes most of his life, and his portly frame, he waddled more than walked down the rows of tables holding ice and fresh seafood. His eyes resembled stab wounds when he selected fish for Emperor Restaurant, one of the finest eateries in China. Besides the fish, crabs, fish stomachs, and shrimp eggs, he purchased dried seahorses and three large scalloped hammerhead fins. Those particular fins created an ideal gelatinous soup. The fin size was also important. When cooked and broken apart, they became hair-thin translucent noodles, and the longer the noodles, the longer the life of the diner, or so believed. Only a basking shark, whale, or great white's fin was more sought after and more expensive than the scalloped hammerhead's, since those other species were supposedly protected. Chin was aware of the increase in price as the quantity of large fins had decreased over the years, a sure sign that big sharks were disappearing, especially hammerheads.

After personally shopping for the best the market offered, he returned to the restaurant and prepared the day's menu for the wealthy businessmen and government officials that were frequent customers. The average poor Chinese man couldn't afford to dine at the Emperor or pay for long noodles from big fins.

Chin placed a dressed chicken and Jinhua ham in a large pot to start the broth, because fins were virtually tasteless. After an hour, he added some Shaoxing wine to the soup. The truck of a food vendor arrived behind the restaurant. The vendor specialized in procuring exotic delicacies, so Chin took a break from cooking and met him in the alley.

"I have tiger today," the vendor said and removed a ten-pound wrapped package. "Very rare. For you, Chin, I give a good price."

Chin opened the package and stared at the steaks. "Wild or domestic?" he asked.

"Domestic, young tiger, not tough old one," said the vendor, and reached for a smaller plastic bag. "Also a male; I have its penis, but very expensive."

Chin knew the tiger had come from the zoo that specialized in raising big cats. The zoo acted as a front for a slaughterhouse. A tiger that entertained children one day would eventually end up on a dinner plate, and its bones and teeth would be in jars at the medicine shops. Tiger parts were supposedly illegal; the law existed mainly to squelch world outcry, but many bureaucrats turned a blind eye when dining on endangered species at the Emperor. Chin purchased the steaks and the tiger penis, a highly desired alleged aphrodisiac.

At noon the restaurant began to fill with customers. The majority were administrators in the communist regime. They were seated at large round tables with a lazy Susan in the center. The bizarre entries were placed on a revolving tray for all to sample. A table of twelve officials wearing smart uniforms was the first to order the shark fin soup. Soon after, eight wealthy businessmen in suits requested the soup in celebration of a coworker's birthday.

It was business as usual. Chin hustled around sampling dishes and snapped out orders to his cooks, making sure each dish was glamorous before leaving the kitchen. He was preparing a bowl of monkey brain when he heard shouts in the dining room and a server rushed in.

"A man is sick at the officials' table. They've called for an ambulance," said the server.

"It can't be from my food," Chin said. "They've had only the soup and less than fifteen minutes ago. Food poisoning shows up a good hour or more later. Is he vomiting?"

"No, he complained his tongue went numb. Now he can't even speak."

Chin took off his apron and headed to the dining room to investigate. The other diners had left their seats and crowded around the sick man at the officials' table. Chin pushed his way through the anxious people and saw the thin older man who had collapsed on the floor, convulsing and gasping for breath. A fellow diner cradled his head and tried to console him.

Chin concluded the old man probably suffered from an existing ailment or possibly a food allergy, but then a second customer in government uniform screamed, "There's no feeling in my lips!" His face was red, and he slapped his mouth, hoping to feel sensation. "I can't. I can barely speak."

Before anyone could grasp what was happening, a third man cried out and complained of the same symptoms, but he wore a suit and was one of the businessmen. The restaurant became utter chaos. Some people fled, fearing an airborne virus, while other chattered in panic. When the ambulance arrived, five men were down, unable to speak and struggling with spasms and difficulty breathing. Fifteen more were experiencing the first warning signs of mouth and skin numbness.

Flushed and rattled, Chin covered his mouth and was shocked to notice that his lips lacked feeling, like they had been injected with Novocain. He had sampled the soup before it was served.

Four hours after the old man ate the shark fin soup and collapsed in the Emperor restaurant, he went into respiratory arrest and died, becoming the first victim. Twenty-four hours later, thirteen of the other diners suffered the same fate. Seven customers and the chef survived.

Because the shark fin soup was the first course and the only thing eaten by all twenty-one people, the police concluded the soup was poisoned. The restaurant was shut down, and the employees with access to the soup pot became the most likely perpetrators. Everyone, from the owner to the dishwashers, was brought to the police department and questioned. A disgruntled employee fired from his serving job that day proved the most promising suspect and was jailed.

The police worked the investigation while pathologists received soup samples. They could detect almost any poison, but, unfortunately, they had to know which poison to test for. They had to start with the symptoms, but because hundreds of poisons could produce similar symptoms, their conclusion could take weeks. Without the test results, the police did not know what to look for, but they assumed it was an isolated incident, as did the local press.

The hypothesis changed three days later when nine diners at another Beijing restaurant became ill after eating shark fin soup. With five of the nine dying, the story got the attention of the national press. The Beijing government scrambled and ordered shark fins be confiscated from every market, grocery, and restaurant. A warning went out to citizens not to eat their dried fins.

The poisonings had only occurred in Beijing, so the rest of China felt secure in enjoying shark fin soup, but in one terrifying night, all sense of security was shattered. In three Hong Kong restaurants, thirty-six diners succumbed to poisoned soup. A wedding in Taiwan claimed the life of three caterers and a cook who sampled the soup before serving it to guests. Ten more people died in a Taiwan restaurant after eating tainted soup. The story of poisoned fins spread on the Internet and international media faster than the body count.

The day before, the *Washington Post* had run the article about the eco-terrorist, Captain Nemo, and his postcard warning, "Eat shark fins and die." The correlation had become clear, his deadly threat serious. Nemo's words spread throughout Asia, and governments yanked the fins from consumer access. With sixty-eight deaths and counting, half the globe was paralyzed, bringing a halt to the shark fin trade in the Far East.

CHAPTER TWENTY-SIX

On the last day in February, the morning weather was a crisp fifty degrees and sunny with clear blue skies. Christian drove to downtown Sarasota and parked at Marina Jack. He cast off the lines on his sloop and sailed out of Big Pass to the Gulf of Mexico. With no set course in mind, he pointed the bow southward, sailing five miles offshore.

He stared at the ribbon of coastline that drifted past and the pristine green water shimmering under his vessel. The only sound was the brisk wind filling the sheets, the slush of waves hitting the bow, and the faint cries of sea birds farther out that circled and dove for a school of baitfish. *This is it, my last voyage.*

For five months he had locked his heart and humanity into a coffin with Allie and had done everything in his power to save sharks. The task, the goal, was over. He had calculated when the poisoned fins would reach their destination, be sold, and used for soup. The postcard's arrival to Trish at the *Washington Post* should closely coincide with the demise of the first victim. With his final masterpiece of terrorism unveiling in days, he knew the authorities would issue an arrest warrant and come after him as the most likely suspect and Captain Nemo.

He had been overly cautious with his terrorist plots, not so much to protect himself, but to safeguard Captain Nemo and his cause. His mission completed, nothing mattered except a final choice that lay before him. He glanced beyond the endless white beaches and imagined what waited: the shackles of police, a fuming public, an annoying press, and then a drawn-out trial ending with a lifetime in a cage or the death penalty. He looked right at the peaceful open sea and then considered the option of using his father's old revolver and joining Allie. *Another no-brainer, but damn, it's hard. If I kill myself and take the easy way out, I'm a coward. If I don't have the guts to do it, I'm a coward. Jesus, why do I care at this point?*

Throughout the day, he struggled with the decision while maintaining his southern journey. Before leaving, he had rid his sailboat of cell phones and electronics, so the law could not pinpoint his location.

At sundown he figured he was somewhere between Fort Myers and Naples. He lowered the sails and anchored a mile offshore, deciding to have one more night to relish life, freedom, and the sea he hoped he had spared. In the cabin he made a Bloody Mary, grabbed a pen and paper, and tossed a bag of chips on the booth table. *Lousy last meal*, he thought. He sat down and wrote a farewell message to his mother. He didn't admit guilt for his crimes, but explained he couldn't live without Allie. He became teary eyed, asking forgiveness for taking his life. Suicide notes supposedly help the grieving and answer unanswered questions. *There you go, Mom.* He sniffled and placed the note in a drawer. He fixed several more cocktails, finishing the half bottle of vodka, and passed out in the berth.

He rose at dawn and set sail for the wide-open Gulf of Mexico. Several hours later and about thirty miles out, he dropped the sails and retrieved the revolver from the berth. "Okay, let's do it," he said and settled back on the bench in the open cockpit. He aimed the barrel under his chin so the bullet would exit through the top of his head. Vince had said a temple shot was a bad idea. Although screwed up, a person could survive the suicide attempt. Christian wasn't religious or much of a believer, but if ever there was a time to pray, this was it.

God, if you're there, I'm not sorry for what I've done. It was war. The shark extermination had to be stopped, even at the cost of lives and my soul. My only regret is Allie. My anger got her killed, so judge me as you see fit.

He closed his eyes and his hand trembled. He started to squeeze the trigger but heard a loud, high-pitched, *"Ha-ha-ha-ha-haab-haab-haab-haab."* The cackling came from a gull that had landed mid-boat and was perched on the railing.

He lowered the gun. "Way too freaky," he whispered, staring at the black-headed seabird with a white chest and gray wings. It was called a laughing gull. This same species had circled overhead in the Bahamas when Allie died and was constantly in Christian's nightmares; its shrill cries accusing him that his wife's death was his fault.

Even stranger, he knew laughing gulls, once a common seabird in Florida, were scarce because of development and the destruction of their nesting places in coastal marches. They, like countless other creatures, were disappearing because of mankind. What were the odds of such a rare seagull landing on his boat miles out in the gulf?

He brushed off the irony, symbolism, or whatever and yelled at the bird, "Go on! Get off my boat! Go find someplace else to rest." He waved his hand and the gull took off. Killing himself was difficult enough without a tormenting bird watching.

He settled back, but as he raised his weapon again, the gull landed on the upper deck. "Allie, if you've come back as this fucking bird to stop me, you're too late. It's taken me all day and night to get up the nerve. Now I've done what you wanted, and I'm tired of hurting. I just want it to be over. Now go on, get lost."

The gull tossed its head back and squawked. It shook its head, ruffled its feathers, and looked at him, but didn't budge.

"No?" he growled at the bird, "I shouldn't die? Well, fuck you." He hastily aimed the weapon at his head and pulled the trigger, but the gun jammed. He breathed hard and shook while examining the weapon. The safety was still on. The suicide attempt had taken every ounce of his courage and willpower. He had to summon what remained and try again. He covered his mouth, and his eyes watered. Was the distraction of a tired bird and the gun not firing a coincidence or a sign from Allie or God?

Tears blurred his vision as he gazed at the gull. "What are you trying to tell me, that it's not my time?" he asked softly. Bizarrely, the bird answered with a cackle and flew away. He lowered his head and shook it. "Jesus Christ, I'm losing it. I don't even believe in reincarnation."

He set the gun down and reflected that this was not the first time that divine intervention had stepped in and saved him. A few years back, a cruel horse trainer and two Arabs working for a sheik had kidnapped him and taken him to the Everglades to execute him over a horse deal. Bound and kneeling in an open grave with an Arab's knife pressed to his jugular, Christian had prayed to his dead father for help. Seconds later, gunfire erupted and the kidnappers were dead. Vince's men had come to the rescue. Christian walked out of the Glades firmly believing his deceased father had saved him.

He glanced up at the blue heavens. *Am I truly not finished here?* It then occurred to him that if he died, so did Captain Nemo, with Wong claiming that Christian was him. Nemo's death also meant the death of his cause. People wouldn't be afraid to eat shark fins again. *It will all be for nothing. Maybe there's more I need to do or else, deep down, maybe I'm looking for an excuse to live.*

He stood, started the diesel, and raised the sails. Without the GPS, he had no clue as to his location, not that had he cared. But he was back in the game and had to consider his next move. He could cruise south and island-hop the Caribbean for weeks, even months, avoiding detection, or he could sail west to Mexico. With paint, he could disguise the sloop and change his own appearance as he had done in Costa Rica. Disappearing in Central and South America, he might not be found for years.

Instead of those alternatives, he turned the sloop eastward toward Florida and an arrest. Sooner or later, he'd be caught, so why put off the inevitable? He also realized the case against him was weak, more coincidence than reliable evidence, with only one shady witness saying he planned the terrorist attacks. In his defense, he had a solid alibi for each crime, but a suspect who runs looks guilty. He wasn't going to give the prosecution that advantage.

• • •

In the late afternoon, he reached the coast, but saw only mangrove outcrops and small, desolate keys. He had made landfall in the southern Everglades. Getting his bearings with channel markers, he set a course for Key West, deciding on one last drink and good time before all hell broke loose. Curiosity had also played a small role in delaying his suicide. With the sloop stripped of communication, he had no knowledge if his latest terrorist attack had succeeded. No doubt the *Washington Post* had received Nemo's last postcard, but had anyone died from his poisoned fins? If so, did mass hysteria stop the fin trade and save the sharks? In Key West, he'd get answers.

He motored into a slip at the Key West marina that was up the street from a Jimmy Buffett store. After paying for dockage, he strolled toward the heart of town. The key was quiet, compared to his prior visit in October during Fantasy Fest, when the streets were closed to traffic for partiers. The event had been a blast, but only because Allie was with him.

He strolled down the sidewalk and picked up the daily newspaper, but decided to read it over a cocktail. With the paper under his arm, he skirted past the window shoppers, the diners coming and going from restaurants, and the drinkers who overflowed onto the sidewalks from the congested bars. Most were tourists escaping the cold North. He felt out of place. *Alone in a crowd takes on new meaning,* he thought.

He reached Sloppy Joe's and entered the quaint, landmark bar. The place was jam-packed, and he regretted making Key West his destination. He should have sailed on to Islamorada or Pine Key, both of which were quieter. Under the dim lighting and ceiling canopy of old parachutes, he saw a group of six older men sitting at a round table. They looked like locals, old salty-dog boaters. He migrated toward them, but halfway to their table, he was seized by two slightly intoxicated girls.

"We saw you come in," one said, running her hand up his back to his hair as the other caressed his arm. "We have an extra chair at our table. Why don't you join us?"

He smiled. "Sorry, I'm taken."

"Where is she?" she asked.

"Sorry." He pulled free of their grasp and approached the old men. "Mind if I sit with you?"

"Come on, young fella," said the closest man with a snowy beard who was obviously going for the Hemingway look. "But those two pretty gals were all over you. You'd probably have more fun with them than us."

"Yeah," Christian said with raised eyebrows. "They're nice, but I just sailed in, and I'm a little whipped. Not in the mood for romance just yet. My name's Christian." He shook their hands before sitting down.

"Sonny, at your age, I never passed up that kind of opportunity," said another man wearing a baseball cap. "So, where'd you sail in from, Christian?"

"Sarasota, it's my home. Been in Florida all my life."

"Hey, we got ourselves a real cracker," said another man. "Not many of them around."

"There are if you know where to look." Christian smiled and opened the newspaper. He covered his gaping mouth to hide his shock, seeing the front-page article that read "Captain Nemo Struck Again. Eco-terrorist Poisons Sixty-eight in Asia." At the bottom, he saw his picture with a caption asking, "Could this be Captain Nemo?" Trish had said she would not release the story and his picture until his arrest warrant had been issued. The photo confirmed that he was wanted.

The old man with the beard tapped the paper. "We were just talking about this Captain Nemo."

"Yeah," said another man from the group. "Poisoning fins, who would've thought it?"

"Wait a minute," said the man with the cap. "You're from Sarasota?" he asked Christian. "Captain Nemo is supposedly from—" His eyes grew big. "Holy Christ, you're him. You're Christian Roberts, the guy in the picture that they suspect of being Captain Nemo." He jumped up, pointed at Christian, and shouted to the whole bar. "It's him. It's Captain Nemo!" The noisy bar instantly became pin-drop quiet, with everyone staring at Christian.

With a hundred faces watching his every move, Christian slowly stood and backed against the wall, preparing for the worst. He was a terrorist, serial killer, a bomber, and arsonist. He expected to be jumped and beaten.

"He is Nemo," screamed a woman several tables over. Other patrons joined in, "It's Captain Nemo."

The bearded old man stood and stepped to Christian with a grin. "You're among friends." He raised his beer mug to the crowd. "Here's to Captain Nemo, the young man who single-handedly did whatever it took to save our sharks and oceans. In my book, he deserves a medal."

The bar erupted into loud cheers. Many shouted, "Nemo! Nemo! Nemo!" Christian was taken aback, not expecting the warm response. Trish must have written one sympathetic story about him. But he was in Key West, a wacky little town surrounded by reefs with residents who cherished sea life. It shouldn't have been a surprise that they lacked empathy for victims half a globe away who died practicing the barbarian fetish of eating fins.

Christian was mobbed with handshakes and pats on the back, and his earlier suicide attempt crossed his mind. *This is the reason I was meant to live. I needed to see the validation for my cause. I'm not alone in my fight.*

Christian sat down with a line of free cocktails on the table. He drank and chatted with people, not denying or admitting he was Nemo. He knew not everyone there was an admirer, and before long, his location would be leaked to the authorities.

The bearded old man must have thought the same thing. "Christian, someone here is bound to call the cops," he said. "Get to your boat and hide out in the Glades or make for open sea or you can come home with me. I'll keep you safe until I can smuggle you off the keys."

Christian put his hand on the old man's shoulder. "Thanks, really, but I'm not running."

Within a half hour, the bar celebration came to a screeching halt with the arrival of squad cars with flashing red lights and sirens. They surrounded Sloppy Joe's, blocking two street exits. The laughter diminished to hushed mumbles, and smiling faces turned to concerned frowns. With a bullhorn, a police captain ordered everyone out for their own safety.

Christian reclined in a chair and watched the exodus. Some women blew him kisses, and men somberly wished him good luck as they filed past on their way outside. He nodded to them and thought the party had been short but so sweet. He sipped on a drink and waited for the police.

When the last patron left and Christian was alone, a dozen policemen with drawn weapons flooded the bar. Several yelled, "Hands in the air, stand up!"

"I'm not resisting," he said, raising his hands. When he calmly rose from the chair, they rushed him. He was slammed across the table, searched, and handcuffed.

Two police officers held his arms, and the captain said, "Christian Roberts, you're under arrest for terrorist attacks and plotting the bombing of two New York stores. And that's just for starters, Captain Nemo." He then read Christian his rights.

When Christian was escorted to the door, he saw that the bar crowd had grown from a hundred to more than a thousand. Word quickly had spread through the little town that Captain Nemo was in Sloppy Joe's and being arrested. Everyone wanted a glimpse of the infamous eco-terrorist. He stepped out on the sidewalk in view of the awaiting mass, and it erupted with boos and curses aimed at the arresting cops. "Let him go," many yelled.

A unified chant then began, "Nemo! Nemo! Nemo! Nemo!" This time it was deafening. The small police force struggled to hold back the angry mob as Christian was quickly placed into a squad car and whisked away. The car drove down the street, yet he still heard the demonstration from his Key West fans.

• • •

At mid-morning, Agent Wheeler arrived in the Miami FBI office. The day before, he and Ralph had driven two hundred miles to Sarasota to arrest Christian Roberts. The trip was a series of dead ends. They finally learned Roberts had sailed off into the Gulf. They arrived back in Miami late last night, the manhunt having moved out of their hands and to the water. They notified the Coast Guard and hoped it would find the Catalina sloop named *Hank's Dream*. Given his recent terrorist attack involving the murder of sixty-eight people, Roberts had to know he was hunted, making a pleasure cruise unlikely.

Ralph was convinced Roberts was a fugitive and on the run, and granted, the kid was smart, knew the waters, and where and how to hide, even in a large, slow sloop, but Wheeler had his own ideas. Depressed with the mounting pressure, Roberts had most likely sailed out to kill himself. That scenario was more his style, being too much of a free spirit to rot in prison. Wheeler liked Roberts, but he had gone too far and had to be stopped.

Wheeler sat down at his desk and went over his notes. He rubbed his injured shoulder. *For once, I hope I'm wrong and Ralph is right, that Christian is on the lam and not dead.*

Ralph slammed his phone down and called excitedly, "They got him, Dave. They caught Roberts last night in Key West."

"He's alive then?"

"Yeah," Ralph said and stepped to Wheeler's desk. "But get this. When he was taken into custody, it nearly started a riot, people chanting for Nemo like he was some kind of hero. Several people were arrested for disorderly conduct and disturbing the peace. What's this country coming to, people cheering for a terrorist?"

Wheeler leaned back in his chair. "Well, Christian is more a vigilante than a terrorist, and people can relate to his cause. They're frustrated and angry that the environment is going to hell, and the government does little or nothing to prevent it. Christian's like the subway rider who shoots and kills his muggers. In the eyes of the law, he's guilty of manslaughter, but the public sees him as a hero, ridding the subways of evil. Finding a jury to convict him is going to be tough." Wheeler rose and slipped into his suit jacket. "He's in the Key West jail?"

"Not anymore. The local police wanted him gone, so US marshals picked him up few hours ago and are transporting him to Miami Metro. He's scheduled for an afternoon flight to New York to face arraignment on the bombings."

"Let's head over there. I want to talk to him before he goes. Also secure a search warrant for his boat. I want to check it out."

An hour later in the Miami precinct, Wheeler sat in the interview room with gray foam-rubber walls for soundproofing and waited for Roberts. He decided to talk to Roberts without Ralph. The animosity between the two young men was obvious. They belonged in a school yard where they could duke it out, but after seeing Roberts in action, Wheeler's money would be on the blond.

The door opened and Roberts was escorted in wearing handcuffs in front. "Dave," he said with a smile, "we have to stop meeting like this." He sat down at the small table, facing Wheeler.

"I'm glad you're all right, Christian."

"Things could be better." Roberts held up the cuffs. "You must be here to gloat, since you know a confession is a lost cause."

"I was actually worried, but I see you're still a smartass."

"To the end."

"That might be closer than you think. New York has a witness that says you were there mid-January, plotting the bombings of two grocery stores. "

"Really?" Roberts grinned. "The witness is lying. I've never been to New York, and the night of those bombings, I was with you, or have you conveniently forgotten?"

Wheeler chuckled. "No, I don't forget when someone saves my ass, but the dinner, that was clever, using me. I'm curious, though, did you rescue me because you needed me alive for your alibi or were you just being a decent guy?"

"Ah, Dave." Roberts smiled and waved his finger at him. "You're trying to trip me up with that question."

Saying he needed or didn't need me for an alibi could be considered an admission of guilt. The kid is good, Wheeler thought. "Okay, Christian, let's move on. You killed a lot of innocent people for eating a cup of soup. How could you do it?"

For the first time, Christian broke eye contact and stared at the floor, chewing his lip. "I told you. I'm not Nemo, but apparently he had to make a choice: save the oceans or spare some human lives." He looked up. "What would you do, Dave?"

"I wouldn't kill people."

"Back to priorities, that's the difference between you and Nemo. He's stopping the greater crime."

CHAPTER TWENTY-SEVEN

Early in the morning, Cliff Lancet, trim and in his mid-forties, hovered over his desk and shoved through the mass of case files. As assistant district attorney for New York City, he was in charge of the Christian Roberts case. The majority of the reports came from the Miami FBI, which had scrutinized Roberts's activities in the Bahamas and Costa Rica where the arsons of several seafood export buildings and trawlers occurred, and Captain Nemo had left his first and second warning messages about shark fins. In the Bahamas, Roberts was also suspected of foul play concerning the disappearance of a long-line trawler and its crew.

Another file contained the New York detectives' investigation into the mid-January bombing of two Chinese grocery stores. Captain Nemo's third warning had arrived a day prior, in the form of New York postcard addressed to a *Washington Post* reporter. Although a witness claimed Roberts had plotted the bombings, the detective had postponed his arrest for six weeks, hoping to find collaborating witnesses and more evidence to build a stronger case.

The newest file came from the CIA with information on Captain Nemo's recent message and terrorist attack, placing poison in dried fins. So far, sixty-eight people had perished in Asia from eating the tainted soup.

Given the severity of the crime, Roberts's arrest was imperative for the public's safety. Lancet issued a warrant two days earlier, and last night he received word that Roberts was arrested in Key West. He was transported to Miami and was scheduled to arrive in New York that evening. The early arrival left Lancet scrambling. He had the jailhouse bond set aside and had a bond hearing scheduled in two days. He planned to argue that Roberts was not a resident of New York and did not have family here, conditions usually required to bond out. He was suspected of being Captain Nemo, an international terrorist, and wanted in several countries for mass murder and arson. Lancet would request that Roberts be held without bond.

The judge would consider Roberts's virtually clean record: one misdemeanor arrest for assault with no conviction, and the current charges in New York that were not earth shattering. The discharge of a destructive device that caused property damage but where no bodily harm or deaths occurred was a level-two felony, fifteen years tops. Since Roberts only plotted the bombing and didn't take part, the charges were dropped even further to a level-three felony, five years max. Normally a judge would set a high bond and release him, possibly with house arrest and an ankle bracelet, but given Roberts's wealth that added to the high risk of flight and the enormous publicity surrounding the case, a judge might consider his own career and detain Roberts.

Lancet brushed back his light-brown hair and jerked his neck, a nervous twitch he developed when agonizing over a case. For the last several days, he had reviewed all the law enforcement files compiled against Roberts. What Lancet learned left him twitching in his sleep. Except for the New York witness, the evidence against Roberts was barely even circumstantial.

In the Bahamas, Roberts initially was a person of interest in his wife's murder, but with no witness, evidence, or confession, he was never charged. He was next suspected of burning an export company on Andros Island and causing the disappearance of one of its blue long-line trawlers. Blue paint scrapings taken from Roberts's damaged sloop matched floating debris found in the ocean, but without the trawler and its paint, it couldn't be tied to Roberts. Furthermore, the trawler was still missing, with no confirmed evidence of foul play.

Computer printouts about sharks and an article on the export company were found on Roberts's sloop, but these things were hardly damning evidence. The same was true of the blood found on a bullet casing aboard the sloop. Its DNA did not match a foot found in the ocean. Without the crew's DNA, the foot and the bloody bullet could not be matched to the crew to prove Roberts was involved. The only real evidence against Roberts was that he happened to be in the Bahamas, a big area, when the trawler disappeared and the export company arson occurred. The FBI's investigation amounted to conjecture only.

Captain Nemo's second attack in Costa Rica was even more disheartening. In Puntarenas harbor, several export warehouses and trawlers were burned, but again, there was no evidence or witness that connected it to Roberts. Worse, he had a solid alibi. His stamped passport, credit card statements, and hotel registry proved he was in Panama on the night of the arson. The FBI had placed him in the two countries where the arsons transpired, but that was it. A defense attorney would have a field day.

Since Lancet was prosecuting Roberts, he was given the CIA report on Captain Nemo's newest attack. It was no help. The CIA along with the FBI researched everything: Roberts's bank statements, cell calls, credit card bills, mail, Internet ties, airplane reservations, and reviewed public camera videos, hoping to spot him. On top of that, the FBI still had Roberts's passport. The agencies came up blank and with no clue where to start. Things looked hopeful when two tampered-with fins were discovered in the Hong Kong market, but the shipping date took place when Roberts was in the US, and his prints were not found on the fins. The poison was so unusual the labs had yet to determine its kind. Big questions remained. If Roberts was Nemo, where did he get the poison and buy the expensive fins, and how did he get them into the Hong Kong market without leaving the country?

The only good thing to come from all the agencies was that Roberts had been a fledgling criminal in the Bahamas and made a few mistakes: the bloody print on the bullet, computer printouts on sharks, and an inconclusive polygraph. Those mistakes had put him on the radar of an FBI agent named Wheeler. As Roberts was a person of interest suspected to be Nemo, his mug shot was sent to the New York police department, and a witness identified him as the mastermind behind the grocery store bombings. Roberts was therefore Captain Nemo, the notorious eco-terrorist.

For twenty years, Lancet had prosecuted high-profile murder cases, but Roberts's low-level felony charge would be the biggest case of Lancet's career. With a conviction, he would expose Roberts. The unsolved cases against Captain Nemo in the Bahamas, Costa Rica, and countries with poison victims would fall into place. A great deal was riding on a conviction.

He put aside the FBI and CIA files and focused on his case, the New York bombings. The detectives had failed to find additional evidence against Roberts. Wong, the Chinese gang member, was the only solid lead. The surveillance cameras and backlogged videotapes in the stores had been destroyed in the bombings, so there was no picture of Roberts or the person who planted the bombs visiting the store. Hours were spent reviewing the Chinatown street cameras, but they also proved disappointing. None of the blond men captured on film could be positively identified as Roberts. A black policewoman said she had helped a tall blond man with a slight southern accent buy a subway ticket to Chinatown. He resembled Roberts, but since the young man wore sunglasses, she couldn't be certain it was him. Passenger lists on planes, trains, buses, and rental car agencies were checked for Roberts's name, but all the lists came up empty. A search warrant issued for his home, vehicle, boat, and property also yielded nothing. The detectives did not know how he came to New York, where and who he had stayed with, or how he left.

Vince Florio, a mobster and no stranger to law enforcement, was a part-time resident of New York. Florio was acquainted with Roberts and was also his alibi in the Bahamas on the night of the arson. He and Roberts were on the sloop, sailing for Florida. A few days earlier, Florio told FBI agents that Roberts was with him in Florida at the exact same time Wong supposedly met with Roberts.

Either the gang member or the mobster was lying. On the night of the bombing, Roberts had a sound, if not outlandish, alibi. He and Wheeler, the FBI agent hunting him, had dinner in a fancy Miami restaurant. The agent's testimony for the defense would go over well with a jury.

The New York City detectives visited Florio's home on the Upper West Side and spoke to a large Italian named Sal, who said Florio was in Florida, and he hadn't seen Roberts in New York. The detectives tracked down Florio's Town Car driver, who also denied seeing Roberts or Florio. The whole trial hinged on Wong's testimony.

Lancet sipped his coffee and rubbed his forehead, the case giving him a headache. He reviewed Wong's statement to detectives and found too many loopholes and unanswered questions. Wong claimed that Roberts had phoned him, but Roberts never mentioned who had given him Wong's number, and Wong didn't ask. It sounded fishy and unrealistic that two strangers would meet and discuss a crime without an introduction and validation from a third party. One of them, Roberts or Wong, would have said so-and-so sent me. There were also no cell records to verify this call. Wong claimed they met in broad daylight in a nondescript alley and discussed the store bombings. There were no witnesses to the meeting, which was unlikely in crowded Chinatown. If Roberts was Nemo, he had proven to be smart and cautious, giving the FBI a chase. Would he really drop his guard and deal with a stranger and lowlife like Wong? Too much of Wong's story didn't ring true, unless he was trying to implicate Roberts without revealing the real meeting place or involving the setup man. That man could be his drug-pushing gang leader, Lee Chow or Roberts's mobster friend, Vince Florio. Mentioning their names at trial would mean Wong's life expectancy was nil. Before long, Lancet needed a sit-down with this witness.

Lancet's phone rang on the desk, and he glanced at his watch, eight p.m. Where had the day gone? He had last checked the time at lunch. "DA's office, Lancet."

"Your suspect's here," said Pat Grady, the detective in charge of the Roberts case. "He's downtown, and I'm getting ready to interrogate him, but you said you wanted to watch."

"Yes, hold off until I get there," Lancet said, rising and removing his suit jacket from the back of the chair.

"Word to the wise, Mr. Lancet," said Grady. "You'd better use the side door, unless you want to be mobbed by the media. Someone leaked his arrest and arrival at JFK. Reporters and camera crews are jammed outside the station. With the breaking news hitting the TV, this crowd is going to grow. Everyone wants a look at the boy."

"How does he look, nervous, maybe a little crazy?"

"Nothing like that. He's as calm as you please. He walked through the press like he was on a red carpet. He's a good-looking young fellow. I spoke to Agent Wheeler with the Miami FBI. He interviewed Roberts several times, and he warned me that Roberts is tough, doesn't rattle under pressure, so a confession isn't likely."

"I'm aware he's cagey. I read his statements from the interviews. Still, I want to see what I'm up against at trial."

Twenty minutes later, Lancet had the cabbie drop him off a half block from the police station. In the distance, he saw the TV trucks lined up on the streets and the crowd of reporters gathered near the front door. The circus had begun.

He skirted the building where the police cars parked and entered through the side door that was not accessible to the public. He made his way through the building and walked into a room with several wall monitors that recorded interviews. The chairs and desks were filled to capacity with plainclothes detectives and uniformed officers. They all focused on the second screen that showed Christian Roberts sitting in the small room and handcuffed to a chair.

Roberts's blond hair fell into his eyes and hung over the collar of a black shirt, the long sleeves rolled up to his elbows. His lanky frame leaned back in the chair, his worn jeans stretched out to his crossed ankles. He looked way too comfortable.

A pudgy Pat Grady broke away from the other detectives and

walked to Lancet. "Well, there's your suspect," he said and glanced toward the screen. "I told you he was a handsome son of a bitch."

"Yes, better looking than in his mug shot. I'll have to make a note to limit women on the jury. Has he said anything? Requested an attorney?"

"Not yet. Just to be sure, I read him his rights again and asked if he understood them. He said yes and gave me his name and address, but other than that, he's been real coy. Tried chatting him up, being friendly, but he didn't fall for it. He knows the game." Grady scratched his silver hair and sighed. "Well, better get started."

Lancet found an empty seat and sat down in the room as he and the others watched the monitor. Grady walked into the interview room with a file and smile. He sat down across from Roberts. "So, Christian," he began, "you're from Florida. Guess you're not used to our cold weather. I heard when they took you into custody in Key West that it created quite a ruckus. You apparently have a lot of fans down there."

Roberts glanced at him and did not respond.

"You understand why you're here and being charged? There're some serious allegations against you. We have proof that you're Captain Nemo. You want to comment on that or maybe deny it, son?"

"What is it with law enforcement?" Roberts smirked. "You all seem to think I'm your son." He leaned forward and stared into Grady's eyes. "Detective, let's get real. I understand it's your job to get friendly and hope I open up. That's not going to happen. You seem like a nice man. I don't want to piss you off."

"You're a smart cookie, but it'd be wise if you talked to me. If you cooperate, maybe I can get you a deal with less time."

Roberts grinned. "I think it's wiser to talk to my attorney."

"Okay, the jailers will put you back in the holding cell until your lawyer arrives." Grady picked up his file and left the room.

Lancet thumbed his chin and studied Roberts on the screen as the detectives nearby broke into chatter about the short and disappointing interview. Grady returned to the room and stepped up to

Lancet. "Just like I figured," he said. "He's too savvy, been through this routine before."

Lancet stood. "When his attorney arrives, let me know who it is." Leaving the police station, he saw the vigilant press, but the crowd now included protestors with signs that read "Free Captain Nemo" and "Save our Sharks and Oceans."

Jesus, this guy and his cause are controversial. Some love him. I'll be facing an uphill battle with this case. Lancet hailed a cab and settled in the backseat, reflecting on Roberts. He was good-looking— far from a dark-eyed, bearded, turban-wearing terrorist who spoke broken English. His appearance alone could sway a jury. If he testified, he would captivate the courtroom, and tripping him up during the cross was not likely. The guy was look-in-your-eye defiant and no idiot.

Lancet considered the testimony and who the jury would believe, the all-American boy or Lancet's witness, Wong, a Chinese gang member with a long rap sheet.

He massaged his forehead, his headache getting worse along with the case. Another problematic issue was Roberts's motives. He did not commit the crimes for self-serving greed or power, and he didn't have a wacko political or religious agenda. He took the extreme measures for the environment. Many would sympathize with his cause, the proof already apparent with the demonstrators outside the police station and the riots in Key West. Lancet's jury pool kept shrinking.

Another problem, certain members of the press adored Roberts. Several articles had already painted him as a champion for wildlife, ignoring his crimes. Lancet felt fatigue creeping in and he regretted he had taken this case. *I wonder if Roberts will go for a plea deal.*

Christian found himself being escorted through the halls to a holding cell. His thoughts were on the dreaded call to Frank. Once again, his poor stepfather would have to procure a criminal lawyer who practiced in New York. *Screw it. I'll go with the initial plan and get one out of the phone book.*

The two guards, one fat, one thin, placed him in the small cell consisting of a toilet and bunk. The fat guard chuckled while removing Christian's handcuffs. "Enjoy the solitude, sweetheart. Before long, you'll join the general populace, and with your looks, I wouldn't want to be you."

"Feeling is mutual," Christian said sarcastically. "I might get out of here, but you're stuck with that body."

"Joe, our boy's a real smart aleck." The fat guard laughed as the two jailers left the cell. He looked through the bars at Christian. "Well, here's a statistic for you, smart boy. More men get raped than women yearly, thanks to our prisons."

The skinny guard nodded. "Yeah, one look at him, and those cons will be fighting over him."

Christian sat down on the bunk, stared at the small concrete cell, and breathed in the stale air with its disinfectant smell. He shuddered, realizing he could have handled confinement better if he had grown up a shut-in, a TV couch potato, or a computer geek sitting in an air-conditioned room day after day, but he lived for the outdoors, open sea, or country pastures, regardless of whether the weather was steamy hot or frigid. He needed to be beneath sky. He glanced at the bars and wondered if he would ever see another sunset. *Fuck it. I committed the crimes, and this is the price.*

He curled up on the cot and closed his eyes, reflecting on the guard's statements about being raped, more than a possibility. In the past, his looks occasionally caused him grief, but the pen was a totally different playground. Trapped and outnumbered with society's worst, he did not stand a chance of defending himself. *With any luck, they'll beat me to death.*

He shook off the thought and tried to maintain an unruffled front, but inside he felt like crying. *Damn seagull, if it hadn't landed on my boat, I wouldn't be here. I'd be with Allie.*

An hour later, the fat guard returned with a small, middle-aged man with a thin mustache under a Roman nose. He wore a suit and tie under his overcoat. "Your lawyer's here," the guard said, and unlocked his cell.

Christian rose, baffled. "I haven't called anyone. You're my lawyer?"

"Yes, Mr. Roberts," the lawyer said and stepped into the cell. "I'm Saul Goldstein. My firm has been retained to represent you." He handed Christian his card.

Christian barely glanced at the card. "Who hired you?"

Goldstein waited for the guard to leave. "Mr. Florio," he said quietly. "I'm his attorney. He called from Florida, and I am to relay that you shouldn't worry. He'll get you out of this."

CHAPTER TWENTY-EIGHT

In New York, Sal marched down the freezing windswept street, cursing under his breath. "I should be in Florida instead of in this fucking weather, dealing with a fucking chink over this fucking kid's bullshit. Plus, I'm in fucking hot water with Vince." He clutched the top of his overcoat, pulled it tight to his neck for warmth, and hustled across the street to the small park in Chinatown. He glanced around the vacant square and settled on a cold bench under a barren tree. A few scrounging pigeons flew in and walked in circles nearby, hoping for a crumb handout. Some thread-thin Chinese men hurried past to get indoors.

As Sal killed time, he reflected on the angry phone call from Vince the day before. "Sal, what the fuck am I paying you for?" he had screamed. "He's been arrested in Key West. It should've never come to that. Do I have to come up there and handle things?"

"No, boss, but that chink's locked up tighter than a drum. Even the cops on our payroll can't get at him."

The phone was silent for nearly a minute. "All right, this is what you do," Vince had said.

Sal stared at a plump, gray pigeon picking the ground near his feet. Sal aimed his index finger at the bird as if shooting it. *Too bad you ain't the right pigeon.* He saw the dark-blue Lexus drive slowly past. It stopped and parked near the corner at the end of the square. "About time that yellow bastard showed up," he mumbled. He rose and strolled toward Lee Chow, who had climbed out of his car and stood, waiting for Sal.

"You're fucking late," Sal growled, approaching the Chinese gang leader.

Chow pulled his hands from his leather jacket pockets and placed them on his hips. "Don't give me shit, fat man. I already made it clear to your boss that I'll deal with him, but not his fucking partners." His eyes squinted even more.

"This ain't got nothin' to do with your drug hustling. It has to do with your rat sitting in jail."

"Wong?" Chow said with a huff. "He's not my problem. The guy knows not to rat on me or my operation."

"He ran his mouth to the cops about Vince's kid and plans to testify in court about the store bombings. You set the meeting up with Vince. That makes it your problem."

"Tell Florio he's lucky I didn't take that fucking blond out myself, coming up here to blow up my neighborhood."

"The boss likes that kid. If you had hurt him, you'd be pushing up daisies about now. Vince trusted you. Your guy screwed his boy over and broke that trust. In our book that makes you just as guilty, but we'll let it slide if you take care of Wong."

"Fuck you, I'm not touching Wong. And Florio doesn't scare me. He's a retired old fart with no backing except one fat Italian."

Sal laughed. "Yeah, punk, just keep thinking that Vince is harmless. You might have a bunch of hired guns, but knowledge is power, somethin' Vince has and you don't. But let me enlighten you, Chow."

"You're going to teach me?" Chow smirked.

"Yeah, if Wong testifies and our kid goes down, so does the person who got paid to plant those bombs. Where's your sister these days? Did she come into some money and leave town? It'd be a damn shame if that little doll ended up in the slammer."

Chow's mouth dropped open and his eyes grew wide. "What do you know about my sister? Are you telling me she helped that Florida fuck? She planted the bombs?"

"The kid and her sure made a cute couple." Sal chuckled and strolled away.

In Washington, DC, Trish pulled her carry-on luggage through Reagan Airport and soon boarded the flight to New York City. Several days earlier, Christian had been arrested in Florida and was extradited to the North. His bond hearing was scheduled for the next day, and Trish wanted to be there, even though his defense lawyer had declined interviews involving his client or the case. With *Post* reporters stationed in New York along with the Associated Press, the story was already being covered, and her editor claimed her trip was a waste of time. She had argued Christian was her friend and he would talk to her.

She arrived at JFK and took a taxi to her hotel. Over a room-service dinner, she reviewed her interview questions for tomorrow. In the end, she crumpled up the papers. She had only one question for Christian: was he all right?

The next morning, she rose early and put on her press badge and a pair of comfortable shoes, knowing it would be a long day. She left the hotel and caught a cab to the courthouse. She arrived and expected the mob of fifty-some reporters and camera crews where Christian would enter for his bond hearing. The surprise was the hundreds of sympathetic demonstrators holding signs supporting Captain Nemo and his crusade to save sharks.

She maneuvered through the crowd, trying to get close to the doors, but her hope of speaking to Christian faded. She listened to the other waiting reporters discussing the case. "No way will a judge let him bond out," one said, and most agreed. An hour later, the squad cars and prisoner van pulled in, and the horde made a mad rush to the vehicles. A line of policemen restrained the crowd when Christian stepped out in handcuffs, surrounded by law enforcement officers.

"Mr. Roberts, Mr. Roberts!" the reporters shouted and pushed toward him. "Are you Captain Nemo? Mr. Roberts, did you bomb the stores? Did you poison the fins?"

The protestors waved their signs of encouragement, and yelled, "Go, Nemo! We're with you, Roberts."

Through the heads and shoulders, Trish caught a glimpse of Christian. Amazingly, he seemed composed in the jostling and noisy chaos. He focused straight ahead and ignored the screaming voices. Guards escorted him to the doors, but before he disappeared from sight, she chimed in, "Christian, it's Trish."

He hesitated and surveyed the crowd. Making eye contact with her, he pursed his lips and gave her a slight sad nod. He was then hustled inside the building.

My poor Christian, she thought and felt guilty and sick. Her article had put him in the spotlight and brought him down. Jim, the office jerk, informed her editor about the arrest warrant that was issued for a suspect thought to be Nemo and that Trish had the exclusive on the guy. Her editor demanded the story containing her Florida interview with Christian. To hold back might have meant her job and would have given Christian only a few extra days of freedom. Jim or some other reporter would have released the story anyway and not portraying Christian in a positive light. Still, her insides churned with the remorse of a traitor.

She suddenly realized the surrounding reporters were staring at her. They had apparently noticed Christian had acknowledged her.

One saw her press badge and put it together. "You're Trish Stevenson from the *Washington Post*," he said. "Captain Nemo sent you the postcards, and you interviewed Christian Roberts and released his story. Why did he pick you? Tell me about him."

The press converged on her, their focal point shifting from the bond-hearing story to her relationship to Christian. She tried to explain. "Several months ago, I wrote an article about the travesty of shark finning. Captain Nemo must've read it, and that's probably why he sent me the postcards."

"How did you learn Roberts was a suspect?" another asked. "Especially before anyone else?" He smiled and held a recording device to her face as others took her picture.

"I followed a lead that the FBI thought Christian Roberts was a person of interest in the Bahamas arson, long before Captain Nemo caught anyone's attention." She shook her head. "All this information was in my article."

"Yes, but you actually met and interviewed Roberts," said a third reporter. "What's your impression of him? Think he's guilty?"

"Roberts is a very sweet, nice guy," she said. "I believe he's innocent."

"Plan to repeat that when you testify at trial about the postcards?"

"Absolutely," she said.

The cell phone belonging to the reporter chimed. In the group another's rang, then another and another's. Something had happened. The reporters migrated away to take the calls. The music from Trish's phone came on. She dug in her purse and saw the call came from her editor. "Yes?"

"Came over the wire Nemo has struck again," said her editor, "but this time it's not Asia. Twelve people were taken to a London hospital suffering from poisoned shark fin soup they ate in two different Chinese restaurants last night. So far, six of the twelve have died. The authorities can't confirm if it's a new attack or part of the original one. Some poisoned fins might've made it out of Hong Kong to London before the initial poisoning. The word is that Europe is removing fins from public access. The panic is spreading so fast we can hardly keep up with the news. Australia just announced a ban on fins, and the Mexican government is considering it. I would not be surprised if the US follows. On top of that several of the world's largest seafood exporters have announced they are destroying their fins. They will no longer buy, sell, or ship fins, regardless of this scare. That puts a stranglehold on commercial fishermen worldwide who practice finning."

"This is unbelievable."

"Yes, it is incredible, the result of one man's actions. Speaking of that man, were you able to talk to Christian Roberts? I sure would like his comment on this."

"We exchanged glances, but it was impossible to get near him. I'll have to wait and see." She saw the press hurrying to the assistant DA, who was leaving the courthouse. "I'll call you back."

Lancet stood before the reporters. "Judge Solemn has ruled that Christian Roberts will be held without bond. My office will be filing charges against him this week. I have no further comment." The demonstrators booed and the reporters fired questions concerning the newest poisoning. The DA ignored all, and left in a car with others on his staff.

As Trish jotted down the brief announcement in her notepad, she was approached by a young man in a suit. "Miss Stevenson, I work for the firm that represents Mr. Roberts." He lifted his eyebrows skeptically. "Against our advice, he'd like to speak to you before he's taken back to jail. Please come with me." She followed the attorney into the building, past security, and down a hallway lined with courtrooms. "In here," he said, and held open the door.

She stepped inside a small conference room and saw Christian sitting at table, his head down, massaging his temples. Three attorneys talked around him.

"Christian?" she said.

He looked up and smiled. "Hey, I saw you out there." He stood, and said to the attorneys, "Could you leave? I'd like to speak to her alone."

A small man spoke up. "Mr. Roberts, she's press, and I've already advised you against talking to her. Let me stay and make sure you don't say anything that will end up in print and hurt your case."

"I'm not a moron, Goldstein," Christian said. "It's my neck and my decision, so leave." The attorneys left the room, and he slumped back down in the chair. "My stepfather's an attorney. I was raised with this bullshit of caution, but sometimes instincts work better. You kept your word and didn't release my story right away. I trust you, Trish."

"I'm glad. I won't mess you over and question you about the case," she said and sat down across from him. "I came to see if you were okay and to say I'm sorry about the article. I didn't want to release your story until after you were arrested, but my editor demanded it."

"It was a good article. It helped more than hurt. You showed I wasn't anywhere near the incidents when they happened, so I couldn't have done the terrorist attacks, but the public still believes I'm Nemo. Just ask those protestors outside."

"Yes, they think you're him. So do I."

"Great," he said mockingly. He leaned back, and gazed at the ceiling. "I hope you're not on my jury. I just heard from my attorneys about London. If they want my head, they'd better get in line."

"Christian, you're not looking at the bigger picture. A lot of people love Nemo and admire his accomplishments."

"Accomplishments?" He frowned, gazing at her. "You mean the burning, bombing, and murdering people?"

"People have died in wars fought for far less important reasons. Nemo has brought the fin trade to a standstill worldwide and saved the sharks and oceans. That's quite an accomplishment. You won the war, Christian. You won."

Cliff Lancet returned to the DA office after Roberts's bond hearing feeling good. He had gone up against Goldstein and his large, prestigious law firm, argued the facts, and won the first round. The judge issued an order that Roberts be held without bond. The news in the courtroom about the London poisonings also put pressure on the judge. If Roberts was Captain Nemo, he was too dangerous to be freed.

Lancet's feel-good moment quickly evaporated when he glanced at the large stack of case files on Roberts. They consisted of nothing but innuendos and coincidences. The witness's statement was the only verification that Roberts had planned the store bombings, and Wong's allegations were problematic. Before filing charges against Roberts, Lancet needed to tie up the loose ends.

He picked up the phone and dialed lockup at the city jail. "This is Assistant DA Lancet. I'd like Charlie Wong brought up for questioning. I'll be over in a half hour."

"That might be a problem," said the clerk. "According to our records, Wong left yesterday. A Chinese law firm put up his fifty-thousand-dollar bond in the form of a cashier's check."

"No, this can't be happening." He hung up and called Pat Grady, the lead detective on the Roberts case.

"Grady, did you know that Charlie Wong bonded out?"

"Really?" said Grady. "He supposedly didn't have the money or friends to help him out."

"I want you to find him and bring him back in."

"On what charge?"

"Vagrancy, littering, I really don't give a damn. Once he's here, we'll put him under protective custody. Without him, I have no case against Roberts."

A few days passed, then a week, and close to two while Lancet waited for Wong's recapture. The clock was ticking on filing charges against Roberts.

Pat Grady walked into Lancet's office shaking his head. "He's gone," he said and slowly sat down. "We've been at it day and night, interviewed just about everyone in Chinatown, his mother, relatives, friends, and no one's seen Wong since he walked out of jail and got into a dark-blue sports car. The officer who saw it didn't get the tag number, but we suspect the car belongs to Lee Chow, an associate of Wong's. We talked to Chow, and he denies picking up Wong. We just finished a search of his car and found no fingerprints or DNA matching Wong's."

"What about the Chinatown law firm? Is it cooperating?"

"Not a chance. They're claiming attorney-client privilege and aren't saying who put up the bond money."

"You have no leads on where Wong might've gone, if he skipped town?"

"Mr. Lancet, Wong didn't skip town. He had a couple thousand in a bank account that's still there. He hasn't used his credit cards or placed one call on his cell phone. Like I said, he's gone. The best we can hope for is a body. Prove he's dead, and you might be able to submit his statement in court."

"That's unlikely. The defense will argue they can't cross-examine the witness, and the statement wasn't a death declaration. A judge will toss it. Oh, Jesus, this stinks. There's only one person who stood to gain from Wong's disappearance, and he's sitting in jail, but it proves that Roberts has some pretty ruthless friends."

"What are you going to do?"

"Without Wong's testimony, it'll be impossible to convict Roberts. I'll have to put the charges aside until another witness steps forward or you and the FBI find new evidence. Of course, I can also hope that another country finds the goods on Captain Nemo and proves Christian Roberts is our guy."

The following day, Lancet entered a nolle prosequi on the record that declared he would proceed no further, but it emphasized that he could still charge Roberts at a later date.

CHAPTER TWENTY-NINE

On his cell bunk, Christian slept and dreamed of the sea and kicking back on his sloop. Nearby the laughing gull perched on a railing and preened its chest feathers. "Will I ever be rid of you?" he asked the bird.

The seagull tossed back its head and made the high-pitched mocking, "Ha, ha, ha, ha, haab, haab, haab." The gull settled and stared at him. "Get up, get up, Roberts," it said in a deep voice. "You're free of me."

Hearing the sound of his cell door opening, he woke and stared at the heavy guard in the doorway. "Get up, Roberts," the guard said.

Christian sat up and swung his legs off the bunk. "What?" he asked, and rubbed his eyes.

The guard chuckled. "Boy, you were out, and that's not normal for you. I've been trying to wake you and tell you you're free to go."

"I am?" he mumbled. His head still in a fog, he couldn't grasp yet that the nightmare was over and he was being released. He stood and walked out of the cell. "Why? Why am I being let go?"

"Your lawyers are downstairs. I'm sure they'll explain it. All I know is the DA announced this morning he wasn't filing charges against you. Word got out to your Nemo fans. There're hundreds of them outside, along with the press, all waiting for you."

Christian changed from his prison clothes back into his jeans and black shirt. He was given his wallet, sunglasses, and the chained pendant of the Spanish coin. Down in Booking, he met Goldstein and two other firm lawyers. "What happened?" he asked them.

"The state witness disappeared, and without him, the DA has no case," said Goldstein. "It doesn't mean you've been acquitted.

Charges can still be filed against you at a later date so, Christian, you have to be careful. Don't do or say anything that can be used against you in court. Our office has been flooded with calls, TV and radio shows wanting to interview you. Even a few movie producers are interested in you and your story, but if you admit you're Nemo, it's over. You'll be rearrested."

"I get it."

"Okay, Mr. Florio flew up, and he's in a car outside to take you away, but you'll have to pass through a crowd of reporters and protestors. I suggest you move quickly without commenting."

Christian tucked in his shirt, swept back his hair, and put on the sunglasses. "Let's go." He followed his lawyer outside and the crowd erupted with cheers.

"Mr. Roberts has no comment," Goldstein said several times to reporters who converged on them, shouting questions.

"Actually, I do have something to say," Christian said, and the crowd grew quiet. On the jail steps, he bit his lip and stared out at them. "I'm a sailor from Florida, so I do believe I can relate to Captain Nemo and his cause. You all obviously feel the same way. It's a travesty to wipe out sharks that protect our oceans, especially when it's done for a lousy bowl of soup. Nemo's crusade wasn't about discrimination against a race or its culture. It was about conservation and saving the environment. Every person on the planet needs to take that message to heart for our own survival. That's all I really have to say, except—" He glanced upward. "It feels great to be out under a sky, even a gray New York one."

The crowd went wild and took up the same chant that had started in Key West. "Nemo, Nemo, Nemo!" Christian walked through them, nodding with a shy smile. He reached the street and the awaiting black Cadillac. Sal stood outside near the passenger door, his round cheeks holding a smug grin. Christian thanked his lawyers, and they parted ways.

Sal opened the back door for Christian, and commented, "Good fucking speech, kid."

Christian slipped in and sat down beside Vince. "God, it's good to see you," he said and hugged Vince. Sal climbed into the driver's seat and the car pulled away.

Vince looked him over. "Several weeks in the cooler, and you don't look any worse for wear."

"Once again, thanks, Vince, for the help and lawyers."

"Yeah," Sal said from the front seat. "Vince didn't realize being your friend was a fucking full-time job."

"Speaking of jobs," Christian said, "I heard the state witness disappeared."

"Sal and I had nothing to do with it," said Vince. "Besides, we couldn't get at Wong in jail. We just informed Lee Chow that his sister planted the bombs, and Wong's testimony might also put her behind bars. Wong also had to trust the person who bonded him out. So much for trust."

"What do you think happened to him?" Christian asked.

"I imagine your sharks have taken care of Wong's remains for ya," said Vince. "Chow has assured me the guy is no longer a worry." He patted Christian's knee. "I bet you're ready to celebrate your freedom with a cocktail and good meal, after jail food."

"Sounds great," said Christian. "I need to borrow your cell and call my parents in Florida, let them know I'm out. They've been worried sick."

Evening approached when Christian, Vince, and Sal arrived in Little Italy. Sal parked on the shadowy street in front of *Vince's* restaurant. A few diners left the restaurant and stood under an awning, talking. Christian and Vince climbed out of the car and stood on the sidewalk, waiting for Sal to join them before going in.

A thin man wearing a dark sweatshirt with a hood over his head hustled to them. He pulled out an automatic handgun that had been tucked into his belt and growled, "For fucking with my sister." He aimed the weapon at Christian, but as he fired, Vince lunged between Christian and the gun, taking a bullet in his stomach.

As Vince collapsed, Christian leaped over his body and knocked the gun out of the man's hand while slugging him in the jaw. The man lay sprawled backward on the sidewalk. He scrambled on the pavement, picked up his weapon, and pointed it again at Christian. Before he fired a second round, Sal unloaded his piece into man's chest. Sal gazed at the dead man's face. "Fucking Lee Chow."

Christian knelt and cradled Vince's head. "Hang on, Vince." Sal pulled out his cell and hastily called 911.

Sal stooped next to Vince. "We got him, boss, the kid and me."

Vince stared at them and said weakly. "Sal, Sal, you remember the promise you made me in Florida?"

"I remember," Sal said, and took Vince's hand. "But you're not going to die. I refuse to let you die."

Vince gasped but managed a smile. "You live by the gun, you die by the gun." He turned his head to Christian. "I'm proud of you, standing in front of that jail, talking to those people. We've both committed crimes, but I did it for selfish reasons. You did it to better this world."

"No, Vince," Christian said with tears, "I did it because Allie asked me to."

The police and ambulance arrived in minutes. Christian rode in the ambulance with Vince as it sped to the hospital. Sal remained behind and talked to the police. With plenty of witnesses, the shooting was clearly a case of self-defense.

Vince lingered for three days before dying from his gunshot wound. He made a death declaration to the police and hospital staff, saying he was with Christian on his sloop when the arson occurred in the Bahamas. Christian had no part in it. Vince also claimed that Christian was with him in Florida prior to the New York bombing. Protecting Christian to the end, he made sure his friend's alibis were in place in case charges were refiled, and the case went to trial.

Christian felt devastated with the loss, having been closer to Vince than to his own father. He felt drained and cursed, losing his wife and now his best friend, but his heartache could not compare to

Sal's. In the hospital and then the funeral, the big guy wept uncontrollably. Christian and Sal, once at odds, were drawn together with the grief. "He loved you, kid," Sal said, blubbering on Christian's shoulder after Vince's burial.

"I got him killed, Sal. My bullshit got him killed."

"Don't feel that way. Shit happens and we all die. It's how we live that's important. Vince said you were the best thing to happen to him, and backing your cause was the most creditable thing he'd done in his life. He made a choice when he jumped in front of that bullet. He wanted you to go on."

Talking to Sal helped ease Christian's conscience; he was tired of the guilt, blaming himself for Allie's death and now Vince's.

Before Christian left New York, he and Sal visited Vince's attorney, Goldstein, for the reading of Vince's will. Sal received twenty million from Vince, but Christian was floored to learn he inherited the bulk of Vince's estate, more than half a billion dollars. "He made a note," said Goldstein. "'You're to use it for worthy causes, save the world, Mr. Bond.'" Goldstein raised an eyebrow. "Whatever that means."

Two months later, Christian sat in a rocker on his shaded porch in Florida and drank iced sweet tea. Close to sundown, two does with fawns had emerged from the wooded wetland and walked across the horse pasture. A crested caracara bird landed on the board fence nearby and cawed to him. "Yeah, Allie, I'm doing okay," he said to the large bird of prey. The bird cawed again and flew away.

On the quiet country road, he saw a black Cadillac slow and turn into his long driveway. He rose, knowing it was Sal.

"Hey, kid," Sal said, stepping out of the car. "Figured you might be back from DC by now."

"Got back last week."

Sal joined him on the porch. "How's the reporter?"

"We had a great time. Trish showed me some museums, and we caught a play at the Kennedy Center. Next month I'm flying to

Hawaii. I always wanted to surf those waves and dive there. I'll also be spending some time with a certain Chinese girl."

Sal chuckled. "So you're spreading the love around and keeping your girls happy."

"I like both of them, but I've made it clear I don't want a serious relationship. After Allie, I'm not sure I'll ever commit again."

"Kid, you're too fucking young to think that way. Someday a babe will come along, and you'll be changing diapers. But in the meantime, you're smart to get all the pussy you can handle."

"Thanks for the advice, Sal."

"Well, sex is like a New York pizza. When it good, it's damn good, but when it's bad, it's still pretty damn good." He laughed at his own joke.

Christian smiled. "That's a good one, Sal. You wanna to come in? I'll fix us a real drink and defrost some steaks for dinner."

"Yeah, let's get out of this fucking heat," Sal said and followed Christian inside. "May and it's already hot as hell. Don't know how you crackers handle this crap year-round."

"Another month or two and the rains will start. Cools the afternoons off," Christian said while mixing drinks in the kitchen.

Sal wandered into the living room, turned on the TV, and settled on the couch. "What's this shit on your tube?" He frowned, staring at the program. "You like these animal and nature shows?"

"Sorry, never been big on sports." He handed Sal his drink.

"Always knew you weren't fucking normal. So what's this show?"

Christian looked at the screen and sat down next to Sal. "It's called *Whale Wars*. I've been watching it for several years. Every season, these guys in The Sea Shepherd Conservation Society go down to the Antarctic and spend most of their time looking for the Japanese whaling fleet. If they manage to find a ship, they zip around in little boats letting out ropes in front of the ship's bow, hoping to foul the propellers. I can appreciate their effort to save the whales and stop the Japanese and their yearly harvest, but their methods are bullshit."

Christian leaned back and took a swallow of his drink,

contemplating. "You know, Sal, it'd be easy to visit the Japanese harbor while the whaling fleet is in port, put on some dive gear one night, and attach plastic explosives to the ship hulls. Boom, it's over, fleet gone, whales saved. What do you think?"

Sal glanced at him and slowly nodded. "Sounds like something Nemo might do."

Note:

July 26, 2013, Governor Cuomo of New York signed into law a bill that bans the possession, sale, trade, and distribution of shark fins, ending New York's contribution to the dire collapse of the shark population worldwide. The law took effect on July 1, 2014.

New York—one of the largest markets for shark fins outside of Asia and the largest port of entry for shark fins on the East Coast—joins seven other states; California, Hawaii, Illinois, Maryland, Delaware, Oregon, and Washington, and all three Pacific US territories; American Samoa, Guam, and Northern Mariana Islands that passed similar laws to protect sharks.

In March 2013, at the world's wildlife summit in Thailand, CITES, the Convention of International Trade in Endangered Species, proposed that five species of sharks; the oceanic white tip, porbeagle, and three species of hammerhead be protected. The proposal passed with support of the nations attending the conference.

In August 2013, shark fin soup was banned in Hong Kong at all government banquets, but the fight to save sharks is still an upstream battle, thanks largely to the opposition of Japan and China and their cultural attachment to shark fin soup. At this writing, 100 million sharks are killed each year.